Praise for *Chef's Kiss*

A *TIME* BEST BOOK OF THE YEAR

May's Top Rom-Com Reads
—*USA Today*

"Like a dish of comfort food you'll want to devour."
—*The Washington Post*

"It's hard to say which aspect of TJ Alexander's novel is sweeter: the slow-burn romance or the drool-worthy desserts."
—*Time*

"One of the most intricate and satisfying queer romances in years. Fans of Casey McQuiston will be wowed."
—*Publishers Weekly* (starred review)

"A luscious dessert of a novel, a romantic comedy as classic as it is modern, as satisfying as it is groundbreaking."
—Camille Perri, author of *When Katie Met Cassidy*

"*Chef's Kiss* is an utter delight, filled with sumptuous food and adorable banter. This is the first time I've read a book with a nonbinary love interest, and I was cheering for Ray and Simone the entire time. At times, it can be heart-wrenching, but above all it is the ultimate feel-good read!"
—Jesse Q. Sutanto, author of *Dial A for Aunties*

Also by TJ Alexander

Chef's Kiss

chef's choice

a novel

tj alexander

EMILY BESTLER BOOKS

ATRIA

New York   London   Toronto   Sydney   New Delhi

EMILY
BESTLER
BOOKS

ATRIA

An Imprint of Simon & Schuster, Inc.
1230 Avenue of the Americas
New York, NY 10020

First Emily Bestler Books/Atria Paperback edition May 2023

EMILY BESTLER BOOKS / ATRIA PAPERBACK and colophon are trademarks of
Simon & Schuster, Inc.

For information about special discounts for bulk purchases, please contact Simon & Schuster
Special Sales at 1-866-506-1949 or business@simonandschuster.com.

The Simon & Schuster Speakers Bureau can bring authors to your live event.
For more information or to book an event, contact the Simon & Schuster Speakers Bureau
at 1-866-248-3049 or visit our website at www.simonspeakers.com.

Interior design by Lexy East

Manufactured in the United States of America

1   3   5   7   9   10   8   6   4   2

Library of Congress Cataloging-in-Publication Data is available.

ISBN 978-1-9821-8910-5
ISBN 978-1-9821-8911-2 (ebook)

Actually, this one's for me.

Chapter 1

Luna O'Shea cracked her neck in four places before pulling off her headset and tossing it onto her desk. Working from home was usually a godsend, but today Luna felt exhausted, and that last call with Tim had not done her any favors.

Her wildly disorganized boss was the CEO of Papr Tigr, the digital-marketing-slash-advertising firm (or was it advertising-slash-marketing? Luna could never remember) where she had worked remotely for almost five years. Tim was normally a scatterbrained weirdo, but today he'd been in rare form. Luna had spent the last three and a quarter hours walking him through yet another Word document with his very personal, very important log-ins listed in Arial font, despite Luna's protests that writing all that down in a hackable file and then emailing it back and forth was a bad idea.

Kind of funny how the head of a company that touted itself as being on the cutting edge was so bad with anything digital. Tim pulled a $600,000 yearly salary, and Luna really couldn't understand why anyone would think he was worth a fraction of that. Lose a zero, maybe, but what did she know? She was just a personal assistant. And today, her job had consisted of babysitting Tim while he anxiously learned how to update and save the doc himself. Her talents had just been wasted on nearly four hours of sixth-grade-level Microsoft Office instruction.

At least she was almost done for the day. She unhooked her phone from its charger and checked her notifications. Simone still hadn't responded to Luna's question about dinner plans; she probably already had a dinner date set with her themfriend, Ray. As usual. Luna silently resigned herself to another night of microwaved taquitos and a Kraft single eaten straight out of the wrapper. You know, for calcium.

At first it had been kind of fun for Luna, having the whole apartment to herself when Simone stayed over at Ray's. But after a few weeks of seeing Simone only when she swung home to grab some clean clothes, all the alone time had lost its appeal. You could have only so many one-person dance parties before it got old. Between that and working from home, Luna could go from one end of the week to the next without speaking to another person in the flesh.

She wondered if Simone would eventually move in with Ray, since they spent so much time together anyway. That would be awesome for them—but a disaster for Luna, who couldn't possibly cover the entire rent on her salary, and who wasn't thrilled with the idea of finding a new roomie. She'd gotten comfortable over the years, living with Simone. Sure, Simone was neurotic about keeping the bathroom clean, and she did take up way more than half of the fridge space, but she was a loyal friend and always made sure Luna was eating well. The perks of having a professional chef as a roommate.

If Simone decided to move out of the apartment, Luna would be holding the short end of the stick in more ways than one.

She checked her group chat for some much-needed human interaction, but quickly deflated. Aisha was telling everyone about the house she and Ruth were buying in New Jersey, and the other girls were asking about how many guest rooms the place had and what they planned on doing with the backyard.

Willow: can u fit a pool? i want a pool

Lily: It's not your house! It's Aisha's. Although, Aisha, if you want to put in an herb garden . . .

Luna tried to compose a suitably cheery message of her own, but the other responses and counterpoints were coming so fast and furious that she couldn't get a word in edgewise. She was happy for Aisha, truly, but the thought of losing friends to the far-off suburbs was a bummer. Soon Aisha and her wife would be wrapped up in their responsibilities and have no time to hang out. Just like Simone.

Luna slapped her phone screen-down on her desk and said aloud, "That is black-and-white thinking, and I live in a world full of color." It was one of her many mantras designed to disrupt negative thoughts. Yes, her friends were growing up and going in different directions, but that didn't mean Luna was being left behind. She was doing fine! Her blood pressure was great. Her pedicure was unchipped. She was a happy, fulfilled person.

She checked the group chat again.

Willow and Sara had moved on to gushing about their new love interests. Apparently, one was a competitive deadlifter and the other had a world record in rock climbing. Abs that you could serve a mezze platter on, Sara declared.

Luna could feel her teeth grinding. She tossed her phone onto her bed, where it bounced once before coming to a stop far out of her reach. "Comparing myself to others does everyone a disservice," she recited to the ceiling, though she had a hard time believing a word of it.

How could she *not* compare? Everyone else had relationships and houses and mezze-worthy abs, and what did Luna have? Her last hookup, a well-read barista with good cheekbones and a bad attitude, had fizzled out weeks ago. Luna disliked ghosting on principle, but in Rick's case, she'd figured leaving his texts on read was the better part of valor.

Luna took a deep, cleansing lion's breath. It would be more productive to focus on gratitude, she decided. She plucked a sparkly purple journal from one of the shelves above her desk and, uncapping a pen with her teeth, began to jot things down in her stubby script: She had a mother who loved and supported her. She was living her truth as a proud trans woman. She had an amazing group of friends. She lived in New York, like she'd always dreamed of doing. And she had a good, steady job. *Even if it is a little frustrating at times*, she scrawled.

As if in response, her work laptop pinged.

Luna frowned at the video chat icon bouncing on the screen. Why would Jennifer from HR be calling, and at the end of the day? They didn't have anything on the calendar.

Maybe it was another Tim-related fire drill. Sometimes he'd close out of a window, think his file was deleted forever, and randomly call whoever he thought might be responsible for a good yell. HR got involved more often than IT.

Luna jammed her headset back over her ears and answered with audio only on her end. Jennifer's glossy, stick-straight brown hair and wide, pearly smile filled her screen.

"Hi, Jen, I was actually about to log off for the day," Luna said in her corporate voice, full of false cheer. She doodled a small sun in the margins of her journal. "Is this urgent, or can we circle back first thing tomorrow?" Tomorrow was a Friday, and Luna knew no one really got anything done on Fridays. Whatever the problem was, she could tackle it the following Monday.

"It is quite urgent, actually." Jennifer mirrored Luna's tone to perfection. "Oh, would you mind turning on your camera? I can't see your video."

Luna grimaced. This fucking company, always asking her to turn on her camera. Like there couldn't possibly be a good reason as to why she wouldn't want to stare at her own face for hours on end—and know other people were staring, too. The dysphoria was real sometimes. Part of the joy of working from home was not being perceived in a corporeal way, but video-chatting with actual video was being pushed as part of the whole "corporate culture of Papr Tigr" or whatever. She put her journal back on its shelf with a stifled sigh.

"Sure thing." She switched her camera on. For fun, she had a cute Zoom background of cartoon bunnies romping through a field of flowers. And there she was, smack-dab in the middle of it, minimal makeup on her pale face—just her usual foundation and a touch of eyeliner—and her blonde hair pulled into a low ponytail so the purple dye that still clung to the last three inches wouldn't be visible on camera. Lately she'd gotten some comments about how unprofessional her hair looked, even though Quin in finance had a blue streak in hers and *she* never got shit for it. But Luna was a team player; she could rock a ponytail until the last of the dye job got trimmed. "What's up?"

Jennifer smiled back from her standard Zoom square, her office wall in the background. "Well, first of all, it's nice to see your face for once!"

"Haha, yeah." Luna kept smiling, glancing at the clock in the lower corner of the screen. It was ten minutes past quitting time.

"I wanted to catch you before the end of the day." Jennifer's smile did not abate, but it did take on a pitying edge. "These things are never easy for me. I want you to understand this is not personal. It's just business."

Luna's brain shorted out for a second. She could see Jennifer's mouth moving on the screen, but only a low buzz of static filtered through. She caught a few words, however.

Termination. Effective immediately.

"Wait. What? I'm being fired?" Her face was hot, the rest of her body cold. This could not be happening. "Why?"

"As I was explaining," Jennifer said, still with that manic, saccharine smile plastered across her face, "the company is going through a lot of changes, and we had to make some tough decisions, one of which was to terminate low-performing positions."

"But—but my performance has always been good. I just had that review last month—I had great feedback!" Luna tried not to look at her own blotchy face on the screen. It was the last thing she wanted to see.

"I can't comment on internal documents," Jennifer said crisply. "I can only tell you this decision is final."

Luna blinked. On her Zoom square, she blinked right back, surrounded by fluffy bunnies. Oh, this was humiliating. "You made me train those two new assistants that were hired last month. Are you firing them, too? Or is it just me?"

Jennifer's smile finally dropped. "I also can't comment on the status of other employees, Luna. You know that."

The answer was crystal clear, then. Of course they were keeping the younger, inexperienced, cheaper assistants and tossing Luna to the curb. That had probably been the plan all along.

Though—if they needed two of them to cover Luna's workload, it wasn't about the money. It was about other stuff. Like who looked more "approachable" on Zoom calls. Who was a better "fit" for the "culture." All the standard code words for cis.

Her face felt like it was on fire. *I will not cry*, she told herself. *I just won't.*

"Please, I know this must be difficult. It's hard for me, too. But I am asking you to remain professional," Jennifer said. She squinted at the screen. "I'm sending all the documentation regarding your severance package to your personal email now. It's extremely generous, as you'll see: two extra weeks on top of your final paycheck."

Generous? That won't even cover a month's rent, Luna thought wildly.

Jennifer bulldozed ahead. "I've asked IT to lock your work laptop, so in about three minutes it will shut down and you won't have any more access to company files."

"You mean Tim's log-in doc? The one that includes all his personal information, including his Social Security number?" Luna bit out. "By the way, you shouldn't let him do stuff like that. You're asking to get hacked. I've tried telling him a thousand times."

Jennifer sniffed. "I shouldn't have to remind you that if you retain those files, you will be subject to swift legal action."

"I don't plan on retaining anything. I'm just letting you know."

"Well, you make it sound very threatening, Luna," Jennifer said. "If I'm being honest, this is a big part of the reason why we have to let you go."

"What, the fact that I'm pointing out very real dangers to the company?"

"No, your whole *tone*." Jennifer's face twisted into a sneer. "It's a very off-putting *tone*."

Luna's mouth hung open, speechless. She fought the urge to bring up her performance reviews again; she'd always gotten high marks for her cheerful and professional demeanor. But obviously that didn't matter right now.

"I don't think I need another three minutes of this," Luna managed to say once her mouth was back in working order. "Just send me a UPS label and I'll ship the laptop back to you."

"Ah." Jennifer nodded jerkily and pretended to rearrange some papers on her desk. "Right. Do you happen to have the log-in for the UPS account or . . . ?"

"Are you kidding me?" She was actually going to explode. Her blood was boiling. No one else at this terrible company knew what they were doing, and they expected her to help them out while she was booted out the door? "Bye, Jen. Thanks for the opportunity," she said, sarcasm rolling off every syllable. She slammed her laptop shut. Hot tears welled in her eyes.

Okay. So that was one less thing for the gratitude journal.

Chapter 2

Luna couldn't stay home alone for one minute more. Her now-bricked laptop sat mockingly on her desk, making her want to scream every time she looked at it. She had to talk to someone about what had just happened. Simone seemed like the obvious candidate.

Luna had enough money saved up to sustain her for a month, maybe two if she was careful, but . . . not if she was responsible for the entire rent. She thought about how Simone had hardly been home at all lately: her favorite coffee mug was missing from the kitchen cupboard, and her toothbrush had disappeared from their shared bathroom cup weeks ago. At the time, those details seemed harmless, simply proof that Simone was settling into her new relationship. Now Luna wondered if it was more than that. If Simone moved out anytime soon, Luna would be well and truly screwed. That could not happen. Luna would just have to use a combination of logic and guilt to make Simone stay put.

She slipped on her running shoes and hopped on the subway. On the way, Luna mentally rehearsed what she'd say. *Please don't move out* was the current thesis statement. Simone was more likely to vibe with direct orders.

Once she got off at her stop, Luna stood on the corner and waited for the light to change, her hands stuffed in the pockets of the hoodie she'd thrown on over her athleisure. Soon it would be too warm for even a light outer layer—the last crisp chill of spring was in the air, but Luna could smell the suffocating heat of summer right behind it. It was hard to breathe just thinking about it.

Shit. What was she going to do about health insurance? Did she have enough bottles of her hormones stockpiled in the medicine cabinet, or would she run out before she found a new job? What if she did find a new job, but her doctor didn't take her new insurance? Where was she going to find another trans-affirming GP who was accepting new patients? It had taken her months to get an appointment with her current one.

Stop thinking about things you can't control right now. She concentrated on her destination, the building across the street. It looked stately with its refurbished windows and curving lines now that the exterior renovations were finally finished. Luna had visited a few times since Ray and Simone had gone into business with culinary powerhouse Lisette D'Amboise, she of the many public-access food travelogs and cookbooks. Since the three partners had purchased the building, it was quickly transforming into a brewery and production space. The plan was to shoot their new baking competition show—spearheaded by the new production company they'd formed with old coworkers from Pim Gladly's The Discerning Chef—right there on the top floor, then rent it out for events in the future.

The older lady in a gray security uniform at the front entrance recognized Luna, and as before, Luna gave Simone's name as the reason for her visit. The guard made a murmured consultation on her walkie-talkie before waving Luna in. Beyond the spare entrance sat huge silver brewing vats and a gleaming network of pipes. Luna could see workers scuttling around behind the glass walls, connecting machinery and bolting stuff down.

She ignored the shiny new freight elevator, which was packed with people and equipment, and made her way to the wrought-iron spiral staircase, now sporting a fresh coat of black paint. She climbed up to the third floor, where the television studio was situated.

That, too, was a beehive of activity. Luna recognized a few of Simone's coworkers from her previous visits, but they either didn't notice her or were too busy to say hello. They ducked in and out of sight with cameras and lights and endless black boxes with silver trim. Construction workers carried huge rectangles of bare plywood and heavy coils of electrical cords. One person raced by with a towering layer cake—three tiers, all bedecked in lilac buttercream. Luna longingly watched it go.

"It's not real," a familiar voice said at her side. "It's just a prop that'll sit in the background."

"Simone!" Luna whipped her head to the side to find her roommate wearing dust-covered overalls and a wide grin. "There you are. You're really letting them put a plastic cake in the background?"

"Otherwise we'll get ants," Simone said with a roll of her eyes, which meant she was probably repeating something Ray had said. She gave Luna an arm's-length sort of hug to save her from the dust. "Sorry I'm so dirty; I can't avoid it in this place. What's up?"

Luna tried to think of a way to break the news. Her carefully practiced request flew from her mind. *I got canned today; do you think you can pump the brakes on your amazingly perfect relationship so I don't end up homeless?* was the only thought running through her head. She needed to reword it just a tad, couch it in a positive light. Anything could have a positive light if you tried hard enough.

"Well, the thing is—"

A tall, lanky shadow sidled in from out of nowhere, gravitating to Simone's side like it was the most natural thing in the world. "Hey, babe, do you know where Petey is?" Ray was also covered in plaster dust, with the addition of paint spatters on their forearms.

"I haven't seen him since lunch," Simone said, tipping her face toward them for their usual hello.

Ray dropped a kiss on her cheek. "No worries, I'll track him down." They finally saw Luna behind Simone. "Oh, hey, Luna. How's it going?"

"Uh." Luna found herself tongue-tied again. Ray was a sweetheart, but they weren't exactly close friends. It was going to be embarrassing enough explaining her termination to Simone. She wasn't really looking to double her audience. "It's going," she finally managed with a watery smile.

"Cool." Ray's answering grin was its usual cheery sunshine. They turned the full force of it back to Simone. "Whose turn is it to make dinner tonight, mine or yours?"

"Mine," Simone said with a wicked little upturn at the corner of her mouth. "You made breakfast, remember?"

It was obviously some inside joke, both of them looking at each other with an air of mischief usually reserved for cats and cream. Luna would never begrudge them their happiness, but she wasn't really in the mood to watch them do their mating dance. Not to mention Simone hadn't found the time to text Luna back about dinner when she'd clearly already made plans, which kind of stung.

Well, no sense in getting angry about it. Luna cleared her throat loudly, capturing Ray and Simone's attention once more. "Working late again?"

"Yeah, long days." Simone shrugged, then patted Ray's arm, not seeming to care about whether the paint splotches were dry or not. "Go find Petey. I'll catch up in a second."

Ray gave her another kiss, this time on the lips, which Simone accepted with a pleased smile. Luna studied a nearby stack of pans still in their plastic casings to give them a bit of privacy.

"Bye, ladies," Ray said as they loped away. "Nice seeing you, Luna!"

"Mm-hm, yep. Bye." Luna gave a half-hearted wave at their retreating back. She saw Simone watching her with narrowed eyes.

"Is everything okay?" Simone asked. "You seem . . . off."

Luna shifted uncomfortably on her feet, stuffing her hands into her hoodie pockets again. "Actually, I—"

Before Luna could finish, a frazzled-looking woman with long braids walked by at a fast clip, checking the smartwatch on her wrist as she went. "Lisette's here for the production meeting, Simone. You coming?"

"I thought that was tomorrow," Simone called after her.

The woman did not stop, getting farther and farther away. "It got pushed up. I sent an update." She sounded like she was at the end of her rope. Luna could relate.

Simone took her phone from her pocket and checked it with a groan. "I'll be right there, Delilah," she said to her retreating form.

Delilah made a distracted sound of acknowledgment before disappearing around a corner. Luna hoped that Delilah's day would improve; someone's should.

Simone turned to Luna with a grimace. "I'm so sorry. I didn't see your text until just now either. I haven't had one minute to pause, you know? We start shooting in a few months—I don't know how we're going to get it all done in time." She started walking backward in the same direction as Delilah. "I swear I want to hear what you have to say. Can you just hang out here for, like, half an hour? Maybe less?"

Luna gave her a weak smile. "Yeah. Sure. Go to your meeting."

Simone gave her an apologetic thumbs-up before spinning around and jogging to catch up with her coworker.

So that went well, Luna thought with a sigh. Now she just had to kill some time. She stood awkwardly against a wall so she would be out of the way as much as possible, what with the steady stream of people brushing by. Surrounded by people, yet totally alone. It was hard not to feel abandoned.

Don't be dramatic; she'll be back before you know it, Luna told herself. She paced a few steps away and was nearly beaned in the head by a boom mic as someone passed by. She was saved only by her quick reflexes, ducking at the last moment and scowling at the sound guy's mumbled apology. Her already frayed nerves were at the breaking point.

She needed to find a calmer environment. Maybe do a little yogic breathing. She slipped through the knots of people and stacks of stuff and entered a blissfully quiet corridor filled with nothing but bare shelves. A few other people were obviously taking advantage of the peaceful spot: a girl wearing a headset checking her phone and two other women holding a whispered conversation. Perfect. Luna leaned back against a bare piece of wall and breathed.

The quiet did not last long.

No sooner had Luna finished taking a single meditative breath—in for seven seconds, hold for seven seconds, out for yet another seven seconds—than a man dressed all in black came careening down the hallway in a cloud of vape smoke that smelled faintly of coffee. He was extremely white, almost ghostly, and his hair was the sort of tousled black waves that reminded Luna of tragic poets. Although it was hard to tell from the timeless aesthetic, Luna estimated he was about her age: twenty-seven, maybe a year or two older. In the hand not occupied with his e-cigarette, his cell phone vibrated aggressively. Before he could come within a few yards of Luna, his progress was stopped by the girl with the headset.

"Oh, sir, you can't use that in here," she said, pointing to where his hand clutched the slim vape pen.

"Would you pretend to be my girlfriend for fifteen minutes?" he replied. If the clothes and the hair and the general European bearing hadn't been enough, the accent made it clear that he was French. His phone continued to buzz.

The girl visibly recoiled. "Uh," she said. "No?"

The Frenchman sucked his teeth and whipped his head

around. His gaze landed on Luna, then skipped right over her—rude—to the two ladies who were chatting off to the side.

"You there," he called to them. "Do you have fifteen minutes to pretend to be my girlfriend?"

The two women stared at him, then at each other.

"Which of us are you talking to?" one said.

At the same time, the other said, "I'm married."

Luna wondered if she should call security, but if the guy had gotten past the walkie-talkie guard, he probably knew someone here. Plus, she wanted to see how this would play out. It was like watching a train wreck. Kind of comforting, actually, after the day she'd had.

"Both. Either." He sucked on his vape pen and expelled a Starbucks-scented cloud toward the ceiling. "Only for a few minutes; I am sure your husband would not mind."

"Wife," the woman corrected with a glower.

Sensing that he'd lost any goodwill he might have had from that corner, he turned back to the girl with the headset. "I will pay you one thousand American dollars," he said, "if you pretend. Just fifteen minutes."

Luna's eyes widened. A thousand dollars? Who the hell *was* this guy?

"You really have to put that away," the headset girl said, gesturing to his vape pen. "It's the law. We could get fined."

"Yes, yes, I'm doing it." The guy shoved his e-cig into the pocket of his black leather jacket. "Is that a no, then?"

"A *hard* no." The girl stalked off with her clipboard clutched in her hand. The other two women also drifted away, shooting judgey glances at him as they went.

Luna watched them go, then looked back at the Frenchman. He was much, much closer now, staring up into her face with huge, dark brown eyes. She gave a startled jolt. Maybe it should have made her uncomfortable, being left alone with an unhinged vaper who was propositioning strangers, but the lure of a thousand dollars was enough to keep her where she was.

"You're really offering that much money? For real?" she asked.

He tipped his head in acknowledgment. "I do not know the exact exchange rate, but I did not think it would be such an"—he glanced in the direction the other women had gone—"insulting sum."

"I don't think it was the number that was insulting." Luna peered at him. "Why do you need a pretend girlfriend for fifteen minutes?"

The guy ran a hand through the back of his unruly hair. His phone stopped vibrating for one glorious moment before starting up again, as insistent as before. "It is a long story," he said. "And I do not have time." His accent made the words sound languid and slapdash. French was mostly a language of mumbles, in Luna's opinion, and not nearly as romantic as English speakers made it out to be.

Now that he was closer, Luna could see he was pretty short. Most people were, from Luna's six-foot-something vantage point, but from a distance he had seemed taller. Must have been the outsized anxiety.

The man checked his phone's screen and muttered something in French that sounded like a cuss word. All of a sudden, Luna realized that she knew him.

Well, not personally, but she knew *of* him. Ray and Simone had mentioned that Lisette had a grandson who was trans and that Lisette was super chill about it. How many French-speaking short kings could there be in this neck of the woods?

"I'll do it," she blurted out.

He looked up from his phone, his face a mask of confusion. "You will?"

"I've worked harder for less." She offered her hand, all business. "Luna O'Shea."

The Frenchman transferred his phone to his left hand and extended his right for a handshake. It was firm without being painful, just a touch of machismo. "Jean-Pierre Dominique Gabriel Aubert-Treffle," he said. "A pleasure."

Luna frowned. Aubert-Treffle? The sound of it tickled her brain. Where did she know that name from?

Still holding her hand, Jean-Pierre held up his phone. It was buzzing with an incoming FaceTime call. The caller ID had no photo and said only *Papi*.

"Fifteen minutes or the length of this phone call, whichever is shorter," Jean-Pierre said in a grave tone. "All you need to do is go along with what I say, and afterward I will transfer the money to you. You can watch me do it on my phone. Do we have a deal?"

"Sure," Luna said, trying to sound casual, like she made a thousand dollars every day by pretending to be someone's girlfriend. "Sounds fair."

Jean-Pierre's hand tightened a little on hers. "My grandfather," he muttered, waving the phone, "that is who is calling. He might— He can be insulting, too. He may see you and say, ah, cruel things."

Luna made a face. "Because I'm trans?"

"I did not want to assume," Jean-Pierre said quickly.

"Well, you'd be right, because I am."

"I only say this to warn you. He may notice, he may not. He has not been the most understanding of my own situation." What a delicate way to call someone a complete asshole. "Are you sure you agree to this, now that you know?"

Luna considered the number of times someone had been a jerk to her for free. At least this way, she'd be making bank.

She slipped her hand from their prolonged handshake. The phone kept on buzzing. "I'm still game," she said. "Let's chat with your granddaddy." She pulled her hair out of her ponytail and finger-combed a few strands to artfully frame her face. If she was going to be on a video call with a weirdo dickhead, she was at least going to look cute doing it.

Jean-Pierre positioned himself at Luna's side, holding his phone out at arm's length so the camera would capture them both. He took a deep, shaky breath. His face was even paler than before, which Luna thought was concerning. The boy needed to eat some carbs.

Too late to back out now. Jean-Pierre tapped the answer button on the phone.

A man's frowning face filled the screen. A face Luna instantly recognized.

Chapter 3

"Bonjour, Papi," Jean-Pierre said.

"Uh," Luna added, not too helpfully. It wasn't her fault, really. Jean-Pierre should have mentioned that his grandpa was famous.

There, on Jean-Pierre's phone, scowling at her with the full force of his French distaste, was Chef Henri Aubert-Treffle. His gray-streaked beard was neatly trimmed, and his eyes were cold, exactly as he looked on TV. He was known—and feared—as the angriest man in the culinary world. His prime-time cable show, *If You Can't Handle the Heat*, had been running for decades. It was one of those shows that Luna had watched in reruns late at night with her mom when nothing else was on. It consisted mostly of Chef Henri screaming at hapless cooks who couldn't possibly meet his high standards.

There was another show he did, Luna recalled, where he tasted different dishes blindfolded and eviscerated them without mercy. In a super-fucked-up twist, half of the cooks were precocious children who ended up in tears when faced with the torrent of nasty comments. The guy was like a cross between a *New York Times* restaurant critic and Satan, if Satan had opinions on soufflés.

And now here he was, staring at Luna with a sour expression that she was already very familiar with. Except this time, there would be no cut to a commercial break.

Jean-Pierre cleared his throat and gestured between Luna and his phone. In English, he said, "Luna, this is my grandfather." Switching to French, he introduced Luna to Chef Henri. Luna caught only her own name, but whatever else Jean-Pierre said had Henri's bushy eyebrows winging upward.

Henri asked something in a demanding tone, also in French, and Jean-Pierre responded with heated words, and soon they were volleying back and forth louder and faster. Luna wasn't sure what to do, so she just kind of stood there with a tense smile plastered across her face. *A thousand dollars is a lot of money*, she reminded herself.

Chef Henri addressed Luna then, sounding just like he did on *Handle the Heat* when a contestant overcooked the fish: "Est-ce bien vrai? Vous êtes amoureuse de mon petit-fils?"

Luna didn't know much French, but she did know the lyrics to the entire *Moulin Rouge!* soundtrack. Plus her Spanish was decent and her Italian passable, and since French was basically those two languages mashed up with a bunch of letters ignored, she could more or less figure out what he meant. Something about love?

"Well, I . . ." she began.

"Elle ne parle pas français," Jean-Pierre said sharply. "Can we please speak English?"

"If we must," Chef Henri said. His accent was even more pronounced than Jean-Pierre's. His steely eyes fell on Luna again.

She gave the phone a tentative wave. "Hello. It's nice to finally meet you."

Henri's eyes narrowed in suspicion. Luna withstood his scrutiny, not letting her picture-perfect customer-service smile slip. If he was going to say something nasty, now would be the time.

Finally, Henri looked back to Jean-Pierre and said, "She is too pretty for you."

Luna fought the urge to slump in relief against Jean-Pierre's side. Passing as cis was not usually her goal, but in this situation, she would take it as a win. She covered her nervousness with a light laugh. "That's so sweet of you to say."

"I am not sweet," he said, swinging his laser focus back on Luna. "I am confused. Why have I not heard of you before? How long has this been going on, supposedly?"

"Oh, a long time. Like, months." Luna looked to Jean-Pierre for guidance. "It's been . . . how many months?"

"So many," Jean-Pierre offered.

"And yet it still feels like we just met!" Luna grinned a bit too forcefully. "You know how it is. Exciting young love. That's us."

"And how did you meet?" Henri asked in the same way a hard-boiled detective might ask for an alibi.

Luna gave Jean-Pierre a questioning glance, her eyes flying wide. He seemed as lost as she was. Why hadn't they spent five seconds before answering this call to discuss their fake dating history?

"It is, um, quite the story," Jean-Pierre said.

"Such a story." Luna nodded. "See, I live here. In New York." She stared at Jean-Pierre, silently pleading for him to help fill in the blanks. This was shaping up to be the worst round of Mad Libs in human history.

"And I was visiting. To check in on one of the restaurants. As a favor to Maman," Jean-Pierre said haltingly.

"Which restaurant?" Henri demanded.

"Le Cloître." No hesitation there. "She worried that the head chef was, how to say, cutting corners."

"And my roommate, she sometimes does restaurant reviews. Or did, at her last job," Luna jumped in. She'd never heard of Lew Clet or whatever it was called, but it sounded fancy. And she didn't even have to lie about Simone's previous gig. The best lies had a dash of truth; she'd read that somewhere. "So I was there with her, having dinner."

Jean-Pierre gave her a sappy look, which was probably just channeling his relief. "I saw Luna from across the room . . ."

"He sent over a bottle of wine," Luna improvised.

"She was very impressed."

"Hard not to be."

"After her friend left, we sat at the bar and talked for a bit."

"And we had so much in common!"

"Like." Jean-Pierre raised his brows at Luna in question. "Art?"

"Yes, we both love art. And"—Luna's mind helpfully supplied that the body she was squished up against felt pretty firm under all those black clothes—"fitness. We're both really into fitness."

"And food," Jean-Pierre offered.

"Right, food. You got to eat." Luna laughed. "Like, that's a no-brainer."

"So you consider yourself a gourmand?" Henri asked Luna.

She nodded frantically. "Oh, yeah. I live for food." This was a tiny exaggeration since Luna didn't even know how to fry an egg, but it felt like the right thing to say to a man whose entire life was dedicated to cooking.

"That works out nicely, seeing as this one"—he gestured at Jean-Pierre—"comes from a long line of chefs on both sides."

Luna fought the urge to frown. Henri seemed to be going to great lengths not to say Jean-Pierre's name.

"I have told Luna all about Papa's Michelin star and Maman's many restaurants," Jean-Pierre said. "She knows."

"She knows about us, yet we know nothing of her. She does not even speak your language," Henri grumbled. "How serious can this so-called relationship be?"

"It's very serious. I just didn't want to mention it before we were ready. It is bad luck to rush these things." Jean-Pierre wrapped an arm around Luna's shoulders, bringing their heads closer together in their little rectangle on the screen. "Do you really think I would travel all the way to New York for a mere fling?"

"I think you might travel to New York to see that D'Amboise woman," Henri said. "Is your grandmother not there to star in yet another vapid little pastry show? You cannot fool me so easily."

Jean-Pierre made a considering noise in his throat. "Is Grand-mère in town? I was not aware." To Luna, he said as an aside, "My grandmother from my mother's side; I have been meaning to introduce you, of course." Then, turning back to the phone: "I told you, I am here to see Luna." It was odd hearing her name in his voice, with its rolling syllables from the back of his tongue.

Chef Henri glared at them both, his gray eyes narrowing to the thinnest slits. "If you and this girl are actually in love—"

"We are," Luna said with what she hoped was a convincing smile. She wrapped an arm around Jean-Pierre's waist for emphasis. The phone wouldn't catch the gesture, of course, but it was the atmosphere that counted. "Deeply. Hopelessly. He's the cream in my coffee. He's the air that I breathe."

Jean-Pierre gave her a silent look that she assumed meant she should tone it down.

Henri's face, meanwhile, took on a gleeful cast. "Ah, I see, I see. Well! Shouldn't your very serious partner support you in the upcoming culinary test?" he said to Jean-Pierre.

"Luna has been nothing but supportive, Papi," Jean-Pierre said, moving his hand to the small of Luna's back and giving her a warning pat there. "Haven't you, darling?"

Luna, who had zero idea what they were talking about, gushed readily. "Absolutely! I tell Jean-Pierre every night when we video-chat, 'I support you, sweetie.'" She was very proud of herself; mentioning details made their story more believable. Probably.

"Cheering you on from afar, yes, that is one thing. But if you are truly a committed couple, then shouldn't you take the test together?" Henri gave them a sharklike smile, teeth bared. "After all, it sounds like she is practically family. And this is a family matter."

A chill ran down Luna's spine. None of this made any sense to her, but it sounded like a threat. They weren't fooling him at all. He was calling their bluff.

Jean-Pierre, for his part, doubled down. "What an excellent idea. Luna has already been helping me prepare, of course, so it makes sense for us to face your test together. Why not?"

"Yes, why not?" Henri sneered.

Luna could think of a dozen reasons why not off the top of her head, number one being she didn't know these people and didn't need to get involved in their drama. She turned up the wattage on her smile. Only a few more minutes, and then she could take her grand and go.

"What do you think, darling? Will you take the test as well?" Jean-Pierre's hand gave her hip a little pinch.

Luna jumped. "Sure!" She batted his hand away discreetly.

"Wonderful. Since there will be two of you in the kitchen, you can complete the menu much faster," Henri drawled. "Let's deduct, shall we say, two hours from your allotted time?"

"That's perfectly fine," Jean-Pierre said, though his face was scrunched up in a way that said the opposite.

"Good."

"Great."

"Super."

"Parfait."

They might have gone back and forth all day and into the night, but Luna broke the stalemate. She had a good work ethic—despite what her erstwhile employer might have thought—and she was determined to finish strong. She glanced at her own phone; the fifteen minutes were almost up. "It was a pleasure to meet you, sir," she said, beaming at Jean-Pierre's screen, "but we should get going."

"Ah, yes, young love." Henri gave them a sarcastic-sounding air kiss. "Farewell."

"Au revoir."

Jean-Pierre ended the call, waited one second, then heaved a loud groan.

Luna extracted herself from Jean-Pierre's side as quickly as she could without seeming too rude. It wasn't that she thought he was gross or anything; he was just a total stranger. Although the coffee smell that clung to his clothes wasn't half bad. It was really making Luna crave an oat milk latte.

More important things, she reminded herself.

"What was he talking about? What culinary test?"

Jean-Pierre pocketed his phone and rubbed at his eyes. He muttered something in French to himself.

"Hey, come on." She placed her hand on his elbow, feeling the creak of his leather jacket under her fingertips. "What does it all mean?"

Jean-Pierre turned to her with a strange look. "It means," he said, "that we are stuck together for longer than fifteen minutes."

Chapter 4

Before Luna could question Jean-Pierre further, Lisette D'Amboise herself whisked into the hall, clearly fresh from her meeting with the production staff.

It was the first time Luna had seen her in the flesh, and she was exactly what she'd expected. She wore her trademark black sack dress and had her long silver hair swept into a stylish chignon. A large statement pendant hung from her neck, and her heels made sharp clicks on the concrete floor. Her eyes fell on Jean-Pierre right away, lighting up at the sight of him.

"Ah, mon chéri!" She floated toward him with her arms outstretched, rattling off a lot of surprised, questioning French. No doubt she had not expected this visit.

"Bonjour, Grand-mère." Though he was short, his grandma was downright tiny, which meant Jean-Pierre had to duck so she could kiss both his cheeks. He answered her in rapid, agitated French. Lisette responded in kind, and soon they were locked in an incredibly loud argument. It seemed to be a pattern with this guy.

Luna tried her best to tiptoe away from the domestic dispute, but Jean-Pierre pinned her in place with a look. "You, stay right there," he said.

Luna stayed. Normally she would be more than ready to defy some stranger's order, but she realized she should stick around, if only for her payout. One thousand dollars would really pad her unemployment fund. Not to mention the conversation that continued between Jean-Pierre and his grandmother was pretty mesmerizing. If Luna concentrated, she could catch the meaning of perhaps every fifth word.

Simone sidled up alongside Luna, munching on popcorn from a gigantic zip-top bag. "Who's the shouty goth?" she asked, tossing another handful into her mouth. She shook the bag in Luna's direction in the universal gesture of offering.

"Oh, that's Jean-Pierre, Lisette's grandson." Luna reached without looking and took a handful. The popcorn was slightly spicy and a little sweet on her tongue. "That's really good. What is it?"

"Sriracha kettle corn. If I'm going to work late, I'm going to have snacks." Simone popped another fluffy piece into her mouth. She looked faintly impressed at something Lisette said, and Luna couldn't take the suspense anymore.

"Hey, you speak French, right? What are they saying?"

"Well, just then Lisette called him a silly boy with more money than sense." Simone chowed down on more popcorn. "Now he's saying it's all Henri's fault that he's in this mess. Whoa—Henri? Like, Chef Henri? From *If You Can't Handle the Heat*?"

"Yeah, apparently that's Jean-Pierre's grandpa from his father's side." Luna helped herself to more of the kettle corn.

"Okay, uh." Simone tried to concentrate on the back-and-forth tennis match that was the French conversation. "All right, Jean-Pierre is explaining that Henri is going to write him out of his will unless he passes some test." She listened intently to the passionate plea that Jean-Pierre seemed to be making. Her eyes widened in recognition. "Okay, I get it now. He has to cook The Menu."

Luna raised a brow. "*The* Menu?"

Simone nodded, not looking away from the action. "See, there's a special menu at Henri's flagship restaurant that's super famous and complicated. We spent a week in culinary school studying a single element of one dish. It's a whole thing. Millionaires are on the waiting list for years to get a table. Everyone on that side of the family knows the recipes except Jean-Pierre, I guess. Sounds like he can't cook much at all, really. And he came here to ask Lisette to coach him so he can pass the test. It's all tied to his inheritance, apparently."

Lisette asked a heated question, which Jean-Pierre answered just as heatedly.

Simone helpfully translated: "Lisette asked whether she's even allowed to help under the terms of Henri's weird test, and Jean-Pierre is saying, 'Of course not, no family members can. I'm not even supposed to be talking to you about it. I had hoped to come here in secret'—oh, this is getting *juicy*—'but Mother must have seen the plane ticket on my credit card and told Grandpa, so I had to come up with a good excuse for visiting New York.'"

Jean-Pierre pointed in Luna's direction, which made Luna startle. She paused mid-chew, her cheek full of popcorn like a squirrel.

Again, Simone translated Jean-Pierre's words. "'Now Grandpa thinks I am practically engaged to this girl, and she will have to take the test with me if I have a chance of—' Oh my god, Luna, what have you gotten yourself into?"

Luna swallowed hastily. "I don't know," she whisper-hissed at her. "He offered me a thousand dollars! It was just supposed to be a few minutes of my time."

Lisette lowered her voice to say a few choice words to her grandson, accompanied by adamant hand gestures. Both Simone and Luna leaned closer to listen, though in Luna's case, she was listening only for the vibe, not the content.

Simone provided that in spades: "Wow, she's letting him have it. Um, it's kind of hard to translate. Basically: while she would normally be happy to teach Jean-Pierre how to cook, she is not thrilled that he's only showing an interest because of Henri's bullshit—paraphrasing, she made it sound much nicer. Plus, she's a very busy woman, which is completely true, and she—" Simone stifled a laugh in the crook of her arm.

"What?" Luna pressed.

"She thinks Henri's signature menu is garbage. She says the people willing to pay thousands of dollars for nine tiny pretentious courses are fools, and Henri is the biggest fool of them all. She doesn't want to waste her time teaching him how to cook food like that."

Lisette pointed emphatically in Luna's direction as she continued speaking, and this time Luna was ready for it. She gave Jean-Pierre and his morose eyes a cheery wave.

"Now she's telling him off for dragging 'some poor girl' into his mess," Simone said. "Which I guess is you."

"Honestly, it's just an honor to be recognized." Luna dug around in the zip-top bag and ate another fistful of kettle corn.

Lisette seemed to finally reach the end of her diatribe. She quieted and visibly softened, reaching up to frame Jean-Pierre's angular face with her thin hands. Her murmurs sounded sweet and warm.

"Aww." Simone, who had only recently gotten in touch with the more tender emotions, gave a sappy smile. "She's saying she loves him and is proud of him no matter what, but she can't in good conscience help prolong this farce. She hopes he understands."

A fire lit up Jean-Pierre's dark eyes, and his jaw took on a steely determination. He took Lisette's hands in his and gently peeled them from his cheeks. "If that is how you feel," he said in English, "so be it. I will just have to do it on my own." His piercing gaze caught Luna's and held it. "Mademoiselle, I will give you an additional $100,000 and a trip to Paris if you continue the charade with me."

Luna choked on her popcorn.

Chapter 5

The security guard tried to wish Luna a good day as Luna hustled out of the building at a fast clip. She managed to register the farewell and call a goodbye of her own over her shoulder only at the last second, just before the glass doors of the entrance fell shut behind her. Through them, she could see Jean-Pierre rocketing down the spiral staircase to catch up with her.

She hurried a little faster and gave thanks for the fact that she was wearing gym shoes. Plus, her longer legs meant she could probably get a decent chunk of distance between them. *Tall girls keep winning.*

"Luna, wait, please!" Jean-Pierre's voice followed her down the sidewalk as he pushed through the doors. "Where are you going?"

"Far away from here." She focused on reaching the corner, where she could cross the street and make a beeline for the subway.

"Why would you want to do a thing like that?" He must have been faster than he looked, because Luna could hear him right behind her.

She stopped and whirled, her hands on her hips. Jean-Pierre was, as she'd sensed, much too close, his big Victorian ghost-child eyes going wide as he moved back a step to get out of her personal space.

"If you think I'm going to get involved in this family feud you've got going on," she said, "think again."

Jean-Pierre stared at her, barely winded, his hair still artfully falling over his brow. By contrast, Luna could feel her heart hammering away somewhere in her throat. She was covered in a light sweat, and not the dewy, attractive kind.

"But I have not even sent you the money that is owed," he pointed out. "Will you at least give me the few minutes it takes to do that while I make my case?"

Luna hesitated. A thousand dollars was nothing to sneeze at, but every instinct she had was telling her to walk away, that it wasn't worth any amount of money to get wrapped up in his family drama.

Her desire to pay the next month's rent won out. "Fine," she said. "Talk fast."

Jean-Pierre whipped his cell phone from the pocket of his leather jacket and began swiping. "Of course. Do you have this app?" He showed her the icon.

"Yeah." She retrieved her own phone to pull up her money-transfer QR code. "So what's the deal with your grandpa? He's making you cook a bunch of stuff before he puts you in his will?"

"I am his only male grandchild, you see." Jean-Pierre made a face. "I know. So old-fashioned. Yet he insists this is how our family has always done things."

"Seriously?" Luna stared at him. "Your family has always forced its heirs to cook secret recipes? You can hear how bullshit that sounds, right?"

He shrugged, then tapped his phone to Luna's in a way that made her imagine the phones were kissing. Their devices pinged happily. "I honestly do not understand his reasoning, but he has always been, ah, eccentric. I must do this if I am to inherit not just his restaurants but the entire estate. Houses, horses, cars—you should see these cars he owns. Stocks, bonds, savings accounts, the family antiques . . . It's not a small thing, his will."

"But why test you at all? Does he expect you to be in the kitchen cooking all day once he's gone?" She checked her phone's screen as she spoke. One thousand American dollars added to her account, as promised. Jean-Pierre's number had also been added to her contacts, along with his full name. It barely fit on the screen.

Jean-Pierre barked a harsh laugh. "Non, non, he knows I have no talent for food. I think that is why he is being so stubborn about all this. He would love nothing more than to leave everything to someone else, but there are no other men available. My father has apparently refused to inherit his restaurants, as he already has his own to manage." He scoffed. "I must prove myself a worthy heir. This outdated notion of birthright. It has only made problems, eh?"

Luna knew she was grasping at straws, but she asked anyway. "What about your parents? Can't your dad get him to see reason? Someone's got to be able to explain to Henri that this is way too wild, even for him."

"My parents." Jean-Pierre looked to the side, licking his lips like he needed to prepare them for his next words. "We are not exactly close."

"No?" Luna was taken aback. "Didn't you say you were doing favors for your mom when we had our fake meet-cute?"

"Our . . . ?"

"How we met! Or how we said we met. You told your grandpa you were here in New York to do something for your mom, so I assumed you got along," Luna said.

"Ah. That." Jean-Pierre waved an unaffected hand through the air. "I work with my parents, yes. I am their—hm—operations man, the one who helps the business parts run smoothly. But my mother and father are quite busy; we all have our own lives, you see? I may go from one end of the month to the next without speaking to them. They leave me to my own devices, as they say."

Luna scrunched up her nose. She and her own mom were so close, they spoke on the phone nearly every day. The majority of those calls involved Luna's mom trying to weasel out every fact she could about Luna's love life, with the best of intentions, of course. In fact, Luna was probably going to miss the window for their usual after-work phone call; it was a Thursday, so her mom would have her aerial gymnastics class that evening. Luna couldn't imagine working for her mother while her mother simultaneously ignored her as a person.

"So your folks are completely fine with Grandpa Henri making you jump through hoops to get into his will?"

"Oh, they find it all very vulgar," Jean-Pierre said, his voice as light as Simone's pastry. "They would rather one or both of us call a truce—that is probably why Maman felt it necessary to gossip with Papi about my comings and goings, I'm sure." He laughed like it was a big joke. "My parents have a point; this is all very silly, these, ah, hoops of my grandfather's."

"So why even agree to take the culinary test? You obviously don't need the money that badly." Luna waved her phone in the air, the dollar amount still glowing on the screen.

"It is not about the money." Jean-Pierre paused, his brow crinkling in thought. "All right, it is *somewhat* about the money. But more importantly, it is about my grandfather losing and myself winning. He does not believe I can do it, which means I must."

Luna shook her head. "See, this type of macho BS does not call to me, to be honest. I really don't think I should get involved in this."

Jean-Pierre regarded her closely. "Not even if I paid you a hundred thousand dollars?"

Luna opened her mouth, closed it, raised a finger in the air and shook it a couple of times. It was the kind of money that could change her life. Her amorphous daydream of becoming a certified yoga instructor and opening a queer-friendly mindful-ness retreat in the Catskills suddenly didn't seem so out of reach.

A hundred grand wouldn't buy a sprawling mountain prop-erty, but it would be a start.

Luna was reminded of Tim at Papr Tigr, earning six times that absurd amount for every year his butt was in his fancy CEO chair when he couldn't even open a Word doc. She licked her lips. The situation was already ridiculous; why not up the ante?

"Make it six hundred and I'd consider it," she said, knowing there was no way in hell—

"All right," Jean-Pierre said. "Six, then."

Luna goldfished for another moment before recovering her-self. "You're honestly willing to pay me that kind of money? You're *that* rich?"

"Well, I don't know what the going rate is to pretend to be someone's lover," he said with a little heat. "If you say six, I say that is fair. I can afford it."

Luna's world tilted and rebalanced. Six hundred thousand dollars was an inconceivable amount of money. Life-changing times six. "What would I have to do? Take this culinary test with you?"

"Yes, and come to Paris with me to do so. All expenses paid, naturally."

"Naturally," Luna echoed.

"And continue pretending to be my lover."

Luna squished up her face in a cringe. "Can we just say 'girl-friend' like normal people?" *Lover* sounded so . . . tragic black-and-white film with a weird ambiguous ending.

Jean-Pierre rolled his eyes. "Yes, fine, as American as you please."

God, he was annoying. Luna wasn't sure she could pretend to be his friend, let alone his devoted girlfriend. It was a lot of money, and sure, she'd always wanted to see Paris, but . . .

"Can I think about it?" she asked. Her hand went to her forehead; she felt a little dizzy. "It's a lot to take in, you know?"

"Certainly!" Jean-Pierre grabbed her free hand and held it between them. "Take all the time you need. There is no rush."

It was at that moment that Luna looked over the sharp point of Jean-Pierre's shoulder and noticed a gaggle of people rounding the corner armed with news cameras, microphones, and long tele-photo lenses on their Nikons. The brewery studio was situated on the tip of a triangular block, so the crowd must have come from the back of the building, where the service entrance was.

Luna squinted at the approaching mass of people. "What's all that?"

Jean-Pierre turned to look, still clutching her hand in his. At the first sight of his face, the crew sprang to life, shouting things in both English and French, all while surging forward in their direction, their cameras at the ready. Some were repeating his name, although Luna was pretty sure a couple of them were mistakenly calling him Jean-Pierre D'Amboise instead of Aubert-Treffle.

"Ah." Jean-Pierre turned back to her, his eyes wide. "There is actually some rush."

"What? Why?"

"*Journalistes*, the paparazzi." Taking a firmer hold of her hand, he began tugging her down the sidewalk, leading her away from the cameras. "They follow my grandmother religiously."

"Really?" Luna looked over her shoulder and was immediately blinded by a flash. "Lisette is that famous?"

"In Europe, yes. I suppose the Americans have joined the hunt now." Jean-Pierre expertly placed a palm over his eyes to shield his face just as a few camerapeople overtook them, surrounding them like water flowing around a river rock.

The questions came hard and fast, Luna only catching every other word: *Are you working with Lisette on this new show? What can you tell us about it? Is your grandmother going to start filming soon? Who is this you're with?*

"Just ignore them," Jean-Pierre said into her ear over the

roar of voices and equipment clicks. "They will lose interest eventually."

Luna sat in front of her laptop with her head in her hands. The paparazzi had very much not lost interest. The media had followed them two and a half blocks yesterday, right up until Jean-Pierre had managed to flag down one of those uptown green cabs so they could both escape. It appeared that, since they hadn't been able to capture any photos of Lisette entering or leaving the studio, the gossip blogs had shifted all their focus to Jean-Pierre, "the brave transgender heir to multiple culinary powerhouses," and his "mysterious new paramour." Now photos of the two of them were splashed over a dozen different websites and social channels.

And Luna had been wearing *athleisure*. Those weren't even her good yoga tights. This was galactically unfair of the universe. If she was going to get her fifteen minutes of fame, she wished it were while wearing something more flattering.

"I don't get it," Luna moaned into her palms. She glanced back at the laptop—her personal one with the sakura stickers all over it, since her work laptop was now shoved under her bed waiting for the day when someone at Papr Tigr figured out how to create a mailing label. "His grandparents cook food on TV. His folks run a few restaurants. Why are they treating him like a movie star? This is so bonkers."

"You'd be surprised," Simone said from her place behind Luna's desk chair, where she was reading over her shoulder. It was Friday evening, so she was finally free from the constraints of work and able to catch up with Luna. "Some people in the culinary world are movie-star-level famous. Folks will read about their lives if it's out there for consumption, just like any other celebrity. That's just how it is."

Luna uncovered her face and stared at the photo of herself that currently graced her screen. It was not the most flattering angle; the photog had practically shoved his camera in her face to get the shot. She was caught frozen in mid-word, her mouth wide open, her eyes mid-blink.

At least her hair looked okay.

"This sucks," she said. "Now that all this is out there, I'm pretty much locked into this weird fake-relationship deal with Jean-Pierre."

"You can still say no," Simone pointed out.

Luna swiveled around in her chair to face her roommate with her arms crossed over her chest. "He said he'd give me six hundred grand and a trip to Paris."

Simone's eyes went very wide. "Uh—wow, six hundred? Really? Not one?"

"I renegotiated."

Simone shook her head wildly as if to dislodge the thought of that much cash. "But it's not like you're hurting for money, right? You've got a good job; you can turn this down if you want."

Luna closed her eyes and tensed as if preparing for a blow. "Yeah, about that. I got fired."

"What!" Simone gaped at her. "When?"

"Yesterday. I meant to tell you earlier; that's why I was at the studio to begin with." She gave a half shrug. "I guess stuff got hectic. Sorry."

As if sensing that this conversation might last awhile, Simone moved one step to the side and sat down heavily on the edge of Luna's bed. "Why did they let you go? You worked your butt off for that guy, always answering emails after hours and working weekends—"

Luna sighed through her nose. "I don't know. They said it was nothing personal."

"Shitheads," Simone muttered. She looked up at Luna, her mouth turned down. "Are you okay?"

It was touching to hear a curse word from a straitlaced person like Simone; it showed how much she really cared. Or how working alongside the television crew was making her vocabulary more salty.

"I'm . . . dealing," Luna said, which was not too much of a lie. She would, at some point, untangle her emotions. Meditate on it. Maybe head to the gym and take it out on a literal punching bag. But all her tried-and-true coping strategies would have to wait; she had a new job offer to consider, kind of. "Honestly, right now money is, umm, top of mind. Can I really say no to Jean-Pierre?"

Simone's face contorted into what looked like pity. "If you're worried about making rent—"

Luna held up her hand. "I can't let you cover me."

"Sure you can! You can always pay me back. It's just money." Spoken like a true recent recipient of an outlandish production advance.

"It's not about money," Luna said, though it really was. Even as she said it, she knew it sounded like she was trying to convince herself more than Simone. "It's about knowing that I have the chance to handle this myself instead of relying on other people to help. All I have to do is help someone win a bet with his shitty grandpa. Isn't that what life is all about?"

Simone frowned. "That's a really specific thing for life to be about."

"You know what I mean." Luna blew a strand of hair out of her eyes. She could feel herself warming to the theme in a way that meant she was about to talk herself into this plan. "Not that he and I will ever be best friends or anything, but Jean-Pierre doesn't seem like a bad person. And he needs help." She thought about that first meeting in the hallway, and how offended she had been not to be asked to be his fake girlfriend until it was clear there were no other takers, only to discover he'd been trying to shield her—a perfect stranger—from his grandfather's acerbic personality. She smiled a little at the memory, then tossed it aside. She needed to focus on what mattered. "And if he's offering a fair price for my acting skills, why not take him up on it?"

Simone hummed in thought. "Well, you would be leaving him in the lurch if you backed out now. I mean, after all of this"—she gestured at the laptop—"you'd be doing a very nice thing for him."

Luna was the queen of doing nice things. She believed in positive energy, for sure: karma, things coming back tenfold, whatever you wanted to call it. She trusted the universe to put what she needed in her path. Maybe Jean-Pierre and his bargain were just what she needed.

Plus, how else was she ever going to get a free trip to France?

"I think this is something I have to do," she said with a firm nod. "Jean-Pierre is counting on me, after all." She was such a selfless person. People could write songs about her.

"Maybe you should invite him over," Simone suggested. "You can iron out all the details. Maybe get things in writing?"

"Good idea." Luna pulled out her phone, then hesitated with a bite to her lip. "And maybe he should stay over at our place for now."

Simone took a sharp breath. "Why in the world should he do that?"

"Uh, because I'm supposed to be in a relationship with him?" Luna pointed back at the laptop, the crisp photos of them still splashed across the screen. "It's weird if he travels all the way to New York to see his long-distance girlfriend and then doesn't even stay with me, right? If he's staying in some swanky hotel, the press are sure to notice."

"Maybe he'll stay with Lisette; it's not as if she doesn't have the space," Simone said with an uncharacteristic amount of optimism. "She has that penthouse in SoHo; I've been over to visit. It's huge."

Luna shook her head. "Jean-Pierre isn't supposed to even speak with her about this whole debacle, remember? He can't crash in her guest room. If the press or whoever catches him there, it'll be ugly. There are rules he's supposed to follow if he wants that inheritance. The only logical answer is for him to stay here."

Simone puffed out her cheeks. "Where are we going to put him? On the couch?"

She had a point. Their lumpy secondhand sofa did not seem like the natural sleeping spot for a guy as fancy as Jean-Pierre. He probably slept on a mattress of handpicked goose down every night. From endangered geese. Who were massaged with feather oil before they were plucked.

Luna considered the problem, then brightened. "Why don't you stay with Ray for a few days? That way, Jean-Pierre can take your room."

Simone's eyes flew wide. "Are you kidding me? That's a terrible plan!" She crossed her arms over her stomach, looking grim.

"You're over at Ray's most of the time anyway. If you're squeamish about having a guest in your perfectly clean and organized sanctuary, I can stay in there while Jean-Pierre takes mine."

"Luna, it's not an issue of cleanliness," Simone said. "It's that I don't want to leave you alone with a strange guy we know nothing about."

Luna couldn't help it. This naked display of actual human feeling from her roommate was enough to make her clutch her hands to her heart. "Aw, Simone! That is so sweet of you. Trying to keep me from being a murder victim."

Simone blushed like she usually did when she was caught being thoughtful. "I'm serious! You have to consider your safety."

"I know, I know, you're just trying to protect me in that practical way of yours. Such a Virgo," Luna said with deep affection. She dropped her hands from her heart and placed them on her thighs in a more businesslike fashion. "But I promise you, Jean-Pierre is not a serial killer. For one thing, he's being hounded by the press, so it's not like he could get away with dumping a corpse even if he wanted to."

Simone's face fell in despair. "This is not helping."

"Look," Luna said, going for the argumentative kill, "if I'm going to get a butt-load of money to pretend to date someone, I'm going to earn it. You know me: I never do anything half-assed. It's full ass or nothing."

Which reminded her: if she was going to pretend to date a Frenchman, she should probably start learning French. She picked up her phone—which turned out to be a mistake. It was lit up like a Christmas tree. Luna tried to parse the notifications but there were just too many. No way was she going to answer every message from a former high school classmate who wanted to know if she was really the person in the pap photos. She swiped them all away, except for one. Aisha—the most online of her friends—had @'ed everyone in the group chat to share the links to the stories. Luna watched as each of her dear friends joined the chat to demand an explanation.

Luna what the actual fuck

Wow they really went with that picture, huh

i ain't reading all that! luna WHATS GOING ON

I'll tell you when I have a minute, she told them, then closed the app entirely. She put her phone on focus/ignore-everything mode and did what she'd originally picked up her phone to do: download a starter language pack from the free app with the cartoon owl that had bullied her into learning Italian. Of course, Luna always picked up languages more quickly via immersion— she'd watched nothing but telenovelas the summer she turned fourteen, and her Spanish was still pretty decent as a result— so she opened up her podcast player and searched the French-language feeds. There were always true crime and creepypasta podcasts to be had, no matter what language you spoke.

As she marked a dozen or so to download, she said, "Bringing Jean-Pierre here not only helps with the whole 'we're a couple' ruse, but it will also give us a chance to get our stories straight, get to know each other. And"—she put her phone into her pocket, content to ignore it for the time being—"it'll give us time to practice these recipes we're going to have to make."

Simone's lip quivered. Her resolve was crumbling, Luna could sense it. "I can't figure out if I'm being transphobic or super affirming by treating the trans man with the same level of distrust I would have for a cis guy."

"Sweetie, there aren't enough lemon tarts in the world for us to get into that question right now," Luna said. Traditionally, Simone was required to feed her if she wanted to hash out her cis guilt.

Simone blew out a breath and stood. "Okay. I'll pack some things and stay over at Ray's. But I want you to call me if you have any trouble with this dude at all, agreed?"

"Totally!" Luna sprang to her feet and followed Simone into her bedroom. It was smaller and much neater than Luna's—no socks on the floor, no sweaters draped over anything, no chair with a pile of laundry waiting to be folded on it. Luna sat on the edge of the hospital-cornered bed and watched Simone take what looked like an old bowling bag out of her closet. "Seriously," she said, "thanks for doing this. It's a huge help."

"Well, it's not exactly a hardship, staying with Ray." Simone's blush was faint, but Luna caught it before she started pulling open drawers and selecting clean socks and shirts. "I guess I've been doing that more and more lately, anyway."

"Yeah." Luna gnawed at her lip. "Good for you." She knew she should bring up their rental agreement's future and gauge how amenable Simone would be to committing to another year or so of living together. But watching her pack her overnight bag, Luna couldn't miss the look of wistful eagerness on Simone's face. Simone saw her themfriend almost every day, what with working together, and she still couldn't wait to see them tonight. Luna didn't want to put a damper on that.

Plus, if this fake-dating scheme really ended up with her

earning six hundred grand, Luna wouldn't have to worry about keeping a roommate, at least not for a while.

"I should call Jean-Pierre, let him know what's up," she said, distracting herself with fishing her phone out of her hoodie pocket. She jabbed at Jean-Pierre Dominique Gabriel Aubert-Treffle's name in her phone's contact list and hit the call button. She put it on speaker for Simone's benefit.

He picked up on the fourth ring. "Allo?"

"Hi, it's Luna. Your, um, not-girlfriend." She grimaced at Simone, who gave her a supremely unhelpful thumbs-up. "Listen, I've been thinking about what you said and—"

"You will do it." It wasn't even a question. He sounded absolutely certain and unsurprised. "Splendide."

Luna rolled her eyes. Okay, presumptuous. "We should go over the game plan first. Can you come over to my place tonight? Same spot you had the cab drop me off yesterday; I can text you the address."

"No need," Jean-Pierre said blandly.

"No . . . what? Wait, why—?"

The buzzer buzzed. Both Luna and Simone froze, looking at each other. Luna looked down at her phone, ready to repeat her question, but her screen informed her that the call had ended. Total slasher-film vibes.

They both went to where the intercom was bolted to the wall in the apartment's tiny entry hall. Simone pressed the button. "Hello?"

Silence.

Simone groaned and tried again. "You have to press and hold the button so I can hear you." She released hers, grumbling under her breath about how no one understood how to work a simple intercom anymore, and what was this city coming to?

The speaker crackled and a very confused French-accented voice floated through. "Allo? You can hear me now?"

Luna elbowed Simone out of the way, stabbing the button with her fingertip. "What are you doing here?"

"You were about to invite me anyway, no?" he crooned. "I am merely being efficient."

"Oh my god." Luna groaned and slapped her hand over the door-release button. They could hear the loud screech of it all the way from the lobby, six floors down.

"Well, it *does* save everyone some time," Simone said. Luna couldn't argue with that.

Jean-Pierre appeared at their door dressed in a pair of black trousers stuffed into the tops of black boots and a black asymmetrical sweater under what Luna was now certain was his trademark leather jacket. He was carrying a duffel bag with a horse-and-rider logo emblazoned on the side. It probably cost more than five monthly MetroCards, Luna guessed. "I hope you don't mind," he said to them, hoisting the bag. "I canceled the remainder of my hotel stay. I believe I should stay here for the time being."

"We were about to suggest the same thing," Luna said, shooting Simone a look. "Although most people would have waited for the invitation."

Jean-Pierre breezed by them both, navigating the narrow hallway with buttery ease. "Do not worry, I am a very good houseguest," he said as he stepped into the living room without waiting for either of them. "I do not eat breakfast, so you need not worry about fixing me anything in the morning."

Luna shut the door and started going through the laborious process of turning all its locks. "Oh! The Little Prince doesn't eat breakfast," she muttered to herself. "Dear me, whatever will I do if I can't enjoy the privilege of serving him eggs and toast?" She took a deep breath and swept out into the living room, only to discover the leather carry-all abandoned on the floor near the TV stand, unzipped with a length of phone charger cable spilling out of it, its owner nowhere in sight. "Uh, Jean-Pierre?" she called out.

Jean-Pierre's answering shout came from the kitchen. "I am here!"

Luna walked the short distance to the kitchen and paused in the doorway. Jean-Pierre was standing at the small counter, arranging what looked to be oodles of fancy coffee paraphernalia: a jar of whole beans, a small bullet-style grinder, a packet of cone-shaped filters, a pour-over set that looked like it belonged in the MoMA, and an electric kettle with a thin spout. Luna knew that some people took their coffee seriously, but this was ridiculous.

"Did you actually pack any clothes?" Luna asked. "How much barista stuff did you bring?"

"Enough," was his clipped answer. "It is a hobby of mine." Jean-Pierre set one of the paper cones into the pour-over setup with fiddly precision.

Luna folded her arms over her chest and leaned against the doorframe to watch the proceedings more comfortably. Simone joined her, stepping more fully into the small kitchen, which was rightfully her domain. They both watched as Jean-Pierre unplugged the stand mixer and shoved it aside to give himself better access to the two square feet of counter space.

"What are you doing?" Simone said in alarm.

Jean-Pierre plugged in his grinder and loaded in the beans, which made a plinking sound as they were poured. "Making coffee, of course. Would you like a cup?"

"No, I would *not* like—"

"Do you have any filtered water?" Jean-Pierre interrupted, brushing past Simone to open the fridge. He clicked his tongue at its contents. "No matter. The city water is drinkable, yes?"

"New York has some of the best tap water in the world," Simone said in a cold tone. She had been born here, so Luna figured she felt protective of its aquatic reputation. "It doesn't need to be filtered."

"I'll have some coffee," Luna said, raising her hand. Chaos was something she was comfortable with. Other people, like Simone, might not be able to enjoy the ride, but for Luna, it was the only way to travel. She tried not to smile too impishly as Simone's face turned red, then purple. "Can you make mine an oat milk latte?"

"Oui, if you show me where you keep your milk frother." Jean-Pierre mimed the action of using a stick blender, and Luna propped her elbows on the edge of the counter to enjoy Simone's sputtering.

"Seriously? Look at this kitchen." Simone waved to indicate the small amount of space between them. "Everything in here is at least dual-purpose. We don't have a milk frother."

Jean-Pierre turned to Luna with an apologetic twist of his mouth. "I cannot produce a proper latte for you, then. Will you try it black like mine?"

"Now how did I know you would take your coffee black," Luna said, letting her eyes rove over his "goth kid who escaped from art school" fit.

Simone took Luna by the arm. "Would you excuse us for a second?" she said to Jean-Pierre. He was too focused on his coffee paraphernalia to pay her any mind, so Simone led Luna to her bedroom, shutting the door behind them. In the distance, they could hear the grinder whir to life with a loud squeal. Simone shut her eyes as if in terrible pain, and then opened them. "I'm going to kill him," she said flatly.

"No, you're not." Luna put her hands on Simone's tense shoulders and squeezed. "We've got six hundred thousand reasons not to, remember?"

"*You* do; I'm not getting paid for this." A loud clatter came from the kitchen, making them both jump. Simone cast a disbelieving look in Luna's direction. "He's impossible," she whispered. "How are you going to manage being around him for days at a time? It's been five minutes and I already want to strangle him."

"Well, you're more sensitive about milk frothers than I am," Luna said, not unkindly.

"Come on, even you can't be this zen. You'd have to have the patience of a saint to put up with this guy."

Luna shrugged, her mouth pulling up at one corner. "The Marquis de Fancypants is pretty annoying, yes, but I've dealt with worse. And I promise I will make sure he doesn't completely destroy the kitchen while he's here."

"Luna!" came the exceedingly French cry from the kitchen. The banging of cupboard doors echoed through the apartment. "Where might I find—? Ah, never mind, cups are here! The coffee is ready!"

Luna winced at the final slam of the cupboards. Simone stared at her, unimpressed. "If I come back and find he's broken anything," she said, "I'm going to make him replace it with the most expensive, top-of-the-line, state-of-the-art, I-would-never-dream-of-spending-this-much-on-myself version available."

"That's fair. He's loaded, apparently; he won't even flinch." Luna nodded at Simone's half-full overnight bag, still sitting on the floor. "Finish packing, all right? I'll—" She gestured vaguely toward the kitchen. "Keep an eye on him."

Back in the kitchen, Luna found that Jean-Pierre had removed his leather jacket and rolled the sleeves of his sweater back to his elbows. His eyes caught hers as she stood in the kitchen doorway.

"Here you are." He handed her a miniscule sage-green cup—a cup that Luna had never seen before in her life and was surprised to find they owned. It held a small amount of fragrant, dark coffee. Wisps of steam rose to greet Luna's face as she sniffed at it. "Careful; it's still quite hot," Jean-Pierre said.

He watched closely as she took her first sip.

Luna didn't drink coffee often—two cups of green tea with honey and lemon were enough caffeine to get her going in the mornings—but even she could tell Jean-Pierre's coffee was good. It tasted rich and creamy despite containing no cream, the silkiness cutting through the bitter flavor. She took another sip.

"You like it?" Jean-Pierre took a drink from his own matching cup, his gaze never leaving Luna's face in a way that made her cheeks heat. It was probably the coffee.

She smacked her lips. "Pretty decent."

Jean-Pierre frowned at her choice of words. "Decent."

"Yeah." She sipped again. "Decent."

"It is perfectly fresh—a Brooklyn roaster I favor when I am in New York, you see. Do you taste the honey and caramel on the back?" He gestured to his own throat as he pronounced every syllable in *ca-rah-mel*.

Luna took another loud slurp from her cup. She pronounced it *car-mal* and couldn't find it even if she cared to. "I taste coffee."

Jean-Pierre shook his head and busied himself with tidying away the used grounds. "Philistine," he said. She smiled cheerfully through another loud gulp. She'd been called worse by better.

Simone reappeared with her overnight bag in hand. She gave Luna an appraising look. "You're absolutely certain about this?"

"I'm positive. And caffeinated." Luna put down her cup and made a shooing motion with her hands. "Go, get out of here. Tell Ray I said hello."

"Okay," Simone said, sounding doubtful. She turned to their guest. "Jean-Pierre, I'm going now. You can sleep in my room, all right?"

Jean-Pierre, who was putting his cone-shaped drip thing into the sink, looked over his shoulder at Simone. "Ah, I took a glance earlier. Yours is the cleaner of the two rooms, yes?"

"Yes," Luna said in her customer-service voice through gritted teeth. "Much cleaner."

He smiled at her, her irritation bouncing off him like oil on Teflon, then directed his attention to Simone. "I am also a person who likes things a certain way." He reached out and cradled her hand in both of his. "Please know I appreciate you letting me stay in your space, very much. I will leave it in perfect order. You will not even know I was here!"

"Uh," Simone said, looking helplessly at Luna, "no problem."

Luna, for her part, just raised her brows. So Jean-Pierre could be charming, polite even. When he wanted to be.

"Well. If everything's good, then I guess I should be going?" Simone said.

"Ah, allow me to get the door; you have this bag to carry. Shall I take it downstairs for you?"

"No, it's fine. It's not heavy," she said, adjusting the strap on her shoulder. "Thanks for offering, though," she added belatedly.

"Have a good time at Ray's," Luna said, following them both to the front door. "I'll text you once things calm down."

"Yeah, let me know when it's safe to come home." Simone gave her a wry look. "Or if you need any help with—anything."

"We'll be fine! Really," Luna said while they lined up like soldiers in the narrow entry hall, Jean-Pierre working the door locks open. "It's only for a couple of days, and then everything will be—"

With a triumphant cry, Jean-Pierre managed to finagle the final lock and swung the door open with a flourish.

"—fine," Luna said, staring at the very familiar face waiting on the other side of their door.

Luna closed her eyes, then opened them again.

Her mom was here. Perfect.

Chapter 6

"Hi, sweetie pie!" said the face, the apparition, the hallucination. This could not be happening. "Surprise!"

Luna's mother beamed at the three of them as she wiped her shoes on their sisal welcome mat. Mrs. O'Shea—Connie to her friends—had Luna's brown eyes and light-blonde hair, though her face was rounder and her makeup game was a touch more dated. The blue eyeshadow was doing her no favors, not that Luna would ever tell her so; it would break her mom's big, squishy Pennsylvanian heart.

"Mom," she said in a strangled voice, "what are you doing here?"

"Your neighbor let me in; nice lady, she lives on the second floor," Mrs. O'Shea said with a light laugh. "Thought I'd pop in and see how my favorite daughter is doing."

Luna was her only daughter—her only child at all, in fact—but it was a running joke of hers.

"But why—?"

Before Luna could even form the question, her mom's gaze inexorably shifted to Jean-Pierre's pale, shocked face as he stood holding the door open. "Oh! And this is your new beau, I presume?"

"Uh?" Luna choked out. This was some kind of nightmare. Soon she'd remember she had to get to high school algebra and take a test, which she would need to do naked. While everyone deadnamed her.

Her mother leveled a look at her. It was similar to the looks she'd perfected years ago when little baby Luna had snuck fruit snacks before dinner. "I have the internet at home, you know," she said. "Imagine my surprise when I saw your pretty face splashed all over some of my favorite blogs. I guess *GlobeTrot* and *Nouveau Lifestyle* get all the news about my child's life before I do, not that I'm bitter!" She put her hands up in the air. "How can I be bitter when the news is so great?" She turned, arms outstretched, toward Jean-Pierre, who boggled at her. "Can I give you a 'welcome to the family' hug, John?"

Jean-Pierre did not even seem to register the mispronounced name as he stood frozen like a marble statue before saying, "Okay."

Mrs. O'Shea wrapped him up in a huge bear hug, rocking Jean-Pierre's slight form back and forth as she squeezed. Over his shoulder, she mouthed to Luna, *Smells good!*

No matter how hard Luna tried to make whatever was happening stop happening by using the sheer power of positive thinking, nothing could change the fact that her mother was here when she should definitely not be.

Her mom finally released a dazed Jean-Pierre and held him at arm's length. "I'm really looking forward to getting to know you. What's that cologne you've got on? It smells expensive."

"Mom!" Luna cried. She tried to wish herself through the floor, but unfortunately she stayed right where she was. "Could you not? And his name is Jean-Pierre."

"John Pierre," Mrs. O'Shea said.

"*Jean*."

"John." She frowned. "Am I not saying it right?"

"It's actually my aftershave," Jean-Pierre said belatedly.

Mrs. O'Shea gave an impressed waggle of her eyebrows.

"Well, I like it." She shouldered her way farther into the entry hall, dragging her beat-up rolling suitcase with green and red Christmas ribbons tied to the handle behind her. "Let me sit down, sweetie. You'd think spending three hours on the bus from Pennsylvania would have me feeling restless, but I'm wiped. Ah, Simone!" She paused in front of Luna's horrified-looking roommate and nodded at the overnight bag still dangling from her hand. "Going somewhere?"

"Yes, I was just—" Simone looked over at Luna, but Luna had no idea what she wanted her to say, so she just made a panicky eye movement. "I'm going over to Ray's for a few nights?" She winced even as she said it, as if she could sense what would logically follow. Luna was one step behind her, groaning internally at the mess her mom was about to make.

"That's wonderful! I had planned on sleeping on your sofa like the last time I visited, but maybe you'd be so kind as to let me use your bedroom? Since you're not going to be here and all." Mrs. O'Shea grinned widely at Simone with all the bubbly energy Luna had inherited and was not particularly feeling at the moment. That bedroom was already earmarked for her *other* unwanted guest. She had to set the record straight, tell her mom the truth—or at least a version of it that was believable—so this could all be hashed out.

"That would be all right," Simone was saying, but Luna barely heard her. She took her mother by the arm and commandeered the handle of her suitcase. The crowded entry hall was no place to have this conversation.

"I've got this, Simone," she said. "Go, don't keep Ray waiting."

"You're sure?" Simone couldn't quite keep the relief out of her voice at being released from this literal French farce of a scene.

"Go! Jean-Pierre, will you lock the door behind her while I catch up with my mom?" She began steering both mother and suitcase into the living room, not even waiting for his disconcerted *oui*.

Her mother practically oozed sunshine as she sat in the IKEA rocker beside the couch. She pitched her voice low beneath the sounds of Simone and Jean-Pierre making their farewells in French and the clacks of the door being shut and locked up. "He seems nice, Luna. So how come you didn't tell me you have a steady boyfriend?" There was a smidge of hurt under all her grinning, which Luna could only see because she knew her mom better than anyone. "Did you think I wouldn't like him? I think it's pretty neat, him being transgender, too, and all. You match!"

"No, Mom, it's—" Luna sighed and pushed her fingers through her hair, scratching at her scalp as she dropped onto the sofa. She had to explain the whole fake-dating deal she had made with Jean-Pierre, but it wasn't easy to come up with the words. It was such a wild story. About as wild as her mom seeing her in the niche culinary gossip rags and hopping on the first bus to the city. "It's just—I really wasn't expecting you. You couldn't have called? Texted?"

"I did," Mrs. O'Shea said, prim as all get-out. She was using that tone that meant she wasn't mad, just disappointed, and it made Luna feel all of one inch tall. "I've been trying to reach you all day."

"What? I never got—" Luna checked her phone and groaned. It was still on "Do not disturb" mode. She had about a million unread notifications across a dozen apps. It had never occurred to her that her mom might be one of the people trying to get ahold of her. "I turned my phone pings off," she explained. "I didn't see any of your calls and stuff. Sorry."

Mrs. O'Shea gave a nod as if to say *There you have it*. "When I didn't get an answer, I thought, well, maybe I should come see for myself. Just to be safe." Her grin grew into something more real. "He's even more handsome in person, I think. *Zhan*-Pierre, I mean." She put a little too much emphasis on the "Jean," but at least she was trying. "Now, the websites didn't include many details, so tell. Me. Everything. Is he Catholic? He must be, right?" She leaned forward in her chair, her face an eager flush of pink.

Luna sighed. Time to face the music. "The thing is, Jean-Pierre and I, we're not really—"

Mrs. O'Shea held up one hand. "Wait. Can I add something real quick?" She did not wait for an answer, instead catching Luna's slack, sweaty hands with her own and squeezing them tight, her eyes practically dancing. "I love you, sweetie pie, and I am so proud of you. You know I worry about you; a mother can't help worrying. When you first moved here, I thought, 'Gosh, this town is so big and moves so fast,' and I hated the thought of you being alone in it." Her eyes went soft, and she squeezed Luna's hands again. "So maybe that's why I've sometimes been a teensy bit nosy, asking if you've met anyone special every time you call. It broke my heart to think you hadn't found anyone worth your time; you're such a wonderful girl, and you have so much love to give." She reached one hand up and brushed a wayward lock of hair behind Luna's ear.

Luna swallowed. This was going to suck so bad. "Mom, that's not—"

"I know, I know." Mrs. O'Shea put both hands up in mock surrender. "You don't like it when I get all maudlin with my negative energy. I'm only trying to say I am so glad you've finally found a good boy who treats you right. It's such a weight off my shoulders. Finally, I can get some sleep at night. But enough about me!" She beamed at her daughter. "What was it you were trying to say before I interrupted with my mushy nonsense?"

The words stuck in Luna's throat. She tried to squeeze them out like toothpaste from a tube, but they just wouldn't budge. She kept picturing what her mom's face would do when she heard the truth. *Jean-Pierre isn't really my boyfriend; I'm still a single loser with no real prospects. Oh, by the way, did I mention I'm only pretending to date him because I lost my job and can't figure out another way to support myself until I find another? You sure raised a good one, huh? That should keep you up at night a little bit longer!*

The smile would fall off her mom's face faster than the blink of an eye. She would probably cry, or go all quiet, or insist Luna come back home to Mechanicsville, Pennsylvania, to recover from the shame in peace. And then Luna would have to disappoint her all over again by refusing to go back. Sure, there were three Wawas within fifteen minutes of Mechanicsville, but she belonged here in the city. All her friends were here, not to mention her community.

Which was why it seemed simpler, kinder, more natural to just say what Luna ended up saying.

"I'm sorry I didn't tell you about Jean-Pierre," she forced out in a smoky whisper. "I was going to. Really soon. I . . . wanted to make sure it was serious before I brought him home to meet you or anything."

"Oh!" Her mother wriggled happily in her seat. "Well, I guess it all worked out, thanks to the eagle eyes at *GlobeTrot*." She laughed, then faced Luna with a more serious expression. "I understand, sweetie, I do. When something's important to you, you want to get it exactly right."

Jean-Pierre, who must have dawdled in the entry hall as long as he was able to without looking suspicious, sauntered in and took hold of Mrs. O'Shea's luggage. "Where shall I put this?" he asked, looking at Luna with meaningful eyes, spelling out the question in lightly accented English: *Have you told her?*

"Let's put it in Simone's room for her!" Luna popped to her feet. "Here, let me help you. I know where she keeps her fresh sheets."

She hustled Jean-Pierre away, grinning back at her mom until they were out of sight. She shut the door behind them to keep their conversation private.

"You have not explained?" Jean-Pierre whispered.

"I can't," Luna said. "She's so happy for me! And she really likes you."

"Likes me?" Jean-Pierre's nose wrinkled. "She knows nothing about me, save for what she might have read in those filthy gossip rags."

"And your aftershave," Luna helpfully added. "She knows about your aftershave."

Jean-Pierre's dark eyes practically rolled out of his head. "That is hardly substantial."

"I know that!" She opened Simone's closet, shoved her face into the fresh linens that were kept on top of a stack of storage cubes, and gave a muffled screech. Once that was out of the way, she said into the soft sheet set, "Why couldn't you be some big beefy meathead that my mom disapproves of?"

Jean-Pierre patted her on the shoulder, but it felt more sarcastic than consoling. "I apologize; despite all my efforts, I remain quite svelte. I am told it is my genes."

Luna lifted her head with a groan. "Would it be okay if we pretended to be dating when we're around her, too? I know that's a big ask, but—" She slumped back against the stack of organizer cubes. "It would mean a lot to her."

"Of course." Jean-Pierre navigated the rolling suitcase into the corner. "It is nothing. Besides, it is good practice for when we must pretend in front of others, non?"

Luna paused to consider that. She had known in theory that this plan would involve hanging on Jean-Pierre's arm and putting on the girlfriend act for his grandpa and the cameras, but now that he mentioned it, she could see it was going to be a more complicated lie than she'd anticipated. Not only would they be playing the role of adoring couple for her own mother, but they'd also be hamming it up for everyone else who didn't already know what was up—which, aside from Simone, was basically the whole world. They would need to be seen in public, at least enough to satisfy the media, which meant they would almost always be pretending. Not to mention—

"You do know this means I will need to sleep with you," Jean-Pierre said, jolting Luna out of her thoughts.

She stared at him. "Sorry?"

"In your room." He gestured to its general direction.

Luna unclenched. "Right! Like, *sleep*-sleep. Not—" She gestured in no direction in particular.

"Yes. Obviously." Jean-Pierre frowned at her. "Naturally, your mother thinks we will share your bed while she is sleeping in this room. It's not as if I can make use of your sofa; she would think it very odd for your boyfriend to be banished there. Unless she is very, ah, what is the word? Conservative?"

"Conservative" was probably the last word anyone would use to describe Mrs. O'Shea. The woman had entered last year's Mechanicsville Library Halloween costume contest by dressing up in a felt uterus suit complete with bobbly ovary bits while she held a sign that read KEEP YOUR OPINIONS ABOUT ME TO YOURSELF! (In smaller script, below that, she had added at Luna's suggestion: SIGNED, ALL UTERUS-OWNERS.) She hadn't won the grand prize—a $25 gift card to, where else, Wawa—but she had made the front page of the county newspaper.

So yeah, Mrs. O'Shea probably expected Luna to share a room with her totally legitimate, long-term boyfriend. She was not the type to quibble about unmarried couples living in sin.

Luna closed her eyes and tried to breathe deep.

"Let's deal with that as it comes," she finally said, opening her eyes. "First things first: we need a super-quick download of each other's life stories. Like, the two-minute version. Right now."

Jean-Pierre made a face. "What? Why?"

"Because once we walk out that door"—she pointed dramatically—"we are going to have to speak to my mother about our beautiful and perfect relationship, and I don't even know if you have any brothers or sisters." She finished on a hiss, trying to keep her voice down as much as possible.

"I have one sister," Jean-Pierre said. "Chloé. She turns eight this year."

Luna wasn't the type to pry into people's family-planning choices, although the age gap between the Aubert-Treffle siblings seemed like a juicy story concerning her not-quite in-laws.

"Great. Only child here. What else is going on the Wikipedia page under your name? Birthday, where did you grow up, that sort of stuff."

"Birthdate, right. Thirty December."

Luna screwed up her face. "Oh. A Capricorn. I should have known."

Jean-Pierre looked offended. "What is that supposed to mean?"

They didn't have time to go through his entire astrological chart. "Nothing. Go on."

He sighed. "We lived mostly in Paris when I was younger. Part of the year in the Virgin Islands. Is this helping at all?" He must have seen the incredulous look on Luna's face growing by the minute. "I do not know what else you want me to say."

"Okay, that's fine. It'll have to do." She held up her hand like a crossing guard. "Here's my CV, so listen up: born March fourteenth, which makes me a Pisces, obviously. It was just my mom and me when I was growing up. Came out as gay in high school—close but no cigar, har-dee-har—then trans when I was nineteen. You got all that?"

Jean-Pierre nodded, a solemn look taking over his brow. "I think so." He paused for a beat. "I began to transition years ago, but I did not explain it to my parents and the rest of the family until last Christmas."

Kind of weird not to mention such a big life change until that late in the game, but okay. Everyone's experience was a unique kaleidoscope or whatever.

"Good to know." Luna turned back to the closet. "Let's finish up here before Mom gets suspicious. Can you strip the bed, please?" She busied herself with collecting a fresh set of sheets.

Jean-Pierre inexplicably stayed at her side. "Sorry, I—don't follow."

"Strip the bed. Take the old sheets off," she said, thinking there was some miscommunication in language. The French probably had some idiom that described the action in romantic euphemisms. "Unmake the bed so I can make it with these." She shook the clean, folded—perhaps even ironed; *Christ, Simone*—sheets in her hands to better illustrate.

"Ah, but you see, I would only make a mess of it, surely," Jean-Pierre said. He drifted away from Luna and then, to her consternation, made his way out the door. He spoke loudly as he went: "I leave it in your capable hands, darling! Perhaps your mother would like something to drink; why don't I see to that, hmm?"

Even though Simone would never know about it, Luna sent a silent apology to her fastidious roommate as she clawed her fingers into the perfectly pressed sheets, balling them between her hands in suppressed rage.

Maybe it was for the best that she and Jean-Pierre would share her bed tonight. That way, she could smother him with a pillow and make it look like an accident.

Chapter 7

Luna lay perfectly still on her back, staring up at the ceiling. She could hear Jean-Pierre digging around in his duffel bag, muttering to himself in French. The rest of the apartment was quiet, her mother having retired to Simone's room long before. The three of them had sat in the living room, sipping Jean-Pierre's coffee, for an hour or so. Mrs. O'Shea had been wired from the caffeine and the excitement of her impulsive trip, so she had dominated the conversation, catching Luna up on the comings and goings of people back home and complaining about her job at the local library. She'd also insisted that Jean-Pierre call her Connie after confirming that he had indeed been raised Catholic, a development that made Luna cringe. She hoped her mom wouldn't invite him to her favorite hippie guitar Saturday vigil mass. It was a good thing he wasn't her real boyfriend, or this would all be too embarrassing.

Before she'd shut herself in her borrowed room, Luna's mom had kissed her on the cheek and said, "Let's get brunch tomorrow, just the three of us." So that was something to look forward to. Luna couldn't wait to awkwardly be a fake couple while eating overpriced eggs Benedict with her mom.

Jean-Pierre stood like he was giving up trying to find whatever he was looking for in his bag, then slipped his e-cig out of the front pocket of his tight black jeans.

"Oh, uh, can you not smoke in here?" Luna propped herself up on her elbows to get a good look at it, and the strap of her bright floral camisole—which made a matching set with her soft sleep shorts—fell off her shoulder and down her arm. She yanked it back into place. "I heard on a podcast once that they don't know if there's any danger of secondhand vapor. I would rather not chance it." Luna gestured to her trim torso. "My body is a temple." Not to mention Simone would kill her if she found out.

Jean-Pierre snorted. "My body is an inconvenience," he murmured, "and it should be thankful I let it exist at all."

For a moment, Luna wondered if she'd misheard him; that was a pretty dark sentiment to be throwing out at bedtime. But before she could question it, a light switch seemed to flip inside Jean-Pierre. He lifted his head and shot Luna a wry smile, his eyes twinkling. "If my loving girlfriend doesn't want me vaping in her house, I will not do it. I respect her too much to even complain." He bowed gravely in her direction like a butler. "I will use the balcony."

"We don't have a balcony, only a fire escape," she said.

"That is fine. I will escape there with my fake fire if need be." His grin widened. "To please my fake girlfriend."

Luna narrowed her eyes at him. "You really crack yourself up, don't you?"

"I do." Jean-Pierre played with the vape pen, twirling it through his fingers. He cleared his throat meaningfully. "Now that we have a moment alone, we should discuss our plan." His light tone was at odds with the tense line of his shoulders as they moved under his sweater.

"Plan?" Luna pursed her lips. "Like the whole 'pretending to be dating' thing?"

"By the time we arrive in Paris, we must appear to be a perfect couple. My grandfather will be looking for any small misstep. If he uncovers our lie, I am certain the entire test will be forfeit."

"Good point. We need to get our stories straight, especially with my mom here." Luna lounged against her pillows, fiddling with the amethyst crystal she kept on a thin silver chain around her neck. "I hardly know anything about you except your sign and your sister. What do you do for a living? Who's your celebrity crush? What's your favorite color? No, wait—it's black, duh."

Jean-Pierre pocketed his e-cig and sat on the very edge of her mattress with his hands clasped between his knees. "I work for my parents' company, as I said." Luna noticed that the rest of her questions went pointedly unanswered.

"Right, but what do you *do*?"

"Not a lot," he said without a hint of shame. "I am a complete bon vivant. I travel, mostly; there are restaurants and hotels around the world bearing my father's name, or my mother's, and I go to check up on them. I assist with some of the financial decisions, the real estate dealings—it's all very boring, I am sorry to say."

"So you don't enjoy it?"

"Enjoy?" Jean-Pierre rolled the word around in his mouth with a frown. "No, I suppose I don't. I do not hate it—traveling, that part I like. But it is just a job. The price I must pay to stay in my family's good graces. Except for Grand-mère, of course; she seems to love me no matter how useless I am." His eyes flicked up to meet Luna's like they were sharing a joke.

Luna didn't think it was very funny at all. She dropped the amethyst so that it fell out of sight below the neckline of her chemise. There wasn't enough money in the world to make her touch those family dynamics with a ten-foot pole. "Okay, but if you could do anything, what would you be doing?"

Jean-Pierre's brow furrowed. "You mean for work?"

"Or whatever. What do you enjoy? What's your thing? Your—your passion?" Luna gestured expansively.

Jean-Pierre affected a careless shrug. "Must I have one? Is it not enough to live and breathe? You Americans, you think everyone must have this calling from god himself to design buildings or manufacture cans of soup or sell soap—some people just want to *be*."

Luna bristled. Of all the things she could reasonably be accused of, being a capitalist was not one of them. The fact that she needed money to pay rent and eat food wasn't her fault. "Hey, I'm just trying to get to know my boyfriend better."

"Well, your boyfriend is a rich, lazy European with no ambition." Jean-Pierre lifted a single black eyebrow. "Does that answer your question?"

In Luna's experience, people who said things like that about themselves had heard others say it about them first. She wondered who had told Jean-Pierre he was lazy. Between his parents and grandfather, there were a lot of likely candidates. But that was none of her business.

"Fine. That's you. Now, what should you know about me?" She tapped her fingertips against her cheek. She thought of Willow, her most theatrically inclined friend, always going on about the actors she worked with. "You should understand my motivation. What do I want out of life?"

Right now, a new job would be nice, something she actually liked, or at least was appreciated for doing. The yoga retreat in the Catskills was a pipe dream, obviously—something she saw herself doing in her golden years, when she could rock a gray streak and maybe have a couple tortoiseshell cats. What did she want right now? Her friends all seemed to be growing up and moving on to the next stage of their lives—she didn't want to follow anyone else's playbook, but she didn't want to stand still either.

She clutched a pillow to her stomach and squeezed it. "I want good things for myself," she said. "I want to be me and no one else. I want to—to fly. And I don't want to apologize for it."

Jean-Pierre looked at her for a long moment. In the quiet,

like this, Luna thought maybe they were sharing a connection. Two people who had had to struggle, recognizing each other from across a gulf as wide and deep as the ocean.

Then Jean-Pierre opened his damn mouth. "I don't think I understood a single word of what you just said."

Luna resisted the urge to hurl her pillow at his face. She rolled her eyes instead. "Well, great talk. Glad we're really getting to know each other on a deeper level." She turned to fluff her pillow. Conversation over. Time for bed.

"Ah, wait. Please," Jean-Pierre said. He shifted on the bed, causing the mattress to creak. "I am trying. Only, it has been a long time since I've—been intimate. In conversation. Or otherwise. With. Anyone." The words sounded like teeth being pulled from him.

"Really?" She noted how tense Jean-Pierre got in his shoulders and in his corded forearms. "How long are we talking?" At his admonishing look, she added, "Hey, you're the one who wants this fake relationship to look as realistic as possible." She gestured between them. "Seems like something a girlfriend would know, but if you don't want to talk about it—"

"Years," Jean-Pierre bit out. His gaze was fastened somewhere on the windowpane. "I have not dated in many years. Not as an adult. My hopes for a normal social life were disrupted." He traced the oval of his face several times with his hand, apparently indicating the stubble on his chin, or maybe his sharp cheekbones. "I had an abundance of gender to deal with."

She regarded him closely. He was still doing a fair impression of a garden statue at the edge of her bed. "Okay, so you're anxious about being out of practice. That makes sense. The French are known for being the biggest romantics in the world, after all."

Jean-Pierre gave a light scoff, cutting a glare at her. "That is a complete stereotype," he said. "The French are no more sex-crazed and affectionate than anyone else. What, you think because I'm from France I am making love on beaches and in restaurant booths all over the world? Perhaps tomorrow is my regularly scheduled ménage à trois!"

"Yikes." Luna held up her palms. "All right, I'm sorry. I shouldn't have assumed."

Jean-Pierre sniffed. "Anyway," he said, taking a sudden interest in his fingernails, "we should probably kiss."

Luna's eyebrows rose. She leaned forward, certain she had misheard. "We should what now?"

"Unless you don't want to," Jean-Pierre said in a rush. "It is only an idea."

"Oka-y-y," Luna said slowly. She'd been expecting Jean-Pierre to remain aloof and untouchable for the foreseeable future, but apparently she was wrong.

"I was thinking, if we have to share a kiss in public or in front of anyone, we do not want it to look—"

"I said okay," Luna broke in. "Okay as in yes."

"Oh." Jean-Pierre turned more fully to her, his lower lip caught between his teeth. "Good. That is, only if you're certain. I don't want to make you do anything you don't wish to do."

She appreciated the boundary-setting, but there was such a thing as going overboard. "It's just kissing. I'm fine with it if you're fine."

He nodded. A lot. "I am fine."

Luna patted a spot beside her on the comforter. "You'll have to come closer. We can't kiss while three feet apart."

Jean-Pierre murmured something in French that sounded both poetic and derogatory. He knee-walked on the bed until he reached the spot Luna had indicated, then fell into a crisscross-applesauce position. He looked more nervous than Luna had ever seen him in their short time together; the sleeve of his sweater was getting worried to threads between his fidgeting fingertips.

Luna smiled in what she hoped was a calming way. "Okay—think natural. Let it flow. It'll look better that way, right?"

"Right." Jean-Pierre stayed where he was. He didn't even

lean in an inch. He looked like he might stay frozen right where he was forever.

Luna blew her bangs out of her eyes. "Do you want to get things started or—?"

Jean-Pierre surged forward before she could finish.

Their mouths met with a harsh clack, their teeth banging behind closed lips with too much force. Luna's eyes flew wide.

"Pardon, pardon, je suis désolé." He backed up rapidly, his eyes squeezed shut like he was too embarrassed to look at Luna. "That was a very poor first kiss."

"It's fine. It's practice," Luna said as she rubbed at her stinging bottom lip. Ouch.

"It's just been a while—"

"You don't have to explain yourself to me. Relax, okay?" She took his soft, sweaty hand in hers and placed it on her thigh so he could have better leverage the next time he leaned in. "Stop thinking about it so much. Just do it."

He took a deep breath, then sighed it out. "Yes. Right." They swayed closer together. Jean-Pierre's hand tightened on her bare leg, brushing the hem of her soft sleep shorts. His other hand came up to touch her cheek, lightly at first, before slipping behind her ear to cup the back of her head.

"Thank you," he breathed in the small space between them, "for not laughing at me."

Oh, that hurt something inside in the sweetest way. "Don't mention it," Luna whispered back, and then they were kissing again.

Luna let her eyes drift shut as the sensations washed over her. Jean-Pierre had very soft lips. They moved over Luna's mouth carefully at first, testing the fit of their different shapes. A nip to her bottom lip made Luna gasp, and Jean-Pierre didn't waste the opportunity. His tongue slipped beside her own in what she could only think of as a gentlemanly way, not forceful but undeniably present.

This kiss was *much* better.

They shifted on the bed, Jean-Pierre moving forward as Luna tipped back. His hand moved from her leg to her waist, holding her steady. It was like being dipped in an old-timey postwar photograph. Luna suppressed the giggle that bubbled inside her at the thought; she didn't want Jean-Pierre to think she was laughing at him, now that he'd finally gotten into the groove. She put her palm against the flat solidness of his chest, not pushing but gripping, her nails digging into the fabric of his sweater. He went where he was pulled.

The kiss deepened.

Luna congratulated herself on her very professional approach to being a fake girlfriend. If she let herself enjoy being kissed, that was simply a perk of the job. It had been several weeks since her last good make-out session with the well-read barista, and for Luna, that was a pretty long dry spell. Jean-Pierre was certainly turning the weather pattern around.

Luna let out a breathy sigh and gave in to the temptation to dig her fingers into Jean-Pierre's thick curls. Whatever product he used must've been expensive, because his hair was as soft as the endangered goose down he no doubt slept on at home. Even the stubble on his face wasn't scratchy or irritating. Good thing, what with how much his face was nuzzling against hers. And her mom had been right: he smelled fantastic.

Remember, this is just a job. She pried her eyes open and saw, all blurry and close-up, that Jean-Pierre still had his closed. *Keep it professional. This is a total stranger. He's just your fake boyfriend.*

For a fake, he sure did sound real. Tiny noises of want fell from Jean-Pierre's mouth and into Luna's, louder whenever she tugged at his hair. His hand moved from her waist so that he was cupping her face in both hands, drinking down her answering gasp.

That was . . . that was actually pretty nice. It was the perfect balance of being kind of manhandled and being in control. Jean-Pierre was acting like he was so starved for her touch, he would do anything to get more of it. It was enough to give anyone a power trip.

Okay, I think we've got it down. Definitely should stop kissing soon. She clawed her fingers tighter in his hair.

In, like, a minute.

The choice was taken out of her hands, though, as Jean-Pierre broke the kiss. He hovered a few inches above her, breathing hard, the air between them warm with their mixed exhales. Luna realized she was now lying flat on her back, her hair splayed all around her head like she was in a damn music video. And she still had one hand in Jean-Pierre's hair.

"How was that?" he asked. He sounded annoyingly unaffected, the slight hitch in his breathing the only clue that he'd just kissed Luna within an inch of her life.

"Good!" She removed her hand from his hair and let it flop onto the mattress above her head. Her scratchy voice sounded like she'd just done fifty chaturangas in a row. "I think that was—pretty good."

"I can try again if you think it could be improved," he said, his lip curling upward at one corner.

If she knew one thing about men, it was that you couldn't let them get too big for their britches. Which was probably why she didn't have a boyfriend at the moment; men loved their too-tight britches. She flattened her hand against Jean-Pierre's chest and gave it a firm shove, putting some more distance between them.

"Now that that's handled," she said, "maybe we should go over other fake-relationship things."

Jean-Pierre rolled to the side, sitting back in his cross-legged position on the mattress. "Other things? Such as . . . ?"

Maybe Luna just didn't know him well enough to tell, but she could've sworn his gaze trained on her mouth for half a second before skittering away.

Luna sat up and combed her fingers through her hair, trying to tame the blonde and purple strands into something less sex-mussed. "Well, kissing is just one level of intimacy. How do we feel about cutesy nicknames? That's a thing couples do. Ray calls

Simone *Mona*, which is sweet. We could do something like that. Do you want to do something like that?" Was she babbling? It kind of sounded like she was babbling. She probably wasn't getting enough oxygen after that kiss.

Jean-Pierre frowned. He ruffled a hand through his messy hair, but that only made it messier. "Un petit nom? I have never had one. What would you call me?"

Luna considered this with all the seriousness it was due. She believed in the power of choosing names well; it had taken her over a year and a half to decide on her own. For Jean-Pierre, she wasn't feeling "honey" or "baby" or any of the usual standbys. He was too—not usual. She'd never met someone like him before.

Oh, she knew other trans guys; that wasn't what made him different. Maybe it was the fact that he had money, or was well traveled, or had a weird sense of humor, like if dad jokes had a baby with French surrealism. He was just—just a strange little guy.

She tried to imagine what it would be like to have really met him over a bottle of wine in a nice restaurant. To have instantly clicked. To fall in love with a man who would commute from Paris to see her and who kissed her like he would die if he didn't. They would talk on the phone or online almost every day, she thought. Doing the long-distance thing would be hard. Every second would be precious. She wouldn't want to waste any time saying what she needed to say; she would make her own shorthand for him.

"JP," she said with a nod as she came out of her visualization trance. "I'd call you JP. Is that cool with you?"

He looked supremely unmoved. "That's it? Just my initials?"

"Yeah. Nothing too sappy. You don't seem the type."

"It is not very creative," he groused.

"Well, excuse me!" She flung her arms in the air. "You give it a try, Shakespeare! Go ahead, make up a pet name for me. Do it."

"Clair," JP said with no hesitation.

Luna stared at him. "Claire," she repeated. "Why Claire?"

"Clair de lune." His eyes skated away again, this time to the ceiling fan slowly rotating above them. "Moonlight. Luna, *lune*. You see?"

Luna's brain ticked over a few times before she smiled wide and gave his foot a happy little kick. "Huh! Guess you *can* be romantic if you try. That's actually really pretty!"

"Thank you."

"Okay," she half-yawned, half-said, "I think that's as much preplanning as we can do tonight. Hopefully it's enough to keep my mom convinced that we've been dating for months." She turned and fluffed her pillow into her preferred shape. "We should probably get some sleep. Left side's yours."

That tense line was back in JP's spine. "I can sleep on the floor if you like."

"I'm not going to make you stay on the floor like some orphan in a Dickens novel. Quit making it weird." Luna, for her part, was already snuggling under the covers on the right side of the bed. "I'll try my best not to crowd you, okay? If I get restless and move a bunch in my sleep, just push me away. I'm a heavy sleeper; it won't bother me to get nudged."

"Wonderful." Jean-Pierre stood with a creak of his knees and what sounded like a soft curse. He pulled his sweater over his head to reveal a black tee underneath. Luna wondered if there was another, smaller black shirt under that. Like a nesting doll, but with depressing clothes.

There was a patch of scar tissue on his forearm, she noticed, a perfect rectangle. A skin graft scar; Luna filed that away but didn't bother commenting on it. That kind of stuff was way too personal.

JP's fingers paused at the button of his jeans. "Do you mind?" he said, meeting her gaze. "Normally I sleep in the nude, so I did not pack any clothes for sleeping. I will have to sleep in my underthings."

Underthings. Was this guy even real?

"Ah, sorry. Didn't mean to look." Luna turned away on her side to let him disrobe in relative peace. She could hear the thump of designer denim on her floor.

"You can look; just don't stare like that."

The snooty tone of his voice made Luna glance over at him, instinctually wanting to fire off an equally snarky reply. What she got was a glimpse of Jean-Pierre in his black tee and lime-green briefs before he slipped under the sheets.

The briefs derailed whatever she was going to say. Lime. Like, *neon*-green lime. With bright white piping.

"So it's a real party underneath the whole goth facade, huh?" she blurted out.

Jean-Pierre offered a grunt in return. He shifted against the sheets, then went still. The room became quiet.

Sleeping next to another person like this was weird. Luna didn't have much experience in it. If she spent the night with someone, there was context for that—sexy context. She was a total limpet, often using her bed partners like body pillows. But she couldn't do that now. This was more like a platonic sleepover, which had not really been a thing during Luna's childhood. She'd only ever gotten invited to sleepovers for boys, which had not piqued her interest at all.

She listened to him breathe in and out, unmoving except for his lungs. How could he sleep on his back like that? Like a damn vampire. Where did he put his hands? Luna could never figure out where to put her hands when she tried sleeping on her back. Like now.

Luna rolled over on her side, facing away from her bedmate and clutching her pillow under her head. Jean-Pierre's breathing was probably no louder than hers, but it was new and unfamiliar, and therefore sounded as loud as a steam engine to her ears. Ugh, she was never going to get any sleep at this rate.

That was probably the moment she fell asleep, but being asleep at the time, she couldn't be certain.

Luna swam back into wakefulness what felt like hours later,

her mind a swirl of confusion. She looked for the alarm clock on her bedside table. She had to swivel her head around to find it: 3:26 a.m., it said. A horrible hour. The streets outside her building were as quiet as they could get, just the odd hum of a truck engine going down the avenue. No car horns, no people shouting. Luna hated this level of quiet. It made her feel like she was completely alone in the world. Why had she woken up at a time like this, anyway?

Her pillow sighed under her hand.

Luna almost jumped out of her skin, blinking in the dark until the pale shape of Jean-Pierre's face and neck resolved in her vision. Oh, this was just perfect. She was curled up against his side, her cheek resting right on his chest.

The thin material of his black undershirt was soft, luxurious under her fingers, a cotton so fine it was almost silky. He gave a sleepy mumble and pulled her closer. Luna nearly had another heart attack when she realized how he was accomplishing this feat: his hand was resting in the hair at the back of her head, and he used that leverage now to guide her back down to him.

Luna let her cheek rest on Jean-Pierre's chest, though she was all tensed up and her eyes were wide open. She wasn't too shocked about where she'd ended up; she was a known cuddler, always seeking out contact in her sleep, apt to snuggle up with any bedmate who would tolerate it. What was surprising, though, was that Jean-Pierre had allowed it. Then again, he had probably been fast asleep when it happened.

Should she say something? Maybe wake up Jean-Pierre? But the guy was dead to the world; she didn't want to take away his chance to get some rest. That would be rude. Right?

No, she chided herself. That was no excuse for indulging in nonconsensual cuddles. Though these were some pretty high-quality cuddles, to be sure: Jean-Pierre was as warm as a bed of coals, and he still smelled good, and his chest was a pleasant, level plane on which to rest her cheek. Luna could feel the lean definition of hard-won muscle under his shirt, in the swell of his bicep at her shoulder.

She fit her cheek more snugly against his chest while she contemplated her options. It wasn't easy to concentrate, though. Even the steady thump of his heart under his shirt had a calming effect. Luna would fall asleep here again if she wasn't careful.

Her lashes fluttered down, then snapped back up.

No, she couldn't go back to sleep. She was going to say something. Or at least slip out of Jean-Pierre's arms and back to her side of the bed. If he would just let go.

"Hey. JP. Come on, I've got to move." Luna began scooting away from him in earnest now, but Jean-Pierre's free hand closed over hers where it sat on his chest, keeping her trapped.

Luna tipped her head up to stare at him, huffing in disbelief. He was going to be so embarrassed when he woke up. He'd probably scramble away from her so fast, he'd fall off the bed and onto the floor. She was already preemptively embarrassed for him.

Wow, up close, his eyelashes were really, really long. The faint light from the street caught them just right, outlining them in a yellow glow. Luna couldn't help staring at them with a mixture of awe and jealousy.

Then, to her silent horror, those mile-long lashes began to lift—slowly at first, then in fits and starts until Jean-Pierre was looking blearily back at her.

"Mm," he said. "It is morning?"

"No, it's still the middle of the night," Luna said quietly.

"Middle. Okay." Jean-Pierre closed his eyes again, or would have if Luna hadn't nudged him in the ribs. "Eh?" He blinked down at her again.

"Don't you want me to move?" she asked. She tugged her hand out from under his, awkwardly curling it between their bodies. "I guess I kind of turned into an octopus while I was sleeping. I'm sorry, I didn't mean to."

She wriggled out of his arms and back to her side of the imaginary dividing line that ran down the center of the bed.

Jean-Pierre's lazy eyes slid shut. "Fine," he said, turning over on his side and giving Luna his back.

Luna grimaced. "Don't be mad. I said I was sorry."

"Apology accepted." He sounded more awake now, and more terse. "Go back to sleep, Luna."

Luna supposed everyone was allowed to be grumpy at ass o'clock in the morning. She sagged onto her back, hands splayed on either side of her head, and closed her eyes. A few deep-breathing exercises and she was sinking back into dreamland.

When she woke up again, it was closer to a decent hour. Miraculously, she was on her side of the bed, though Jean-Pierre's hand had flung out at some point in the night and nestled against her arm. That was fine. The cuddling had been fine, too; it was just touching. People touched, especially in small spaces like beds.

Moving stealthily, she slipped out of bed and pulled on her sunflower-patterned silk robe. The fabric whispered as she wrapped it tight around her. Jean-Pierre gave a quiet sigh in his sleep and burrowed his face deeper into his pillow, but did not wake up. He probably wouldn't even remember their weird late-night snuggle.

Probably for the best. Luna headed to the bathroom to take the longest, chilliest shower of her life, and resolved not to mention the lapse in personal space once Jean-Pierre was conscious.

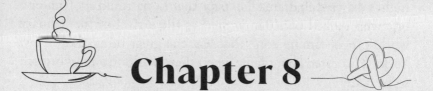

Chapter 8

Mrs. O'Shea insisted on treating them to brunch at the twee "New American" cafe on Amsterdam that she'd found after clicking around on Google Maps for ten minutes. It was called The Rare Parrot, and the menu offered all-you-can-drink mimosas for $35 per person with purchase of a brunch entrée, which, in Manhattan, was a pretty good deal if you were the type of person who would house $35 worth of cheap sparkling wine alongside your home fries. The O'Sheas were the definition of that type of person, so Luna agreed to her mom's plan.

They arrived a few minutes before noon, prime time for the brunch crowd. The cafe was decorated in shades of mint and pink with lush plants hanging in every corner. With the mild weather they'd been enjoying, the French doors at the front were flung open to let in the sunshine and the noise of traffic along the avenue. The usual weekend suspects were packed in shoulder to shoulder: old-timers who haunted the Upper West Side and would never leave, tourists in ugly sneakers, young couples rocking their baby strollers with their feet while they downed Bloody Marys, and groups of gay guys loudly recounting last night's dance club drama. No paps that Luna could spot, and no one who looked overly interested at the arrival of the culinary world's most famous son. That was the great thing about New York: Who cared about fame when there was bottomless brunch to be had?

Luna tried to muster a sunny smile at JP as he pulled out her chair for her like a good boyfriend would. They had shared . . . not an awkward morning, just a strange one. After her shower, she'd returned to her bedroom and found no sign of her erstwhile bedmate and cuddle buddy. She'd followed the sounds of morning voices to the kitchen, where Jean-Pierre was making coffee while chatting with Mrs. O'Shea.

"Good morning, darling," he'd said, and pressed a fresh cup into her hand. Less than thirty-six hours into this fake relationship and he was already deploying "darlings" at every opportunity.

Luna would have preferred her usual tea, but she couldn't complain in front of her mom. Now she was wired in addition to the fake-dating stress. Her heart felt like it was going to rocket out of her chest. Every comment her mom made, every little glance she shot in Jean-Pierre's direction—it seemed like disaster could strike at any moment and she'd realize they were not really a couple. Which meant Luna would be caught lying to her mom about something major for the first time in her life. Which meant her mom would realize Luna was the worst daughter in the history of daughters, and that could not happen.

Jean-Pierre didn't seem to have a care in the world, though. He couldn't possibly have gotten much sleep the night before, but he wasn't showing it. He just breezed along in his charcoal button-down and sleek trousers tucked into heavy black boots, his damp hair curling as it dried. He looked like he'd be at home walking along the Seine with a paper sack of groceries, iconic baguette poking from the top. Slickly European. Effortlessly better at life. And that aftershave, now freshly applied, smelled really fucking good, damn him.

The waiter appeared to ask for their drink order, blessedly interrupting that line of thought. He introduced himself as Toby and asked, "What can I start you ladies off with?"

Luna shot a glance over at Jean-Pierre. If being lumped in with the women bothered him, he didn't show it; he just stayed behind his menu. Then again, maybe the waiter just meant it was ladies first in the ordering process. Luna hated this kind of social calculus. She wished that servers would stop using gendered salutations altogether, but she wasn't going to rant about it to someone who was probably pulling minimum wage with tips.

Luna's mom went first. "I'll do the bottomless mimosa, please, the peach and pineapple one. And keep them coming."

"And for you, miss?" The waiter turned to Luna.

It did sound delicious. "The same."

"And for you—?"

Jean-Pierre glanced up at the waiter. His profile was downright gorgeous, Luna thought. She felt the urge to file a complaint. He also had a rakish hint of stubble on his chin and upper lip, the same black as his hair, which glinted in the sun streaming in from the open-air entrance.

". . . sir?" the waiter said helplessly, like he wasn't sure if he'd picked the right word and wasn't feeling confident about his chances. "I'm sorry, I said 'ladies' before, didn't I? That was my mistake, uh—"

"Sir," Luna said in an effort to help move everything along.

"Sir." The waiter nodded several times in Luna's direction. "I didn't mean to offend anyone, really, miss—unless? Um?" He scrutinized Luna's face in a way that made her want to pick up her butter knife and start stabbing.

"I will have the Irish coffee," Jean-Pierre announced, drawing all eyes to him. He flicked his menu into the center of the table, coming daringly close to melting the corner in the tealight candle that sat there. "Any whiskey is fine." He didn't make eye contact with anyone and went into a statue-like stillness.

"Yes, *sir*." The waiter ducked his head to the table at large. "Sorry. Again."

Mrs. O'Shea stared at the waiter as he disappeared into the maze of tables. "That was bizarre. How could he have thought you were a girl?" she whisper-hissed at Jean-Pierre. "You have facial hair, for crying out loud. It's like, get a clue."

"Mom, I have facial hair when I don't feel like shaving," Luna pointed out.

Mrs. O'Shea made a face. "Yes, but you're wearing a dress."

She was: a very cute violet A-line with stars printed all over it, but that wasn't the point. Even though Mrs. O'Shea was a rainbow flag–waving ally and the best mom any trans gal could ask for, she still didn't *get it* a lot of the time.

"That doesn't automatically mean anything. Anyone can wear a dress if they want. There's no law against it." Luna thought for a moment. "Nowadays," she added.

"Well, either way, that couldn't have been very fun for you, being misgendered like that," Mrs. O'Shea said to Jean-Pierre. She sounded very proud to have remembered the term. "I'm really sorry. Oh, and I picked this place . . ." She shook her head in self-recrimination.

"No one's blaming you, Mom," Luna said, reaching over the table to pat her mom on the arm. Just a quick one, because between her mom's guilt and JP's . . . whatever he was going through at the moment, the latter was clearly the winner in terms of needing her attention.

She looked in JP's direction, trying to gauge whether he was going to come back to life anytime soon and whether he might need an arm pat of his own. He was still frozen, though she couldn't tell if it was in rage or mortification or some combination of the two. A real girlfriend would offer comfort, but the real Luna would, too, no matter who needed it. She slipped her hand onto his leg under the table and gave it a little squeeze. "You okay?"

That got the gears going again. He blinked over at her and,

with a deep breath, hooked his arm over the back of her chair like he was as comfortable in this cafe as someone could be. "Just fine," he said. The picture of nonchalance. "It has been a while since someone got it wrong. I was wondering what I may have done to cause such confusion." He idly reached up and played with the thin gold chain he was wearing today, visible only in flashes where the top three buttons of his shirt were undone.

Luna wondered if he was already blaming the jewelry. She hoped not; it looked good on him. "You didn't do anything. It's the waiter's mistake, not yours."

Jean-Pierre looked at her like he didn't entirely believe her, but wanted to. His hand found hers under the table. Their fingers threaded together. "Merci. A weight off my mind."

"I hope he doesn't charge you for that drink," Mrs. O'Shea broke in. Luna quickly slid her hand away like her mom had caught her sneaking cookies. "I can complain about it, if you want. I'm a white lady; it's what I'm good at."

"Mom!" Luna wasn't usually so embarrassed by her mom's skill in weaponized whining, but for some reason, having Jean-Pierre witness it made her feel self-conscious. She hoped he didn't think they were cheap. "Can you please just let it go?"

"I appreciate the offer, madam," Jean-Pierre said, much more smoothly than Luna would have ever given him credit for, "but Clair is correct. We can let these things go."

Mrs. O'Shea cocked her head. "Claire?"

"That's what JP calls me," Luna mumbled. She began shredding her paper napkin into tiny squares. Maybe it was silly, but she felt like all the tension that had just supposedly bled out of Jean-Pierre had been magically transferred to her. The perils of being an empath.

Jean-Pierre explained his moonlight pet name to Mrs. O'Shea's palpable delight. She cooed at the sweetness of it all. JP shot a toothy smile over at Luna like he'd won a prize for picking the better nickname. It was nice to see him back to his usual arrogant self after that little hiccup.

"See, that's the sort of thing a good boyfriend does," Mrs. O'Shea said, nodding at Luna. "I don't recall any of those people you met through that Campfire thing being so sweet."

"Tinder, Mom. It's called Tinder." Which reminded her: she needed to take her profile down while she was fake-dating JP.

"Whatever. He's sweet, is my point." She waggled her finger at Jean-Pierre's beaming face.

Luna took a deep breath. She seemed to be doing that a lot these days. "Yes," she said, "JP is very, very sweet." No time like the present to practice her new role. She eased the muscles of her face into a warm smile and imagined herself as a loving girlfriend. The glance she tossed Jean-Pierre was nothing short of Oscar worthy. Sandy Bullock herself could do no better. "I'm really glad we found each other," she said. "Isn't it wild how one little thing, like going to the right restaurant at the right time, can change your whole life?"

She was shocked when JP put his hand over hers on the table, squeezing it gently. Her eyes widened a bit, but he just gave her a doting grin and leaned in close. Very close.

Oh, okay. So they were doing this now. The kissing thing that they'd practiced, it was happening.

His lips brushed her cheek.

"I have to believe, my Clair," he murmured, "that fate would have brought us together no matter what. To think otherwise is too painful to contemplate."

Okay. So he could do a decent Keanu. Luna looked across the table at her mom, wondering if she was buying this whole thing.

Mrs. O'Shea didn't even seem to be paying them a lick of attention. She was too occupied with coolly accepting her mimosa from Toby, who had returned with their drinks. Once he left, she whispered conspiratorially, "Are we going to leave him a tip, though?"

"Yes, Mom," Luna groaned. "We're not monsters, okay? Unless he sets the table on fire and tells us god is going to strike us down, he gets twenty percent."

"Isn't she an angel?" Jean-Pierre said with more than a hint of sarcasm curled around his words. "She is kindness in human form, my Clair."

"Well, I'm so happy you're both happy." Mrs. O'Shea raised her glass. "To my new favorite couple."

They clinked, though JP looked disturbed at the idea of tapping his overflowing coffee mug to their brimming wine glasses.

"So, JP," Mrs. O'Shea said after they'd all enjoyed a healthy swig, "I feel like all I know about you is what I read in *GlobeTrot*. What's your story? I want the whole enchilada."

"The, erm?" He looked to Luna with mild panic painted across his face.

Luna downed more of her drink. "She means she wants to hear everything."

"Ah, of course." He relaxed slightly. "You will forgive me; English is only my third language."

"Third?" Mrs. O'Shea squeaked.

He counted on his fingers. "French is first, then Italian, followed by English"—he nodded to them as if to say *You're welcome*—"then German, Portuguese, and a smattering of Norwegian, Spanish, Tagalog, Japanese, and Mandarin." That got him up to ten, the fingers of both hands spread like starfish. "One picks up these things when you travel as much as I do."

"That's impressive," Luna's mom breathed out. She turned to Luna. "So that's another thing you have in common, isn't it?"

Out of the corner of her eye, Luna could see JP quirk a brow in confusion. She reached under the table to pinch his leg, hoping he'd take the hint to roll with it.

"Yes!" she yelped to cover his resulting gasp. "Of course, my Italian is nowhere as good as JP's. He gets to use it so much more than I do."

"I wish I could speak Italian," Mrs. O'Shea said wistfully.

"You speak Italian?" JP asked Luna in that language. "Why didn't you tell me?"

"Because we've known each other for about twenty-four hours and I couldn't have possibly mentioned every single fact about my life," Luna answered in the same.

Her mom smiled back and forth between them. "That sounds so beautiful. What are you saying?"

"I was just telling Luna that she knows very well her Italian is flawless." JP touched her once again, this time on her forearm. "Isn't it remarkable how talented she is?"

Luna gave a little laugh and, since they were apparently touching each other all the time now, reached over and gave his arm a squeeze. She hoped he got the message that he should pull it back just a tiny bit. This level of adoration was sure to be suspicious.

"It's not *that* flawless," she demurred.

"Oh, sweetie pie, don't sell yourself short!" Mrs. O'Shea turned to JP with a frustrated, fond sigh. "She's always doing that, you know. I'm glad you don't let her get away with it. I've been telling her she should really keep up with studying her languages. There are programs she could be taking advantage of! I know the libraries here offer them. Just because you didn't finish college doesn't mean you need to stop learning." She directed this last comment at Luna, just like she had a dozen other times over the years.

Luna braced for Jean-Pierre's reaction. This was probably one of those things that she should have foreseen would come up, but it was too late now.

"Hm, yes," JP said, turning to her with a hint of concern flashing in his eyes. "Why *didn't* you finish college, Clair? I know you told me before, but my memory is so bad sometimes, I've forgotten."

"Oh." She flapped a hand through the air, keeping the other locked on JP's arm in a death grip. It was a good thing his shirt's fabric was so supple; otherwise, there might have been a risk of her nails stabbing holes through it. "You don't want to hear all that again; it's so boring."

Two things were simultaneously true about Luna's failed college career: She knew there was no shame in not finishing her degree. Lots of happy, successful people didn't have college degrees! The university system was a classist dinosaur, anyway.

And also: She deeply, deeply did not want to tell the whole story to Jean-Pierre, who probably had three different degrees across various disciplines.

Her mother, however, seemed to have no such battle raging within her when it came to this topic. "It's not boring to me! I'll tell it." She held her glass out to the waiter for her mimosa refill without looking away from Jean-Pierre. "You know, nothing made me prouder than when Luna decided to drop out of college."

"Really?" JP's eyebrows winged high. He pried Luna's clawed fingers off his arm and held them loosely under the table instead. In his lap.

Luna fumed helplessly, her mom still running her mouth.

"So halfway through her freshman year, end of the first semester, I get this call." Mrs. O'Shea made a phone out of her hand with thumb and pinkie extended, despite the fact that phones hadn't had that shape in decades. "She says, 'Mom, I don't think I can do this anymore,'" she said in a high-pitched voice.

"I did not sound like that," Luna deadpanned. "I don't even sound like that now." After years of being on HRT and a couple of voice lessons, she had decided that her gravelly, jazz club voice was just fine, actually.

"I know, I'm just trying to create a mood." If there had been any question where Luna had gotten her sense of drama, the answer was now clear. Mrs. O'Shea focused on Jean-Pierre, her audience of one. "Okay, so she's upset, clearly, and I'm going, 'I know it's hard, you're probably really homesick right now, I miss you, too.'" She dropped her phone-hand as her eyes bugged out.

"I didn't get it at all. Here she is, trying to come out to me, and I'm like, 'Everyone's going through this, sweetie, you're not alone.' Boy, talk about the wrong thing to say!"

Luna glanced over at Jean-Pierre, nervous at how he was absorbing all this. He seemed relatively unmoved by this reenactment of her coming-out story. His pale face displayed a polite amount of interest and, mercifully, no judgment so far. She thought they should speed by the more rocky parts, so she took over the storytelling.

"Once we'd both calmed down a little and I explained what was going on with me," she said, "we decided it would be best if I came home." Penn State was a good school, but Luna had been a baby trans woman and a freshman to boot, with very few close friends and nothing in the way of a support system.

"Not to mention how badly we needed the tuition money for other things," Mrs. O'Shea butted in.

Luna stared at her mom in disbelief. Even if JP were her very serious and real boyfriend, he still wouldn't need to hear that particular detail. She reached for her mimosa.

"What things?" Jean-Pierre asked, because of course he would.

"Well! Luna wanted to transition, to live her life the way she wanted—am I using the correct terminology, sweet pea?" Luna was in the middle of gulping down her drink, but she gave her mom an affirmative lift of her eyebrows. "Anyway! She needed new clothes, and therapy, the paperwork fees, and then there were the doctors' appointments, plus—"

Luna slammed her glass back onto the table with more force than was necessary. "Okay, we really don't need to get into all of that at *brunch*."

Her mom had clearly been on the cusp of mentioning the biggest financial investment of all: her bottom surgery. That was a personal topic, meant for close, personal relationships. Not total strangers. Luna could wax poetic about her surgery— the one procedure she had really wanted, not that she could afford any others after that was done, anyway—but only to her trans femme friends; she didn't feel the need to trot it out in front of JP.

"What's wrong?" Her mom blinked. "I mean, it's not as if your boyfriend doesn't know all this already, right?"

"Right," Luna said way too quickly, "but still—" She glanced over at Jean-Pierre, then at the bustling restaurant at large. "There's a time and a place, Mom."

JP, for his part, looked as panicked as a cat in a dog park. He gulped his coffee as if to save himself from needing to comment. The whipped cream left a little mustache on his upper lip. Luna watched him lick it away.

Mrs. O'Shea heaved a sigh. "Okay, I'm sorry. My point is, that was all pretty expensive, so Luna decided we would use the money I'd saved for her college expenses. Which meant she couldn't go back to finish her degree."

"Which I was fine with! *Am* fine," Luna said, looking between the two of them. "I'm totally fine."

Jean-Pierre turned to look at her, his head almost whipping with the swift motion. "There was not enough money for both?" He looked like the concept was completely foreign, like money wasn't a finite resource, which Luna supposed was true. For him.

She wished the waiter would show up to take their food order, or at least top off her bottomless mimosa again. She sucked the last few drops from her glass. "It wasn't like some huge tragedy," she said. "I don't think college was for me, anyway. I never even declared a major; the money was better spent elsewhere."

His face looked a little flushed. Probably from the spiked coffee. "Do you think you would ever want to finish your degree? If you had the chance?"

Luna fiddled with the tiny salt and pepper shakers that sat in the center of the table. "Oh, I don't know. That ship's sailed, probably." Then, because she felt like a jerk for relying on idioms all the time around JP, she added, "It's too late for that."

Her mom rushed to back her up, which was refreshing. "Besides, Luna is doing just fine without a degree! She's got a good, steady job with a decent paycheck, benefits, health insurance—she makes way more than I do, that's for damn sure."

"Mom."

"What? It's true. Librarians don't make chicken scratch," she said to Jean-Pierre, whose face scrunched as he probably tried to parse what chickens had to do with it. "And in my county? Forget it; the only raises they give us are these measly cost-of-living increases. One percent a year? Give me a break. But Luna's boss can't function without her. Isn't that right, sweetie?"

There were only so many falsehoods Luna could juggle at once. She didn't want to keep her firing a secret from her mom, too. She was going to find out about it sooner or later—JP also, come to think of it. Might as well be now. She set the shakers down with twin clicks.

"I've been meaning to tell you, I was let go a couple days ago. I don't work there anymore."

"What? Let go?" Her mother rocked back in her chair so hard, Luna worried the spindly metal thing would tip onto the floor. "They can't fire you!"

"Jen from HR would disagree," Luna muttered.

"You have been, ah, released?" JP asked, brow furrowed. "From your job? I didn't know that."

Mrs. O'Shea gaped. "She didn't tell you either? Oh, Luna." There was nothing in the universe that could match her mom's patented disappointed tone.

"I'm sorry!" Luna gestured expansively, her hand almost swiping her empty glass off the table. JP saved it before it had a chance to fall over. "The last couple days have been pretty busy for me, what with my boyfriend visiting and, um, the paparazzi, and my mom coming into town unexpectedly and—" She looked down at her lap. "Anyway, I'm telling you now," she finished, feeling very silly.

Her mom leaned over the table. "Are you going to be okay?

Do you need me to float you some cash to keep you going before you find something new?"

"Mom, you were *just* complaining about how librarians don't make any money."

"That doesn't mean I'm incapable of helping my only child if she needs it!"

"I'm fine. Seriously. I have some money saved up and—" She looked over at Jean-Pierre, who looked as pale and wan as an old-timey consumption patient. Any remaining color seemed to be draining from his face right before her eyes. Maybe the mere idea of discussing finances like this was anathema to him, something only the poors did. She looked away, focusing on her mom. "I have a new job in the works, actually."

"Already?" Mrs. O'Shea looked equal parts impressed, relieved, and proud. "That's amazing, honey. What's this new job going to be?"

"It's a . . . freelance gig." Out of the corner of her eye, she watched as Jean-Pierre drained his coffee cup, throwing his head back to catch every last drop. "And the pay is good. Like, really good. It'll tide me over until I find something more permanent. You don't have to worry about me."

"I'm your mother; I'm never going to stop worrying about you," Luna's mom said, her smile wide and soft. That was another thing Luna had gotten from her mom, her smile.

"I know." Luna smiled back. Even though her mom could be a lot, she really was awesome. "Thanks, Mom."

"Well!" Mrs. O'Shea swiveled her blonde head this way and that, peering into all the corners of the loud, packed cafe. "I need to visit the ladies' room. If that server comes by again, get me the bacon salad." She pushed her chair back and stood. "Oh, and a refill," she said, snapping her fingers at her mimosa glass.

"Sure thing," Luna said. She watched her mom bustle through the obstacle course of tables and tray-laden waiters. A little of the tension went out of her shoulders as her mom moved farther away.

Jean-Pierre cleared his throat. "I did not know you were so recently unemployed," he said.

And the tension was back.

She folded and refolded her torn-up napkin in her lap. "I didn't think it was relevant. Does it matter whether or not I have a job?"

"You need this money very much, then," he said slowly. "The money I am paying you."

Luna tried to catch the eye of a passing server, but no dice. "Uh, yeah. Duh. Why do you think I agreed to do this?" She got no snappy comeback in response, which was worrisome. Even after knowing Jean-Pierre for such a short amount of time, she felt like she had a good handle on his energy. He was the type of guy who always had to have the last word. She turned back to him. "JP?"

Jean-Pierre was quietly rotating his empty cup on the tablecloth. "I'm sorry. I didn't realize."

"What, you don't want your fake girlfriend to be jobless? Is that too embarrassing for you?" She rolled her eyes. "We can just lie to your grandpa, tell him I'm a fashion model, or a florist, or a—"

JP shook his head. "Non. It's not— We don't have to lie about that. It makes no difference, I suppose."

"Oh. Good." If JP really didn't mind that she was unemployed, why was he acting so weird? Maybe he just felt guilty about being uber-rich. Which, fine, he could afford to feel a little guilty.

Toby returned, bearing another Irish coffee for Jean-Pierre. "On the house. Seriously, once again, I apologize." He set the whipped cream–topped cup on the table in front of him. "I love the LGBT community. Trans rights." He inexplicably raised his fist in what was actually a Black Power salute.

"Please stop," Luna said, grimacing up at him. "You're just making it worse."

"Uh. Okay." Toby lowered the ill-advised fist and stood

there awkwardly, the handle of a mimosa pitcher clutched in his other hand.

Jean-Pierre picked up his fresh drink with a face of stone. "I think we're ready to order."

They rattled off their food order to Toby as quickly as possible while he refilled the mimosa flutes: salad for Luna's mom, the Florentine eggs Benedict for Luna (with extra home fries), and the same for JP. After Toby made his escape, JP said, "You can have some of my meal if you like; I doubt I will finish it."

"You don't like eggs Benedict?" Luna gasped. This was more comfortable territory: judging Jean-Pierre for his bad taste.

"I told you, I do not normally eat breakfast."

"But eggs Benedict is the best. If you want to see how good a brunch spot is, you've got to get a Benedict. Have you never gotten a little thrill from cutting open a perfectly poached egg?" Now Luna was actually getting hungry. She closed her eyes and hummed in anticipation. "All that silky eggy goodness— whoosh! All over the plate. And then you get to sop it up with the English muffin, maybe drag a few potatoes through it. Mmm-mm-mm." She wrapped her arms around herself and rocked side to side. "What's not to like about that?"

When she opened her eyes, JP was staring at her like she'd just done a strip tease wrapped in Canadian bacon. "You really are odd," he said.

She flicked a strand of hair behind her shoulder. "You're the one fake-dating me."

Mrs. O'Shea returned from the bathroom, weaving in and out of the packed tables. She smiled at Jean-Pierre as she dropped back into her chair. "While I was washing my hands, I realized we got majorly sidetracked. I still don't know anything about you besides how many languages you speak." She smacked him playfully on the arm. "You're not getting away that easy. Tell me about yourself!"

"What would you like to know?" he asked.

"Well," Mrs. O'Shea drawled, "where did you grow up?"

"Paris, mostly. My parents sent me to a boarding school in Switzerland when I was about seven years old," JP said. "A girls' school, of course."

"Oh." Her smile fell. Then she rallied to ask, "What about your folks? They're pretty successful restaurateurs, aren't they?" She addressed Luna. "The articles I read happened to mention that; I'm not being nosy."

"You kind of are?" Luna said, but she was ignored by everyone.

"Yes, my parents operate several establishments." Jean-Pierre watched another server, not Toby, deliver a huge platter of food to the table next to theirs. "They have enjoyed some success in that area."

This was starting to sound like an interview in the *Economist*. Luna propped her chin on her hand and fought off a yawn with a quiver of her upper lip.

Then her mom, fortified with a sip from her freshened mimosa, said, "Could I ask what it was like when you told them you were trans? Is that rude?" She whirled in Luna's direction. "I don't know any other parents who went through that. It would be helpful to hear how different folks handled it, is all I'm saying."

Luna gestured generously to indicate she wasn't going to stop anyone from asking questions, not that she could if she wanted to.

"I do not mind the telling." Jean-Pierre picked up his fork and examined the stamp on the back of it. "They were not upset, nor were they particularly pleased. My mother claimed to have never heard of the concept of transgender people before, and she maintains she still does not grasp what it means. My father is largely ambivalent; he tends to take his cues from her." The fork was replaced on the table. "She said something along the lines of, 'Whatever you wish; it has nothing to do with us.'"

Mrs. O'Shea looked like she'd just witnessed someone stomp all over a nest of baby ducklings. "That doesn't sound terribly supportive."

"They did not stand in my way." Jean-Pierre lifted his cup and lipped away the mound of whipped cream. "That is enough for me."

Luna's mom seemed to sense that a change in topic was in order. She swerved accordingly.

"I'm so curious," Mrs. O'Shea said. "Growing up with that family of yours, all those chefs—whose food do you like best?" She crossed her fingers on both hands. "I hope it's Lisette's. She's my favorite. Not that your grandpa's shows aren't entertaining! But I love nothing more than coming home from a long day, kicking off my shoes, and watching reruns of Lisette on PBS."

Jean-Pierre smiled, not the alligator-teeth smile he had been deploying through so much of their brunch, but a smaller, quieter one. "My relationship with food, it is complicated," he said as he stirred his coffee with a spoon so the whipped cream melted into a whirl. "My parents' restaurants were like another child I had to compete with for their attention. I spent very little time with them, what with nannies and tutors and, later, boarding school. You could say I resent cooking because of that."

Poor little rich boy, Luna thought with an internal eye roll, then felt guilty for judging him. Having everything you ever needed growing up was an enviable position, sure, but Luna didn't think she'd trade all her mom's hugs for that.

Jean-Pierre glanced at her, and for a moment Luna worried he had somehow divined her thoughts. But he continued, turning back to Connie. "My only truly good memory about my family and food does indeed involve Grand-mère. When I was very small, I would be sent to her country house to spend the holidays. Restaurants are exceptionally busy during the holidays, you see." He said this last part to Luna, who nodded in understanding. She vaguely recalled that JP's birthday was also around Christmas, but this story was already sad enough without her pointing that out. "Grand-mère would make croque monsieur for me. I was a, hm, fussy eater at that age; I would fixate on one simple meal and want nothing else for months on end. Grand-mère indulged me. Every day at the cottage, croque monsieur, perhaps a small green salad beside it." He made a cage out of his fingertips and tapped them against the table, like he was putting an invisible pile of lettuce on an imaginary plate.

Luna raised a hand in the air. "Wait, what's a croque monsieur?"

"Have you never eaten a croque monsieur?"

"I guess not."

"It is a sandwich with sliced ham, Gruyère, and then"—JP dipped an invisible ladle and unleashed its contents into the ether—"covered in a béchamel sauce and toasted with more cheese on top."

"So it's a ham and cheese, but wet?" Luna made a face. "Why would you cover a sandwich in sauce? That sounds messy."

"You eat it with a knife and fork," Jean-Pierre said.

"Completely defeating the purpose of the sandwich as an on-the-go food item," Luna countered.

"Where am I rushing off to that I cannot eat my sandwich on a plate?" He turned to Mrs. O'Shea, probably sensing she was a more sympathetic audience. "My grandmother must have made me croque monsieur a thousand times. *Never* croque madame. Even though I don't mind eating eggs on their own, that, I would refuse." He shot Luna a rueful look. "I did not want a lady sandwich, you see? Very silly, but that is how I was. A tiny monster of a child."

Under the table, he took out his phone and began swiping at the screen. Was he looking up an escape route?

"No!" Mrs. O'Shea gasped. "You were a delight, I bet! Now you want to talk about a fussy eater?" Her mom pointed at her in classic j'accuse fashion. "This one went on a mac-and-cheese kick for about seven years. From age ten till she left the house, all she wanted was mac and cheese."

"I still only want mac and cheese," Luna said with feeling. "It's *mac and cheese*."

Luna felt her phone buzz in her dress pocket—hell yes, it

had pockets—and took it out to see who was trying to reach her. It was JP. His bank, to be exact. He had just wired her $50,000.

It took all of Luna's self-control not to stand up and shout like she'd won the lottery. Fifty thousand dollars. She'd never had a payday like this before. She glanced at her mom, certain that she'd notice Luna's shock, but she was still wrapped up in her conversation with JP. Luna took the opportunity to stare at her phone some more.

The message said she should receive the funds in two to three business days, since it was an international transaction. The whole tone was very apologetic, as if the bank assumed she was expecting fifty grand in her hand right that minute. She and JP hadn't even discussed a payment schedule yet. Why was he jumping the gun like this in the middle of brunch?

Luna's mom was going on and on about how Luna had had a horrible fear of baby carrots as a child, but Luna wasn't paying attention to the story. She watched as another text popped up on her phone, this time from Jean-Pierre directly: I will need to initiate the transfer of the remaining funds in person. Is this sufficient in the meantime?

Luna texted back under the table while her mom used the salt and pepper shakers as stand-ins for the poor teachers who'd been terrorized by Luna's "Question everything, especially why carrots are babies" phase.

Yeah I think I'll manage.

The food arrived, and any questions Luna may have had about her payment schedule went out the window. When she cut into her eggs Benedict, the yolk was too firm to run.

Chapter 9

The rest of Mrs. O'Shea's weekend visit went off without a hitch. After brunch, JP had kissed Luna goodbye on the corner of her mouth as they parted on the sidewalk, saying he had a few errands to run and that she and her mom should enjoy some quality time. Luna managed to snag appointments for them at the salon: fresh color for her—a deeper purple with highlights of candy pink, since she didn't have a day job that frowned upon such things anymore—and a mani-pedi for her mom. While Luna waited for her foil to be unwrapped, her phone buzzed. Willow had sent the group chat a screenshot of a *DeuxMoi* blind item: *A certain heir to a culinary empire was seen brunching at The Rare Parrot on the UWS earlier today with two unknown women. A new acquisition for the restaurant portfolio?*

Luna groaned. Looked like the media attention wasn't going away anytime soon. Also, *unknown* women? Excuse you, anonymous.

Her mom, seated in the chair next to hers for ease of conversation, left off the small talk with her manicurist to ask, "Something wrong?" Luna wordlessly showed her Willow's message. You would have thought Christmas, Easter, and the

Ascension had all come early for Connie O'Shea. "That was us!" she squealed. "That was where we were."

"Yeah, only an hour or two ago. Don't you think it's a little creepy?" Luna put her phone away before the rest of her friends could chime in.

Connie patted Luna's arm. "I think it comes part and parcel with dating Jean-Pierre."

Right, she was supposed to be madly in love, not complaining about how rich and famous her boyfriend was. "I guess a teensy invasion of privacy is worth it." She avoided meeting her mom's eyes directly or in the mirror in front of them.

When they'd emerged freshly coiffed and polished, Jean-Pierre was waiting for them with three orchestra tickets to a matinee of a new Broadway show, causing Connie to squeal with joy. After that, at JP's suggestion, they'd all shared an early nosh of hummus platters in a tiny Mediterranean cafe that Luna must have walked past a thousand times and never known was there. When asked, Jean-Pierre said he'd been taken there once by a business colleague, and he'd filed it away in his mind as he did with all the restaurants he visited in his travels.

The day had been shockingly nice. All in all, it was a successful maiden voyage for the good ship O'Shea–Aubert-Treffle.

Even if, that night, Luna and JP had to share her bed *again*. This time, Luna had the forethought to construct a pillow fence down the middle of the mattress. JP took one look at her creation, sighed heavily, and crawled into bed. He must have been tired from their long day entertaining Luna's mom; he fell asleep within minutes while Luna—unused to only having one pillow under her head instead of three—took much longer.

When Connie finally left in a taxi bound for the Port Authority Bus Terminal, the apartment felt eerily quiet. Minus the constant burbling of Jean-Pierre's gooseneck kettle.

Luna puttered around, taking the sheets off Simone's bed, tidying away the little gifts her mom had left along with a sappy note on the kitchen counter. (*Thanks for letting your silly old*

mom crash the party for a couple days! I love you, sweet pea. xoxo.)
Jean-Pierre peered over her shoulder at the package that accompanied the note.

"Your mother left you treats?" he asked.

"You bet." Luna clutched the slightly greasy bag to her chest
protectively. "They're stuffed pretzels from Wawa, and they're
the best things humans have ever invented."

JP blinked at her. "I understood . . . perhaps half of those
words."

"Okay, so Wawa is— Do you have any stores in France that
are, like, on every corner, and they're always open, and they sell
sandwiches and sodas and also you can get a tank of gas?"

"A petrol station," he said. "You are describing a petrol station."

"Wawa is so much more. Here." She opened the bag, tore
off a chunk of pretzel, and held it out to Jean-Pierre. "Eat this.
Even cold, it's amazing."

He balked like a horse ridden to a cliff's edge. "Tell me what
it's stuffed with first."

"Cream cheese and jalapeños."

"Oh, in that case: absolutely *never* will I be putting that in
my mouth."

Luna scoffed. "What? You can't handle a little spice? Your
loss." She popped the morsel into her mouth and chewed, her
eyes closing in bliss. "This is proof god loves us and wants us to
be happy."

"No, that is champagne," Jean-Pierre said. He raised an
imaginary champagne flute up to the light. "They say when
Dom Pérignon invented it, he cried, 'Come quick, I am tasting
the stars!'" He dropped his hand. "A children's story, of course,
but the spirit of it remains. Champagne is the best that human-
ity has to offer."

"Yeah? Well, champagne isn't exactly in my budget. Pretzels
are."

That seemed to shut him up. He looked away, probably embarrassed about once again forgetting their financial disparities.

Luna ate more of her pretzel with loud moans of appreciation. "So, what do you think?" she said with her mouth full. She wasn't about to stop eating the holy grail of snack foods for any reason, even politeness. "We've got the kitchen to ourselves now. Should we start practicing for the culinary test?"

"Oui." JP pulled a slim, black Moleskine from his back pocket and began flipping through it. "Is there a shop nearby that sells rabbit meat?" He looked over the top of the notebook.

"Rabbit?" She licked a smear of cream cheese and pickled jalapeños off her thumb. "I think there's a Caribbean grocery store in Morningside that sells goat. Does that help?"

"Are you not aware of the vast, *vast* differences between a rabbit and a goat?"

"I know they're both super cute," she said with a sprightly grin. "And there's a petting zoo on Staten Island where you can see them, so they have that in common." Luna shoved the last piece of her pretzel into her mouth, chewing obnoxiously. JP looked so disgusted, she almost laughed it down the wrong pipe. The Little Prince was too easy to rattle.

He gave a puff of frustration through his nose before turning his attention back to his Moleskine. "No rabbit, then. Perhaps we should concentrate on the final dessert course. I understand that is the simplest of these recipes."

"Cool." Luna tossed the Wawa wrapper toward the trash can. It bounced off the rim and had to be scooped up again for another, better shot. Yeah, she was a real threat to women's sports, that was for sure. "So what's for dessert?"

Jean-Pierre consulted his notes. "It is my grandfather's version of the marjolaine cake."

"Marjolaine." Luna rolled the word around in her mouth. "What's that mean?"

"It is, ah, an herb? A spice?"

"Oh! Like marjoram?" Luna had no idea what marjoram was supposed to go into, but she remembered seeing it on one of the labels in her mom's dusty lazy Susan–style spice rack back home.

"Yes," Jean-Pierre said. "That is the word."

"So it's like an herbed spice . . . thing?"

JP frowned down at his notebook. "Non, it contains no marjolaine at all."

Luna pursed her lips. "So why—?"

"I do not have every answer, Luna," he snapped. "That is the name of the cake. I only tell you what I know."

"Fine. All right. Let's just calm down." Luna snatched a hair tie off her wrist and put her long purple-pink hair into a high pony. "How do we make this thing?"

It turned out the first step was to go to the grocery store—not the one at the end of the block, but the fancier, more expensive store that was five blocks north and always had pomegranates and dragon fruits arrayed in perfect rows in the outdoor stand displays. Jean-Pierre had been doubtful that the closer store would carry everything he needed, including a metric ton of hazelnuts.

"They do not look as fresh as the ones I am used to," he mumbled as he molested a bag of nuts that cost more than Luna's monthly manicure, kneading it over and over like that was going to tell him anything about the product. "They will have to do."

Luna grabbed the bag of nuts and dropped it into their plastic shopping basket. "What else?"

They traipsed up and down the maze of aisles together, doubling back more than once in their quest for all the ingredients. Into the basket it all went: farm-fresh, cage-free eggs; European-style unsalted butter in huge blocks; bars of organic dark chocolate that promised all the humans involved in its harvesting had actually been paid; a carton of cream with a very specific percentage of fat that JP made a huge deal about; and actual vanilla in real fucking pods.

"This stuff is going to run you a lot of money," Luna said

as she placed the jar of vanilla beans carefully in her basket. She had the sense that this store was a "You break it, you buy it" kind of place.

JP swiped a second jar from the shelf and added it to their haul. His dark eyes swept up to meet hers, his lips twisted in a lopsided smirk. "I can afford it."

Well, as long as Daddy Warbucks was paying . . .

Luna ducked into an aisle lined with refrigerated cases. Wheels of Parmesan cheese and slabs of imported Gruyère nestled among chunks of stinky bleus and artisanal, cave-aged cheddars. Luna's mouth watered at the sight. At heart, she was a dairy queen, and she wasn't about to miss an opportunity to grab some. She selected a hunk of French Brie wrapped in cling film, hefting it in her palm.

An amused voice came from behind her. "There is no cheese in the cake recipe, Clair."

Luna turned with the full force of her deepest pout already on her face. "If we're going to spend the whole afternoon baking, then we're going to need energy. Protein. A healthy snack." She lifted the wedge of Brie for Jean-Pierre's inspection. "And look, he's French, just like you. Can I keep him? Please?"

JP rolled his eyes, though his mouth twitched slightly at the corner like he was fighting a smile. "Absurde," he muttered, which Luna was pretty sure meant exactly what it sounded like. Then, as if he knew he was not going to win this lactic acid–laced battle, he gestured at the cheese. "Yes, yes, fine, we will buy it."

Luna gave a cheer and tossed the Brie into the basket before hustling past Jean-Pierre toward the snack aisle. "We're going to need crackers. The good ones with the seeds and stuff on top."

JP followed at her heels. "Okay, but remember, we must carry all this back to your home."

"What about grapes?" Luna smoothly stepped around a parent wrangling a baby carriage. "We can't have cheese and crackers without grapes. Oh, and wine, of course. This kind of spread calls for wine. We'll stop at the liquor store on the way home."

"Luna," JP groaned.

"Just a few more things!" Luna shot him a smile before disappearing behind a display of pita chips.

By the time they were done and checking out at the cramped registers at the front of the store, they had managed to amass an impressive collection of overpriced gourmet products. Luna was desperately happy. She had forgotten how fun it was to share the chore of grocery shopping with someone else. The fact that JP's budget seemed to be limitless was a definite plus, too.

"This is going to be fun. I may not know how to cook—yet," she said as she selected the lightest of the five bags to carry, "but I can sure as heck put together a mean charcuterie board."

"Charcuterie is meat," Jean-Pierre said, hefting the remaining four bags. "What you are talking about is a cheese plate."

Luna decided not to mention the fancy upstate saucisson she'd smuggled into the basket when JP wasn't looking. "Po-tay-toe, pa-tata," she said, putting some Italian funk on the final word.

Back at the apartment, they unloaded all their consumable treasures and stood surveying the pile they'd made on the counter. The cheese and assorted snacks were put away, "So we can have them as a reward later," as Luna said, but the ingredients for the marjolaine cake towered before them in a way only the most intimidating task could.

"Right." JP took the Moleskine out of the back pocket of his jeans and consulted the page. "So we . . . hm."

"Hm?" Luna raised her brows. "What's *hm*? And what's that notebook of yours about, anyway? Did Grandpa Henri write all his recipes down there for you?"

"Ah, non, Papi never writes down his recipes." Jean-Pierre

frowned at the notebook, flipped a page to frown at the back of it, then flipped forward again. "He is a bit paranoid about other chefs stealing his so-called brilliant ideas. This cake, for example, it is a classic, found on a thousand different dessert menus in Paris, but he supposedly executes his with elevated methods." He flipped three pages ahead and brought the notebook within an inch of his nose to squint at the writing there. "I had to find a retired pastry chef who used to work at Papi's first restaurant and beg him to tell me how to make it. We got very drunk together. These are my notes from that conversation." He shot Luna a look of chagrin. "I do not take very good notes when I am drinking, I suppose."

"Well, it's just a cake, not rocket science. We can figure it out between the two of us," Luna said.

"True." JP propped up his notebook on the counter, using Simone's salt cellar to hold it in place against the kitchen wall. The handwriting was a messy scrawl of French that Luna couldn't decipher even if she were fluent. "Step one," he read aloud, "make the dacquoise."

"Awesome." Luna looked at him. "What's a dacquoise?"

"Well, it's—" Jean-Pierre paused. "It's like—ah. It is a kind of cake?"

Luna felt her blood pressure tick upward. "Yeah, we know that. That part of the mystery is solved. How do you *make* it?"

"I do not know! I have only eaten dacquoise, I have never made it! I've watched Papa make it once or twice." He began to mime whipping something in a bowl held in the crook of his arm. "I think it is meringue. With other things in it. Nuts!" He tapped the bag of hazelnuts that sat slouched on the counter. "It contains the nuts," he said with pride.

"Don't we have to blitz the nuts in the food processor first?" Luna hefted the bag of shelled raw hazelnuts. "You said they needed to be powdered, right?"

For a moment she considered calling Simone to beg her for the world's fastest lesson in making a cake, but it would be too selfish to interrupt her in the middle of a workday. Plus, Luna was certain that between the two of them, she and JP could figure this out on their own. Despite what her former employer said, she had a great attitude—a wonderful *tone*. And she could prove it by baking a single ridiculous cake.

"Yes, that is step one." Jean-Pierre wrangled the Cuisinart from its spot on a high shelf and plugged it in. "I do not see why this is such a big deal," he said. "You were right; it is just cake."

Five minutes later, they had made hazelnut butter. The nuts had been processed way past powder and into paste just like peanut butter, if peanut butter were thirty dollars a jar. There was a faintly smoky scent in the air from the poor overworked Cuisinart motor. Luna and Jean-Pierre peered into the bowl of the food processor in total silence.

Luna, of course, had to break it. "We can probably still use it."

"Do you think so?" JP asked.

"Sure, why not? It's still nuts in tiny bits. They're just . . . wetter than most bits."

"Won't that affect things?"

"You're asking me?" Luna stared at him. "The only cakes I ever made were with the help of Duncan Hines."

Jean-Pierre looked pained. "A former, ah, boyfriend?"

"No! A box mix! A premade, just-add-water type deal. I've never baked a single thing from scratch."

"But you are a woman," Jean-Pierre said. "How can you not know how to make a cake?"

Luna reeled back, her eyes going comically wide. "Oh! Okay, restaurant heir who can't cook for shit! We're bringing gender into it now? Because I have some *thoughts*." What she actually had were Simone's thoughts, which she had adopted as her own. Her roommate had complained often enough about the bullshit ways most restaurants still operated. Head chefs were still overwhelmingly men; women tended to be shuttled into the pastry departments—not that there was anything wrong with pastry, but when it was still thought of as the "girly" kind of cooking, that translated to lower salaries and higher expectations. Luna knew just enough about it to be furious.

JP held up his hands in defeat. "Apologies, apologies. Of course you can be a woman and not know how to bake." He gazed down at their hazelnut butter like it had personally insulted him. "I do not want to waste this. Perhaps we put it into the meringue and see what happens? That is what chefs do, yes?"

Luna snapped her fingers. "Now we're talking. See? We've got great instincts."

"We do," Jean-Pierre said, sounding a little more confident. He found a rubber spatula and began scraping the paste out of the food processor's bowl. "Although . . ." He squished up his face like he was unsure whether he should say what he had just thought.

Luna's heart sank. "What?"

"Should we have toasted the nuts first?" He looked up at her. "Or do you think they are fine raw?"

"Raw is good. Things that are raw have more flavor, right?" Luna thought hard. "Okay, you know what? We're going to learn how to do this the way I learned how to do everything at my old job." She whipped out her phone and opened YouTube. "We're going to find a video of someone who knows what they're doing and just copy them." It was how she'd learned about spreadsheets, photography touch-ups, gift basket arrangements, curtain rod installation, condolence card messages, and light graphic design in her capacity as a personal assistant. YouTube had never failed her.

A simple search brought them to a video of someone's hands as they quietly began assembling the marjolaine's dacquoise. Helpful subtitles spelled out exactly how much of each ingredient to use and what to do to them. Luna and JP huddled over her phone screen, their heads practically smushed together as they watched. Step one was definitely *toast the nuts*.

"Okay, I will do this again," JP said, tearing open another

bag of hazelnuts. He nodded at a stack of egg cartons. "Perhaps you can start by separating these for me. We will need" he squinted at the propped-up Moleskine—"nine egg whites. Be sure not to get any of the yolk in the bowl. That matters, apparently."

"No problem," Luna said. Had she ever separated an egg in her life? No. Was she going to tell JP that? Also no. She flipped open the carton and got to work.

Her first attempt smashed smartly against the lip of the metal mixing bowl, spraying flecks of eggshell and goop everywhere. She stood there with egg white dripping down her hand, wondering how Simone always made this look so easy.

She peered into the bowl. Bits of yolk and shell swirled in what little of the white had made it into the bowl instead of onto the counter. Clearly, that had been her practice egg. She got herself a new bowl and reached for another egg from the open carton.

"So." Jean-Pierre was deep in the weeds measuring out more nuts, laser-focused on the kitchen scale's digital readout as he spoke. He plucked one hazelnut out of the bowl, frowned at the numbers, then chopped the nut in half and tossed one piece back in. "I thought we were quite convincing this weekend. Was Connie convinced?"

Luna cracked another egg. This time, only three or four tiny pieces of shell made it into the bowl. She considered this a huge win. "Probably," she said. "She was practically walking on air when she left, she was so happy for us. Then again, that's my mom: always seeing the best in everything."

JP paused in the middle of opening a bag of chocolate chunks. "Really?"

"Oh, yeah. Runs in the family, I guess."

She tried to separate the whites from the yolk the way she'd seen Simone do it, using the two halves of the broken eggshell as little cups, passing the yolk back and forth between them so the white could drip down into the bowl like strands of snot.

More bits of shell came loose in the course of this exercise. Luna worked faster, thinking that might help, but then the yolk broke on the jagged edge of the shell and oozed into the bowl in spots of sunny yellow.

She took a deep breath, then got a new bowl. Her stack of failed attempts was growing.

Jean-Pierre tore open the chocolate and looked at her. "This is terrible news," he said. "My grandfather is the opposite: he always sees the worst. What if he sees through our lie right away? What if he declares the whole test void? All of this will have been useless." He motioned to all the cake makings.

"Hey, take a breath. We're going to be fine, both with the cooking stuff and the lovey-dovey stuff." She clicked the egg gently, gently, gently against the lip of the fresh bowl, but nothing happened. Not even the thinnest fissure appeared in the eggshell. With the tiniest bit more force, Luna tapped it again. The egg burst open, casting off a huge bit of shell the size of a thumbnail into the bowl.

She glared up at JP, who was watching all this in silence, eyebrows raised to high heaven. Luna put one eggy finger in the air. "Don't say a word."

"I am saying nothing." Then, because he apparently couldn't keep his big mouth shut for long, he said, "I think we should establish our rôles. If we can agree what we are like in relation to each other, then no matter what happens, we will be able to react like a real couple would."

"Uh, sure. I guess." Luna fished around for the piece of shell, but it seemed impossible to get ahold of in the slimy pool of egg. "How about a classic *Dharma & Greg* double act?" The show had been one of her mom's favorites back in the '90s. She'd said with total earnestness during Luna's transition that Luna was a dead ringer for Jenna Elfman. They certainly shared the same height, not to mention the same penchant for yoga.

"I don't know what that is. You are saying words like I'm supposed to understand them."

Luna gave up on trying to de-shell her egg and reached for the last clean bowl. "It's an old sitcom, Like, a comedy about a . . . situation? Sorry, I keep forgetting you were probably raised on a diet of sad black-and-white movies and perfume commercials."

"Excuse me," Jean-Pierre huffed, "but I will have you know my people invented the farce."

Luna hooked an unimpressed brow at him. "Whatever. The *Dharma & Greg* premise is simple: one of us is the lighthearted, spirited one—me, clearly—and the other is the serious, no-nonsense one. That's you."

JP crossed his arms over his chest. "I can be spirited. My heart can be light."

"I'm sure you contain multitudes," Luna said dryly, mopping up the wet egg on the counter with a paper towel. "Would you rather be the Dharma? For six hundred large, I'll glower all day at you if that's what you prefer."

He rubbed at his chin, where his five o'clock shadow was getting darker. "Non. I will be the . . . Greg." He said the name with more distaste than it deserved, in Luna's opinion. "That should work as long as we pretend to truly— What is the phrase? Support, loving support?"

"'Lift each other up?'" Luna suggested.

"Yes, exactly. You think this is, ah, believable?" He squinted at her like the answer was important to him, and he wanted to make sure she didn't lie.

"Sure." She cracked the egg smartly—on the first try—and started the delicate process of separation again. "Every queer couple I know is like that." Aisha and Ruth, Ray and Simone, the two adorable gray-haired butches who worked at the gay-friendly salon Luna liked—they all thought their partners walked on water.

Jean-Pierre frowned. "But we are not a queer couple."

Luna lifted her head, not paying attention as her yolk dribbled over the edge of her eggshell, breaking badly. "What do you mean, we're not? How do you figure?"

He gestured between the two of them, at the small amount of space between their bodies as if that indicated the bodies themselves. "I am un homme. You are une femme. Transgender or not, that makes us a straight couple."

Luna laughed. One sharp, high, almost hysterical laugh. Then she realized Jean-Pierre was not laughing along with her. His face was as serious as a cigarette label. Her own fell to match. "You honestly believe that?"

"Of course." He stared at her. "You don't?"

Luna dropped the ruined egg into the bowl with a plop. "I am not *straight*." She said it with all the disgust someone might use when describing the Great Pacific Garbage Patch, or a particularly nasty strain of cholera. "I'm a lot of things, but that's one thing I have never been. Not only did I date a few girls back when I was still in my boy disguise, but I have since had the pleasure of being courted by all sorts of genders. I would say I'm—is there a word in French meaning pansexual?"

"Yes. Pansexuel," Jean-Pierre deadpanned. "That's very good for you—I, however, am a straight man. Do you make me queer by merely existing in my orbit?"

"No," Luna said with fraying patience, "of course not. But you don't make me straight in the same way either!"

"If we are walking down the street, hand in hand, what do you think people see? Hopefully, if we are looking our best, they will see a heterosexual pair. Un homme et une femme, nothing more. That is a straight couple."

Luna reeled, her palms in the air, her eyes blinking wildly up at the ceiling. "Wow. Okay. There is *so* much to unpack there, I'm going to need a fucking bellhop."

"A maid," Jean-Pierre said. He opened the oven and shook the pan of toasting hazelnuts.

"What?"

"Bellhops do not help you unpack luggage. A maid might."

"Oh my god, can you stop being fancy-rich for one second? You know what I meant." Luna ticked off her fingers, which were sticky with egg. "First of all: Why should I care what other people think when they see us? And second: What the hell does 'looking our best' mean? Are you talking about passing? Because I care even less about that, if that's possible!"

"You cannot tell me you do not care about your appearance," JP said with a patented Gallic sneer. He retrieved the nuts from the oven and put the pan on a wire cooling rack. "Obviously you take great pains. The dyed hair, and the lipstick, and the, the—" He gestured with an oven mitt at her body in a frantic way and said something in French that sounded kind of flattering.

Not that Luna was going to let that sidetrack her.

"I do those things because I want to. It's for *me*. No one else. And I spent way too many years in therapy working through the difference, so fuck you if you think I don't know myself well enough to say so." She turned back to her bowl and cracked another egg. This time it didn't explode, and shell didn't fly everywhere, and she didn't get egg goo all over her fingers. She managed to separate the egg into an empty bowl with only a couple flecks of yellow yolk dotting the slimy mass. Luna chewed her lip. Surely a tiny bit of yolk was fine? It's not like this was brain surgery; no one expected her to be that precise.

Jean-Pierre started spooning the nuts, which looked a tad dark and smelled burnt to Luna's nose, into the wiped-clean food processor. "Well, fuck you if you think I am foolish for wanting to be treated like a normal person. Not all of us have achieved nirvana like you have."

"Now you're just putting words in my mouth. Where's the whisk?" Her eyes darted around the kitchen until they landed on the utensil caddy Simone kept in the corner of the countertop. Luna leaned well into JP's space to retrieve the wiry implement, ignoring his affronted grunt as she did so. "Of course it's fine to want fair treatment; we all want that. What's not fine, in my opinion, is bending over backward so cis people don't get uncomfortable. I have no interest in blending in with the crowd. The crowd kind of sucks."

She jammed the whisk into the bowl just as she remembered she needed eight more egg whites. Back to cracking she went, speeding through until she had enough.

"Well, some of us don't want to stand out. We just want to live our lives unbothered. Where is the milk?" Jean-Pierre looked around until he spotted the carton.

"I've got news for you: the whole angsty Beat poet schtick you've got going?" She gestured from his head down to his toes. "It's not exactly the best camouflage." She turned back to her bowl and started whisking as fast as she could. "You look like a reject from a Swedish metal band. Like, if they had a violin player."

"Actually, I played the viola in school," JP said primly, "not the violin."

"See?" Luna whisked more aggressively. "Always got to be a little bit special, don't you?"

Jean-Pierre regarded her with narrowed eyes. "So says the grown woman with the candy-colored hair and the grammar-school accessories."

The bowl fell from the crook of Luna's arm and back onto the counter with a bang. She gave a shocked gasp, her hands clapping to her throat where her lacy choker sat. "I've gotten a lot of compliments on this necklace."

"Ah, oui. From nine-year-olds, I assume?"

Luna's upper lip trembled in anger. Sure, the choker was kind of a throwback, but it was a throwback to a time that Luna had missed out on. She hadn't exactly been in a position to wear stuff like this when she was a nine-year-old herself, so what was the harm in indulging in some good old-fashioned wish fulfillment?

"These," she said gravely, touching her fingertips to the dangling silver charm in the center of the choker, "are coming back in style."

"I will have to take your word for it." He turned back to the various bowls on the counter filled with half-whipped meringue and nut paste and sugar. "Perhaps we should stop insulting each other long enough to bake this cake, hm?"

"You started it," Luna muttered, even though, as she replayed the mental tape in her head, it seemed likely that she had been the one to lob the first verbal grenade. She sullenly returned to whipping her egg whites, then stopped. Her elbow twinged in pain. "Isn't there a better way than doing this by hand?"

Almost two hours and some liberal use of the stand mixer later, Luna and Jean-Pierre stood in the kitchen staring at the thing they had created.

It wasn't a marjolaine cake. It could not, in good conscience, be classified as a cake at all. It was more like—Luna tipped her head to the side, thinking another perspective might help—a sticky lump of stuff layered with other stuff, none of which looked correct. The dacquoise had not puffed into a light and airy meringue as planned; it had instead congealed into a flat brown mass in the oven, like someone had melted a soda bottle filled with root beer into a pancake. Still, they had forged ahead with what they had, agreeing that once everything was arranged in the proper stack and slathered with buttercream, it would look better.

It did not look better.

The vanilla buttercream had taken on a grayish appearance, and the hazelnut one had failed entirely, becoming more of a pudding that oozed from the layers of the not-cake to puddle on the cutting board they had used as a serving platter. The less said about the chocolate ganache, the better. According to JP's notes, it was supposed to be as glossy and smooth as a piece of volcanic glass. (Retired French pastry chefs were real wordsmiths, apparently.) But their version of the ganache was a nightmare of lumps and grit.

Jean-Pierre sighed and plopped the three candied whole hazelnuts they'd managed to produce—coated in burnt caramel, naturally—on top of the quasi-cake. Luna noticed he placed them strategically to try and hide the worst of the rips in the dacquoise, which was peeking through the too-thin coatings of chocolate and failed icing.

"Maybe it tastes good," Luna offered.

JP gave her a look. "Do you want to try eating it?"

Jean-Pierre was paying her a lot of money, but not enough to contract food poisoning. "No. You want a slice?"

"I want to throw this in the garbage."

Luna scrubbed a streak of powdered sugar off her cheek with the back of her hand. "You said this was supposed to be the easiest recipe out of the nine, right?"

"That was the impression I was given, yes."

"Then we're doomed," Luna said. "It's going to take a miracle for us to produce anything edible."

JP turned a well-placed glare on her. He had hazelnut powder clinging to his black hair and on the tips of his eyelashes. "Maybe if you had concentrated on the dacquoise like we agreed instead of trying to rip my throat out—"

Luna rolled her eyes. "Maybe if you'd learn how to properly handle nuts—"

"Maybe if you could stop nagging me for one minute—"

"Maybe if you didn't care so much about what your fucking grandpa thinks!"

They stood facing each other in the too-hot kitchen, breathing hard in the residual heat from the oven. Luna could see a tic in JP's jaw. She wondered if she had gone too far.

Well, someone had to tell it like it was.

"I see," JP said in a slow, dangerous sort of voice. "My grandfather, his opinions should just—?" He tossed some imaginary weight over his shoulders. "Roll off like a duck's back, yes? That would be wonderful, wouldn't it? Of course, you would be six hundred thousand dollars poorer for it."

"Small price to see you get your head out of your ass," Luna shot back. "I may need money, but I can get that lots of places. You can't find another fake girlfriend named Luna that your grandpa will recognize from FaceTime. So don't act like you're holding all the cards here, okay?"

Jean-Pierre's nostrils flared. His mouth opened like he was about to launch another searing volley, but he clapped it shut and looked away. "I . . . don't want to fight with you," he said in a halting way, like he was unused to giving ground in conversations like this. "We need to learn to work together. Not just as a couple, but in the kitchen."

Luna couldn't help but laugh, a disbelieving sound that echoed through the small apartment. "Okay, seriously. This?" She pointed at the congealing mass of un-cake. "Does not bode well for our chances."

JP stared at the lump of failed dessert. He didn't seem to have any witty comeback, no plan for how to improve their chances of success. He just looked defeated, slumped there against the kitchen wall with nut dust in his hair.

It was almost enough to soften Luna's heart. Almost.

She turned to the fridge and started taking out the remaining cheeses and grapes plus the reasonably priced bottle of chardonnay that was now chilled, piling them all up in her arms. "Well, I'm going to enjoy my charcuterie."

"Cheese plate," JP said automatically.

"Whatever. You're welcome to join me—after you clean up the mess in here." She looked pointedly at the sink, which was overflowing with dirty bowls and baking implements. "Or do you normally have a maid wash the dishes?"

She swept out of the kitchen without waiting for an answer, slamming her bedroom door shut for emphasis.

That night, since Luna's mom was finally absent, they were able to sleep in separate rooms. Luna lay fuming in her bed, wrapped around her biggest pillow. Of all the guys in all the baking competition soundstages, he had to walk into hers. She could hear Jean-Pierre moving around in Simone's room across the hall. Probably getting ready to sleep in the nude; Luna made a mental note not to tell Simone about that particular quirk lest she burn all of her sheets.

She turned onto her other side. It was impossible to get comfortable tonight. Too hot, then too cold, then too hot again.

Luna shut her eyes and willed herself to become unconscious. She stayed on the very edge of sleep for a long time, half-thinking, half-dreaming of eggs being separated, whites in one bowl, yolks in another.

Chapter 10

The moment Luna woke up—much too early and alone in her bed, which didn't seem fair—she grabbed her phone off its charging station on her bedside table and flicked open the group chat. She'd been putting this off for far too long, but between her mom's visit and dealing with Jean-Pierre, there hadn't been a free moment for her to catch her friends up on the situation. She typed with a half-twist of her lips. It was hard not to feel a little smug when you were, for once, the one composing a message that would derail the chat for at least a day.

Sorry I was AWOL for the last few days! I'll cut to the chase: I now have a fake boyfriend who's paying me over half a million dollars to pretend to be his girlfriend and I think we may be on the verge of breaking up WHAT DO I DO

Sara never woke up before ten if she could help it, but Luna knew Aisha and Willow were early risers, and Lily never seemed to sleep at all, so she wasn't surprised by the flurry of responses. She grinned as they came in, her phone pinging wildly.

WHAT

ok literally tho what the fuck

THAT'S why you were getting papped with the French restauranteur guy??

Maybe it was petty, but Luna couldn't help the thrill that surged through her. Finally, she was getting some time in the spotlight, basking in the glow of her friends' undivided attention. Who cared about what wall color Aisha and Ruth had decided on for their open-concept living room when *this* was happening? Today, she was the most interesting girl in the chat, and that felt good.

She gave everyone a rundown of what was going on with Jean-Pierre, right up to their disastrous attempt at cake making the day before. It was impossible to tell it quickly with just the bare facts; the girls kept chiming in with color commentary and pointed questions.

so is he hot or not, O'Shea??? he looks hot in these pics but what about for real.

Luna demurred, saying they needed to focus on the real problem, and could Lily please hold all her questions until Luna was done telling the story. Even Sara joined in eventually, backreading the whole thing in record time so she could put in her two cents, which basically amounted to:

for half a mil he could have six heads and a dozen tentacles and I would not care.

we all know for you that would be a feature, not a bug, Willow said.

Enough about Sara's monsterfuckery! Tell me what I'm supposed to do about JP, Luna typed furiously.

Oh, definitely don't bail.

yeah mackerels don't happen everyday

*miracles

Lil's right you can't just turn down HALF A MILLION DOLLARS just because the guy is DIFFICULT.

Honey, think about what you could do with that amount of money. Clothes. Shoes. Electrolysis. New boobs. New cheekbonesssss.

if you WANT that stuff.

Do you want that stuff?

Luna bit her lower lip in thought. She tapped the corner of her phone on her knee. It had been a long time since she'd even considered getting additional gender-affirming surgeries. There was no real point in thinking about it, after all, when they were so expensive as to be out of her reach. Like the yoga certification courses that were step one of one hundred in her daydreams. But now that there was a possibility of a windfall, did she feel different . . . ?

I'm not sure, she told the chat. It would be nice to have the option, though.

Then fucking get back in there and fake make up with your fake man!

whoa let's try not to call the trans boy fake

Mm, good point. Fake make up with your very real sugar daddy!

Willow dropped in a gif of a cartoon kitten doing some kind of cheerleading dance. It made Luna smile, which was a nice change from sulking in her too-empty bed. Sugar daddies expect sugar, she reminded them. He's not getting a taste, okay?

u serious?

Not even a little?

Luna tried not to think about the kiss they'd shared in that very spot. That had just been practice.

I should go, she said instead. Time to face the music/the weird French guy that's crashing in my apartment.

A chorus of well wishes and good lucks flooded the chat, and Luna closed the app with a smile still lingering on her lips. Talking with her friends had cheered her up, sure, but more importantly, she had gotten some much-needed perspective. A little tiff over a bad cake was no reason to lose out on such a huge amount of money. She needed to suck it up and smooth things over with Jean-Pierre.

She got up, threw on some yoga pants, fixed herself a cup of green tea with honey, and drank it while taking stock of the kitchen. Jean-Pierre had clearly made an effort to clean up. All the bowls and whisks and baking sheets were scrubbed and sitting in the dish drainer in a precarious Jenga stack, but at least they were washed. The counters had been wiped down and all the appliances put away. There were still a lot of leftover baking ingredients piled on top of the stove, and the overflowing trash can hadn't been emptied, but that wasn't so surprising. JP had likely run out of steam, and who could blame him?

Luna took herself into the living room and uncoiled her yoga mat. It had been five days since her last session, and she intended to remedy that with a long, indulgent practice. The real world fell away, and the only thing she had to hold in her head was the rhythm of her breath and the movement of her limbs. Sun salutation, forward fold, down into plank, chaturanga into a cobra, back into downward dog, then a hop into mountain pose to start the whole cycle again.

She needed this; there hadn't been a spare moment to recenter since being fired.

Jean-Pierre emerged from the hallway just as Luna was arching her back into her third salutation. She cracked one eye open to take him in. He was wearing newly purchased running shorts and the same shirt from yesterday. His hair was a wild tumble of curls shooting off in all directions. As Luna watched, he ran a hand through it and regarded her with the sleepy squint of the just awakened.

"Coffee?" he croaked.

She chose to believe he was offering, not asking her to make him some. "No, thank you. I had some tea earlier." The words came out much less clipped than they could have been, which Luna was very proud of. She floated down into her forward fold, her face pressing very close to her knees, her eyes falling shut again.

She endeavored to tune out the shuffling of JP's bare feet in the kitchen. The clinks and taps of his pour-over ritual floated to her ears, but she tried her best not to be distracted from her breathing. She went through the last of the cycle before coming into warrior three. That pose always made her feel strong, her feet planted solidly on the mat, her arms outstretched on either side. It reminded her of shooting an arrow for some reason, the way that her shoulders and hips were stacked.

Deep breaths, in and out. She visualized her energy circulating through her body like warm, golden honey. Healing and eternal.

"May I join you?"

Luna opened her eyes once more to find JP standing right in front of her yoga mat, a half-empty cup of coffee in his hand. His head was ducked and his shoulders hunched like he was expecting to be told to fuck off.

Luna let go of a breath she had been holding. She stuck her chin toward the corner of the room, where another yoga mat was leaning in a neat roll tied with a Velcro band. The mat was ostensibly Simone's, but it hadn't been used since they'd done yoga together in the park last summer. "Be my guest," Luna said in what she hoped was not too sarcastic a tone. She was trying to smooth things over, after all. She began yet another flow that would take her back to her sun salutation.

By the time she was back into warrior three, this time with her other knee bent, JP had unrolled his borrowed mat and nudged the coffee table out of the way to make space. He copied her pose fairly well; she was facing his way and could see that his spine was nicely stacked above his hips.

"You do a lot of yoga?" she asked as she held the pose.

"Off and on." He made a small adjustment, pulling his shoulders farther back. "My doctors say it will help recover my range of motion after my various surgeries. I should do it more often, if I'm honest, but I would rather go for a jog most days."

"Jogging is terrible for your joints," Luna said automatically. She flowed down into another cycle, and Jean-Pierre followed suit. "And I read somewhere that going for a run in a place as polluted as Manhattan, like, negates any health benefits just because of the amount of gunk you're breathing in."

"It helps clear my mind," JP said, his voice slightly strained as they lowered into downward dog together.

"Hm," was all Luna said. She closed her eyes and let her head hang between her shoulders, her purple hair brushing the mat. Peace was hers; contentment was hers. That was the mantra she breathed into her lungs.

"Can we talk?"

Luna's eyes popped open and she turned her head to stare at JP through their forest of arms. She wasn't sure she was centered enough for this conversation, but okay. "About?"

"Yesterday"—he flowed decently out of downward dog and into a tree pose, of all things—"I realized you and I can be quite similar. We are both, how to say—hard in the head? Stubborn." He balanced on one leg, the other foot planted high on the meat of his calf, knee pointed out to the side, hands clasped in prayer position in front of his chest. "I would like to move past this, if we can."

Luna copied the pose, though she lifted her foot to her inner thigh; she was more bendy. Not that it was a competition, but if it were, she'd be winning. "I completely agree," she said. Her friends would be so proud of her. "You're the one paying for this fake relationship. If you want to call it straight, then what's it to me? It's not like we're really dating."

Jean-Pierre wobbled on his leg and only caught himself from falling by holding his hands out to his sides for balance. He recovered after a few seconds, his gaze locked ahead at the wall. "But you are not obliged to do whatever I say just because I am giving you money. It's not as if you're some paid—woman," he finished with a wince.

Luna switched legs and looked over at him, her hands still folded in prayer. "You mean a sex worker."

"Yes. That. You're not that, I mean." It was hard to tell if he was turning pink from exertion or embarrassment.

"I don't see a huge distinction," Luna said. "You're giving me money in return for the illusion of intimacy, a fantasy; what is that if not sex work?"

"But we're not having sex!" JP's foot came crashing to the floor with a thump. He swung it up and clasped it in a clumsy quad stretch. He glanced at Luna with a huff.

"A lot of sex work isn't about sex at all, you know."

"Then the English language should have a better word for what you are describing," Jean-Pierre retorted.

Luna rolled her eyes. "It's not something to be ashamed about. I sold my underwear online for the first year I was living in New York." She transitioned smoothly into a half moon pose, looking up the long line of her arm pointed at the ceiling. "I never met any of the people who were ponying up the cash for panties, but it wasn't *not* sex work. Just like what I'm doing now isn't *not* being an escort."

Jean-Pierre gave up any pretense of working on his leg and stood on his mat, staring open-mouthed at Luna. "You sold your—?" His gaze flicked slightly downward before rocketing back up to meet her eyes. "Were they already worn?"

She clicked her tongue. "Don't sound so scandalized. If that's someone's thing and they're willing to pay for the privilege of owning my laundry, who am I to judge?" Luna released from the balancing posture and switched sides. "Besides, I usually didn't have time to actually wear them. Just spritzed them with perfume, rumpled 'em up a little, stuffed 'em in a Priority envelope—bam, that's fifty bucks right there."

Behind her, Jean-Pierre made a sound like a distressed kettle.

"My point is," she continued as if JP wasn't having a pantie-induced heart attack in her living room, "you're the client here. If you say we're playing a straight couple, okay, fine. Let's play a straight couple." She dropped out of her pose entirely and faced him with her hands on her hips.

Jean-Pierre adopted his own power pose, crossing his arms over his chest with a frown. "I do not want to be thought of as your—client." He couldn't even manage to suppress the shudder as he said it.

"Well, that's what you are. Unless you think pretending to date me is too gross, now that I've spelled out that it's kind of, sort of exactly like sex work."

His pale face went through a series of twists and scrunches as he chewed on that. "I do not think— That is, there is no shame in that line of work, of course. But I do not want to be some tyrant, ordering you around. It makes it all seem so—" He groped for the right phrase. "Cheap."

Luna laughed, a real hearty one. "It's not cheap at all. It's costing you a lot of money."

"Please don't remind me," he muttered. His gaze drifted away across the room. For someone who said there was nothing shameful about this, he was sure radiating a lot of guilt.

Luna could feel the embers of their last argument flaring to life in her belly. Maybe she hadn't exorcised all of that anger with deep breathing and mindful movement after all. "Oh, okay. So it's not enough for me to simper and giggle and hang on your arm while playing the adoring girlfriend. You think I've got to do it with a smile—even when the cameras aren't pointed at us."

JP took a step back, almost colliding with the television stand. "That is not what I meant. It is— Argh." He growled in frustration, like he couldn't find the English words quick enough.

Her rage only built as she remembered flashes from Zoom calls with her old boss Tim. *You need to be a team player. We expect you to give 110 percent just like everyone else. All I'm asking for is a little flexibility.*

This should be more than a job to you; we're like a family here.

Luna was done giving her all for some boss who didn't give a shit about her. She was over it, being treated like a machine that cranked out productivity and never needed to be oiled. And she was certainly not going to fall back into the same trap of doing a job that pretended to be her entire lifestyle.

She advanced on him, not caring if she was crowding him. "You don't want to be reminded that this is a paid transaction? Then maybe I'm not the right fake girlfriend for the position, because there is no way I am ever going to let you forget it."

His mouth worked open and closed. She scoffed at the sight of him, gasping like a fish out of water. They weren't getting anywhere like this. This was just yesterday's confrontation: part two.

"I need some air," she said and snatched her purse and cozy oversized hoodie from where it hung on the back of the rocking chair. "I'll see you later."

Jean-Pierre didn't even call a goodbye as Luna left the apartment.

She headed to the only place that made sense: the brewery studio. Luna needed to talk to someone about the latest development in their fake-dating scheme, and Simone was one of the few people in the world who knew about it and wasn't under the impression that she had this thing on lock. Right now, Luna didn't feel like she had anything on lock. Six hundred thousand dollars was a lot of money, but was it worth all this . . . hassle? Luna couldn't imagine pulling off the ruse of being a loving couple, not to mention passing a Black Diamond–grade culinary test.

They just weren't working well together. On any level. Maybe it was better to stop now before it was too late.

These were the thoughts that plagued Luna as she entered the building and clomped up the stairs in her slip-on sneakers. On the third spiral upward, she ran into Petey Zhang, Simone's old cameraman, now the show's director. Luna had hung out with him a few times over beers with the ex–Discerning Chef crew, and was thankful to see his friendly face.

"Hey, Petey, is Simone around?"

Petey paused on his way down the stairs, stopping three rungs above her. "Oh, hi, Luna. Yeah, she's around, but I don't know if she's got time for a visit." He hooked a thumb over his shoulder in the direction of the studio. "They're doing lighting tests for the confessional rooms—you know, where people talk to the camera to provide commentary? She'll be in there for a while longer."

Luna bit the inside of her cheek. It was always something on this set. But of course Simone and everyone else was super busy getting everything ready for the first day of shooting.

"Do you think I could hang out and wait for her?" she asked.

Petey shrugged. "I don't see why not. Just do me a favor: do one of those breathing exercises or whatever with her."

Luna's eyebrows rose. "Is she in need of a little calm?"

"We all are," Petey said. "It's getting pretty wild around here." He glanced at his cell phone. "I've really got to run. See you later." He inched past her on the narrow staircase and practically zoomed out of the lobby.

Luna stuffed her hands into her hoodie pocket and continued climbing the stairs with a sigh. She had some time to kill and nothing to murder it with.

As with the other times Luna had visited the set, she found herself trying to stay out of everyone's way. The beehive of activity had become a swarm, with more people and equipment crammed into the space than seemed possible. Luna edged around a stack of cardboard boxes that someone with a headset was tearing open. Inside were deep-blue Dutch ovens, all gleaming new. Luna recognized the brand name stamped on the lids as one that Simone often sighed over when it appeared on cooking shows. Before, just one of those pots had been too expensive to own at home. Now it looked like Simone would be working day in, day out in close proximity to a million of them.

It sure was funny, Luna thought, the way things could change. The universe had a plan for everyone, and she was glad that Simone's plan included her dream enamel cooking vessel. She made her way along the edge of the chaos, keeping her eyes peeled for a place to sit where she wouldn't be mowed down.

What she found instead was one beleaguered boss. Standing in the middle of the whirlwind was a woman Luna had seen before in passing—Delilah, one of the show's producers. She looked more overwhelmed than any one person could be. Her mass of braids was gathered into a knot at the top of her head, and two pens were stuck in it. She was juggling an armful of printouts, two cell phones, a walkie-talkie, and, most tellingly, an industrial-sized bottle of Tums.

"No, no, that's not what we agreed on," she said into one phone, then switched to the other. "Are you still there? I said this needs to be done by EOD. The delivery is coming first thing tomorrow." A tense pause. She hopped up onto the half-built counter of a competitor's workstation and shoved the phone between her ear and her shoulder so she could wrestle with the Tums cap. "I'll be here. Yes, at five a.m. You're breaking up again. Hello? Hello!"

Luna slowed, then stopped as Delilah muffled a mixed sob-scream into the pile of papers that were stuffed in the crook of her arm. Luna did not know this woman very well, but still, it seemed insensitive to walk right by without offering some kind of support to a fellow human in the midst of a breakdown.

"Tough day?" she asked.

Delilah picked her head up, papers spilling. The Tums bottle lay tightly sealed in her limp hand. "Are you the scene painter?" She scrambled through her printouts as if the answer was contained somewhere in there. "You were supposed to be here yesterday, but I didn't have time to follow up and—"

"Ah, no." Luna held up her palms. "Not a painter. I'm just Simone's roommate."

"Oh." Delilah deflated. "Sorry, I—" She shook her head. One of the pens dislodged and tumbled free, hitting her in the arm as it fell. Delilah didn't seem to notice. "I knew that. Luna, right? I've seen you around here before. My brain is complete mush today, I guess."

"You seem super swamped." Luna stooped to pick up the pen where it had fallen on the concrete floor and placed it atop some of the papers that had spilled onto the counter. Delilah stared at it like she'd never seen it before in her life.

"Yeah," she said, slowly lifting a hand to her hair and pulling out the second one. She stared at it, too. "Oh my god, is that where they're all going? I'm putting pens in my hair. I'm turning into the kind of person who sticks stuff in their hair and forgets where they put it. What is happening to my life?" She dropped the pen into her lap and gazed into the middle distance with a glazed look in her eyes. "I'm turning into that white lady from the *Cathy* comic strip. What's her name?"

"Um, I think it's Cathy?"

Delilah's eyes filled with an alarming sheen. "I couldn't remember that Cathy is from *Cathy*," she whispered. "I. Am. Losing it."

Luna glanced around to see if anyone more qualified was nearby, but everyone else seemed to be focused on their own tasks, oblivious to the imminent crying jag from their fearless leader.

"Can I get you a coffee or something?" She reached out and tugged the phones and assorted papers from Delilah's lax grip before they fell onto the ground. "How do you like it? Cream, sugar?"

"I could do an herbal tea," Delilah said, still teary. "I try not to have any caffeine after lunch. Oh my god, lunch." She looked at her smartwatch.

Sensing that this breakdown might require some space to really unravel, Luna began collecting all the other bits and pieces from the counter: the walkie-talkie, the Tums. "Do you have an office? Somewhere you can sit for a second? I'll bring the tea to you there."

"Yeah, it's—" Delilah gestured with vague disgust down a hallway. "Not that I ever get a chance to use it. I'm on my feet all day. This is the first time I've actually stopped moving since I got in this morning. Whoa." She put a hand to her head as she stood. "Huh. Sorta dizzy."

Okay, things were dire. Spiritually and medically, this called for an intervention. Luna put a steadying hand on Delilah's arm. "Let's go use that office, then."

She followed Delilah down the hall and into an airless room packed with binders and boxes. The desk was buried beneath an avalanche of paper—what looked like contracts, to Luna's eyes. At least what she could see of the top strata. Delilah flopped into the only chair, a creaky office chair, and spun around, groaning at the ceiling. "I can't be crying in front of you," she said. "I don't even know you, really."

"That makes me the *best* person to cry in front of." Luna deposited her armload of stuff on top of the desk pile, balancing it precariously at the peak. "Just consider me one of the random, anonymous New Yorkers who have seen you cry in semi-public. Have you ever cried on the subway? Top-tier place to cry."

Delilah looked at her like she was a bit concerned—whether for Luna or her own safety now that she was in a room alone with someone who rated public crying spots, it wasn't clear. "I'm not usually a big crier, to be honest. Today is just— I don't know what's wrong with me today."

Luna had some ideas. But first, tea. And food. "Wait here," she said, even though it was clear that Delilah was not capable of moving at any point in the immediate future. Luna dashed down the hall and poked around until she found the staff break room. It looked like every break room at every retail and office job Luna had ever had: arranged haphazardly, like it was an afterthought, a collection of mismatched plastic chairs and a beat-up table. The walls were adorned only with the required safety posters provided by the city.

But it had a coffee and tea station, and that was all that really mattered.

Luna selected a packet of sweet cinnamon tea from the carousel of options on the kitchenette counter and found a clean mug on the shelf. Hot water was available from the single-serve coffee machine, which Luna figured out how to work in under twenty seconds, grinning to herself the whole time. JP would hate this thing, she thought. As the tea steeped, she turned her attention to what she supposed was a ubiquitous sight in the break room of a show dedicated to cooking: platters of food scattered down the center of the table. Luna wondered if there was a team of chefs already working on testing recipes that would be used in the show, or if it was just Simone doing that thing she always did—feeding everyone with all the determination of a nagging mother.

The food was pretty picked over, but Luna managed to scrounge up a decent array on a paper plate: mini croissants stuffed with ham and cheese, turkey-and-vegetable pinwheels, a tiny tart shell filled with what looked like caramelized onions (in case Delilah turned out to be vegetarian), and a glossy lemon bar dusted with powdered sugar.

Delilah was still staring up at the ceiling with a blank look when Luna returned. She accepted the mug of tea without really looking, cupping it between her hands like she needed to soak up its warmth.

"I don't know if I can do this," she said in the same tone someone might use to say the Mets had lost a game. Disappointed, but not surprised, with a certain removed air.

Luna placed the paper plate of nibbles within easy reach on a low metal filing cabinet, then took a seat on the only patch of floor that wasn't playing host to overstuffed boxes.

"Want to tell me about it?" she said.

Delilah blinked, then looked down at her. She must have seen the aura that Luna was trying to project, a crisp light blue of sincere concern tinged with a royal purple lack of judgment. "I'm not sure I'm cut out for this job," she whispered. It sounded like a secret, never before said aloud. "I mean, what the hell am I doing? I was a secretary before this, for god's sake. An assistant to some rich weirdo."

"Wow, small world." Luna hooked both her thumbs in her own direction. "Same here. What was your weirdo like?"

"Intense. Pim was—" Delilah grimaced. "She was the kind of boss you really should be going to therapy about, if only you were being paid enough to afford therapy."

Luna's mouth fell open. "Pim—as in Pim Gladly?"

"You know her?"

"I've heard stories." Simone had had some choice tidbits to share from her time at The Discerning Chef. Luna had also caught a few episodes of some culinary competition show where Gladly was one of the snooty judges. "Is it true she has, like, fifteen purebred dachshunds with names like Grand Marnier and Aperol?"

"More like seven. Still, a lot." Delilah lifted her mug, but lowered it without taking a sip. "She was always *such* a lot. It didn't matter how hard I worked, she was never satisfied. I'd try to present my own ideas, and she'd dismiss me like *that*." She snapped her fingers. "Every day I worked at that place, she made me feel like the stupidest, most worthless person in the world. And I know I'm not; I *know* that! But . . ."

"It gets to you," Luna said softly. "The last guy I worked for? He would expect the impossible, then send all-caps emails when I tried to explain how airlines and the laws of physics worked. Like, I'm not the clueless one here, Tim! Sorry I can't get you from JFK to Santa Barbara in under three hours." Heat infused Luna's words. It was kind of nice to talk about this stuff with someone who'd also been in the trenches.

Delilah shook her head in a commiserating fashion. "The way they treat us. Like we're disposable. No appreciation, not even a glimmer of thanks."

"But you're the boss now," Luna pointed out. "All the nonsense? That's behind you. You should be proud! You got out from under Pim Gladly's thumb." She gestured around the messy office. "This is all yours. I think that's worth celebrating."

"I don't feel like celebrating lately." Delilah's voice cracked on the last word. "I'm not qualified to be a showrunner; I've never even worked in television. Why am I in charge? Whose bright idea was that?" The tears, which had receded since their first appearance, came back in full force. "There are so many people working on this thing, who are depending on me, and I'm afraid I'm going to let them all down."

"You don't know that," Luna said gently. "No one has a crystal ball."

Delilah wiped the edge of her hand along her eye, but delicately, like she was scared of ruining her lash set. Luna understood. "I can do the math. I get here at the crack of dawn every morning, and I don't leave until it's night, and there's still never enough time. There's always more to do, and then more right behind that. I am more than overwhelmed; I am—I'm hollowed out. I don't feel like a person anymore, just a machine. And not even a very efficient one!" She let out a shaky sigh. "Maybe I need to admit I've bitten off more than I can chew."

Oh, okay, we are spiraling.

Luna loved a spiral, to be honest. When it came to her own typhoon of emotions, nothing felt more cathartic than to lay on the couch like a vintage pulp-art model and sob beautifully. But she could do that; she was a Pisces. Delilah was giving off major earth sign energy, and for earth signs, there was nothing more frightening than being unmoored.

Her hand hovered over Delilah's ankle, which peeked out of her scuffed tennis shoes. "How are we feeling about being touched right now?" she asked. "I know I'm kind of a stranger, but—"

Delilah nodded jerkily. "It's okay."

Luna squeezed her ankle. "You're working so, so hard. No wonder you're exhausted. You're trying to do the work of ten people all on your own." She spotted a box of tissues squashed beneath some forms on the desk and liberated it to hand over to Delilah.

"Exactly!" Delilah put down her unsipped tea and plucked a wad of tissues from the box. "I haven't seen my husband with my own eyes for weeks. At least, not awake." She pressed the tissue to her cheeks, soaking up her tears.

"Oh, you're married?"

"Yes!" She sobbed. "I have a life! Not that you would know it, the way I'm always here. And I've got to keep up the perfect facade so that no one knows how close I am to falling apart every minute of every day."

"Hey, you are more than this work. You deserve your life and your conscious husband." Luna rubbed her ankle in what she hoped was a soothing gesture. "It doesn't have to be gaslight, gatekeep, girlboss twenty-four/seven. No one expects you to be perfect."

Delilah let out a surprised laugh. "I'm a Black woman in charge of a new series with a ten-episode order. *Everyone* expects me to be perfect."

"You got me there," Luna said. She gazed up at Delilah's tear-streaked face. "Sorry. I know that's got to be a ton of pressure. I also shouldn't be moving on to the solution-oriented portion of the conversation if you're still in the feeling-your-feelings portion."

"No, please!" Delilah tossed her used tissues into a nearby trash can. "Let's talk solutions." Definitely an earth sign. "I need to figure out how I'm going to pull this off instead of, like, going straight to Penn Station, buying a ticket for whatever train is at the top of the departure board, leaving the city forever, and starting a new life in Bumfuck, Ohio."

"Wow." Luna reached up and grabbed the errant tea mug, pressing it back into Delilah's hands. "You've really got your escape route all mapped out, huh?"

"Except I can't leave," Delilah said, finally gulping down her tea. "How can I blow a chance like this? I don't want to live in Ohio!" The tears welled up again.

"You won't have to. All you need is a way to—" Luna sat up straighter. The wheels in her head were spinning. "To take some stuff off your plate."

"And how am I supposed to do that?"

Luna stood. She fidgeted with the strings of her hoodie. Tried to pace the length of the room, but the overflowing office made that impossible, so she just bounced on her heels in place. "Hire me," she said.

Delilah looked at her like she'd suggested they build hats out of bread loaves. "What?"

"Just hear me out. Hold on." She took out her phone, wildly scrolling through her emails, looking for an attachment. "Okay, this is not how I would normally make a pitch, like, at all, but—" She yelped in victory as she found the right file. She opened it and held the phone in Delilah's line of sight. "Here's my résumé. Four-plus years as a personal-slash-executive assistant in a startup environment, five or six years before that in customer service. If you call my last job for a reference, they'll tell you I have a bad attitude but that's because they're all assholes. Sorry, I know that's unprofessional to say, but it's the truth."

Delilah took the phone in one hand to squint at the small type. "I don't get it. What job are you hoping I'll give you?"

"The role of your assistant," Luna said.

She had expected pushback; she did not expect Delilah to laugh out loud. "My what?"

"Your assistant," she repeated. "You really need one. And don't tell me it's not in the budget; I saw all those Le Creusets being unpacked. This production has got money to spare." Money that could find a nice, comfortable home in her own bank account, please and thank you. Getting a job—a *real* one, not a fake-relationship one—would mean insurance, which would mean no more worries about her meds. And no more relying on JP's whims and schemes.

Delilah scrunched her face. "Why would you want to be my assistant?"

"It's wild, I know, but I have this theory that working for someone who actually gives a shit might be fun for a change." Luna paused. "Sorry I cursed. I swear, I'm usually *super* professional."

"Oh, I don't fucking care if you curse."

"See? This is what I'm talking about. You treat me like a person." Luna shrugged, half-smiling. "Maybe that's a low bar, but as far as bosses go, it would be pretty new for me."

Delilah blinked. "Do you even have any experience working in television?" she asked.

"No," Luna admitted, "but neither did you. I can pick things up pretty fast. I learned how to walk in heels in one afternoon. I can do all those things with spreadsheets that other people hate doing. And!" She pointed to the mug of tea. "I know about your caffeine intake already, which is like seventy-five percent of an assistant's job, so I'm way ahead of the curve."

"Luna—" She glanced at the résumé header. "Ms. O'Shea. I was an assistant for a long time. The only people who have assistants, in my experience, are people who don't do a damn bit of real work." She handed the phone back to Luna. "I'm not the kind of person who needs an assistant. No way."

Luna felt her body's energy focused and zinging through her meridians. She was a being of power, and she was going to go for what she wanted. "I totally get what you're saying. That's been my experience, too." She clasped her phone to her chest, imagining its bright light filling her heart. "But it doesn't have to be that way. Just because you're a capable, hardworking person doesn't mean you have to do everything yourself. You've already done so much. Imagine what you could accomplish if you let me help you. Please," she said, "I want to help."

Delilah watched her closely, then put her tea back down on the desk. Her silence was unnerving, but Luna withstood it.

"I'll think about it," she said.

Luna tamped down on her instinctual fist pump. She managed to edit it into a tiny hop instead. "Of course. Take your time. It's a big decision." She waited a beat. "Should I, like, email you with my contact info or . . . ?"

"Oh! Yes." Delilah was also switching on her Real Adult Mode; Luna could tell by the set of her shoulders. "Here, why don't I—"

There was some awkward back-and-forth with phone numbers and email addresses and sending a copy of the résumé as an attachment and making sure Delilah could open it without any trouble, but once that was done, Luna felt good. She actually wanted this job. She could picture herself enjoying it, maybe. This was a cosmic miracle. What more could she want? As long as her bills were paid and her healthcare was good to go, she didn't need anything else. Plus, it was a way more sustainable solution than getting weird lump sums from an even weirder millionaire who thought it was okay to yell at her in her own kitchen.

"Give me a shout if you're open to discussing further details," she told Delilah as she was preparing to leave, her hand on the doorjamb. "It's your decision, obviously, but I think— Listen, do you believe in fate?"

"No," Delilah said flatly.

"I didn't think so." Luna smiled. "That's okay. I can believe enough for the both of us." She tipped her head to the paper plate of food that sat untouched on the desk. "Don't forget to eat. Not that you need me to baby you. Hashtag girlboss!" She struck a pose in the doorway, crossing her fingers into a makeshift hatch of squares.

Delilah looked like she might crack a smile for the first time all day. Maybe all month. The corner of her mouth was fighting its slow rise upward. "Goodbye, Luna. I'll be in touch if I have news. And if you could keep my little pity party between us, I'd appreciate it."

"Of course. My lips are sealed. Confidentiality and all that." Luna gave her a little wave and made her way out of the building. Talking things through with Simone didn't feel as urgent as it had before; she could always catch her up later.

Once on the sidewalk, she allowed herself a giddy shriek and a Mary Tyler Moore–esque leap into the air. If she could pull off a beret, she'd be flinging it into the sky. Nothing was certain, of course, but for the first time since she'd been fired, Luna felt a sense of hope. She was going for it; she had prospects. Even if Delilah didn't hire her, it was enough to know she still had the drive to fight for herself.

Maybe relying on Jean-Pierre's scheme wasn't her only option. Maybe she had a bright future that she could grab all on her own. For a moment, she allowed herself to visualize working alongside Simone and her friendly crew every day. It felt exceptionally good to visualize it.

She gazed up at the brewery's facade, immediately pinpointing the square of light that was Delilah's office window. As she watched, Delilah's elegant silhouette came into the frame, paused for a moment like a work of art, and then moved on. Luna took this as a sign that she was in a contemplative mood.

Her phone buzzed in her purse. Luna rushed to check it, her heart pounding. There on her screen was Delilah's newly added number and a text message: I'm done thinking about it. When can you start?

Chapter 11

Luna returned to her apartment with a spring in her step and a cold mini bottle of pink champagne in her purse. A celebration was in order. She was embarking on her new job—working title: assistant to the producer—in a couple of weeks. After a flurry of emails and texts from Delilah and the HR person, Luna had secured a slightly higher salary than she'd had at her last job—win. Plus the paperwork she'd skimmed on the subway ride home promised that the company was committed to being a safer space for all employees. Single-stall gender-neutral bathrooms were the norm, for example, a perk that gave Luna quite a bit of comfort.

A million ideas about how to organize Delilah's schedule were buzzing around in Luna's mind. She couldn't wait to get started. She'd already called her mom and told her—between breathless squeals of delight from Mrs. O'Shea—that she would be working on an actual TV show. And that she'd secured the position all on her own, with no help from Simone or anyone else.

The best part? She could tell Jean-Pierre and his entire fake-dating plan to go straight to hell. Money wasn't everything;

as long as she had a steady paycheck, health insurance, and the people she loved around her, Luna was happy. JP would be fine without her. He had more money than god. He'd figure it out.

Her phone buzzed while she was kicking off her sneakers into the coat closet. It was a text from Simone.

Delilah just told me you're going to be her assistant!? This is so awesome, why didn't you tell me you were interviewing here??

Luna toyed with the idea of trying to explain over text, but then she realized something in the apartment smelled good. She and Simone could have that conversation in person, she decided. Right now, she needed to investigate the kitchen.

Ever since Simone had begun pulling long days at the studio and spending more time over at Ray's, yummy kitchen smells had been few and far between. Curious, Luna edged her way down the hall.

What she found in the kitchen was more than a surprise. It was bordering on an impossibility. Luna was starting to think she'd hit her head doing yoga that morning and everything following it had just been a coma dream, because that would make way more sense than this: Jean-Pierre at the kitchen counter, one of Simone's plain white aprons draped over his black-on-black outfit, tugging an oven mitt patterned with grinning cats off his hand. Even more wild, he was smiling—actually smiling, not a smirk, not a smug grin—down at a steaming casserole dish.

A casserole dish filled with—

"Is that mac and cheese?" Luna blurted.

JP glanced up at her. "Ah, yes. Welcome home." He tugged the apron off, and Luna felt the world tilt under her feet. "I thought I would try my hand at something simpler than cake."

"You made mac and cheese." Luna stared at the simple square metal baking dish brimming with cheesy goodness. There was a light dusting of bread crumbs on top—an addition that Luna normally felt ambivalent about, but she now felt herself wanting nothing more than to dig a fork into the golden little crispies. Were those green flecks parsley? Where the heck had JP found parsley? The fridge had been sadly devoid of fresh vegetables for weeks, owing to Simone's busy schedule.

"Your mother said it was your favorite." Jean-Pierre put his hands behind his back and stood at a kind of parade rest, though what he was waiting for, Luna couldn't guess. She remained where she was, still shocked. JP cleared his throat. "I thought, considering how I behaved yesterday and this morning, you may appreciate a small gesture."

Her brows quirked up into points. "Where did you get parsley?"

Now Jean-Pierre looked confused. "At the shop? That is where one normally buys herbs, non?"

Luna shook her head. "You went out and bought—what, a whole bunch? Just to sprinkle a couple bits of it on top?"

"The recipe called for it," Jean-Pierre said, "and I had to pick up more milk anyway." He took his phone from his back pocket and showed it to her. "See? It is one of Grand-mère's. I wanted to do it properly."

Lo and behold, there was a recipe for classic gratin de macaroni on Lisette's website, complete with a short video of the chef herself urging everyone at home to make this ultimate comfort food from scratch.

"I used some of the Brie you had left in the fridge. I hope you don't mind," Jean-Pierre said. "I thought you would like the taste."

"I don't . . . mind." Luna hadn't even known you could put Brie in mac and cheese. Why hadn't anyone informed her? This was pertinent information.

JP slipped his phone away. "Also, Grand-mère says a béchamel is the building block I need to cook many things, so I should practice that. But more importantly, I want you to know—" He glanced down at the floor. "You were right, of course. What we are doing, it is only business. I must make peace with that."

"Oh. Okay." Luna's stomach sank. This was not how she had pictured her triumphant "in your face" resignation from the position of fake girlfriend. "Well, I'm glad you've started to see it my way. It's just that, after I left today—"

"Please, one moment. I need to say this before I lose my words." Jean-Pierre took a deep breath in and let it out through his mouth in a rush of air. "This is a job for you. Work. Yes, as it should be. But if we are to do this, I want us to work together. Just because I pay you does not give me all the power here, as you said. We need to act as a team. In the kitchen and out." He dared a glance up at her. "I know I can be . . . difficult."

Luna laughed. "Yeah, a little."

"But I am willing to bend if you are willing to, uh—" He made a face like he knew what he was about to say was a mistake, but he was saying it anyway. "Bend me?"

Luna screwed her mouth to the side. "I don't really—"

"That was not what I—"

"Yeah, let's not—"

"Sorry, okay, yes." He gave another huff of breath, this time more frustrated. "What I am saying is, I need to be more flexible."

Luna opened her mouth, desperate to get a word in edgewise so she could put an end to this awkwardness, but once again JP barreled ahead.

"After all, what you are doing for me, I cannot say how much it means." He lifted his lashes—all ten miles of them—and looked at Luna like she was the most important sight in the world. "Perhaps I should not care so much about being named my grandfather's heir. Perhaps it would be best if I walked away. But if I do, I am admitting I am an unfit steward to his legacy. And I am not unfit, Luna. I refuse to be made to feel unworthy of my own birthright." He tipped his chin up and, for a moment, Luna was reminded of swaggering musketeers in adventure stories. Did he know how to fence? He'd look right at home with a rapier in his hand, she thought. Not to mention the tight bodysuit. Did those things come in black?

Maybe she should focus on the conversation at hand, she reminded herself.

"What am I doing, chattering away while your food goes cold?" Jean-Pierre jerked his head toward the mac and cheese. "Eat, eat. Bon appétit."

How was Luna supposed to give JP the proverbial finger after that little speech? Normally she didn't mind being a bit of a bitch when necessary, but in the wake of Jean-Pierre laying his soul bare, the idea of telling him to fuck off didn't sit well. She'd just have to power through.

"You sound pretty determined," she began, thinking that was a good way to lay the groundwork. Jean-Pierre would realize, once she let him down gently and with all the sympathy he was due, that he would find a way to jump through his grandpa's hoops without her.

"Yes, but here—it should have cooled down enough by now," Jean-Pierre said. He took up a serving spoon from the utensil caddy and began dishing out a huge portion of the mac and cheese onto a plate. Fragrant steam spilled from the dish, redolent in cheese, butter, a hint of onion, and spices Luna couldn't begin to identify. She watched closely as the food was lifted out of its dish, strands of cheese pulling long and thin as it ascended. Her mouth wasn't just watering, it was positively flooding.

Maybe she could hand in her resignation after lunch. It would be rude not to taste JP's first successful dish, after all. He seemed so proud, his cheeks glowing with ruddy color as he served her the plate. A fork clattered alongside the oozing mac and cheese as Jean-Pierre fumbled to include it.

"I thought about those petrol station pretzels you like so well, so I tried to re-create that. A lot of soft, white cheeses and a small can of— What were they called? Jalapeño pickles."

Luna was taken aback. "You added pickled jalapeños? For me?"

JP looked up at her through his eyelashes. "The recipe, she is very forgiving."

Luna tried not to smile. *Okay, buddy. I get it, it's all very on theme.*

He pushed the plate toward her across the counter. "The topping is crushed pretzels instead of plain bread crumbs. I tried to find a soft pretzel but the shop only had the little hard ones in bags. I hope it tastes all right," he said. "Whisking the sauce together was not as easy as it looked. There might still be a few lumps."

Luna would gladly suffer a lump or two if she could eat the whole pan of carbs and dairy. She tried not to drool as she accepted the plate. "I'm sure it's fine. Smells good," she said.

Jean-Pierre busied himself with hanging up the borrowed apron, though he kept one eye firmly on Luna as she maneuvered her fork into the food. She felt his gaze on her as she constructed the perfect bite: several pieces of elbow macaroni dripping in the cheesy sauce with plenty of the crumb topping. Her fork hovered in the air as she surveyed her work. Yes, it looked just right.

"Please just eat it," Jean-Pierre said.

Luna clicked her tongue. "Don't rush me." She blew on the bite to cool it down, since it still looked molten hot. Then she slipped the fork into her mouth.

The taste came to her in stages. First, the creaminess of her leftover Brie married to the tang of cheddar and what she thought might be Gruyère—it was inspired. All her favorite cheeses were at the party, and they were dancing. There was a hint of heat—Maybe cayenne? Hot sauce? Paprika? All of the above?—that delighted Luna to no end. And then, right behind that was the sour tang of the jalapeños—more briny than spicy—and the crunch of the pretzel topping.

It was not perfect. There were, as JP had warned, some lumps. The onions had not been diced as finely as they could have been. It was a little heavy on the salt—probably because of how salty the pretzels were, but Luna didn't mind that so much. All in all, it was an acceptable first attempt at a very simple dish.

Luna could have eaten the whole tray.

"Well?" Jean-Pierre came back into view as Luna managed to tear her eyes away from her plate. "How is it?"

Luna was still chewing, so she put her hand in front of her mouth and made a kind of garbled *mmmm* sound. The hand clutching her fork gave a thumbs-up, and to underscore all of this, she tossed in a firm nod.

"It's all right?"

"Yep," Luna said with her mouth full, then swallowed to say, "not bad at all. Can I have more?"

JP slumped in relief, like all the air had gone out of him. "Please! It's all for you."

"The whole thing?" She dug her fork in for a huge, cheese-stringy bite. "Awesome."

As she ate, Jean-Pierre did what most home cooks did, which was detail all their food's failings. "Next time, I will dice the onion smaller, I think. Perhaps add garlic. It is not traditional but there is nothing wrong with a pinch of garlic. My instincts are developing, yes? Just in time for the test."

Luna put her fork down. She didn't have to be cruel about it, but she should explain that she had just gotten a new job and probably wouldn't have time to learn how to cook gourmet food and fly to Paris and pretend to be Jean-Pierre's girlfriend. Shouldn't she? That was still the plan, wasn't it?

JP quietly fished his own fork from the utensil caddy and took a bite of the mac and cheese. He chose to dig out a morsel right where she had taken a bite, Luna noticed. He could have easily eaten from the other side of the plate, but he seemed starved for these kinds of small intimacies. His brows did a little dance as he chewed.

"Not bad, as you say. Less salt next time, I think." He looked over at Luna, then back down at their shared dinner. "I know this is not an adequate apology, but I do hope it is a start."

She swallowed around the lump in her throat. "Hey, JP—"

"I cannot do this alone." He turned to face her fully. "I swear I will respect you as my equal in all things. Like any good business partner should. Please, will you see this through with me?"

Luna's breath caught. The part of her that had so been

looking forward to flipping off Jean-Pierre was gone. It didn't feel right to abandon the plan now at the first little hiccup. A mere hour ago, she'd been convinced that her new job as Delilah's assistant was a sign from the universe that she needed to cut ties with Jean-Pierre. Now she wondered if seeing this new side of JP—deferential and chastened and with a lot of carbs in tow—was a sign that she should rethink her plan.

"If we do this," she said slowly, "you really want me to have veto power over our fake relationship? Same as you? Total equals?"

"Yes, exactly."

"And when we disagree?" She ate another bite of mac and cheese. "Because we will disagree," she said as she chewed.

"Then we must discuss it like the adults we are. Like with our differing views of how to classify our fake relationship." JP scratched his stubbled chin. "My instinct is to call us straight; yours is to say we are queer. Fine. What does it matter? Who will be asking us to assign a word? If anyone is gauche enough to do so, we will merely say that it is our private business, just as we would if we were really dating."

"I guess," Luna said, swallowing.

JP dropped his hand. "We need not have all the answers. I think it is more realistic if we do not, oui? Real couples must work these things out over time." He gave her another one of those piercing looks. "We can give ourselves time."

Luna searched her heart. She wanted to help Jean-Pierre, she really did. But she also wanted to have the space to do her own thing. "If I agree to stay the course," she said, "we'll need to plan our cooking practice and all that stuff around my schedule. This is nonnegotiable for me."

"Of course," JP said quickly. "What sort of things will be in your schedule that I must avoid?"

"So, for starters, I just got a new job today."

His face lit up like the sun cresting over the skyline. Luna knew how to spot a disingenuous smile, and the one Jean-Pierre was sporting looked absolutely real. "Fantastique! Clair, congratulations. How wonderful for you."

"Yeah, I'm actually going to be working on your grandma's new show with Simone and Ray and everyone." She was feeling excited about the prospect all over again. "It was the strangest thing; it just sort of happened."

"We must celebrate." JP grabbed up her hands in his. "Dinner?"

His hands were really warm. Luna tried to play it cool in the face of his cultural touchy-feely stuff. "Isn't this my dinner?" She arched a brow at the mac and cheese that still sat between them.

His face turned a little pink. "Ah, of course. Tomorrow, then?"

"That sounds good—no, wait." Luna pulled her hands from his grasp so she could dig her phone out of her purse. She checked her calendar app. "Shit, tomorrow's my monthly hang with the girls. Hm." She grinned at him. "Why don't you come with?" Their get-togethers weren't strictly trans gals only; Aisha's wife, Ruth, joined once in a blue moon, when she was free.

His eyes went round. "Really? You wouldn't mind?"

"It'll be great. You can meet my friends, and if the paparazzi are around it will establish how serious we're getting, right?" Luna beamed at her phone as she composed a message in her group chat. She was so smart.

JP, on the other hand, seemed to lose some of his earlier enthusiasm. "Yes. Of course. It will establish seriousness. For the plan."

"Yep! Don't worry, I've given the girls the short version," Luna said as she typed. "They know we're not really a couple, so there won't be too much pressure. If no cameras show up, we can just chill like normal people."

"Bien entendu," Jean-Pierre murmured, which, to Luna's ears, sounded fairly melancholy. "Normal."

Chapter 12

Southie's was their usual haunt for group hangs, a local chain specializing in vegetable-forward dishes (since Willow was vegetarian) and boasting an extremely decent selection of happy hour deals (since they all needed to get tipsy once in a while without breaking the bank). When Luna arrived with Jean-Pierre, Sara and Willow had already claimed a large circular table by the huge bay windows draped in crimson velvet at the front. Her friends spotted her entrance and immediately rose for their hello hugs.

"Hey! Long time, no see!" Luna pulled Willow into a tight embrace, giving her a squeeze around her middle before doing the same for Sara. "Is Aisha on her way?" It was just going to be the four of them, plus JP, since Lily couldn't make it. Getting five New Yorkers together was damn near impossible, after all.

"Yeah, she texted me. Her train is slow." Sara looked shyly over Luna's shoulder. "So this is the *boyfriend*," she said with all the reverence the word was due.

Luna turned to find JP standing with his hands shoved as far into his tight pockets as they would go, a clear indicator that he would not be participating in the hello hugs. His smile was genial but aloof. He nodded to the two women in turn. "Enchanté."

Willow bit down on a girlish giggle. She nudged Luna with her elbow. "As far as fakes go, he's not so bad," she stage-whispered.

Aisha arrived just then in a flurry of jangling bracelets and earrings. She had informed them weeks ago that she was in her accessories era. "Lovelies!" she cried, and another round of hugging commenced. Jean-Pierre stood as far out of the way as he could while they dispensed with their ritual greetings, avoiding both the hellos and the stream of tray-carrying servers who needed to pass by.

When they finally all took their seats, Jean-Pierre made a point of pulling out Luna's chair for her, a gesture that did not go unnoticed by her three friends.

"Oh damn," Willow crowed.

"Look at this gentleman." Aisha grinned wide. "If he treats you this good now, imagine how he'd be in a real relationship."

JP snorted at that; Luna could feel the puff of it on the back of her neck.

"If you could all please keep your voices down?" Luna scooted her chair up to the lip of the table, glancing around furtively. Southie's was packed as usual, and no one was paying them much mind, the hum of the dining room's conversation drowning out all but the loudest laugh or clatter of dropped silverware. Still— "We're trying to maintain an image here."

Jean-Pierre took his own seat at Luna's side. His profile was perfectly composed. The only reaction to her friends' shenanigans seemed to be a slight curl of amusement at the corner of his mouth. "It's such a pleasure to meet you all," he said.

Sara gave a dreamy sigh. "Your accent is so—"

"French," Luna said. She went to work unrolling her silverware from her napkin. "It's just French. There's, like, fifty million people in the world who sound exactly like him. It's nothing special."

"It's more like seventy-five million, I believe, so even less impressive," JP said. He turned the full force of his charming smile across the table. "Thank you, anyway, Sara." Luna was not imagining the extra French twist he put on Sara's name. *Sarr-AH*. Ugh. "It is nice to be appreciated."

Their usual waitress, Fiona, appeared and greeted them warmly with her patented, "Hello again, all!" One of the quirks of meeting up in a large-ish group of trans women was that you tended to stick out in people's memories. Luckily, with Fiona, it worked in their favor. "Happy hour margaritas all around, right?" she correctly guessed. "Extra salt?"

"Ah, a glass of the house red for me, if you could," Jean-Pierre said, because he just had to be different.

"And two orders of the mixed pickles to start, please," said Aisha, holding up her fingers in a V. "Oh, and some of that fried Halloumi."

Luna and the rest of the girls nodded in approval. Pickles were like gold to them. *God's perfect food*, Sara once called them, and she wasn't wrong.

"So," JP said once Fiona had left them, "how did you all meet?" He looked around the table with a bemused expression. "Work, perhaps?"

Willow laughed. "Is he serious?" she asked Luna.

"He doesn't like to assume," Luna said, dry as day-old bread.

"I think you can safely assume there's never going to be more than one girl like us at any given corporate job," Aisha put in.

Luna hesitated. "Should we tell him?"

"I don't see why not. We know all his big secrets," Willow said, and the other girls nodded their agreement.

"We met at a support group for trans women," Sara told Jean-Pierre, because she was too sweet to make fun of him. Luna was usually circumspect about mentioning the support group to outsiders. There was an expectation of privacy that she didn't like to break.

Willow poured glasses of water for everyone from the

provided carafe and distributed them around. "I think we all joined up around the same time? Anyway, there was this one session where this older white lady took center stage and would just. Not. Pass. The mic!"

JP's brow furrowed in confusion.

"You're supposed to give everyone a chance to speak if they want to," Luna explained. "We're all supposed to support each other. It's right there in the name."

"Ah." He nodded gratefully to her. "I have never attended such a group."

"Right, well, this lady was hogging all the air in the room," Aisha said. "I started looking around, like, Is anyone in here going to make eye contact with me so I can silently bitch about this behavior? And lo and behold—"

"We were all staring right back." Sara laughed.

"We just kept catching each other's eyes and almost bursting into giggles." Willow scrunched her nose up in delight. "When the meeting ended, we went to the diner down the block so we could scream about it. I don't even think we caught each other's names until the check for our milkshakes came!"

"That's the foundation of true friendship," Luna said with a sage nod. "The ability to complain about other people for hours on end."

"So true, bestie." Sara raised her water glass, and everyone but JP followed suit.

Then the drinks arrived, and there was a flurry of activity centered on trying to help Fiona pass out the margs without spilling the oversized, frosty glasses. Once that excitement was over, Jean-Pierre sipped at his wine and pulled a face that said it was beneath his usual standards.

"Group selfie?" Willow suggested, already pulling out her phone and angling it high above her head to get the whole table in the frame.

"Oh, maybe not, since—" Luna looked to JP. "We're on the down-low today, right?"

Willow's phone drooped.

Jean-Pierre gestured magnanimously, "Non, non, please, take a picture."

"You're sure?" Willow asked, hand rising again. "Want me to tag you?"

"No need. If you use my surname as a hashtag, though, you might be approached by some outlets. You may as well make a bit of money, hein?"

"Wait, is that true?" Aisha stared at him.

Sara fumbled her phone out of her purse. "Hold on, let me make sure we're spelling it right. Is it A-U-B or A-E-B?"

Luna nudged his foot under the table. "You really want this to get picked up by some niche gossip blog?"

"Why not?" He threw up a peace sign as Aisha leaned in to get her selfie. "I'd rather these lovely ladies profit from it than the table over by the window."

Luna twisted in her chair to see a very frustrated guy jerking his camera phone this way and that, trying to get more than the back of Jean-Pierre's head. Well, if that was how it was going to be . . .

She ran a hand through her hair, making sure to tweak a few strands to frame her face. "Don't forget to smile," she said, leaning into him so her friends could get them both in the picture.

Once the flurry of posting and tagging was done, everyone gleefully turned their attention to their drinks. Except for JP, who moved his wine glass over to the left and reached for his water instead. Luna listened to Sara and Aisha compare the photos they'd taken and sipped at her margarita.

"It must be very strange," he said to the table at large, "having so many friends who are also transgender."

"Strange?" Aisha frowned. "Why would that be strange?"

"Yeah, it's kind of natural," Willow said.

"Do you not have a lot of trans friends?" Sara sipped at her margarita, dipping her head to meet the salty rim instead of taking the risk of lifting the overly full glass.

Luna regarded him closely as he seemed to think this over.

"I don't think I've ever had a conversation with another trans person until I met Luna," he said.

The women around the table reacted like a bomb had gone off. Even Luna, who knew that JP was a bit of a loner, reeled. How could you not surround yourself with queer and trans people? They were the best!

"Not even one?" she asked.

Sara clutched her hand to her chest. "How is that possible?"

"Who do you talk to about"—Willow gestured wildly—"guy stuff? Like, trans guy stuff?"

Jean-Pierre looked confused. "A doctor?" The assembled ladies let out various noises of disbelief and dismay, while JP just rolled his eyes. "Please do not take offense," he said in a tone that Luna assumed meant he was about to say something offensive, "but being transgender is not the most important part of my life."

A chorus of booing met this statement, and Luna's boos were the loudest.

"If you surround yourself with only cis people, you're doing yourself a terrible disservice," she said. "I could make concessions for people who were isolated or whatever, but there's always the internet! And you clearly are not isolated; you travel all over. You're seriously telling me you don't have a single gender nonconforming friend?"

"You have got to, got to, *got to* have community." Aisha leaned forward in her seat. "You have to have trans friends for when cis folks start getting on your last nerve, just like I've got my Black friends for when white folks get on my nerves."

Willow, possibly the whitest girl in the world, nodded with feeling. "That's true."

"Well, I am extremely easygoing," JP said. "I have no nerves for others to get on, not anymore." He slipped his e-cigarette from his jacket pocket. "Do you think they will let me use this in here?" he asked Luna.

"No," the women all chorused.

"He's got no nerves, but he's got a vaping habit," Sara muttered to Willow. "Sure. Totally."

Luna was about to open her mouth—whether to defend her faux boyfriend from her friends' judgment or to join them in ragging on him, she'd decide once some words tumbled out—but she was interrupted by the sudden appearance of a newcomer who approached the table. She had a gorgeous cloud of dark hair swirling around her face and a happy glow to her deep brown skin.

"Hello," she said in a timid voice. She glanced around the table. "Willow, when you said I should come meet you for drinks, I didn't know there would be so many people."

Willow shot up out of her chair. "Britney! Wow, sorry, I totally forgot—" She grimaced at Luna, who was making big, questioning eyes at her. "Uh, I meant to tell you all, but I guess it slipped my mind." Classic Willow. She gestured to her guest. "This is Britney. She's an egg, freshly cracked. We met while working on a play that's never going to get off the ground. Is it cool if she joins us?" She looked directly at Luna as she said this, since Luna would be the one who would want to send away the stranger who didn't know about her fake-dating scheme.

Luna groaned internally. While playacting for an audience of one was not how she'd envisioned spending her relaxing evening catching up with the girls, she couldn't say no to that face. Britney had the hungry look of a newly out trans woman who desperately needed to talk to other trans women and had so far not had the chance.

You couldn't say no to a hatchling. That was the rule. They'd all been there. Luna forced a smile on her face. "The more, the merrier," she said. The others echoed her in agreement.

Willow made introductions around the table. When she got to JP, she said, "And this is Luna's boyfriend. He's French."

"A pleasure to meet you, Britney. A lovely name."

"Actually," the new girl said as a shuffle of chairs commenced to make room for her between Willow and Luna, "I don't know if I'm going to keep using it. I've been trying out a few others?"

"Oooh, like what?" Aisha said. "Tell us what we should use for now."

A pretty, shy smile spread across her lips. She smoothed the hem of her jade wrap dress over her knees. Luna's heart twinged; her first Big Girl outfit had been a wrap dress, too, with little yellow birds printed all over. "I was thinking Beatriz?" she said. "For now. Bea for short."

"It's a good name," Willow said, then began chattering away about all the names she had gone through before landing on hers.

While the girls exchanged name-game tips, Luna texted JP under the cover of the table. He barely glanced at his screen when the text came in.

i don't know her so we're gonna have to Pretend again

JP replaced his phone in his pocket and shot her a bored look. "But of course, Clair."

Right. It was probably obvious.

She sat stock still in her seat while Jean-Pierre stretched out his arm and, like a cat, laid it across the back of her chair. His fingertips brushed against her hair, a small gesture that Beatriz definitely noticed from her position next to Luna.

"How long have you two been together?" she asked.

"Oh, it feels like forever," JP said.

"Five months," Luna said at the same time.

Beatriz gave them an awkward smile. "That's nice."

Luna tried to turn the spotlight away from them. "How about you, Beatriz? Anyone special in your life?"

"Me? No. No, no, no." She laughed a little too loud. "It's kind of—early. For that. Don't you think? I mean, maybe I should just be focusing on myself for now."

"Smart," Luna said.

"Silly," JP drawled. "I think that you should always leave yourself open to the possibility of love, because it will come to you when you least expect it, every time. Take my Clair de Lune here," he said, touching her neck in a way that made her shiver. *Damn him.* "I do not think when we met she was looking for anything serious, were you, love?"

Luna twisted in her seat to give him a sharp-edged grin. "You know I wasn't, *love*," she said. She turned back to Beatriz. "He really had to convince me. Strikes a hard bargain, this guy of mine." She ran her fingers playfully through JP's curls, and if she tugged a little harder than was necessary, well, that was between the two of them. Jean-Pierre, for his part, gave a muted grunt at the pull, then smiled serenely at her, his eyes half-lidded.

Damn. He was enjoying this. Maybe in more ways than one.

Luna tore her hand away from his hair and placed it in her lap, where it could do no more harm.

Bea gave a dreamy sigh. "I wish I could find someone like that. I want what you have."

Trust me, you don't.

Fiona the server returned to ask Bea what she wanted to drink, and the girls vocally recommended the BOGO margaritas. As Bea was inquiring about all the different fruit flavors, Jean-Pierre leaned over to whisper in Luna's ear. He really didn't have to, what with how noisy the restaurant was, but it wasn't easy to be annoyed with someone who smelled that good.

"She wants what we have," he said, his breath caressing her ear. "A good sign, eh?"

Luna put her hand on his knee and leaned in to caress an ear of her own. "Try not to let it go to your head, okay? She's new; literally any example of a T4T couple is impressive to her."

"Tea for . . . what?"

"T for— Oh my god, you really need to get out more, in the queer world specifically." Luna bent closer to his ear. "Trans for trans? When two trans people date each other, thereby cutting out the need for cis coddling? It's the dream. The pinnacle."

"Really?" He pulled back a few inches, his face pinched. "I had no idea."

"Stick with me and you'll get a lot of new ideas." Luna dipped her head to sip at her margarita like a gazelle drinking at a watering hole, the glass still way too full to pick up.

"Shall I get you a straw, darling?" Jean-Pierre asked, amusement thick in his now-normal-volume voice.

"No thanks." Luna continued to slurp. She caught his eye as she made the loudest sucking noise possible against the rim of her margarita glass. "This way, I can get all the salt."

JP shook his head, but in that fond way that meant *Ah, my girlfriend is so quirky and fun; how lucky I am to be allowed to bask in her joie de vivre.* Not a bad Greg to her Dharma, actually. Luna smiled as she licked the rock salt from her glass. Maybe they could actually pull this off for real when they got to Paris.

"So, Jean-Pierre," Willow said as Fiona took her leave, "Luna tells us you work in the restaurant business."

"I do," he said. "It is not so exciting, though. A lot of finance and contracts." He waved his hand in the air. "What about you ladies? What do you do for a living?" He lifted his wineglass to his lips and took the tiniest non-sip Luna had ever seen.

"I'm a computer programmer," Willow said, "but that's just my day job. My real passion is theater."

"Ah, bien."

"I'm also a programmer," Sara said. "Mobile platforms."

"Programmer here, too." Aisha stuck her hand in the air.

Bea giggled shyly. "And me, of course."

Jean-Pierre boggled at them. "But you said you do not work together. You are, ah, pulling my legs?"

"Nope," Luna said, popping her *p*. "They're all computer nerds."

"But that is bizarre," he said, looking at each of them in turn like one would crack and tell him it was all a joke after all. "How can this be?"

Aisha regarded him strangely. "Don't you know?"

"It's kind of a running joke among trans women," Luna explained, adopting the patient tone she thought a loving girlfriend might use in just this situation. "Like, we're all in tech so we can hide behind a screen?"

"And make good money," Sara pointed out.

"Yeah, that sure doesn't hurt," Aisha said. "Shit's expensive for girls like me."

"And when we finally come out"—Willow made a grand gesture, her hands spreading apart to encompass the entire world—"we're less likely to get fired because no one else knows how to fix the fucking app."

The girls all howled at that and lifted their sloshing margarita glasses in a toast. All except Luna, who kept sipping at her drink gazelle style and avoiding eye contact with everyone. JP had to duck his head down toward the table to meet her shifty gaze.

Luna braced herself for the questions. *Why don't you work with computers? Is it because you never finished college?* But instead Jean-Pierre said, "Are you all right?"

She sat up straight and put on her very normal smile. "Why wouldn't I be?"

He indicated the rest of the party with a flick of his eyes. Bea was in the middle of telling them a funny story about some corporate meeting she'd been in last week, and no one was paying Jean-Pierre or Luna any attention. "I know how it feels to be left out," he said in a low voice.

Luna mustered a smile. "It's fine. Really. And besides"—she grinned over at her girls, who were now doing their best impressions of their managers, two of whom were named Brian—"I'm proud of them. They're kicking ass in their careers. How can I be sad when my friends are so happy?"

Jean-Pierre made a considering noise and took another swig of his house red. The more he drank, the less he cared about the taste, apparently. "You can be pleased for your friends and at the same time feel whatever it is you feel about not having the same."

"Jealousy is toxic," Luna stated decisively. "That's not my style."

"Is it jealousy?" JP shrugged. "I am not you, of course, but I myself feel a burning anger that you had to choose between your schooling and your true self, and at such a young age. Aren't you furious with the world for doing that to you?"

Luna's brain whited out for a moment. This was some deep shit to be getting into before the apps even arrived. Yet despite the serious nature of Jean-Pierre's line of questioning, the only thing she could seem to grasp was—

"You feel a . . . burning anger?" She cocked her head. "For me?"

"On your behalf, yes. Anyone would." He mumbled this last bit into his wineglass before setting himself to the task of draining it in one fell swallow. Luna watched his throat bob as he did so. "Sometimes, things—suck, as you would say. Just plain suck. You do not have to try to turn them into gold."

She relaxed back into her chair. "That's true, I guess." She thought about it for a moment, and opened her mouth to say something else, but Jean-Pierre pushed away from the table before she had a chance.

His chair scraped as he stood. "I must visit the washroom," he said. "Ladies." He nodded to the rest of the table before disappearing into the busy dining room.

To their credit, Luna's friends waited until he was well out of sight to explode into JP-related chatter.

"Okay, so he's adorable," Aisha said. "Cute, cute, so cute I want to tear my eyes out."

"He might prefer to be called handsome," Sara pointed out in a quiet whisper.

Willow gave a thoughtful hum. "Is that something trans guys are sensitive about?"

"Sometimes. I dated a trans guy once who hated being compared to anything even remotely girly."

"Hm, I get that," Aisha said.

Willow sucked her teeth. "I don't. What's so bad about girly stuff? An attitude like that will drag you down into toxic masculinity, no?"

"But if Jean-Pierre has been pressured for most of his life to be feminine, there's nothing wrong with him rejecting girly stuff for himself, right?" Bea said, blushing as she did so. "I mean, that's how I feel about guy stuff these days. Maybe I'm going kinda overboard with pretty clothes and makeup and shoes—"

"No!"

"Never."

"Well, it's really Jean-Pierre's personal choice whether he gets to be cute, or handsome, or both. Luna, which does he prefer?" Aisha turned to her, her impeccable brows raised in expectation.

Luna had been zoning out while watching the Intro to Gender Theory play out in front of her, but she realized she should have had a ready answer for her waiting friends. After all, who knew her boyfriend better than she did?

The thing was, she wasn't 100 percent certain where Jean-Pierre fell on the "secure enough in my masculinity to be called adorable" scale, and it would really suck if she got it wrong and exposed him to all sorts of schmoopy, frilly compliments that he did not want.

"I think, in general," she said slowly, "JP gravitates toward the more manly side of things. He didn't even like feminine sandwiches as a kid."

Everyone around the table looked at her like she was speaking in tongues.

"Sandwiches can be feminine?" Aisha asked.

"They're masculine in Spanish. French, too, I think?" Bea said.

"No, I mean— Forget the sandwiches." Luna drank more of her margarita before plunging ahead. "My point is, he'll stick with the most masc option available. Unless he's really comfortable. Like, in private." She had a flash of memory of Jean-Pierre wearing Simone's apron to cook the mac and cheese, which, while plain, was cut for someone with curves. Not to mention the adorable kitty oven mitts. There had to be about a gazillion sets of oven mitts in the kitchen drawer, but JP had chosen the cutest ones. So he couldn't be *that* deathly afraid of the feminine.

"Oh, so if it's just the two of you, he doesn't mind being a little less *grrr*?" Willow said, adopting a pro wrestler big-shoulders pose.

"Yeah," Luna said. She paused, realizing it was true. "Yeah, I guess so."

Bea sighed and stared into her freshly delivered marg. "You two are so good together, seriously. It's like you know each other inside and out. I wish I could find a guy who had that kind of love and respect for me."

Willow, Sara, and Aisha all looked at Luna with matching grimaces of disbelief. Luna tried to communicate the need to chill by making a discreet slicing motion with her hand.

"Well, you know." She fumbled for the right words that a real girlfriend would say about her doting boyfriend. "I just got really lucky."

Bea's head popped up as she stopped contemplating her drink.

"Do you think he's The One?" Bea asked.

Everyone else froze in what they must have thought was a totally natural, not-freaking-out posture. Willow had propped her chin on her fist, Aisha studied the little happy hour menu card in the center of the table, and Sara looked back and forth between Luna and Bea like it was a tennis match. If tennis matches involved lying to a sweet girl about who you were dating.

"Uh." Luna looked to her dearest friends for help, but no one was making eye contact with her. "Who knows? I've never really thought about marriage." Luna knew she was babbling, but it was her only defense. "The whole institution is fucked, right? Ever since they decided gay marriage was the most important goal we could shoot for—"

"Instead of *liberation*," Aisha put in, abandoning the happy hour menu in favor of their favorite topic to bitch about as a group.

Luna nodded her thanks to her. "—I've been kind of *whatever* about the whole idea of getting hitched."

But Bea was not to be dissuaded. She hummed and lifted her drink for a long sip, not spilling a drop. When she was done, she replaced her glass perfectly in the center of its white napkin and said, "Well, if you ever change your mind about that, I would tell you to lock that man down. When a guy looks at a woman the way he looks at you, you don't want to let him go. Trust me."

Luna blinked, a confused smile spreading across her face. "How does he look at me?"

"Like you hung the moon, girl," Bea said.

A tiny scoff left Luna's mouth before she could stuff it back down. She glanced at the other ladies around the table, the ones who knew what she and JP had was all fake, but again, none of them seemed willing to meet her eye.

"No he doesn't," she said.

"Oh, come on." Bea nudged Willow with her elbow. "Am I wrong? Tell her."

"He does kind of give you heart eyes, like, constantly," Willow said. Probably just to help with the story and continue the ruse.

"Maybe you don't notice it because it's happening twenty-four/seven," Sara put in, "but yeah. It's definitely happening."

Aisha just pointed at Sara and said, "This."

Luna forced her smile to grow into something a pleased girlfriend might wear when being told her beau was clearly head over heels for her. How cool and nice of her friends to play along with the ruse. Could she force a blush on command? Her face felt hot already, so she was probably doing a great job there. "Ah, thanks, everyone. That's so sweet."

"You two are what's sweet," Bea declared. "I'm telling you: marry him."

Because the universe was a cruel and uncaring mistress, Jean-Pierre chose that exact moment to return from the restroom.

Unaware that the subject of their conversation was right behind her, Bea kept talking. Luna sat there like a bump on a log, watching it all happen in mortifying slow motion.

"I wouldn't even wait for him to pull out the ring. I'd just inform him the wedding was on for next summer. Or, ohhhh, maybe a winter ceremony. You don't seem like the traditional type. Would you take his name, do you think?"

Jean-Pierre's brows lifted in Luna's direction. He looked like the most amused cat swimming in cream. "Yes, Clair, would you?" He ignored the way Bea jumped about six inches off her chair. "I admit I am curious."

Luna sighed. "Well," she said, "I guess I have until next summer to decide, huh?"

Jean-Pierre rounded the table, immune to the appraising looks of all the women, and reclaimed his seat next to Luna. "Or this winter. Since you're not the traditional type," he said, and kissed her on the lips. It was just a quick kiss, the kind any couple might share to say *Hello, I'm back* or *Hello, you're so funny* or *Hello, we're the best actors in the world if this lady is buying this*.

Luna managed a watery smile in return. "Sure. Winter." The joke wasn't so hilarious anymore, now that he was the one making it.

Fiona dropped off their apps, and Jean-Pierre graciously ordered them all another round of happy hour margaritas. He pushed his wineglass aside and told the server, "I think I will have one as well. They look very refreshing."

Fiona made a note on her order pad. "Do you want salt on that?"

"Oh, yes. *Extra* salt." His eyes met Luna's. "You can lick it off if you wish."

Low catcalls sounded from the women around the table. Luna felt simultaneously proud of their performance and frustrated with how red her face was getting.

Yeah. The best actors in the world.

Chapter 13

After dinner, Luna exchanged goodbye hugs with her friends outside Southie's, their voices overlapping as they told each other how great it was to see everyone, and they really needed to do this more often, and Lily was going to be so sad that she missed out. Even Bea gave Luna a tentative squeeze, whispering in her ear as she did so, "Seriously. Lock that man down before someone else does."

What could Luna do but laugh?

Once all the girls scattered to their different subway stations, Luna turned to JP, who had been waiting without complaint for her to wrap things up. He was lounging against a streetlight and vaping lazily. Something buzzed through Luna in that moment. Probably the four happy hour margaritas she'd had. Fiona always made sure theirs weren't watered down.

"Feel like going for a post-dinner walk?" she asked. "It's a nice evening."

Jean-Pierre pocketed his vape pen in his leather jacket. "Yes, let's." He actually offered his arm for Luna to take like they were in some kind of Hepburn movie. Audrey, not Katharine, although Luna was a sucker for either.

Luna eyed his arm with all the appropriate caution. "It's just us, you know," she said. "We don't have to be all lovey without an audience."

JP shrugged. "You never know when a camera will flash. Better safe than sorry." His face fell. "Unless, of course, you would prefer—"

"This is fine," Luna said quickly, and took Jean-Pierre's arm like it was the last available seat on the A train: fast and with all her focus.

They meandered around the Village, passing outdoor cafes with packed bars whose patrons were already spilling out onto the sidewalk. The side streets had the narrowest sidewalks in the entire city, and a lot of the real estate had been claimed by the outdoor cafe tables and crowds of people waiting to get into one of the hot new restaurants that populated the crooked lanes. Luna reluctantly let go of JP's arm since it was quickly becoming impossible to walk side by side. She slipped behind him so they could pass between the stoops of some old brownstones and a dog walker with one extremely yappy terrier.

"Here," Jean-Pierre said over his shoulder, and reached back to take her hand. His eyes were dancing like this was a very funny joke. "I don't want to lose you."

Luna fought the urge to roll her eyes. "I can keep up," she said. She kept her tone light and flirty in case anyone overheard.

JP squeezed her hand in his. "Indulge me."

Well, since he was asking so nicely, Luna let herself be led.

Jean-Pierre weaved expertly through the meandering people on the sidewalk, guiding them through a few stubborn knots of idle crowds, heading north and west in a way that made Luna think perhaps they did have a destination. They eventually strolled out of the Village and through Chelsea toward the High Line, the hipster-ish park built on the bones of the old 10th Avenue elevated railway tracks. The park was long and narrow with a great view of the Hudson, though in recent years that view had become somewhat obscured by douchey condos.

The thin paths were packed that evening with all sorts of people: screaming children, tourists toting selfie sticks, groups of high schoolers eating bags of chips, couples walking hand in hand. Luna darted through the throngs of slow walkers to nab a seat on a bench that was situated in an out-of-the-way cut-out, shielded from the main thoroughfare by trees so leafy they looked like something out of *Jurassic Park*. She plopped onto the wood slats of the seat with a happy sigh, patting the open space next to her.

"You have to see this view," she said.

JP sat next to her and stared at the New Jersey waterfront that stretched out before them, just visible between a gap in the high-rises. "It is nice, in its way." He cocked his head to look at her. "You love this city, don't you?"

"How can I not?" Luna watched an airplane towing a banner fly low over the Hudson: MARIJUANA JUSTICE NOW, it said. "You can be whoever you want here, and no one cares. Well, real New Yorkers won't care. When you're living right on top of each other, you learn to get really chill about everyone real quick. People say that this town is stressful, and I guess that's true. But for me, it kind of shoots the moon."

Jean-Pierre made a questioning noise that Luna had come to understand meant *Your idioms are not universal.*

"That means you get so much of one thing that it kind of turns into the exact opposite. Like, it's so hectic here that it goes all the way around into peaceful." As if summoned just to prove her wrong, a series of vibrations jiggled inside Luna's jacket pocket. She checked her phone to find her Insta notifications going wild. Apparently, her friends' photos had been discovered and reshared by food bloggers and gossip columnists alike, because a ton of randos were leaving comments. She switched to airplane mode. The evening was too pleasant to be distracted by all that. "Sorry. What was I saying?"

"The city," JP reminded her. "Will you live in New York forever, do you think?"

"I don't know." Luna smiled at the sight of two boats passing each other on the river. "I have this vague idea of retiring to the Catskills or something when I'm older, but who can plan that far ahead? For now, this is my city." She directed her smile toward him. "I once saw Jake Gyllenhaal drop his wallet in a puddle on Christopher Street. You can't top that; it's impossible."

"You haven't been to Paris yet," Jean-Pierre said. He leaned back with his elbows resting on the low back of their Scandi-inspired bench, his legs kicked out in front of him.

"You think it'll impress me?" Luna raised an eyebrow. "It's got to work hard to reach Gyllenhaal levels of schadenfreude."

"Paris is not out to impress anyone. That is what makes her so impressive." JP shot a grin her way. "I think you'll love it. I hope you do," he added, quieter, his gaze dropping.

Luna felt squirmy in her middle. "I'm really looking forward to it. I've never been outside of the country, really. Unless you count the trip we took to Montreal for Aisha's birthday last year, but that was by train." She shrugged. "So: first time in Europe and first time on a plane. It'll be a red-letter day for me."

Jean-Pierre's mouth fell open. "You have never flown on a plane before?"

"Nope."

"Merde." JP looked out over the Hudson. "I did not know that was possible in this day and age."

Luna couldn't help but feel defensive at that. "Well, I guess when you're a lowly peasant like me—"

"Non, non, I didn't mean it like that." He turned on the bench to face her. "You must understand, I spend so much time on airplanes. Sometimes I feel I am in the sky more than on the ground. It is difficult for me to imagine not living that way; that is all."

He seemed sincere, though Luna was loath to be so easily mollified. "I guess I'm looking forward to seeing how the other half lives. Or the other ninety percent; I'm not sure how many people have flown on planes."

The sun began to dip toward the tops of the Jersey high-rises. JP shielded his eyes. "Ah, shall we stay to watch, ah —? Le coucher de soleil?" He gestured downward with his hand.

Luna had just learned the word for *sunset* on her app, though the context clues made it obvious anyway. "Sure, we can—"

"Excusez-moi," said a heavily accented voice behind them.

They both twisted around on the bench to find a pair of thirtysomething folks, clearly tourists of the French variety, standing behind them. The man wore tiny round glasses and a lightweight scarf, and the woman wore her dark hair in a stylish half-twist. He was clutching a guidebook in his hand, and his companion had a small child strapped to her chest in a posh-looking sling.

"You, ah, speak French?" the man said. "I hear you."

Jean-Pierre launched into his native tongue, reaching for the guidebook and asking the couple what they needed help in finding. The woman gave a relieved exclamation of some kind, which JP waved away. He conducted the conversation in a more animated way than he ever spoke in English. If the tourists recognized him, they were very low-key about it. The man nodded along and asked questions, which Jean-Pierre answered in rolling, liquid French. He seemed more alive when he was using it, and Luna was glad she could follow along with her beginner's knowledge. The other day she'd listened to a podcast about a small child going missing in Bordeaux in the '30s, so understanding a simple conversation like this was a walk in the park. The man mentioned their dinner plans for that evening—a place that had been in SoHo for years that Luna had never gotten around to trying.

"No, no, do not dine there," Jean-Pierre said to the tourists. "It is no better than any middling brasserie one might find back home. There are so many superior options." He began listing the names of restaurants that Luna had heard of only in passing.

At one point the baby in the sling made a series of burbling noises that sounded like a crying jag was imminent. The parents and Jean-Pierre all made identical sympathetic coos. The mother even offered the baby's downy head to JP to pat, which he did, all the while whispering soothing French somethings. The kid calmed down right away, and the couple made a lot of exclamations about JP's skills.

"Do you have one of your own? You must; you are so good at this," the woman said.

"My sister was this small not so long ago," he answered. "I miss her at this age. Now she talks too much." The three of them shared a laugh at that.

Luna watched all this with both eyebrows raised to their limit. Who could have guessed that Jean-Pierre was good with babies?

The conversation started to wind down. The man shook JP's hand, and the woman kissed her fingertips and sent the kiss over the baby's head. They parted like old friends with an overflow of well wishes. JP waved to them until they turned down a staircase and went out of sight.

"Ah, sweet people," he said. "And such a small world. They are from the neighborhood right next to mine."

"The baby was cute," Luna said in the hopes that it would prompt Jean-Pierre to explain what was up with that interaction.

"Hm. She is eight months. How brave they were to take an infant on an international trip." He smiled to himself.

Luna glanced up to see the sun gracing the river with rays of gold tinged with purple. "Oh, it's starting," she said, wriggling on the bench in excitement.

There was a moment when the light just started to dip behind the New Jersey skyline and everything was thrown into fractured pieces of color as it hit the glass and water in just the right way. It was like magic. Luna didn't want to miss a second of it.

"It's nice." Jean-Pierre put his arm along the low back of the bench.

"Very nice," she said.

If she leaned a little bit into Jean-Pierre's side, it was only because the bench was so small, and she was so tired from their long day of pretending to be a loving couple.

When they got back to the apartment, it was quiet and empty. Simone was probably working late again, or was over at Ray's. Which reminded Luna: she never had gotten around to begging for Simone's help with cookery. She whipped out her phone and texted her while she was thinking of it: Hey I know ur busy but do u have time to teach me and JP how to make a cake? Or like any of the impossible french food we're supposed to cook?

Hopefully she'd get a response this time. She cracked her neck from side to side, wincing at the popping joints. Her phone buzzed in her hand. Not a reply from Simone, but a calendar reminder. Oh, right, it was a Thursday. She was supposed to do her injection every other Thursday.

Luna left Jean-Pierre to his own devices and opened the hall closet. Her hormone stuff was arranged in a cute little plastic bin on a high shelf, so she pulled it out, giving it a quick rattle to make sure there were plenty of needles still stocked inside, then headed for her bedroom to get everything ready.

She was interrupted by a ping on her phone. Her mom had sent her an email. Quaint. No subject line, just a link in the body. Luna clicked on it, and an article popped up from *Let's Dish*, one of the food celeb gossip blogs that had run the original pics of her and JP leaving the TV studio. This time, the story had a bit more meat. "Lisette D'Amboise Slated for Appearance at Upstate Food & Wine Fest," the headline blared.

She scrolled down to read the nonstory about how Lisette was preparing to shoot a new reality baking-competition show with Simone and Ray (with plenty of links to previous articles rife with speculation about the format and air dates), but before that, she would be attending some event. Big whoop, food celebrity does food stuff. Luna kept scrolling until she found the reason her mom must have sent her the link: the final paragraph.

Lisette isn't the only person in her illustrious family to be making waves recently. Rumors are swirling around her grandson, transgender restaurateur Jean-Pierre Aubert-Treffle, who may be involved in a high-stakes culinary test put on by celebrity chef Henri Aubert-Treffle of If You Can't Handle the Heat *fame. We'll have more details as they emerge.*

Great, the test itself was in the news. Now Luna knew without a doubt that any failure would be breathlessly discussed in the comments section of LetsDish.net by a bunch of self-described foodies.

A knock on her doorframe made her turn around. Jean-Pierre stood there, silhouetted in the light from the hallway.

"Would you mind if I joined you?" JP said. He held up a sleek black leather case that looked like it could be a luxury shaving kit. "These time zone differences. I was supposed to take the testostérone yesterday, but what with all this excitement . . ."

"Sure. Pull up a chair." Luna kicked at her wheeled desk chair with her foot, nudging it away from the wall. She herself took a seat on the bed.

Jean-Pierre nodded his thanks as he sat. He opened his kit on the desk to reveal a neatly arranged set of syringes and needles of varying sizes.

She held out a small white square packet. "Need an alcohol swab?"

"Ah, thank you. I am always forgetting to restock this." JP took the square and laid it atop the barrels of the syringes, then began wriggling out of his tight black trousers.

Luna tried very hard not to stare, even though she was kind of curious. Would it be lime briefs again, or some other color? She concentrated on drawing her estrogen from its little bottle. "Where do you usually give yourself the shot?"

"Sometimes, I am so weary from traveling I can barely roll up my sleeve and use my arm. Tonight, I can manage a thigh,

I think." He looked up at her, flashing a cheeky smile. "And you?"

Luna returned the smile with one of her own. "Butt, most of the time. Thigh in polite company." She couldn't stop herself from glancing. The briefs were sky blue today. Very jaunty.

"Do not change your habits on my account. I will look away, if you wish." JP fitted a needle to a syringe and began drawing his own medication. "I am quite impressed, actually; le derrière is ideal, I hear, yet I can never seem to twist around well enough to see what I'm doing."

Luna held her syringe up to the light and flicked the barrel a few times to make sure there were no bubbles. "I'm very flexible," she said. "Leg is fine for tonight. Do you want an ice pack?"

JP shook his head. "I am fine, thank you." He held up his own needle, eyebrow raised. "Shall we?"

Luna had never actually done this with someone else before. Sure, there had been nurses present when she was first being taught how to inject herself, but she'd never had an injection buddy, even though plenty of her friends were on HRT. It felt like such a private thing, like tweezing your eyebrows or scrubbing behind your ears. And yet, she was not bothered by the idea of doing this with him.

She gave JP a nod, feeling strangely shy as they ripped open their alcohol swab packets in unison and rubbed circles on their bare thighs. Jean-Pierre's quads were nicely formed, Luna noticed. Probably all those morning jogs. His legs were covered with a dusting of black hair that got thicker and more unruly past his knee. There was a collection of small, dark freckles on his pale skin just to the right of where he was prepping for his injection. Luna wondered if he used the freckles as a kind of guide, a star map to remind him where to insert the needle.

What a weird-ass thought.

Luna set aside her used swab and readied herself, holding the skin of her leg taut like she was trying to zoom in on a phone screen. They both went for it at the same time, sitting in silence while they pressed down slowly on their syringe plungers. Luna looked up mid-injection to find JP grinning back at her.

"This is nice, too," he said.

Luna startled a bit. "Too?"

"Like the sunset, no?"

"Yeah," she said, surprising herself with how quickly she agreed. "It is."

Chapter 14

Simone texted her back during the weekend, full of apologies but also good news.

I've got a plan for teaching you the entire menu! We have the holiday weekend off from work and Lisette is going upstate to some fancy farmhouse. She said we should use her kitchen. Technically since she's not present it doesn't count as helping JP. It's HUGE and gorgeous and I've always wanted to cook in it so please say yes?

Oh, right. Next Monday was Memorial Day. Luna had completely lost track of the calendar while she'd been unemployed, and one week into her new job as Delilah's right hand, she was still a little iffy on what month it was.

Luna texted back her enthusiastic agreement to Simone's plan. Once she had her first week at her new position under her belt, Luna was ready to tackle her other major life-changing task. Their kitchen at home was nice for normal people living in New York, but she was eager to see how the one percent lived. Best of all, according to JP, the paparazzi would follow Lisette up to the Hudson Valley culinary event to snap pics of her and all the other celebrity chefs who would be in attendance, so no one would notice or care if they used Lisette's place as headquarters for their cooking boot camp.

She and JP took an Uber there with a couple overnight bags, arriving late because of the horrible traffic that always plagued the streets of SoHo. Lisette lived in a converted warehouse, the kind that artists used to squat in and now probably cost five million dollars for one unit. The elevator took them up to the very top floor.

When the doors opened, Luna was expecting to find herself in a hallway or outside Lisette's door. Instead she found herself stepping right into the kitchen. Penthouse living, indeed.

She looked around, her eyes bugging out of her head. "Oh my god."

It wasn't like Luna had never been in a rich person's house before. Her old boss Tim had sent her to fetch documents from his place on the Upper East Side several times. That apartment had looked the way people with more money than taste preferred, all white-on-white walls, shining chrome, overly curated art, and cavernous space. Luna hated when rich people decorated as if they didn't own anything. That starkly modern, empty look was such a bullshit move.

Lisette's penthouse was not like that at all. She lived in, while not exactly *clutter*, an atmosphere of comfortable sumptuousness. The kitchen Luna found herself standing in was bigger than her entire apartment. It was full of sparkling stainless-steel appliances, gorgeous marble countertops with deep whorls of gray and white, and copper pans hanging from a rack in the middle of the ceiling, right above the gigantic island. The cabinets were painted a soothing sea green with thin gold hardware.

Luna had never been jealous of cabinets before. Maybe she was just getting to that age where she wanted to nest or whatever, but those cabinets were making her hands itch with the urge to rip them out and take them home.

The open-plan kitchen flowed into a living room-slash-dining room-slash-entertaining area complete with a fireplace stocked with real wood—who the fuck had a fireplace in New York?—and a dozen flourishing houseplants in a riot of colors. Luna's eye was especially drawn to a collection of African violets that lined the mantelpiece in shades of deep blues and luscious purples. They set off the wallpaper perfectly: a damask botanical print done in a soft, buttery yellow. The space was filled with items one might collect during a long and interesting life. Antique cookware was mounted on the walls alongside framed photos of the French countryside. On a delicate side table, an old-timey camera sat next to a magnum of champagne, the comically oversized bottle topped with a jaunty hat sporting a long green feather.

But it wasn't just the colors that set Lisette's home apart. It was the personal touches, the soul. There were handwritten notes and recipe cards attached to the giant refrigerator door with magnets shaped like tiny baguettes and croissants. There were books on the coffee table in front of the fireplace, actual books that someone was reading, if the bookmarks between the pages could be believed. On the kitchen island, there was a cute cake stand made of milk glass covered with a clear dome, under which sat three-quarters of a cake studded with fresh raspberries and blackberries and dusted with powdered sugar. A note in flowing handwriting told them in French to help themselves. Thanks to spending every spare moment on her language app and listening to French podcasts, Luna could decipher the note pretty easily.

"Look here," JP said, and took her by the shoulders to turn her.

There were framed family photographs arranged on the wall next to the elevator, before the hexagonal backsplash began. In one of them Luna could make out the face of a young Lisette in a kitchen with an apron tied around her waist, her hair done up in an amazing retro style like something out of *Mad Men*. Another photo depicted a little kid with cake smeared around their mouth, grinning gap-toothed at the camera and clutching the rest of the slice in a tiny hand. And another showed Lisette, older but not quite present day, holding a swaddled baby crying in pink-cheeked rage.

"My mother," Jean-Pierre said, pointing to the picture of the cakey kid. "And myself as a child." He pointed to the baby picture.

"Wow." Of course JP had been a fussy baby. That tracked 100 percent. Luna stared at the pictures for a second longer, then turned in a circle to stare some more at the beautiful kitchen. "I mean, this is so cool."

"This is not even her main residence," Jean-Pierre said with a laugh. "You should see her house in Fourcés. Now that is an impressive place."

"Luna? Jean-Pierre? Is that you?" a muffled voice called. A hidden door that blended seamlessly with a wall popped open, making Luna jump. She settled down only when she saw Simone's head appear in the gap.

"Christ on saltine crackers, Simone," she said, clutching her heart. "I thought you were a burglar. Or a ghost. A burgle-ghost."

"Sorry. I forgot how well camouflaged the pantry is." Simone grimaced in apology.

Ray's head appeared above Simone's like they were stackable Tupperware. "You have got to see this pantry. It's like pornography for label-obsessed nerds."

"Hey," Simone said, somewhat defensively. Her head tipped back so she could glare at them.

"No, babe, I mean *me*. I'm hard-core into it." Then, to Luna and JP, they said, "Seriously, look."

The door was shoved open the rest of the way, allowing Luna to gape in wonder at the organizational heaven that was revealed. It was a pantry that most people could only dream about. Everything was arranged in neat rows, giant bins of flour and sugar on the floor along with crates of wine and bottled water. There were canned goods lined up like they would be in the fanciest of grocery stores, not a single one out of place. And the baking supplies—oodles upon oodles of different chocolates, sprinkles, nuts, dried fruit, and a ton of stuff Luna wouldn't have been able to identify if it weren't for the labels that adorned each shelf. They were written in both English and French, which was handy for Luna's growing vocabulary.

"How come—?" she started to ask, pointing at the bilingual labels.

"Grand-mère hires staff, of course, to stock the penthouse before she arrives from abroad. There have been a few miscommunications in the past, so I suggested she do this. Now the English-speaking assistants can more easily see what needs to be purchased," Jean-Pierre said. He plucked an apple from an overflowing rattan bin and bit into it with a loud crunch.

"That's . . . actually a good idea," Luna said, unsure what it meant that her first reaction wasn't disgust at how rich people could just pay for someone else to do their boring chores like grocery shopping; maybe she was getting used to the concept of first-class living.

"Lisette was kind enough to order all the ingredients we need to re-create your menu," Simone said.

JP perked up. "Including the rabbit?"

"Yes. Including the rabbit."

Ray looked a little queasy at the prospect. "It's not, like, a whole rabbit, is it? We're not going to butcher a cute little bunny ourselves, are we?"

"I'm sorry," Jean-Pierre said to Ray, "but you are . . . ?"

"Oh, my bad!" Ray stuck their hand out, though not very far since they were all crammed into the pantry and there wasn't a ton of elbow room. "I'm Ray. I work with your gram-gram. They/them."

"They—?"

"My pronouns."

"Ah." JP took their hand but did not shake it, looking instead to Simone with wide eyes and saying something in French. Luna could catch only a few words in the rapid stream of sentences, like *what* and *he*.

"No need to be embarrassed," Simone said in English. To Ray, she said, "He's never used the singular 'they' before. He wants to know if you would prefer— Well, just tell them, Jean-Pierre." Simone gestured to Ray.

Ray looked delighted. "What's up?"

"I was asking," JP said slowly, retracting his hand, "how I should refer to you if I am speaking French. It is difficult, yes?"

"There's a gender-neutral pronoun in French now," Luna said. "They added it to the dictionary a few years back. It's *iel.*"

Everyone turned to stare at her.

"What?" Luna shrugged. "I heard about it on a podcast." She'd decided that adding a couple general-interest shows on her French feed might be a good idea so that she could learn how to say more than "skeletal remains" and "chain of evidence," which, hopefully, she would never need to use in polite conversation.

"And for, ah, accords? Words that describe?" Jean-Pierre asked. Just like in Spanish and Italian, French adjectives changed slightly depending on their subject's gender. "How do I—?"

"You can just use the masculine if it's easier," Ray said.

"Non, non. I want to do it correctly." JP pulled out his phone and started typing. "I shall look it up, yes?" He glanced up at Ray. "If I make a mistake, I am sorry. English is not my strongest, and it will take some practice to get it right in French."

"Hey, it's cool," Ray said. "I don't speak French anyway, so I wouldn't even know if you mess up."

"*I* would know," Jean-Pierre said, and in that moment, Luna felt a completely inappropriate urge to do—something. Something that no one should do in a beloved elderly TV cook's perfect pantry. Like shove JP against the labeled shelves and grind like a freaking pepper mill until he said more hot shit. She couldn't help it; she loved it when a man respected other people.

Okay, wow. Where had that come from? Time to be professional.

They all tumbled out of the pantry and back into the kitchen.

"So!" Luna turned to Simone with a bright, near-manic smile. "Food? Cooking? Cuisine of the French variety? Where do we start?"

"Right, we're here to cook." Simone clapped her hands, then consulted a piece of paper on the counter. It was neatly printed, a list divided into nine sections.

"Is that the menu?" Luna asked. "I haven't actually seen the entire thing yet. Can I take a look?"

"Sure." Simone handed it over.

The menu read:

CHILLED SUNCHOKE SOUP
roasted cashews, chive oil, local watercress

CAVIAR ROYALE
housemade black sesame crackers, melon pearls,
custard au champagne

SALAD OF GREENMARKET PEACHES
compressed kohlrabi, pickled blackberries, mint dust

BEEF TARTARE
sabayon, lavender mustard, quail egg jus

BUTTER-POACHED SEA SCALLOP
bacon smoke, marinated fava beans,
mango-sweet potato crumble

BRAISED SADDLE OF RABBIT
tomato medallions, suggestion of fennel,
blood pudding emulsion

DUCK LEG CONFIT WITH FOIE GRAS TERRINE
marmalade blanchette, whipped ramps,
rhubarb scented foam

FLOATING ISLANDS DE FRUITS
cinnamon meringue, caramelized pear crème anglaise,
coriander-pineapple syrup

GÂTEAU MARJOLAINE À LA AUBERT
biscuit dacquoise, praline buttercream, glace au chocolat

Simone rapped her knuckles on the marble countertop. "We should probably get started on our mise en place."

"That means 'little containers of all your shit, ready to go,'" Ray said.

Jean-Pierre rolled his eyes. "I know what it means."

"Yeah." Luna scoffed. "I may not be a classically trained chef or whatever, but I've seen every episode of Lisette's public-access show, like, three times, thanks to you. I've picked up some knowledge, I'm sure, just from osmosis alone."

Simone was laser-focused on opening drawers and setting up bowls and cutting boards. "We'll need eggs for the cake, the meringue, and the egg wash for the crumble. Luna, think you can handle that? A dozen whole, another dozen separated."

Luna tried not to think of the last time she'd tackled eggs. Today was a new day, after all. She gave a snappy salute. "Aye-aye, Captain."

She stood at the counter, shoulder to shoulder with JP, as she opened the cartons of cage-free organic eggs that had apparently been shipped from a farm upstate that very morning. The brown shells gleamed under the soft kitchen lights. Luna picked up the first egg carefully. She began tapping it against the rim of a metal mixing bowl, conscious of Simone's eagle eyes boring into her back.

"What are you doing?" Simone asked.

Luna looked over her shoulder. Simone was standing with her arms crossed over her chest, looking as severe as a schoolmarm in a period piece.

"I'm cracking an egg."

"Not like that, you're not." Simone squeezed between her and Jean-Pierre, who was busy chopping onions and shallots into large, irregular pieces. "Let me show you." She took the egg from Luna and held it between her thumb and forefinger, narrow tip to rounded bottom. "If you whack it against the edge of something, what happens? The shell gets penetrated, crushed inward, and you're more likely to get pieces of shell in your product."

"Oh god, are we going to be calling food 'product' all weekend?" Luna moaned.

"Pay attention." Simone tapped the egg lightly down on the countertop. "Flat surface. See? No penetration."

"We're saying 'penetration' a whole lot, too, huh?" said Ray, who was sitting on a slice of counter way over by the sink, feet swinging as they sipped at a bottle of beer. Luna wondered if there was enough beer for everyone, and when she'd be allowed to have one. Her throat was parched.

Simone lifted the egg, which now sported a hairline crack down the equator, and showed it to Luna. "Now all you need to do is—" She held the egg over the bowl and did a trick with her thumbs, but it happened so quickly that all Luna caught was the sight of the sunshine-yellow yolk and glossy white slipping into the waiting vessel. "Got it?"

"Yep, sure," Luna said, even though she hadn't really gotten it at all.

Simone's attention shifted to Jean-Pierre, who was cutting the biggest onion ever grown in the continental United States like it was a rival who had personally offended him. "Um, let me show you a better way to do that. Before you slice off your fingers."

Luna relaxed slightly now that JP was the target of Simone's nagging. She meant well, really, but Luna was not a little kid. She didn't need a babysitter in the kitchen.

She took another egg and rapped it against the countertop, just like Simone had demonstrated. No explosions, although she did get egg on her fingers as she parted the shell over the bowl. Now she just needed to do that a few dozen more times. She reached for another egg, but her progress was stopped by JP.

"Clair, could you hand me that dish?" He tipped his chin toward a clear Pyrex bowl that sat just out of his reach on the massive island, but well within Luna's.

Luna grabbed the bowl and started handing it over.

"Whoa!" Ray squawked.

"Ah!" Simone practically screamed.

Luna froze, bowl hovering in midair. "What?" Her heart was hammering. "Why are you shouting?"

"Your hands." Simone's horrified voice came out almost in a whisper. "They're covered in raw egg."

Luna glanced at said eggy hand, which was holding the Pyrex dish. "Yeah?"

"You can't touch a clean bowl that vegetables are going into with a contaminated hand," Ray said from their perch across the kitchen. "It's not sanitary."

"I don't get it." Luna looked between the two of them. "The vegetables are getting cooked, right? So who cares if they touch eggs?"

"Because— It's . . ." Simone whipped her head around to look at Jean-Pierre as if for backup. "You get why this is a problem, right?"

JP shrugged. "If they're getting cooked . . ."

"Oh my god." Simone backed away from the counter with her hands pressed to her forehead. "Oh my *god*."

Luna glanced at Jean-Pierre, and they shared a look that confirmed they both thought this was a tad dramatic. She lowered the supposedly contaminated bowl to the counter, which, she assumed, was now also contaminated.

"Babe?" Ray hopped down from the counter and crossed the kitchen in three strides. They held Simone by her upper arms. "Breathe. We can wash a bowl."

"It's not the bowl, babe!" Simone dropped into a hissy whisper, which Luna could hear clear as day. "Neither of them know anything. Not the first thing! Not about food safety, or knife skills. Nothing at all!" She looked like she was about to pass out. Her face was as white as her apron. "I can't do this. I can't teach people to cook if they don't have basic knowledge."

Ray's face creased in worry. "Well, that's unfortunate, seeing as we're about to make a TV show where the premise is you doing that, like, every episode."

Simone gave a helpless wail. Ray grimaced at Luna.

"Why don't we take a break for a few minutes?" They hustled Simone into the pantry and shut the door. Luna could hear the hushed tones of a classic Simone becalming. Ray was kind of an expert at that.

Luna heaved a sigh and crossed the kitchen to wash her hands. "Are we really that hopeless?" she asked Jean-Pierre over the sound of running water.

"I think Simone is just a bit stressed." He popped an unpeeled hazelnut into his mouth and chewed, making a face immediately. "Oh, they are—"

"—not good like that," Luna said.

"Terrible."

"Yeah."

They looked at each other from across the gigantic island. The complete ridiculousness of the situation hit them both in the same moment. All Luna needed to see was the telltale twitch of JP's mouth and she was laughing harder than she had in— shit, maybe months. She doubled over with it, howling while Jean-Pierre joined in. There was nothing to do but laugh, really.

"Oh my god," Luna wheezed, "we are *hopeless*."

Jean-Pierre valiantly tried to get his breathing under control through fits of laughter. "Non, non," he said. "It will be fine."

"Really?" Luna straightened and wiped at her eyes. She was crying, she was laughing so hard. "We haven't even applied heat to anything, and we've already driven our instructor to a panic attack."

That set them off on another round of laughter, both of them losing it. Luna had to prop herself against the counter with both arms so she wouldn't collapse in a heap. She tried not to catch JP's eye because every time she did, she just started giggling all over again.

Jean-Pierre was the first to recover some semblance of normalcy. "I still think we can do this," he said. "It is possible."

"This isn't the movies, though," Luna said, trying to effect a serious tone. "We can't just buckle down and learn to cook in three days when it takes most chefs a lifetime. There is no such thing as a *Rocky* montage in real life, okay?" She paused. "*Rocky* is a film about a boxer in Philadelphia—"

"I know what *Rocky* is. I have seen many American films." Jean-Pierre rounded the island and came to stand directly in front of Luna. "And I say, why can't we be Rocky?"

Luna shook her head. "You know Rocky loses in the first movie, right?"

"Exactly. We do not have to be perfect. We do not even have to be particularly good." Jean-Pierre shifted from foot to foot, like he was actually gearing up for a fight. "According to the stipulations of my grandfather's will, we only need to produce a *decent* re-creation of the dishes. We can achieve decent."

Luna chewed her lip and thought. Despair would get her nowhere, so best to put it aside. JP was right. Cooking was a skill, just like anything. You could learn it with practice and hard work; nothing was innate, not really. Even with things that came to Luna easily, like languages, she needed to start somewhere.

Jean-Pierre owed it to himself to try, and Luna—she was getting paid pretty handsomely to work through the pain.

She met JP's gaze with the fire of determination burning in her stomach. "Okay," she said. "Let's go the full fifteen rounds."

He almost cracked a smile. Luna pursed her lips and fought the urge to laugh again.

The pantry door swung back open. Simone shuffled into the

kitchen, smoothing her hair down and clearing her throat. "All right," she said, "I'm sorry about that tiny hiccup. I'm calmer now."

Luna stepped forward, knowing exactly what she needed to do. "Simone? You're in charge here."

Simone blinked at her. "Okay?"

Behind her shoulder, Ray stuck their head out of the pantry and gave a thumbs-up.

"I mean it," Luna said. "You're the boss. Whatever you tell us to do"—she gestured between herself and Jean-Pierre—"we'll do it. No questions, no backtalk."

"You can ask questions—" Simone started to say.

"No, we don't have time. We don't need to know why. It's literally do or die."

"Well, not literally," JP mumbled.

Luna cut a glare over her shoulder at him before turning back to Simone. "We have until Lisette comes back Monday night to work on this menu, right? That's"—she checked her phone—"less than sixty hours from now. Now, I don't even know what the hell a sunchoke is. I don't care. I just need you to show me how to make it into a chilled soup so that Jean-Pierre's grandpa can fucking gag on it when we serve it to him. Can you do that?"

Simone stood up straighter. "Yeah. I can do that." She looked at JP. "But you two have to do exactly as I say. Actual kitchen hierarchy applies. I can keep you safe and teach you what you need to know, but you have to trust me. All right?"

"Yes, Chef," they said in unison.

Luna grinned at him. "Oh, we said the same—"

"The same thing." Jean-Pierre nodded.

"That was cool."

Simone took a huge copper pot from the hanging rack over the island and let it drop with a loud bang onto the counter. "Luna, fridge. I need the rabbit, the duck legs, butter, the tub of duck fat, every fresh herb you can find, and the sunchokes. They look like weird potatoes. Go." Then, as Luna scampered, she said to JP: "Pantry. Red wine, a really robust one, garlic, onions, and every dried herb you can get your hands on. Got all that?"

"Oui, Chef." He slipped by Ray and into the pantry.

Simone pulled a clean knife from the block. "Let's make some goddamn food."

Chapter 15

"This is all going to come down to timing," Simone told them as she toasted spices in a pan for the duck legs. "In the real world, almost every component of these dishes would be made ahead of time and then just assembled at dinner service. That's the only way a busy restaurant like Chef Henri's can function. You two won't have days to marinate or let things set, which is why the rules say you only have to make a 'decent' approximation of the dish."

"Babe, you read that whole will? In French?" Ray was on the opposite side of the counter, demonstrating how to butcher the rabbit, which thankfully had already been skinned. "That's hot."

Luna made a note to herself to ask Simone for a copy of that document. It would be good French practice.

Simone gave a curt but pleased nod. "Thank you. But focus." She dumped the toasted spices into a grinder and turned to Luna and Jean-Pierre as it whirred to life. Simone's voice rose to be heard over the noise. "So I'm going to give you a step-by-step timeline of what to do and when to do it. That's the only way you're going to be able to cook this menu in seven hours."

"And that's why we're starting with the things that will take the longest to cook, like the meats," Luna said. She felt a little like a student again. She even had a notebook and pen in her hands to take copious notes on Simone's technique. She couldn't wait to make a spreadsheet about this later.

"Correct," Simone said, and Luna beamed like she'd just earned a gold-star sticker in kindergarten. "The duck confit needs to marinate before being slow cooked. Chef Henri probably does this overnight, but you'll only have four hours. I'm tweaking the recipe so that hopefully the meat will break down quicker and still get tender without going mushy. Careful, though: a little apple cider vinegar goes a long way here." She switched off the grinder and added a small glug of the liquid. "Now we rub that onto our duck and let it sit in the fridge until it's time to throw it in the oven."

Luna made a note of that, then tried to concentrate on how Ray was trimming the weird shiny bits of flesh off the rabbit meat. "We're going to need to decide which one of us does what," she told JP. "Do you want to be on Bugs Bunny or Daffy Duck duty?"

"Hm. I like eating duck more than I enjoy rabbit," Jean-Pierre said, "but then again, I don't want you chopping through bones. That requires some, ah, muscle."

"Hey, I can chop through a bone. My arms aren't that weenie."

Simone put a heavy Dutch oven lid down on the counter with enough force to make everyone else jump. "We don't have time for this! I decide who does what." She stabbed a finger in their direction. "JP, you take the rabbit. Luna, you take the duck. Toasting spices is just like making a grilled cheese, and I know I've seen you make grilled cheese."

"Yes, Chef," they both mumbled.

"What was that?" Simone snapped.

They stood at attention, coming out of their twin slumps. "Yes, Chef!"

"That's what I thought. Now we make the baked components so they have time to cool. Cake, crackers, crumble. Get me flour, sugar, butter, eggs, nuts, sesame, and salt. Plus the mango and sweet potato."

"On it," Luna said, and jogged toward the pantry while JP took the fridge.

The rest of the evening went like that, everything going at full speed with not a second's rest. Luna had known in a theoretical sense how demanding restaurant work could be; she remembered when Simone was still putting in long hours in restaurant kitchens, coming home exhausted in the middle of the night smelling of onions. But Luna hadn't realized it would be a grueling marathon where every move you made had to be done with the utmost efficiency: a trip to the pantry or the fridge for a single item was a fool's errand. She needed to load up her arms with everything she could carry. She needed to get something going on the stove while she turned her attention to chopping vegetables while simultaneously keeping an eye on the simmering pot. She needed to do everything right—or as close to it as she could—the first time, or else she would have to waste precious minutes redoing it. Her feet were killing her, but her brain felt like it was going to explode with all the stuff she had to remember and keep track of.

"How do you do this?" Luna gasped after chugging a giant glass of ice water that Ray had blessedly deposited at her elbow. She was melting, standing over the heat of the stove while she stirred a broth that was going on some fucking dish; she didn't even know which. "How does anyone do this for eight hours straight, five or six days a week?"

Ray snorted while sorting through microgreens. "Right, just eight hours. That's cute."

"A dinner shift is usually closer to ten or twelve hours," JP informed her. He jotted something down in his Moleskine while he watched Ray make the vinaigrette.

"But in a real kitchen, you'd have a lot more people working together," Simone said as she washed some truly freakishly shaped heirloom tomatoes. "You just get used to it, I guess."

"Or you blow out a knee and then you're out of luck," Ray said. "That happened to a lot of cooks I worked with back in the day."

JP's head jerked up from his notebook, a deeply concerned look painted across his face.

"But I'm sure you two will be fine," Ray added, a little too late to be comforting.

The complete meal of nine courses was ready shortly after midnight. Some of the plates didn't look exactly like the helpful photographs that Simone had scoured the internet for so they could compare—piles of meat and vegetables were meant to be neat stacks; the floating islands had become more like a continent when all the meringues had merged together in the custard sea; and the sesame crackers on the caviar dish all dipped in the middle. But there were four complete plates of each course, exactly as the rules demanded of them, lined up on the counter in neat rows.

It wasn't perfect. But was it good enough? They all bellied up to the kitchen island, the silence tense and prolonged.

Simone passed out forks and spoons. "Remember, this is only the first attempt. We have all of tomorrow and most of Monday to refine things."

Luna's stomach gave an unhappy gurgle. She normally didn't eat dinner at such a late hour. Plus, just the thought of doing all this over again made her tummy hurt. She dipped her spoon into the sunchoke soup and took a bite.

"Hm." She took another bite, and so did everyone else. "I don't know if I'm just starving and cardboard would taste okay to me right now, but this is—fine?"

"It's edible," Jean-Pierre said as he gathered a little more of the chive oil that floated atop the soup into the curve of his spoon. "Although I still don't understand why it's served chilled."

"It's a power move," Ray said, slurping up a bite. "Throw your customers a curveball, make them think you're some kind of mad genius who knows more about soup than they do. People are spending hundreds of dollars to eat this stuff. They're primed to accept fancy bullshit." Simone coughed meaningfully, and Ray glanced up at JP with wide eyes. "Not that your grandpa's food is bullshit."

"Non, c'est vrai." Jean-Pierre sampled the caviar with a satisfied nod. "Much of this menu is shit. It is certainly not the food I would choose to make, if I had the skill." He let the remainder of his floppy cracker fall back to the plate with a plop. "Actually, I'm not even that fond of French cuisine."

Simone almost choked on her bite of salad. "That's, uh, kind of unfortunate for you."

"Wait, so what kind of food *do* you like best?" Luna asked. "You've traveled a ton, right? So you must have tried, like, everything."

JP smiled down at his low bowl that held a near-perfect poached scallop—it had just caught a little on the edges, turning the caramel crust slightly more black than brown. "Honestly? Thai." He took a bite of the scallop's accompanying sauce and made a note in his notebook. "Thai cuisine is as complex and sophisticated as any other, of course, but how many upscale Thai restaurants do you see? Perhaps one for every fifty French restaurants. Why? Because we insist French food is better? That it requires more skill? Ridiculous."

Luna took a bite of the rich, buttery rabbit dish. It was definitely missing something. "Maybe we could learn to cook some Thai dishes," she said.

"Not this weekend, you won't," Simone said. "You've got to concentrate on this menu, remember? You have less than two weeks to get this right."

"Yeah, I know. I meant, like, maybe later we could . . ." She trailed off. There wouldn't be a later, would there? There was no point in making future plans for cooking lessons with JP. Once they passed the test, their arrangement was over. Luna swirled her spoon sullenly through her crème anglaise. Why did that thought make her stomach feel like it was full of rocks and not a pretty-okay rendition of a nine-course meal? "Never mind," she said at last. She was probably just overly tired.

They ate their way through all the dishes, Ray and Simone pointing out where they'd made mistakes and what could be improved, Luna and Jean-Pierre trying their damnedest to pay attention and absorb all the information. The beef was underseasoned. The rabbit was raw in the center. The salad was a mess. And on and on until Luna couldn't keep another thought in her head.

She wasn't the only one dead on their feet. In the middle of explaining why the rhubarb foam had deflated much too quickly, Simone caught sight of Ray propping their head on their fist, elbow braced on the counter, eyes slipping shut. She paused and put her fork down. "I think we've done all we can for today," she said, even though she seemed to still have energy to burn. "Why don't we stop here tonight?"

"Aw, babe, there's still cleanup to do," Ray said, sleepily glaring at the mountain of dirty pots and pans and mixing bowls and utensils that loomed in and around the kitchen sink.

"We can tackle that first thing in the morning. Come on." Simone grabbed up her two dessert courses and headed for the sitting area. "Let's get off our feet."

Luna shot JP a look that said, *Is this not the cutest thing you've ever seen?*

JP looked at her blankly as he collected his own plate of gâteau marjolaine. "What?"

She tipped her chin at Ray and Simone, who had already claimed the sofa for themselves, sinking into the luxuriously deep cushions and laughing at something Luna couldn't hear. "She saw they were tired, so she's acting like we all need to take a break. It's just sweet, you know? How she looks out for them."

"Well, I *do* need a break." Jean-Pierre cracked his neck. Loudly. "I'm going to sleep like a marmotte tonight."

JP took her by the elbow and steered her toward the pair of armchairs that flanked the—again—actual fucking fireplace.

"Come, have a seat. I know where Grand-mère keeps the good wine," he said, as if someone like Lisette would ever have bad wine in the house. "Red or white?"

"Uh, white, please," Luna said. She took her cushy seat, balancing a half-eaten plate of floating islands on her knees. The dessert course, pillowy meringue mounds arranged in a bath of custard, had been her favorite bite of the night, and she planned on cleaning the plate of every morsel. She barely heard Jean-Pierre asking Ray and Simone if they would like to imbibe; she was too busy spooning up spiced mouthfuls of pear and clouds.

JP returned with three glasses and a bottle, plus another beer for Ray. Soon they were all settled in, dirty plates on the coffee table or at their feet, drinks in hand. Ray complained about being overheated from their long stint in the hot kitchen and shucked their button-up. They were wearing a sleeveless shirt underneath, and Luna noticed Jean-Pierre noticing the peek of scar tissue under Ray's arm.

"Oh," he said, sounding surprised. "I did not know you, ah—" He gestured. "The surgery?"

"Hm? Oh, yeah." Ray placed their palm in the center of their chest, rubbing lightly. "I got mine about seven months ago. You?"

"It has been perhaps five years. Yes?" Jean-Pierre looked up to the ceiling. He always did that when he was doing mental math, Luna noticed. "No, six."

Luna hid her shock behind her wineglass. If JP had gotten top surgery that long ago, but hadn't come out to anyone in his family until a year or two ago—that was a lot to unpack. Luna couldn't imagine what the recovery would be like without your loved ones around to take care of you. Plus, had they not noticed when Jean-Pierre started to look different? She knew people could be oblivious, but this was on another level.

Ray sipped at their beer. "Did you go to a doctor in Paris or—?"

"I chose a surgeon outside of Madrid." JP shrugged airily. "The best on the continent. Full service, cliffside views, excellent meals."

"Whoa. That sounds amazing. And expensive." Ray wagged a finger at Jean-Pierre's black shirt, a sleek button-down pieced together in panels of silk and leather. "Hey, sorry if this is weird, and you can totally say no, but—could I see?"

"Babe." Simone's tone held a note of warning. She barely paused in her long gulp of wine.

Luna smothered a laugh as Ray swiveled their head in the direction of that one-word reprimand. "What? He can say no! Would it be better if I went first?" They leaned forward and reached for the hem of their tank, rucking it up halfway on their long torso.

JP cast a helpless look at Luna, telegraphing his plea for her to intercede. Luna didn't understand what she was supposed to do about it. It was JP's call, not hers, and her answering look said that clearly. Her sip of wine was loud and pointed.

Jean-Pierre's jaw jutted out at a stubborn angle, and for a moment Luna was certain he was going to tell brash, loud, quintessentially American Ray to please remain fully clothed. But then his fingers lifted to the buttons on his shirt and started working them free.

"We can do it together," he said with a determined gleam in his eye.

"Awesome. Okay, ready?" Ray's goofy grin widened as they watched JP reach the end of his buttons. "On three: one, two—"

Luna tried not to look more than was polite, but she *was* going to look. It was, after all, two attractive people taking their shirts off in Lisette D'Amboise's well-appointed penthouse. She was allowed a glance, surely. As long as she didn't stare too hard.

Ray let out a long, low whistle. "Holy shit, look at you! Your surgeon was an artist, man. You can barely see the scarring; it's, like, perfectly positioned." They leaned far over the coffee table to get a better view of the thin, pink twin dashes that lined the bottom of Jean-Pierre's not-inconsequential pectoral muscles.

"Yours are— It is well done, for so recent a surgery," Jean-Pierre said.

Ray stood to their full height. Their hands went to their hips to better display their flat chest and the slightly thicker, reddish lines there. "Thanks! I'm pretty stoked about the results. Just wish I could sleep on my side without that weird pins-and-needles feeling. Did you get that?"

Jean-Pierre nodded. He looked more relaxed now, like he was warming to the topic. "For the first year or so. It will fade, eventually."

"That's a relief." Ray stared down at JP and clicked their tongue. "I mean, damn. Seriously. You look so good. That nipplework is— Babe, are you seeing these nips?"

Simone lifted her wineglass in a salute. "They're very nice nipples, Jean-Pierre," she said.

"Merci," JP said in something of a daze. His gaze tracked over to Luna, and Luna wondered if he was expecting her to weigh in as well. She wasn't certain how she should phrase her opinion about the appearance of her fake boyfriend's nipples. There was no Hallmark card for something like this.

"Um, *cuuuuuuute*," she said like she was reacting to a friend's new shoes. Then, because Luna was nothing if not a supportive person, she added, "Good color, natural placement." She was blushing before the first word had even left her mouth. What in the world was she doing, talking like that? Even if it was the truth: Jean-Pierre's nipples were objectively lovely. Shell pink, like his lips when he bit them. Not too close, not too far apart. Goldilocks nipples.

Dear lord, she needed to get out more.

Luna cleared her throat. "So where are we supposed to sleep tonight?" she asked. "Just curious."

Jean-Pierre shrugged his shirt back on and buttoned it up. "Ah, there are many guest rooms. Please, help yourselves. I assume Simone et Ray shall take the largest?"

"Yeah, we should probably hit the hay." Ray struggled to get their tee back over their head, saw it was backward, and then struggled to get it right with their arms all bound up inside it. "Another big day tomorrow."

Luna shifted in her armchair, tucking her feet under her. "Didn't mean to ruin your masc bonding moment, sorry."

"Hey, no worries!" Ray did finger-guns at JP, a gesture that both alarmed and intrigued him, if his eyebrows were any indication. "We can hang out after your whole training weekend is over."

"All right," JP said easily.

Simone rose from the sofa as well, leaving her wineglass on a side table. "Good night, you two."

A chorus of good nights followed while Simone and Ray stumbled their way down the hall. Luna looked into her empty glass and wondered if she could convince Jean-Pierre to have one more drink before bedtime.

"Shall I open up another bottle?" JP asked before she could.

Luna quirked a brow at him. "Aren't you tired?"

"Not in the least." He tried to stifle a yawn by not opening his mouth at all, which kind of made it look like he was sniffing really, really hard. When Luna laughed, instead of looking offended, he just grinned. "Come on. One more glass."

"Sure," Luna said. The wine was making her feel warm and cozy. "One more glass."

One more glass turned into two and a half. It made sense to finish the bottle, just like it made sense for JP to swap his armchair for a seat on the sofa, where Luna joined him—only because it was easier to converse in whispers when they weren't sitting across the room from each other.

"So tell me about Thailand," Luna said softly. Jean-Pierre had turned down most of the lights, and the only real illumination came from an old Tiffany lamp on the sideboard. It cast JP's face in blues and greens, like he was underwater in some fairy-tale pond. "What did you eat there that was so amazing?"

"There was this one dish, I do not know its name." He topped off Luna's glass for her. Such a gentleman. "I believe it was made to suit a tourist's tastes; not too spicy, very simple. But it was divine. Chicken and green onions and slivers of ginger—probably an entire root's worth of ginger—all simmered in this thick sauce. I dream about that ginger sauce. I wish my Thai was better; I tried to ask the woman at the stand how it was made, but I couldn't catch what she was saying. Something about tamarind, I think, or maybe tomato . . ."

Luna nodded, and then really nodded. She was falling asleep where she sat, but for some reason, she couldn't force herself to move. The deep burr of Jean-Pierre's voice was so soothing, and the sofa was actually very comfortable, and Luna wanted to close her eyes, just for a second—

She was woken by the familiar click of a camera app making a fake shutter noise. Her fuzzy head took a moment to register the sound—and to lift from its spot on Jean-Pierre's shoulder.

"Hm—? Wha—?" Luna brushed her hair out of her eyes and saw, with sudden, chilling clarity, several things. One: she was curled up on the sofa right against JP's side with her hand on his thigh. Two: Jean-Pierre was thankfully still asleep, his head tipped back and his arm around her shoulders. Three, and the weirdest of all: Simone was standing in front of the fireplace taking photos of them with a huge grin on her face.

"You two are the cutest," she whispered to Luna. "You fell asleep like that."

Luna blinked muzzily. "Why would you . . . ?"

Simone gave her a funny look. "Because you're pretending to be a couple, remember? This is pretty solid evidence for the internet. I'm sure my twenty-six thousand followers on Insta will buy it, anyway." Her fingers flew over her phone screen.

That snapped Luna into wakefulness. She wriggled out from under JP's heavy arm as quickly as she could without disturbing him. Their two wineglasses were sitting side by side on the coffee table. She didn't remember putting hers there. He must have taken the glass out of her hand as she was falling asleep and placed it gently—

"Yeah. Yeah, evidence." She rose from the couch and hurried in the direction of the hall bathroom. She needed to splash water on her face, brush her gross-tasting teeth. Most of all, she needed to leave the scene of the crime. Exhaustion aside, there was no excuse for a slumber party with her very-much-not-real boyfriend.

"Don't forget," Simone's hushed cry followed her, "you're on dish duty!"

Chapter 16

Luna and Jean-Pierre stood in Lisette's kitchen, sweaty and exhausted, while they watched Ray and Simone take small bites of the food they'd made. It was Monday afternoon, and this was the last round of practice cooking they'd been able to squeeze in. This time, they'd managed to finish every dish within the time limit. There were still a few half-assed elements, and their aesthetics left something to be desired, but everything that was supposed to be on the plate had made it there.

Simone finished chewing her forkful of cake and swallowed. "I think you did it," she declared.

Luna sagged against the counter in relief. "Thank god."

"The rabbit was cooked through?" JP asked, still clutching his notebook. "You are sure?"

"Tender as hell," Ray assured him. "And the salt was on point this time."

"You two should be very proud." Simone beamed at them. "Of course, with a teacher like me, there was no way you'd fail."

Happy to just have survived the practice test, Luna didn't bother pointing out that Simone's confidence in them at the start of this exercise had been somewhere below sea level.

Then she turned around and saw the mountain of dirty dishes that needed to be washed. They'd used practically every single piece of cookware and cutlery in Lisette's well-stocked kitchen to produce the meal, and now Luna was almost in tears at the thought of the cleanup they had ahead of them.

Simone must have noticed her distress. "Why don't you two go home? Ray and I can handle the dishes this time," she said.

"Yeah, get some rest. You deserve it." Ray ate another bite of duck. "What you accomplished? Kind of miraculous."

Luna grinned over at JP, then rounded the kitchen island to wrap Simone in a huge, sweaty hug. "Thank you for helping us with this," she said. "If we win this thing, it's all because of you."

"My pleasure," Simone said, though her words were somewhat muffled in Luna's boobs, given their height difference.

Jean-Pierre offered their saviors a more stoic handshake, and then they were out of the penthouse for the first time in days. Luna clutched her overnight bag in one hand and used the other to shield her eyes from the sun. "I feel like a mole coming to the surface after a lifetime underground," she muttered. Her feet ached, and her knees throbbed, and the less said about her back, the better. The weekend had been a real ordeal. "All I want to do now is—"

"Let's go out tonight," Jean-Pierre said at the same time Luna said, "—sleep for a week."

They stared at each other in silence, the foot traffic weaving around them as they remained rooted to the sidewalk.

"Are you serious?" Luna blurted out. "You want to go out after all that?" Maybe he had picked up more chef-like habits from his parents than he realized; only restaurant people had this kind of stamina.

JP shrugged, hoisting his duffel bag over his shoulder. "I think it's only natural to blow off some steam. We worked hard; we should celebrate."

Luna shook her head. "I mean, if you really want to, go for it. I'll pass, though." Her pajamas and the couch were calling her name. She wanted nothing more than to curl up with some takeout and chill. Fine-dining French cuisine was definitely not meant to be eaten for six straight meals. She craved something light. Maybe tofu. Or a nice green mango salad with grilled shrimp.

Jean-Pierre's face went from open to closed in the blink of an eye. "Are you forgetting who we're supposed to be? If I am seen alone in a nightclub, people may wonder where my beautiful girlfriend is."

Luna groaned. She had totally forgotten about that piece of the puzzle. "Right. Yeah, I can see how that would be bad."

JP frowned. "But if you truly do not want to—"

"No, no." Luna ruffled a hand through her limp hair. "You're right. We haven't, uh, been seen together for a while. Out in public. On the 'Gram. Doing couple things." Her stomach sank. She really didn't feel like going dancing, but this was the job, right? This was what she'd signed up for. She forced a cheery smile onto her face. "Let's go for it."

Jean-Pierre looked like she'd just told him Christmas was coming and Midnight Mass had been replaced with an ice cream social. His whole face was aglow. "Fantastique." He expertly spotted their Uber and waved the driver over. "A quick shower, a bite to eat, and I will take you out on the town."

"Great," Luna said. Her smile, she resolved, would never waver.

It was wavering. Hard.

Luna could tell the place was the douchiest club in all of NoHo, and she hadn't even seen the inside yet. The line outside the door snaked down the sidewalk, corralled by a blue velvet rope. The hopeful patrons were all dressed in various interpretations of Bridge & Tunnel Chic: a lot of exposed skin and too-tight pants. As she and Jean-Pierre walked past the long queue, Luna could hear a girl who didn't look a day over eighteen screech into her phone, "Well, fuck her! Her eyebrows are way too thin."

"Chill place," Luna murmured to JP. She self-consciously tugged at the hem of her stretch lace minidress—black, of course, to match JP's $500 shirt. "I feel like I can really relax with this crowd."

Jean-Pierre didn't seem to be listening. He was too focused on their destination at the front of the line, marked by the tall shape of the bouncer. As they neared the entrance, Luna could see that essentially two lines had formed: the long one, presumably for the plebeians, and a shorter, more informal scattering of people who felt it unnecessary to stand in the long line. The bouncer, a white, bald man sporting an unfortunate goatee, was currently arguing with someone in the latter line. He did not look friendly or accommodating, which was probably part of the job description.

"Are you sure about this?" Luna asked. They had reached the outskirts of the smaller line and were now milling around with the rest of the inmates. "We could just go somewhere else."

"This place has something we need," Jean-Pierre said to her in a quiet undertone. Not that anyone could hear him above the aggressive shouting from the angry wannabe patron. "Cameras."

As if on cue, Luna saw a photographer across the street wearing a many-pocketed vest raise a huge telephoto lens and point it right at them. JP lifted his hand in an insouciant sort of greeting. Flashes went off like fireworks.

Luna tipped her head toward JP with a saccharine smile. If she was going to be papped, she was going to make sure they got her good side, damn it. "Wouldn't they follow us wherever we decided to go?" she hissed through clenched teeth.

"I am told this is one of the better locations for people who wish to be noticed." His gaze flicked over her shoulder, where the flashes were still going off. "Shall I put my arm around you? That might make for a better picture."

"Why not?" Luna took his hand and guided it around her waist to rest on her hip. She snuggled into his side. "We could try a kiss, if you're up for it."

"Perhaps once we're inside," JP said. His eyes landed on her lips—Magenta Dreams, that was the name of her lipstick; designed to get attention—before darting away. "Once we're more comfortable."

The people in line began to notice that the camera was trained on Luna and JP, and murmurs started to grow about who they were and why they were worthy of being photographed. JP must have been banking on that, because he used the momentum to push his way forward to the front of the smaller-line crowd, claiming an audience with the bouncer. The patron who'd been arguing must have sensed he'd lost, because he finally stalked away with a glare at JP.

"I believe we're on the list," JP said to the man at the door. "Jean-Pierre Dominique Gabriel Aubert-Treffle. And guest." He reeled Luna in closer, squeezing his arm around her waist.

She felt some show of affection was in order, so she giggled—ugh—and tipped her head to rest it atop JP's dark curls. Their height difference made it easy. She hoped it looked cute.

The bouncer barely looked at her, just stared down at the clipboard in his hand. "You can go in," he said, pointing a pen in Jean-Pierre's direction. "You can't." The pen stabbed toward Luna.

She frowned and straightened. "Why not?"

"I am permitted a guest, am I not?" JP craned his neck to get a look at the clipboard. "It says right here, oui?" His finger tapped against the entry under his name, which indeed said so.

"A guest, yes," said the bouncer. He cut his eyes at Luna. "Not this guest."

"Why not?" Luna repeated. Her voice got louder. She was on the verge of making a scene, but she didn't care.

The bouncer shrugged. "It's not that kind of club."

In the relative silence that followed, Luna could hear a voice in the long line behind her: "If she wanted to pass, she should have at least worn flats, you know what I'm saying?"

Luna felt the cold fire of adrenaline lighting up through her. She crossed her arms over her stomach and spoke only to Jean-Pierre. The bouncer, she knew, wasn't worth the breath she'd waste. "This place is trash," she said. "Let's just go."

But JP was wearing that stubborn lockjawed look, his eyes burning into the man at the door. "What do you mean?" he demanded. "Explain it to me."

"I don't need to spell it out, man," the bouncer said. "Take it or leave it."

Luna tugged on JP's sleeve. The fabric was so expensive and lush, she could barely feel it. "Seriously. There's a million other places we can go instead."

It was like he wasn't hearing her at all. Like she was invisible. He only had eyes for Danny McDoorman. "You can't treat us like this. Do you have any idea—"

Jean-Pierre's words faded into the static buzz in Luna's head. Or maybe they were just being drowned out by the whispers she could hear from the line behind them. Someone called her something—something really bad, but when she turned to see who'd said it, no one would meet her eye.

Fuck it, she thought. Fuck it directly up the ass. She didn't have to stand here and take this. She was out. Gone. Goodbye, losers, and that included JP, who wasn't fucking listening to her. Even if he could successfully argue their way into this club, why would Luna want to be inside a place like that?

She held her clutch purse under her arm, turned on her very high heel, and walked away.

She didn't even know where she was going, really. She didn't know the area all too well, and it was dark, the street signs unreadable in the flash of passing headlights. The sidewalk was packed with late-night revelers, some of them in huge groups and already drunk, hooting and stumbling their way to the next bar, the next club, the next super-cool and safe (for them) ad venture. Luna crossed the street to avoid them. Her feet hurt so bad, it felt like the straps of her heels were burning into her skin. But she kept walking at a fast clip. She just had to keep moving.

After a few blocks, her surroundings solidified into things she recognized. The throngs of college kids gave way to more relaxed sidewalk bistros with wineglasses upside down on white-cloth tables, waiting for their next customers. Luna glanced at the cross streets. Her addled feet had brought her back to the West Village.

She almost laughed in relief. Even in the midst of a tiny, totally manageable panic attack, she could still find the subway station that would bring her home.

The sidewalk was blocked off on the avenue because of construction, so Luna ducked down a side street, the kind that sometimes snaked through the Village and made you feel like you'd been teleported a few decades or centuries into the past. Her heels click-clacked on the pavement, loud in the relative quiet. Wait, had she even brought her MetroCard with her? She dug around in her purse, trying to locate the elusive slip of yellow plastic.

A hand brushed her bare arm.

She turned, thinking that Jean-Pierre had finally caught up with her. A sarcastic greeting was already on her tongue. *What took you so long, Napoleon?*

But the words died in her mouth.

The guy touching her arm was definitely not Jean-Pierre. Luna had no idea who he was. She stared at his face, trying to figure out if she could place his blue eyes and dishwater-colored hair. Did she know him from the gym? From a one-off Tinder date? She really didn't think so.

"Excuse me?" she said. She hated that it came out as a question.

The man stroked her arm again, staring at where his hand

was touching her skin. He wasn't even looking at her face, wasn't saying anything. And that was creepier than anything Luna could dream up. The tiny hairs on the back of her neck stood on end. It was fight or flight all over again.

This time, she picked fight.

"Oh, you are messing with the wrong bitch tonight," she muttered, reaching into her purse.

Luna wasn't sure if it was against the law to carry the tiny canister of pepper spray within the City of New York, but Mrs. O'Shea hadn't been about to send her only daughter into the wilds of Manhattan without some kind of protection. Luna had been carrying it with her for years. Did pepper spray expire? It might not even work, she thought wildly. Still, maybe the threat of it was enough to get a weirdo chaser to back the fuck off. She brandished it like a badge.

"Get your hands off me." She felt the thrill of satisfaction at seeing the guy's eyes go wide. *That's right, motherfucker.* He pulled away, curling his arm into his chest like she'd snapped his wrist or something. Loser.

Now that there was a little distance between them, Luna was considering the pros and cons of macing this dickhead. Her brain ran through the mental calculus of it all (pro: it would probably be fun; con: he might press charges) when a ball of rage inserted himself unannounced between Luna and the creep who'd been groping at her.

"Laisse-la tranquille, connard!" Jean-Pierre shouted, advancing on the guy with all the power of a five-foot-five Frenchman with a bone to pick. "Get the hell away from her!"

The stranger stumbled back a step with his hands raised and finally spoke: "Hey, I didn't even do anything—"

JP unleashed another round of French curses that Luna couldn't even begin to translate. The Duolingo owl had never prepared her for this.

JP took one more step forward, and the guy turned and bolted, disappearing around the corner, where the lights and sounds of the comedy clubs and dive bars and ice cream shops swallowed him up.

Jean-Pierre turned back to Luna. He was panting like he'd run all the way there, and maybe he had. There were two bright spots of red on his otherwise wan cheeks, and his hair was a tousled mess. "Are you all right?"

Luna still held the can of pepper spray tight in her hand, and for a brief moment, she considered deploying it on a new target. "No, I am not fucking all right!" She shoved the Mace back into her purse before she got too trigger-happy. "What is your problem? I had that handled."

JP looked askance, his head jerking back like he needed more room to take her in. "*My* problem? That man was—! I do not even know what he was doing, but it could not have been good. So you're welcome."

"I'm not about to thank you," Luna snapped. "I didn't need you to swoop in like some white knight to save me. I was saving myself! I was staying sexy!"

Jean-Pierre looked up at the sky and put his hands on his hips. Like he was the one who deserved to be pissed. "There is no need to get hysterical."

Luna's mouth dropped open. "*I'm* being hysterical?" She pointed in the vague direction of NoHo. "You're the one who just had to swing your dick around the second you couldn't get what you want! Do you have any idea how *humiliating* that was?"

"I was trying to fix that," Jean-Pierre said, staring hard at her. "If you hadn't left in such a rush, they would have let us in."

"I didn't want to be let in! I wanted to go home and eat chips."

His face fell from anger to disillusionment; it was all in the crinkle of his brow. "How can you be okay with being turned away like that? It's not right."

"So you're going to fight for something I don't even want?" Luna shot back. "Wake up, JP! It's a shitty game that they've tricked you into playing, and the only prize is some dickhead bouncer patting you on the head and saying, 'You're a real boy.'"

She didn't hear how cruel her mocking tone sounded until it was echoing through the tiny street all around them, ringing in her ears. Somewhere in the back of her head, Luna thought maybe she should apologize, but her anger still overrode everything else. She swallowed and stood her ground. No take-backs.

Jean-Pierre, for his part, just looked at her, his nostrils flaring. His jaw worked like he wanted to say something but couldn't find the words in English.

Luna couldn't help herself. She loved having the last word. She leaned in a little, cocking her head. "Have fun pretending to be normal. I'm going home."

And she stalked off down the dimly lit lane, not even pausing when Jean-Pierre called after her.

Chapter 17

Luna pulled her hair into her third messy bun of the day. Somehow, it kept slipping loose and making her look like some kind of mad scientist. Not that a mad scientist would be out of place on location in the brewery studio, but Luna wanted to at least project a sense of calm and normalcy in that tornado of an environment. That was what she'd been doing the last week she'd been employed, anyway. She'd managed to wrangle Delilah's overclocked schedule and delegate the tasks her fearless leader hadn't had time to delegate herself. Now Luna was the one who felt like she could use an extra set of hands.

The thing was, her workday hadn't actually been that bad. Sure, there had been a few hiccups—cancellations and getting bumped were a part of life as an assistant—but it wasn't anything Luna couldn't handle. No, the real reason she was off her game was all the bad feelings still churning in her stomach from the night before. After their screaming match in the middle of the street—nothing like giving the tourists something to tweet about—Luna had not seen or spoken to JP. She wasn't even sure if he had come back to the apartment last night. He certainly hadn't been on the couch when Luna had left for work in the morning.

The whole ugly episode had left her frazzled and distracted. Their fight remained unaddressed. She didn't know what she would say to Jean-Pierre when they crossed paths again. Would he call the whole fake-dating thing off? It wouldn't be the end of the world for Luna, financially, now that she had this new job. But it didn't feel right, letting it end this way. Besides, she was still pissed at how he'd acted, and in the hours since their argument, she had come up with at least five or six new ways to tell him so.

"Luna, thank you; just what I needed," Delilah said, taking the cup of steaming tea from her hands.

Luna blinked. Apparently she had gotten Delilah her usual afternoon herbal tea and delivered it to her desk on autopilot. Damn, she really needed to focus. Or have a nap in the storeroom. The huge bags of flour were surprisingly comfortable. She had certainly indulged during lunch breaks.

"No problem, boss." Luna stuck her hands in the back pockets of her jeans and tried to look like someone who was not losing sleep over whether their fake boyfriend was going to break up with them or not.

Delilah sipped deeply, then said, "I have a favor to ask. You're not busy for the next twenty minutes, are you?" She looked up from her seat in her office chair, newly purchased by Luna. The old one had offered zero lumbar support.

"Uh, no, I don't think so."

"Great. One of the contestants is here early for the intake interview. Normally I'd handle it myself, but I've got a call with Lisette in five. Think you can do it for me?"

Luna hesitated. On any other day, she'd be jumping at the chance to help with actual producer-y stuff. Today, though, she wasn't sure she was up for the job. "I wouldn't know what to say," she pointed out. "I haven't even sat in on any of the intakes yet."

"It's really simple. I have a list of questions already prepared." Delilah handed over the very official-looking clipboard.

"You don't have to stick to them, though. Just get the contestant talking so the camera can get some nice B-roll. As long as the personality jumps out, we're golden."

"Okay." Luna took the clipboard. "I can do that." Probably. Maybe.

"Awesome, thank you." Delilah sighed. "I'd ask Simone to do it, but she wants to finalize the challenge timeline even if she has to stay all night to get it done. That girl works too hard."

Luna wisely held her tongue about pots and kettles who had been, up until a few days ago, working their own fingers to the bone.

Instead, she walked in a complete daze to the tiny room they used for these interviews, a literal converted closet that had probably housed car parts or whatever in a past life. Now it held a brightly colored shag throw rug and two clear plastic chairs that attempted to make the space as un-claustrophobic as possible. Luna poked her head in and saw her contestant already waiting in one of the chairs, fiddling with a mobile game.

"Hi there!" She turned on her cheeriest voice as she shut the door behind her. "I'm Luna; I'm going to be chatting a bit with you today."

"My name's Cam. Uh, he/they pronouns," Cam said, rising from his chair and extending their hand for a shake.

"Cool. She/her," Luna said, taking the offered hand.

Cam sat back down with a grimace. "Would you mind, though, if I just used he/him on the show? I'm not sure—you know." He flicked his gaze at the camera mounted behind the lights and reflectors in the corner of the tiny room. "If I'm ready for . . . all that."

"Oh my god, of course that's fine." Luna took her own seat and fumbled with uncapping a pen. "No one expects you to do anything you're not comfortable with."

"Really?" Cam blew out a long exhale. "Okay. That's a relief. I wanted to tell you because, you know"—they gestured to Luna's denim jacket, which confused her for a second before she remembered the trans pride pin that sat on the collar alongside a button with the Pisces symbol—"I figured you would get it, but I wasn't sure if you'd *get* it, you know? I don't like the idea of drawing attention."

"Hey, listen." Luna leaned forward and smiled gently. "This is just a TV show. We're baking cakes here. There is no reason for you to share that part of yourself unless you want to. You don't owe it to anyone, okay?"

"Yeah, but." Cam made a face. "I know Ray is—like, *out* out! I feel like a fraud, kind of."

"Trust me: Ray is the last person on earth who would judge you for this. There are a million valid reasons why someone might—" Luna stopped, her tongue going heavy in her mouth.

Everything she was saying to Cam was true. So why hadn't she been ready to extend the same kind of grace to Jean-Pierre? Was his stance on trying to fit in really so different?

Luna frowned down at her clipboard. Maybe that was why she'd felt so shitty about their argument: because deep down she knew, even if she didn't agree with JP's desire to pass, she shouldn't judge him for wanting to.

Ugh. She hated being even technically wrong.

Cam stared at her. "Someone might . . . ?" he asked in a leading way.

"Oh! Make a decision like that." She tried to stay bright and cheery. She was supposed to be putting a contestant at ease, not using this as her own private confessional. "So no need to worry. Let's use he/him on set for now, and if you ever want to change it up, just let me or one of the production assistants know."

Cam blew a huge breath out of their mouth. "Awesome. Geez. That's a load off my mind."

Luna's face was going to snap if she smiled any harder. "Okay! So." She pretended to write something on her clipboard. "Tell me about how you started baking."

While Cam detailed the very funny and interesting story of his first attempt at making cookies as a kid, Luna found her thoughts drifting back to Jean-Pierre. She wasn't a fan of how he'd ignored her when she'd made her feelings about leaving the nightclub abundantly clear, but she saw now where he was coming from. He wanted to be treated the way cis people were; he expected to be given the same level of respect. That wasn't crazy. It was normal. She couldn't really hold that against the guy.

Well, she could, but she didn't plan to. In fact, she planned on talking all this through with JP like adults. Later. After this endless workday was over.

"And that's how I ended up baking my ex's wedding cake," Cam said.

Luna shook herself out of her Jean-Pierre-induced stupor. "I'm sorry, can you repeat that?"

Definitely endless.

That evening, after surviving the workday with minimal damage, Luna walked into her apartment to find a party already in progress. The hollering voices died down as she stood to survey the sight in her living room. Her gaze tracked from Jean-Pierre to Ray to her other new coworker, Petey. Not the atmosphere she'd expected when she came home, hat in proverbial hand.

"Why are you all shirtless?" she asked.

All three glanced down at their bare torsos as if to confirm that their shirts were, in fact, missing. JP crossed his arms over his bare chest to obscure the patch of dark hair between his pecs. Petey poked his exposed belly while Ray gave an expansive shrug, their incision scars pulling into straight lines.

"It got hot," they said.

Petey picked up a capped brown bottle from among the crowd of dead soldiers and offered it in Luna's direction. "Want a beer? We were sampling Ray's latest."

"It is very strong," Jean-Pierre said. A slight slur made his accent more pronounced than usual. He snagged the bottle from Petey and sauntered into Luna's orbit. "I do not drink beer, but I drank this beer, and I liked it very much. You must try." He pressed the bottle into her hands.

Luna made no move to uncap it. No one had thought to give her a bottle opener. "I didn't know you folks were all friends. So you're just—hanging? Like, a bro thing? Sorry—gender-neutral pal thing?" She directed this last bit to Ray, who made a so-so gesture with their hand.

"For the purposes of tonight's hang, I will allow bro-y language," they said.

"I was shown a baseball game." JP leaned in close and whispered like he was sharing a secret. "Your Mets, they are very bad. They were murdered by Philly."

"We're used to it," Petey said, throwing himself down on a pile of throw pillows and reaching for his beer. Ray, meanwhile, dug through some blankets for their shirt.

"The Phillies are my team, ostensibly," Luna said, "so I guess I should be happy. I don't really follow sports, though." Unless the players were cute.

"Still, my condolences." JP slouched back to the sofa, where he sprawled like a true libertine, one leg hooked over the couch's arm. Luna couldn't help but notice his rangy build, set off by the light dusting of chest hair and the even darker line running from his navel down into his low-slung jeans.

She forced herself to look away and instead took stock of the living room. Besides the empty bottles and the fact that the throw pillows had been thrown in random directions, nothing was really out of place. Maybe they'd had a tamer night than she'd initially feared. Then her eyes landed on the sleek laptop glowing on the coffee table. "Were you working on something?"

"Ah, non." JP reached across the short distance to the laptop and clapped it shut before Luna could get a good look at the screen. "We were just—"

"Did you know Jean-Pierre is, like, *really* fucking loaded?" Petey said. His Queens accent was making itself known as well, all nasal and aggressive on the consonants. "I mean, you must know; you're dating him, kind of. Like, fakely."

Luna's eyes flew wide. "JP! You told him? We're supposed to be keeping that on the down-low."

"But Peter is a friend." As soon as Jean-Pierre said it, he sat up and looked over at Petey in shock. Like he wasn't sure if he'd been mistaken. "A friend, yes?"

"Fuckin' A, man." Petey lifted his bottle in JP's direction before taking another swig.

The sigh of relief from Jean-Pierre was audible. "You see? He will not tell anyone."

"If I have one more of those stouts Ray made, I won't fucking remember it anyway," Petey added.

"How many is that for you, bud?" Ray asked, gingerly taking a half-empty bottle from Petey's lax grip.

"Like, three? I can't be this gone after three beers. Oh my god, am I getting old?"

Ray hummed. "Well, yeah, we all are. But the imperial stout is also, like, fifteen percent ABV, so—"

"Ah, fuck me," Petey moaned. He caught sight of Luna and his face fell. "Hey, I might not make it home tonight if that's okay."

She gave a cheery grin. "That seems completely reasonable."

"Thank you for your understanding," Petey said, and then promptly fell asleep right where he sat, his snores picture-frame-rattling loud.

Luna watched Petey sleep for a moment. "Cool." She turned to JP, who was acting squirrely, stowing the laptop away under a side table. Like Luna was going to miss that. "So what were you all doing with JP's buckets of money? An online shopping spree or something?"

Jean-Pierre turned a faint shade of pink. "Of course not. We—"

"JP got to play Santa Claus!" Ray interrupted. They finally found their T-shirt and shrugged it on. "Like, trans Santa Claus. It was so awesome."

Luna pursed her lips. "Sorry, what?"

"Here, I'll show you. Excuse my reach." Ray's long arm easily caught up with the laptop even as Jean-Pierre attempted to kick it farther under the table. They plopped down on the couch next to him and opened the computer on their knees. "It started as a joke, right? I was like, 'Bro, with that much money, you could pay for a million top surgeries.' And Petey was like, 'Bro?' And JP was like, 'Bro!'"

"I did not—I was not like that," JP told Luna with a serious jut of his jaw. "'Bro' is not a thing I say."

Luna ignored him and squeezed herself between the two on the sofa so she could see the screen. Her eyes nearly bugged out of her head when she realized what she was looking at. "Oh my god."

Ray was clicking through tabs as fast as they could—which, granted, was not so fast; apparently they weren't used to using a trackpad—so that Luna could see page after page of online fundraisers, all of them for trans folks crowdsourcing for their surgeries or therapy bills or voice lessons or the fees it took to legally change their names and birth certificates.

All of them had met their goal.

"Amazing, right?" Ray said.

Luna turned to Jean-Pierre, who was still shirtless and groping around in the couch cushions, probably looking for said shirt. "JP, you donated money to all these people?"

"Most of them needed just a little bit to get to their goal," he muttered, trying to reach under the cushion he was sitting on. "It is nothing."

Ray snorted. "Buddy, you single-handedly funded, like, twenty transitions tonight. That ain't nothing."

"How much did you spend?" Luna asked. It was impossible to suppress the note of stunned awe in her voice.

"I really did not keep track—"

"Just over ten thousand," Ray said immediately.

"Ten—? Holy shit!" She smacked Jean-Pierre on his arm out of sheer joy. "That's sainthood-level stuff right there!"

To his credit, Jean-Pierre didn't even flinch from the smack. "You are not disappointed?" He retrieved a black shawl collar sweater from under Luna's ass, tugging it free and pulling it over his head.

She frowned. "What? Why would I be disappointed?"

"Because I—" JP licked his lips and looked away. "It was just a few people I helped. There are so many others. Hundreds, thousands. I have solved nothing, have I? As Ray says, I am only playing Santa."

Luna stared at him, then turned her head to cast a pleading look in Ray's direction. She didn't know what to say, but Ray was the kind of person who could get someone out of even the deepest funk. They had to be, what with dating Simone. Ray caught her eye and nodded.

"Hey, bud." They reached across Luna's lap and patted JP on his hunched shoulder. "No one's expecting you to—what?—fix the American healthcare system tonight. You don't even *go* here."

"No, but that doesn't mean I shouldn't support my brothers and sisters and— What is the nonbinary word?"

"Siblings," Ray said.

"My siblings. Wherever they are, I must help them, no?" He looked confused. "What is the point of me otherwise?"

"But it's not all on you." Ray's hand slipped away. "It would be wild to put that on one person."

"Ray's right," Luna chimed in. She slid her hand onto Jean-Pierre's thigh, which was bouncing up and down with nervous energy. It stopped at her touch. "And maybe twenty people out of thousands is a drop in the bucket, but for those twenty people, it mattered. You can't even imagine what a few grand would have meant to me when I was first looking into surgery. That's not nothing."

Jean-Pierre looked at her, his eyes a deep, sad darkness. "The only thing I have is money," he said. "I have nothing else to offer, do I?"

Luna sucked in a sharp breath. "What are you talking about? Like, as a human being? You have tons to offer."

"Like what?" He slumped back against the couch cushions, staring into space.

"Like—" Luna looked to Ray for help, but they just held their hands up as if to say *All yours, O'Shea*. Supremely unfair. She turned back to JP. "You make a great cup of coffee, for instance."

Jean-Pierre gave a derisive scoff.

"I'm serious. I don't even drink coffee, but yours is good. And you're funny—in a kind of sad goth way, but hey, it makes me laugh." She nudged him in the side, hoping to get at least half a smirk out of him, but none was forthcoming. He didn't even meet her eyes. "You're good with kids," she rambled on. "My mom is completely charmed by you. You've got great hair. And you can cook now."

Jean-Pierre finally deigned to glance at her. "You really like my hair?"

Luna nodded. "Smells good, too," she said, and then, realizing how weird it was to say something like that, added, "I smell everyone's hair, so I know what I'm talking about."

Yeah. Like that was better. JP scrunched his nose at her, but for once was too polite to point out how bizarre she was acting.

"Okay! Well, I should call it a night." Ray slapped their palms on top of their thighs and rose swiftly from the couch, the cushions shifting so that Luna tumbled against JP's side. "You kids have fun. Try not to wake up Petey, although"—they contemplated his snoring form in the pillow pile—"he could probably sleep through a tornado. God, his back is going to be killing him tomorrow if he stays like that. Help me put him on the couch?" Ray bent down to grab hold of Petey under his arms.

"Uh, Petey's staying on the couch?" Luna watched helplessly as JP got up and took Petey's ankles.

"On three, capisce?" Ray said to Jean-Pierre.

"Un, deux—" The two of them hoisted Petey off the ground. Luna scrambled to get off the sofa so they could deposit the sleeping director into its warm embrace. "It's just that JP has been staying on the couch."

"I will use Simone's bedroom, I suppose," he said, his voice even and light as he arranged Petey's arm so it wasn't hanging off the edge of the cushion.

"No, you won't," Ray said. "Not unless everyone involved is a lot more chill than I gave them credit for." At Luna and JP's questioning stares, they said, "Simone and I are sleeping there tonight. She's in there right now." They flapped a hand toward the hallway.

"She's—? Simone's home? I thought she was pulling an all-nighter." Luna's heart sank. If Simone's bedroom was occupied and so was the sofa, that meant—

"Nah, I told her she isn't allowed to burn out. She's been working too hard lately. So I brought her home, put her to bed early, told her I'd make pancakes in the morning."

As if summoned by the mere mention of breakfast food, Simone's bedroom door opened, and Simone herself shuffled into the living room wrapped in a fluffy bathrobe. She looked like she was still half-asleep, her eyes squinched shut. "What are you all doing out here?" she croaked. She looked down at the sofa. "And why is Petey half-naked?"

"Long story. Go back to bed, babe. I'll be there in a second." As Simone complied with a grumble, Ray flashed Luna a smile and, for no reason Luna could fathom, a thumbs-up. "Have a good night, you two."

They disappeared with Simone into her bedroom, the door shutting behind them with a soft click.

Luna shared a look with Jean-Pierre, who looked even paler than before, if such a thing were possible. He really needed to get a little sun; he was a poster boy for vitamin D deficiency. "I guess we're spending the night together. Again."

"I guess so," JP said. "After you." He waved Luna down the hall.

They ended up once again side by side in Luna's bed, though this time there was as much space between them as was humanly possible. Luna lay flat on her back with her hands folded on her tummy. She didn't know what to say, or if she should say anything. Maybe Jean-Pierre had totally forgotten about the argument they'd had last night? A few of Ray's stouts could do that; she knew from experience.

She hadn't even teased JP about tonight's underwear color— a shocking hot pink that he wore pretty well. This was all so awkward.

"Your lady friends were right," Jean-Pierre said into the silent dark.

Luna's heart stopped. Right about what, exactly? Had he been reading her group chats? Because Willow and Aisha had been teasing her mercilessly about how her fake relationship had lasted longer than most of her real ones.

"Having a friend like Ray is—it is necessary," he said. "A friend who is not cis."

A breath left Luna's body, along with a good chunk of her soul. "Yeah, I'm glad you two got a chance to bond."

"I, uh, told them about what happened last night." The click of JP's throat as he swallowed was loud in the room. "They are of the opinion that I was an asshole."

Luna couldn't help smiling a little at the ceiling. "Well, so was I. I guess that makes two of us."

He took a deep breath. "I'm sorry. I should have respected your wishes when you said you wanted to leave."

"I shouldn't have shamed you about wanting to be treated like a human being," Luna said. "And I could have been a little less of a bitch when you scared off that creep. I was just so mad."

"As was I."

"For valid reasons."

The mattress shifted as Jean-Pierre rolled onto his side. Luna turned her head to see him looking at her with his head propped on his hand. "This is becoming *habituel*, no? We disagree, we argue, and later we both try to say we were in the wrong and the other is right."

"Yeah." Luna sighed. "We're not great at this." She looked back up at the ceiling. "Good thing we're not really dating, I guess."

JP was silent for a moment. "Yes," he finally said. "Good thing." There was an interminable pause in which Luna could swear she heard her own heartbeat thundering, and then—then she felt the brush of Jean-Pierre's hand against hers under the sheets. "Clair," he whispered, "I know this is not real. I know. But tonight, do you think I could—?" He shook his head like he didn't know where to find the words. "Hold you?"

Luna turned her head so fast, she could've gotten whiplash. Her eyes were huge, she was sure, catching all the light that filtered through the curtains. "Exactly how drunk are you right now?"

"*Je ne suis pas ivre*," JP mumbled.

I am not—something. Not drunk. Luna squinted at him. "What was that?"

"I'm not sure," he said, louder. What a fucking liar. "I do not remember how many I had." He retracted his hand and flopped onto his belly, shoving his face in the pillow.

Luna winced. This was supposed to be a truce, not another battle of wills. Plus JP was not drunk, albeit unwilling to admit it. Would it hurt to play along for a bit if it soothed his ego? "Just didn't peg you as a cuddly drunk," she said. "It's cool if you are."

Slowly, a corner of the pillow lowered and JP peeked over the stark white case of it. "It is?"

This was probably more selfish than anything, but Luna had been jonesing for a good snuggle. And she knew from early on in their acquaintance that JP could snuggle like a champ. Also, what better way to cement their little apology exchange? If it gave Jean-Pierre, the prince of touch starvation, some small measure of comfort, what was the harm?

Luna flipped over on her side, facing the door. "Come on." She waggled her hand over her shoulder. "I'll be the little spoon."

For a moment, nothing happened, and Luna was convinced she was going to look like a huge dork when Jean-Pierre laughed her off. But then—oh—he was slotting himself up against her back, and his knees were curling into the backs of her knees, and they were every inch of them pressed together.

His nose—colder than she'd thought a tipsy person's could be—pressed against the nape of her neck. When he spoke, she felt it more than heard it as it vibrated across her skin. "This is all right?"

She didn't trust her voice not to do something embarrassing like crack or squeak, so she nodded instead of speaking. His hand hovered above her hip like it wasn't sure where to go, so she laced their fingers together and brought their joined hands to rest against her ribs. He had nice hands. They fit well in hers.

Well, that was a dangerous thing to think.

This was nothing, Luna told herself firmly. Just two tired people who needed a tiny bit of physical closeness for whatever reason. Did everything have to be analyzed to death? JP was right: some things just *were*.

She brushed her thumb back and forth over Jean-Pierre's knuckles. Every breath he took, every small shift of him, was amplified times a thousand. He sighed against her neck, soft and shuddery. It made her eyelashes flutter in sympathy.

If placed on the stand in a court of law, Luna still wouldn't be able to say with any conviction exactly what happened next. Someone moved. Who? She had no idea. Their hands definitely unclasped. It was entirely possible Luna pressed her hips back into him first, but even so, it was a shock to feel JP's palm cupping her breast.

She inhaled sharply.

His lips were on her neck. "Luna—?" he said. It was a question, and an obvious one.

Luna's hand tightened atop his. This time, he was the one to suck in his breath.

This was a bad idea.

She didn't care.

She rolled over to face JP and kissed him just as he was about to say something else. He made a shocked noise that Luna smiled into as their mouths slid together. She liked keeping him on his toes. She might keep him in other positions, too, if she could. That thought startled a laugh out of her, the puff of it landing along Jean-Pierre's jaw.

"Is this funny?" he murmured as he kissed her again. His lips were pulled into a smile, so he couldn't be that offended. He tasted like the beer he'd been drinking, which actually wasn't so bad. Artisanal and malty.

Luna shook her head. "No, no. Don't mind me." Her hands trailed over his corded arms. "So this is cool? A fun little—interlude."

"Interlude." Jean-Pierre said with the blankest of stares.

"Yeah, like, just messing around?" Did that translate? Luna tried to think of a better way to phrase it. "A one-time thing. Nothing serious." There was no need to pressure the guy, especially since it had been a while for him.

"Ah." She couldn't see his face too well in the dark, but his voice sounded—strange. "Of course, of course. One time, hein?"

Luna was privately pleased with herself for mentally spelling the French version of "Eh?" when JP said it. She liked picturing all the silent letters pouring out of his mouth. She bit at his bottom lip, making him groan. "Now you're getting it." She snaked a hand between their bodies, plucking at the hem of his shirt.

Jean-Pierre answered the silent question by fumbling his shirt over his head. It was getting warm under the sheets, so

Luna got rid of her camisole, too, flinging it at the foot of the bed. She pressed against him while they kissed, sliding her fingertips along the front of his briefs. The fabric was almost buttery, it was so fancy. She found the waistband and ran her fingers along it, another teasing question.

His hand closed over her roaming one, pinning it to his hip. "You know I—?" He bobbed his head, his hair brushing along her face. "My surgery, it is, ah, extensive?"

"I kind of figured." The graft scar on his arm was a big clue. Clearly he could afford a complete phalloplasty.

Jean-Pierre's mouth traveled down her neck, kissing along her skin. "I should probably tell you how it . . . works." He said that last word into the curve of her collarbone.

"Sure," Luna said as she tilted her head to give him better access. Willing student, that was the vibe she was going for. "Give me the rundown."

"There will be no—" JP pulled away to shove his face into the pillow with a groan. "You see? This is why I haven't been with anyone in so long. So fucking—ugh." The words were muffled almost into silence.

She bent to nibble at his ear until he squawked and shot up. She grinned to herself, pleased to have flushed him out of his hiding place. It was better like this, the both of them lying on their sides and facing each other. "Who cares if it's awkward? Sex usually is." Especially for folks like them. "We may as well try to have fun with it. Come on, tell me. There will be no . . . ?"

Jean-Pierre gestured to his pink briefs with an expansive, whooshing motion. "Any—fluid. At the finish." He waggled his head. "If we get that far."

"So no ejaculation." That was kind of handy. No muss, no fuss. Not to mention—how should she explain it to him? He seemed so nervous, and so was she, if only because this wasn't how she had expected her evening to go. Luna brought their joined hands down between them, guiding JP to touch her over her flimsy sleep shorts. It was way faster than explaining in words. "Same with me. See?"

"Oh!" Jean-Pierre sounded genuinely surprised. His mouth kept flapping open and closed. "Oh, I— Oh."

Luna tried not to laugh. "You didn't realize I'd had bottom surgery? That whole thing at brunch? How I had to drop out of college? You didn't put that together?"

"I am not a detective!" He huffed. "And I do not care either way."

That was—that was kind of sweet. She leaned in, their noses brushing. "A true gentleman."

"I try," he whispered.

He kissed her, but missed her mouth, getting her chin instead. With a soft curse, he reoriented himself, his lips finding hers. His careful hand slipped her shorts along with her panties down her thighs. Once those last bits of clothing were gone, Luna was naked alongside Jean-Pierre. He was as hot as an oven, with the steely look to match.

Her fingertips fell to the waistband of his fancy underwear once again. "Maybe we should get rid of these, too?"

He pulled down his briefs so quickly, Luna had to laugh. His own self-effacing chuckle joined in. "I should be more cool, yes?" He kicked his underwear free of his ankles under the sheet.

"Nah, it's better like this." Luna was sick of cool guys, she decided. Eager nerds from here on out. Especially if—oh, especially if they touched her like he was now. Confident, like he was finally getting over whatever nerves had plagued him before. Her hands grasped at his shoulders for stability as they rocked together. He stuck his fingers into his own mouth, getting them wet before reaching down to touch her again.

"Good?" She could hear the self-satisfied smile on his face as he pressed his thumb to just the right spot. Her hiss of pleasure got swallowed in his kiss.

Hard work deserved a reward. She slipped a hand between

them. He was soft, the shape of him a pleasant weight in the curl of her fingers.

"It has to be turned on," he said breathlessly, still touching her. "There is a—" He hesitated. "A mechanism. But we don't have to—"

"You have a power button?" She didn't try to hide her delight. She was practically bouncing on the bed. "Can you show me?"

"You are so very strange," he said. He sounded faintly impressed. "Whenever I think you cannot possibly get any stranger, you do."

"Whatever. You like it." She kissed his stubbled chin. "Show me."

With a put-upon sigh—drama king—he took her hand once more and guided it to cup one of his balls. "There," he said, clipped. "You squeeze. *Gently*."

She hadn't quite realized until that moment how much trust this must take on JP's part. She was holding him—a very tender, vulnerable part of him—in the palm of her hand. Her fingers tightened just the slightest bit until she could feel something give beneath his skin. "Whoa." She dropped a quick kiss to his hunched shoulder. "Is that good?"

"A few more times," he said, his voice tight and struggling to get out.

"It doesn't hurt?"

"No—just the opposite."

Luna stared down in the shadowy space between them, watching her careful progress. She had made plenty of people hard before, but this was the first time she'd done it so literally. His cock filled with each delicate squeeze until it was standing firm against his belly.

"Sorry, I don't want to make it weird," she breathed, "but this is really cool. Like, cyborg-level cool. Damn, I love science." She moved her hand to his shaft, giving it an experimental tug, swiping her thumb over his pink cockhead.

"I am feeling very appreciative toward science myself right

now," Jean-Pierre said, still straining to speak. His eyes were screwed shut, lashes a black smudge on his cheeks.

He was really gorgeous. Luna realized he probably hadn't been informed of that, not recently, and she decided it was high time he heard it. "You look so hot right now."

His eyes opened into dark slits. "Do I?" He tipped his head forward to kiss Luna's ear. There was barely enough space in the warmth between them to fit their roving hands. "And you—" His breath sighed out against her cheek. "Oh, look at you." His words came out all shaky, like he was holding on through an earthquake.

"Okay, don't take this the wrong way, because if the answer is yes then I'm going to be insufferably pleased with myself," Luna said, "but are you already close?"

"I told you, it has been a *very* long time."

"I *said* don't take this the wrong way."

"What way am I supposed to be taking it?" He batted her hand away from his dick. "Stop that before I finish."

"Geez, fine, take all my toys," Luna muttered. "If you want this to go in a penetrative direction, there's lube in the— Oh! Okay." She reshuffled on the mattress, making space for JP as he dove under the sheets. "That's cool, too; we can do that instead."

"This, I am already an expert at," he said from beneath the duvet. His hands slipped under her thighs and propped them up on his bare shoulders. "May I?" His breath was hot against her skin.

"Yeah, I'm going to give a resounding yes to that, personally. I mean, if you're an expert and all—oh, *fuck*." She clapped a hand over her mouth. Any louder and Ray or Simone might come to investigate, which was the literal last thing they needed.

JP's tangle of black curls poked out from the bedsheets. His grin was wide and wet. "Any further jokes you would like to make? Or shall I continue?"

"Who's joking? Get back to work." She put a hand on the top of his head and shoved.

She didn't have to shove very hard. He went willingly and with a self-satisfied laugh, disappearing under the sheet.

Luna stared up at the ceiling, biting her lip while Jean-Pierre licked into her very center. He took his time, like there was no rush at all to drive Luna out of her mind. Maybe being locked away in a girls' boarding school for the entirety of his teenage years had given JP skills heretofore unseen in an ordinary man. She reached down and threaded her fingers through his hair with a groan. Okay, new rule: no cool guys, and no ordinary ones either. They were never half this enthusiastic.

He took hold of her hips and pulled her forcefully against his face. Luna could feel how wet he was getting her, his spit running down his chin. With her legs up over his shoulders, she was bared completely to him, but oddly she didn't feel vulnerable. In fact, with her strong legs cradling his head, she felt pretty powerful. She hooked a calf over the back of his neck and listened to his answering moan as he rocked even further into her.

Jean-Pierre sat up on his knees, and Luna gasped as her hips were lifted higher in the air. The bedsheets fell away and she saw, in the dim light, that JP was stroking himself with an urgency that made Luna's mouth water. And the noises he was making against her—it was enough to make her grab a pillow and hold it tight over the lower half of her face.

She wasn't *not* going to scream, so that was the best she could do.

That perfect lightning feeling lit her up from the tips of her flexed toes to the arch in her back. Jean-Pierre did not let up, not while she muffled her sounds into his pillow, not while she jerked and shuddered in the aftershocks against his tongue, not until he, too, came with a bitten-off gasp, pressing his face into the damp skin of Luna's thigh.

Their breathing was loud in the quiet dark, open-mouthed and chest-heaving. Luna dragged the pillow away from her face. The pillowcase looked soggy where she had bitten it, but she couldn't be bothered to worry. It was all she could do to starfish on the mattress and sink into the embrace of residual pleasure.

Jean-Pierre eventually dragged himself back up the bed to flop at Luna's side. He did not say anything, just breathed hard and long and, once in a while, pressed his face to Luna's shoulder. Their breathing was slow to return to normal, but normal was overrated anyway.

"Well," Luna said on a gusty sigh, "I guess we answered that question."

He twirled a strand of her purple hair around his fingers. "What question?"

She turned and smiled at him. "You *do* have something other than money to offer." He found a pillow squashed between them and weakly batted her in the face with it. Luna considered retaliating, but she curled up against Jean-Pierre's firm, sweaty chest instead. Squishing him was the best revenge. Annoyingly, he didn't complain, just kept playing with her hair, smoothing it strand by strand behind her ear.

"Shall we dedicate ourselves to practice tomorrow evening?" he asked. "We should try cooking the menu once or twice more before we leave for Paris."

Oh, right. The test. Paris. Luna had managed to put all that from her mind if only for a little while. She wished she could extend that vacation a tad longer, but duty called. "Yeah, good idea." She was so tired all of a sudden. Like she wouldn't be able to move from that spot, not even for $600,000. "Your soup is still pretty bad," she said, already halfway to dreamland.

She fell asleep to the sound of his laughter, stifled behind his lips.

Chapter 18

Luna threw another pair of shoes into her already over-flowing suitcase. "Mom, I'm a grown woman. Of course I remembered to pack my meds," she said into the phone tucked between her shoulder and her ear. She grabbed her prescription bottles of antidepressants and anxiety pills from their usual place on her bedside table—where she had very much forgotten about them—and dumped them into her carry-on.

"Just making sure!" her mother said on the other end of the line. "I know you're responsible; I can't help but worry."

"Well, no need." The lie was easy. She was getting used to it, she supposed. "JP is taking care of all the travel details, and it's going to be a fun trip."

Her mom squealed so loudly Luna had to pull the phone away from her ear and hold it at arm's length. "All the gossip blogs are talking about this culinary test you're doing! They say if you two win, Jean-Pierre inherits a ton of moola?"

Luna stifled a groan, trying to keep the sarcasm out of her voice. "Yes, but what's really important to him is his family's respect, not further material wealth." She threw her handwritten pack of flash cards into her suitcase with more force than necessary. With the culinary test only three days away, she figured she should use every spare minute to study cooking times and protein temps. Their last two practice sessions had been successful but slightly truncated due to Luna's tiny apartment kitchen, and she didn't want to rest on any laurels.

"Material wealth isn't a bad perk, though," her mom chirped. "I can't wait to hear how it turns out. Call me as soon as you finish, okay? I know you're going to knock it out of the park." Her voice dropped to a whisper. "And I'm sure Chef Henri is going to love you once he gets to know you. A good Catholic girl like you, what's not to love?"

Luna rolled her eyes. "Fingers crossed," she said, trying to sound bright and chipper. She felt more like a wrung-out dishrag. After their handsy encounter a few nights back, she and Jean-Pierre had barely had a moment to themselves. Luna's new job was keeping her busy, and although Delilah was the chillest boss in history for allowing her to take a long weekend so early in her tenure as assistant, there simply hadn't been time to talk to JP about anything other than travel logistics and the culinary test. Which was fine. Everything was *fine*.

Luna put a hand on her chest, right over her rabbiting heart. She was just on edge because she hadn't been to the gym or done yoga or any of her usual self-care stuff in a while. Once this Paris trip was over, she'd have some breathing room. Just a few more days.

Holy shit, she had only a few more days.

"Honey?" her mom said through the phone. She sounded worried, like she'd been repeating herself for some time.

"Sorry, Mom, I kind of spaced out for a second. What did you say?"

"I said give JP my love."

"Yes! Will do." She tossed a few random hair ties and clips into the suitcase on top of the pile of clothes.

"And whatever happens"—she could hear her mom's sweet smile over the line—"I am so proud of you."

Luna's hand tightened around the phone. *Wait until you hear how I had to break up with my super-real boyfriend when I get back from Europe.* "Thanks, Mom. I'll text you when we land."

"Clair?" Jean-Pierre's tousled head popped into her bedroom. "The car is downstairs. Are you ready?"

"Yeah, one second." She turned back to the phone. "That's my ride. Love you."

"Be good!" her mom said. "Have a blast!"

Luna hung up feeling sick to her stomach. She stared down at the mess of her overstuffed suitcase, then looked up at JP. "I'll sit on it if you zip it shut."

The airport, of course, did nothing to stop her feelings of dread.

Luna frowned as they joined the freakishly short security line for rich people, which was apparently a thing. Instead of her having a good half hour or more to psych herself up, it looked like she was going to reach the security checkpoint in about ten minutes. The body scanners loomed ahead of her like terrible obelisks out of some sci-fi movie with a misunderstood moral. Soon she'd be walking right into one of them. Her whole body froze up at the thought.

At her side, JP stopped rummaging in his carry-on for his passport. He slipped his huge cup-style headphones off his ears and gave her a look. "What's the matter?"

Luna shook her head. "Nothing. I'm fine." She could feel her face going all blotchy and hot like it usually did right before she had a panic attack. She hoped JP didn't notice.

JP looked between her and the security scanners with a furrow of his brow. "We are not even close to boarding the plane yet. You are already scared?"

Luna wanted to laugh despite also wanting to cry, scream,

knock over old women and children, and run away into the wilds of Queens. "I told you, I've never flown before. The whole idea makes me nervous." The family ahead of them got to the front of the line, and they stepped forward to take their spot. Almost there. Luna thought she might pass out, her heart was going so fast. "This part especially," she murmured, almost to herself.

"This part? It is only security."

Luna almost choked on her harsh laugh. "You've clearly never traveled with a trans woman before."

Jean-Pierre took her gently by the elbow and guided her to the side, motioning for the people behind them in line to go ahead. "I have not," he said. "Will you explain it to me?" His passport was in his hand now, but he turned back to his carry-on and feigned looking through it for something else while the line passed them by.

Luna crossed her arms over her chest and shot a glance at the TSA agents at the front of the line, but so far nobody seemed to be paying them any mind. Normally she wouldn't be interested in teaching JP all about issues he clearly had no clue about, but if it kept her from approaching those scanners, even for a few more minutes, she would take it.

"This whole system is a scam," she said, hugging her arms as she talked. "I've read tons of articles about it. When you go into those things, a TSA employee has to push a button: blue for men, pink for women. So Ray's shit out of luck, I guess."

JP followed Luna's gaze, taking in the monolithic scanners. "I did not realize. I have gone through security in so many countries; I assumed these are merely another kind of metal detector."

Luna shook her head. "No, they literally scan your body shape. There are preprogrammed outlines that the machine thinks a man or a woman should fill out. If you don't fill the outline completely, no big deal. They usually don't care if something's missing, only if something is there that 'isn't supposed to be.'" She stopped hugging herself long enough to make quote marks in the air with her fingers.

A look of horrified understanding passed over Jean-Pierre's face. "I see," he said. He gave up pretending to look through his bag and took a step closer to Luna, holding her upper arms before she could wrap them around herself again. His voice was a bare whisper. "But you have nothing to fear, non? Your surgery—"

"That doesn't matter." The panic was rising in her again. "If I get clocked before I go through the scanner, they're going to make me disclose—out loud, in the security line, in front of all these strangers. And then they'll take me to be strip-searched, which is what happened to my friend Sara the last time she flew, and they wouldn't even let her have a woman do it, and—"

She bit her lip shut with a whimper and looked down at her slip-on shoes. For someone who didn't care about passing, it was moments like this that made it suddenly, cruelly significant.

Jean-Pierre gave her arms a light squeeze. He then took her hand in his and led her back into the quickly moving line. "Come on. It will be okay," he said. He sounded so determined, so sure.

Luna tried to respond, but her throat seized up like the rest of her, and she could only be tugged along as they reached the front of the line. JP handed over their passports and made small talk with the agent checking boarding passes. It was all Greek to Luna. Her energy was focused on breathing and getting through this. Was she making a big deal out of nothing? Jean-Pierre probably thought she was completely cuckoo bananas.

Then JP's voice filtered through the static in her brain.

His accent was thicker than usual for some reason. "My wife," he said to the TSA agent as he wrapped an arm around Luna's waist, "she hurt her shoulder a week ago. The doctor says no lifting arms above her head, yes? Is there a way she can go through security without the—?" He mimed putting his hands over his head in the classic body-scanner pose.

"Oh, sure." Now that Luna could focus, she saw the agent was an older woman, perched on the little black stool. She barely gave Luna a glance. "One second. I'll get someone to wand her." She waved to another guard milling around the knot of passengers struggling to get their bags onto the conveyor belt.

"Darling, let me take that for you," JP said. Luna felt the strap of her backpack slip out of her hand as JP shouldered it. "You go ahead, yes? I'll be right behind you."

"Okay," Luna mumbled. You could just *ask* not to go through a scanner? Did that only work if a fancy-looking Frenchman pretended to be your husband? Her body didn't feel solid as she moved from the security line to the old-fashioned metal detector, guided by another lady in uniform. It was all very polite. The agent even asked her which shoulder was giving her trouble. "I don't want to bump it or anything," she explained.

Luna gestured to her right side; if she had to pick one, it seemed like a reasonable choice. The agent passed a wand in a cursory sweep over her body. She patted at Luna's hips, realizing with a laugh that her exercise leggings didn't have pockets, and sent her on her way.

The whole thing was over in about thirty seconds. Luna felt shell-shocked as she waited for JP in the area immediately behind security. Adrenaline zinged in her bloodstream. All around her, parents helped their kids put on their shoes, or struggled with their own, shouting over each other's heads about who had which bag. Luna hadn't even been asked to take off her shoes. The definition of painless.

Distantly, she felt anger welling in her gut. Why couldn't it be that easy all the time, for everyone? What was the point of all this nonsense?

She caught a whiff of old leather and coffee before she caught a glimpse of tousled black hair out of the corner of her eye. Jean-Pierre materialized by her side, holding both their bags. "Ready to go, sweetheart?" he said, even though the closest TSA agent was several yards away. Luna wondered who the endearment was for.

She nodded, letting him carry both bags. They made their

way through the chaos of the post-security area and into the terminal. JP consulted the big board of departure times that hung like a massive tombstone from the high ceiling. Luna eyed his profile.

"Why did you tell them I was your wife?" she asked.

Jean-Pierre squinted at the brightly lit screen, zeroing in on *P* for Paris. "It sounds better than 'the woman who is pretending to be my girlfriend,' no?"

"You swooped in to save me," Luna pointed out, "again."

JP shrugged before turning away from the departure board to face Luna head-on. "I considered asking for your permission first, but for one thing, we were within the hearing of that security person. And for another"—here his imperious look dimmed into real concern—"you were like, ah, a deer trapped in light."

"Headlights," Luna corrected automatically.

"Yes. That. I thought, *Act first, apologize later*." He hitched the strap of Luna's backpack higher onto his shoulder so he could free his hand. His fingers played nervously through his mop of hair. "I am sorry. I should have consulted you."

"No, it's okay," Luna blurted out. "I actually—I really appreciate what you did."

"You do?" Jean-Pierre blinked. "You are not mad?"

"Oh, I'm plenty mad. Not at you, though. At—" Luna gestured behind them to the buzzing hive of the security theater. "I'm mad that all *this* gets done in the name of keeping people safe. It doesn't make me feel safe at all. Not one fucking bit." She turned back to JP with a sigh. "All you did was tell a tiny lie, and it saved me a lot of grief. So. Thanks."

Jean-Pierre looked like he'd been smacked in the face. "You—" He seemed to be struggling to form his response. "You are very welcome," he finally managed.

Did anyone ever thank this guy?

Luna smiled sadly at the thought. Then another, sadder thought gripped her tight: in four short days, she'd be back here in this very terminal. Paris and the culinary test would be behind her—and so would JP. Win or lose, it would all be over soon. The thought was unsettling for reasons she couldn't begin to understand. A few weeks ago, she couldn't wait for it all to be over, but that was before she saw what a sweetheart Jean-Pierre could be. She was realizing she wasn't ready for their time together to end, but she didn't have a choice. The wheels were already in motion; she couldn't bail now.

"So what gate are we going to?" she asked, turning back to the big board. "Do we have time to grab a sandwich?" A sad, floppy airport sandwich for a sad, floppy girl, she thought.

"They will serve dinner on the plane," JP reminded her.

"I know I'm new at this, but isn't airline food supposed to suck?"

"Not in first class, it won't," JP said, and proceeded to walk off in the direction of their gate.

Luna stood there for a full ten seconds, watching Jean-Pierre move away, before finally absorbing the words. "Sorry, what?" She hustled after him. "First *what?*"

First class was an entirely different world. Luna was welcomed aboard the plane before anyone else (including passengers who needed assistance or had small children, which seemed kind of fucked up). As she took her window seat—huge, clean, covered in supple silver leather—a flight attendant appeared out of nowhere to offer her a flute of champagne from a tray.

"Oh, I didn't order anything," Luna said.

The flight attendant—name tag: Charles; mustache: pencil thin—opened and closed his mouth, not losing his perfect smile, clearly unsure how to explain.

JP laughed as he dropped himself into the aisle seat next to her. "Darling, it's complimentary. They give it to everyone when they board. Helps pass the time."

"Perhaps the lady would prefer something else?" Charles swung his gaze to Jean-Pierre. His accent was French-ish, maybe Belgian. Luna supposed she should be thankful he was at least speaking English, even if he was deferring to her fake partner instead.

"She would love some water," Luna said with an aggressive smile.

JP accepted his own glass of champagne and watched the flight attendant escape with an amused smile playing along his lips. "You will make it awkward if you don't accept these little perks, you know. They expect you to take what is given. It's just the way things are."

"It's bougie nonsense, is what it is."

"Boo . . . ?" His brow raised.

"Like bourgeois."

He shook his head. "Will the butchering of my language never stop?"

Luna watched as Jean-Pierre sipped at his glass. His throat bobbed as he swallowed the pale liquid, fizzing with strings of bubbles. *Come quick! I am tasting the stars!* "How is it?"

JP righted the glass and made a neutral sound. "I would call it middling." He offered Luna the glass, holding it expertly by the stem. "Would you like to try it?"

Luna made a face. "If the flight attendant sees me do that, he'll think I refused a glass just to be difficult."

"Since when does my moonlight care what other people think?" Jean-Pierre's face morphed into a secret kind of smile. The flute drifted closer to her hand. "It might help with the nerves, after all."

Luna watched the tiny bubbles rushing to the top of the champagne. "Just a sip," she said, and took the glass from JP. Their fingers brushed, warm and dry. As her lips touched the rim of the flute, Luna recalled how Jean-Pierre's had been there mere moments ago. The idea of sharing an indirect kiss like that made her cheeks heat, which was ridiculous. They'd already actually kissed, after all. And then some.

Stars flooded over her tongue, sharp and bright.

"Not bad," she agreed, passing the champagne back.

The plane quickly filled with other passengers, though Luna could only hear them from a distance; the first-class cabin was situated upstairs in the double-decker plane so the economy people didn't have to file right past them. It made Luna feel kind of like royalty, and not in a good way. She pictured everyone squishing together in the smaller seats, definitely not being offered free sleep masks and fuzzy socks. If she were back there, she'd probably be cursing the fancy folks in first class.

The flight crew began making their safety announcements in both French and English. Luna knotted her hands in her lap and followed along with both. She wasn't fluent yet, but she had a good enough grasp not to need the English translation.

As the plane taxied down the runway, JP reached over and touched Luna's knuckles. "It is natural to be nervous," he said. His eyes were dark and clear. "Would you like to hold my hand?"

"Huh?" Luna's mouth went dry. They had barely touched since the night they'd messed around. Their stolen moments of practicing in the kitchen were strictly businesslike. Except for their little performance in the security line, they hadn't so much as bumped shoulders. She got her mouth back in working order to say, "That's nice of you to offer, but I have to figure out how to do this on my own, right? It's not like you're going to be with me on the flight back." Her lips fought to form a smile, but it was a losing proposition. She pictured that lonely return trip next to an empty seat where JP should be. Well, she'd probably have a stranger there instead—this flight was fully booked, at least. But metaphorically, she'd be alone. Again.

Jean-Pierre leaned in close, his lips brushing the shell of her ear. Luna shivered. "I cannot be certain, but the woman two rows behind us, she is a journalist, I think. *Vogue France*. I recognize her from events and the like."

Oh. Right. The whole pretending-to-be-a-couple thing. The entire reason she was even here in the first place. JP was concerned only with the optics.

His fingers slipped between hers, coaxing them out of their shaking fist.

Luna looked at their joined fingers. It actually was kind of nice, holding hands. A little childish, but sweet.

The flight attendant collected their empty glasses before takeoff. The whole plane rumbled as it rushed down the runway. She clutched JP's hand tighter than she meant to, but he never complained. The wheels left the ground, and Luna felt her stomach go weightless for a moment inside her body. It was like an elevator, but weirder. The plane jerked a couple times as it climbed into the sky, and Luna shut her eyes tight in an effort not to panic.

Then JP's lips were back at her ear, his voice loud enough to be heard over the engines. "A few bumps are normal. It is like a car on the road, yes? Never completely smooth."

Luna nodded, her eyes still closed. "Kind of like life."

Jean-Pierre did not comment on that, instead saying, "Open your eyes; you're missing the best part."

"What part?"

"Look at your city. Say goodbye."

Luna opened her eyes and peered out the window. It was dark, and the night was clear, so no clouds obscured her view of the lights of New York shrinking beneath them. There it was, all laid out in bright rectangular blocks, a big burst of light once in a while denoting a baseball field or some huge shopping center in the outer boroughs. Tiny specks of red taillights raced up and down the arteries of streets. Luna could see where the land met the black, undulating line of the water. The Rockaways, the beaches. Houses and boats dotting the darkness. Then: the huge nothing of the ocean.

It was all so beautiful. She was no longer afraid, not when she could see the world like this.

"Goodbye," she whispered.

"Au revoir," Jean-Pierre said to the window, leaning in to get a look for himself. "À bientôt."

Luna watched him in profile. His black hair was hanging in his eyes again. It made her want to tuck it back behind his ears. She cleared her throat and slipped her hand free from his. They couldn't hold hands for the entire flight. "You know, I was kind of expecting the whole air-travel nightmare you see in sitcoms. No leg room, screaming babies, that kind of thing."

"Mm, no screaming babies in first class, not tonight, I think," JP said, rising a little to survey the seats around them. He dropped back into his seat with a grunt, almost like he was disappointed.

Luna grinned. "I bet if any were around, you could do that baby-whisperer thing like you did at the park." She clicked through the movie menu on the huge screen in front of her. Oh, they could watch *Some Like It Hot*. Her favorite problematic cross-dressing flick. "You've got a magic touch, you know that?"

JP gave a careless shrug and fiddled with the buttons on his armrest, making his seat recline, then come back again. His pale cheeks were flooding bright pink. "I think children are very dear," he said, almost under his breath.

Luna sensed this meant something more to him than just a throwaway comment. Most people thought kids were cute, but then again, most people wouldn't feel much sympathy for a screaming baby on an airplane.

"Do you ever want kids of your own?" she asked.

The question landed like a javelin. Jean-Pierre jolted in his seat like he'd been struck in the chest. He turned to Luna with a wild look in his eyes, his hair flopping over his brow. "What a silly thing to ask," he said. His voice was a hollow thing. "Kids of my own. How exactly am I to produce those, hm? I don't have any of the necessary parts. For either rôle."

"No, but there are other ways—" Luna began.

"And who would give them to me?" JP said. "What person or, or, or orphanage or what have you would look at me and say, 'Hm, yes, that is fine'?"

Luna squinted at him. "What are you talking about? Like, no offense, JP, but you're rich. No one's going to stop you if you want to adopt or use a surrogate or whatever."

Jean-Pierre blew out a frustrated lungful of air. "I am not talking about being stopped. I am talking about—" He made a *quick, quick, quick* gesture with his hands, rolling them in circles in front of his chest. "Men are not supposed to want this. Men do not dream of starting a family and doting on the children and keeping house. I know with every bone in my body that I am a man, but if I do these things, how will that look, hein?"

"Sorry. Hold up." Luna twisted herself in her seat, pulling one leg up so she could fully face JP. This seemed like a full-on-eye-contact sort of conversation, if he would only meet her eyes. "Are you saying you want to have kids and be a *househusband*?"

He became far too interested in adjusting his armrest. "I know that is somewhat abnormal, but . . ."

"Are you kidding? That's hot as hell." She laughed at JP's answering look, incredulous bordering on pissy. "I'm serious! Do you have any idea how many women out there dream of snagging a guy who wants to do all the 'women's work' so they don't have to? Holy shit, if I had someone I could come home to, and he's cooked and cleaned and made sure the kids had their bath . . ."

Her words slowed to a stop. She could picture it: some cute little house with a funny welcome mat out front; Jean-Pierre standing in the doorway with an adorable child perched on his hip.

Wait a minute. Never in her life had Luna considered starting a nuclear family, so why was she all of a sudden—?

She looked over at Jean-Pierre. He had not noticed her internal meltdown over the image of him in their fantasy household's doorway, and was chattering away.

"The cooking, perhaps only very simple things." JP raised a finger in the air. "I am still learning."

"That's . . . fine," Luna said, still in a daze. "Kids don't eat complicated things, anyway."

"No, they don't. They like bland food." He stared at the seatback in front of him as if lost in thought. Then he whipped his head back around to stare at Luna. "Have you ever thought of having kids?"

"Uh." *Quick, say something that doesn't indicate you have but only in the last five minutes and only with him.* "Yeah. I guess so."

JP's face inexplicably brightened.

"Not like it's ever going to happen, though," Luna said with a dry laugh. "Think of climate change. Is there even going to be a habitable world for them to grow up in? Not to mention the cost. One kid would be impossible enough, but kids, plural? Forget about it. And if they wanted to go to college, hoo-boy! I'd be in debt until I died." She leaned back into her cozy chair. "Honestly, I'll be lucky if I can just get my yoga teacher certification and open my dream retreat in the Catskills when I'm ready to retire."

She glanced back over at JP, who was now wearing the most dejected, morose look she'd ever seen, like someone had taken a ball-peen hammer to his hopes. "That is what you want?"

"Just one of those daydreams, you know? Probably won't ever happen." *Like a lot of things.*

"Yes. Perhaps." He gave her one last long look, then reclined his seat. "I think I will get some rest."

"Oh, but—" Luna pulled the spreadsheet printout from her backpack and held it up for his perusal. "I thought we could spend some time memorizing our timetable? For the test? See, I colored all your tasks in gray." She pointed down at the dark rows stretching out across the page. "I would have gone for black but, well, it wouldn't be legible. And mine are in purple here, and the shared stuff in the middle are this kind of orange color."

He put on his huge noise-canceling headphones. "Email it

to me. I will look it over in the taxi later." With a whiff of dismissal, he shut his eyes.

"Yeah. Sure. Good night." Luna spread the pages on her tray table, determined to at least get some studying done on the flight. She put in her earbuds and started the movie for something to keep her company in the background. Tony and Jack played out their silly antics on the screen while her heart thudded in her ears.

She barely missed the feeling of JP's hand in hers. Barely.

Chapter 19

Jean-Pierre's place was not what Luna had been expecting. She had pictured something dressed up the way JP always was: expensively, sure, but in blacks and grays with no hint of color. A kind of gothic man-cave situation.

But when she walked through the door that Jean-Pierre held for her, she saw his apartment wasn't austere at all. It was done up in lush fabrics of every type: soft velvet and fantastical damasks in blues and golds and greens. There were arched entryways leading into every room, and all the walls were adorned with elaborate scrolled cornices that lapped at the ceiling. The rugs were piled high, and at the first step into the sitting room, Luna's foot sank into what felt like six inches of plush. Best of all, there was a skylight dead center in the middle of the ceiling, framed in a grid of oxidized green like a jewel case. Luna stared up into it, looking at the achingly blue sky and the wisps of clouds, not caring that her mouth might be hanging open.

Her mom had had a point. Material wealth sure did have its perks.

"You like?" JP kicked off his boots and tossed his leather

jacket over the arm of the sofa, which was a confection of robin's-egg blue velvet and fuzzy throw pillows.

She put her own coat atop his. "It's gorgeous." It was also, she noticed, very neat. It looked like no one had ever set foot on the polished floors or touched the stainless-steel appliances she could see through the kitchen passway. There were no extra vape cartridges scattered on the low coffee table, no socks abandoned on the carpet, not a speck of dust on the mantel. Maybe it was old-fashioned of her, but she'd expected a single man's home to be at least a little messy. "You live here? Like, most of the time?"

"Well, I do travel quite a bit." JP padded toward the kitchen in his bare feet. "I am not here as often as I would like."

Luna felt something in her deflate. Right. JP belonged here, in Paris, the most impressive city in the world. He would probably stay here all the time if he could—that might even be his plan, once his inheritance was secured. Luna couldn't hold it against him. She would certainly stay here all the time if she owned a place like this.

She watched him open the fridge. The gleaming contents seemed to consist only of liquids: cartons of protein shakes and blue bottles of sparkling mineral water were all arranged in neat rows. Luna wondered where the white wine and champagne were—she had pictured JP keeping both chilled and on hand at all times—but then she spotted the wine fridge under the kitchen counter where a dishwasher would usually go.

Priorities. Nice.

"Would you like something?" He held up a blue bottle of mineral water. It looked like a sapphire jewel in the kitchen lights.

Her stomach rumbled. She gave a sheepish shrug. "I'm more hungry than thirsty, I guess." The meal on the plane had been shockingly decent—quenelles stuffed with crab and sea bass—but that had been ages ago. Her eyes flicked to the beautiful but empty kitchen with its beautiful but empty fridge. "We'll have to go out, right?"

JP perked up. "Ah, there are many good brasseries in this neighborhood, or we could do Ladurée if you want something light, or there is ramen, or—"

Luna held up a hand to stop him. Her head was spinning with all the options, and she was drained from the long day of traveling. "Why don't you pick? It's your city; you know what's best."

Jean-Pierre's brow furrowed for a moment, then smoothed. "All right," he said. "I will take care of everything, then."

Luna considered herself a totally hashtag independent woman, but there was something about a guy saying that exact phrase and meaning it that made her want to swoon. Was there anything better than someone else doing all the work when you were too exhausted to?

Luna was in the middle of wheeling their luggage out of the small foyer when she noticed JP standing by the sofa, his recently discarded shoes dangling from one hand by their laces. He was frowning down at his phone in his other hand.

"Something wrong?" she asked.

"Henri." He almost spat his grandfather's name. "Or rather, one of his media people."

Luna sidled over to him and peeked over his shoulder at the screen. The text message was in French, but she could read it well enough—mostly boring logistical stuff, the address of Henri's flagship restaurant where the test would be conducted, the official start and end times. The last message seemed pointedly personal in contrast.

Can you confirm the American girl will be accompanying you? Chef seemed to think she might not, in the end. Something about her finding a more suitable man?

Okay, seriously, fuck that guy. And his lackey.

"What's it say?" she asked, feigning ignorance while simultaneously resisting the urge to reach through the phone and punch someone.

Jean-Pierre hurried to slip the phone into his pocket. "Some details for the test. Nothing to worry about." He grabbed his leather jacket and headed for the door. "Come, let's eat."

Luna considered pressing him—no one, not even the coolest, most unaffected guy in the world—could endure this level of nastiness from a grandparent and be okay with it, surely. But he obviously didn't feel like sharing. At least, not with his pretend girlfriend who was really here only on pretense.

With a sigh, she followed him out the door.

JP's neighborhood was incredibly fancy and extremely charming. The closest equivalent Luna could come up with was New York's brownstone streets, even though there was not a brownstone to be found here. These buildings were older, and ornate, and exuded the kind of historical significance that America could only dream of. There were a few tourists on street corners squinting at street signs, but thankfully there weren't hordes of them. As far as weather went, Luna couldn't have asked for better: a perfect summer day in Paris, clear skies and a good breeze. She felt like Madeline could come around the corner at any moment with the nun and other schoolkids.

"So where are we going?" she asked as they walked down the street.

Jean-Pierre made a hedging noise. "A few places."

They indeed made many stops, the first one being a produce stand where JP engaged in polite chitchat with the greengrocer, an elderly man who wore an honest-to-god newsboy cap and sold Jean-Pierre a pint each of raspberries and blackberries at a one-euro discount. Then there was the cheesemonger—a real, actual monger—who was tucked away in a fairy-tale cheese shop. JP purchased several small rounds and cuts of cheeses with names Luna couldn't parse even though they all sported helpful little handwritten chalk signs. After that, they made a stop at a bakery right next door, and Luna started to realize what was happening.

"Are you collecting ingredients for charcuterie?" she asked.

"Again, it is called a cheese plate," Jean-Pierre said as he exchanged a few euros for a long loaf of crusty bread. "Unless you would like to pick up meats as well?"

Luna wasn't going to say no to prosciutto, so JP bought some at a quaint butcher shop down the block, sliced so thin you could read the dictionary through it. When Jean-Pierre saw her making puppy eyes at a display of handmade pickles in glass jars, he picked one up as well.

"I feel like we're miles away from your place by now," Luna said as they left the shop.

"We are not going back to my place."

"We're not?" Luna stopped in the middle of the sidewalk. "Then where are we going?"

JP stopped as well, his many purchases dangling from his hands in brown paper bags with twisted handles. "You will see," was all he said before ducking into a wine shop and cajoling the owner into giving them two actual wineglasses with their bottle of Château Climens Barsac.

"Do not break them," the middle-aged shopkeeper said as she rolled the glasses in butcher paper and carefully packed them in their own little bag. She winked at JP. "You must promise to return them intact, all right?" Was she flirting? Or just French? Either was possible.

Jean-Pierre smiled and agreed.

Back on the street, Luna noticed Jean-Pierre was kind of loaded down with bags. "Can I carry something?"

"Non." He looked at her with those lazy eyes. "It is not so heavy."

They walked up the street until they hit a river. "Is this the Seine?" Luna asked. The water was a dishwater brown, chugging slowly. It reminded her of the Hudson back home.

"Mm. Follow me." Jean-Pierre led the way across a street and onto a bridge. Luna gasped as the bridge's guardrails came into view.

"I know this place! It's famous, right?" She ran right up to the wrought-iron fences that lined the footpaths down to a little spit of land below. The fences bristled with padlocks of all shapes and sizes. Most had writing on them, two people's names scrawled in permanent marker. Luna picked up one, then another, holding them up so she could read them better. *Marc and Celine. Erik and Hilda. Gustav and Georges.* Oh, nice. "Look! I found a gay one!" Luna crowed, jingling the lock for JP's benefit.

Jean-Pierre came abreast of her, moving slowly on account of all his bags. "This is not even the famous lock bridge," he said. "You're thinking of Pont des Arts, that one." He gestured with his chin to a bridge some distance upriver. "This is merely the overflow. These fucking tourists, they'll put a lock on anything they can reach." He brushed by Luna and made his way down to the little triangle of a park below. "The city has been cutting them off for years, but that doesn't stop them from doing it anyway."

Luna frowned, letting the gay lock slip from her fingers. She thought it was sweet, but whatever. If JP didn't have a single romantic bone in his body, that wasn't her problem. She followed him down the steps.

For a tiny park, the place was packed. Luna could see why: they were on a small island in the middle of the Seine with a fantastic view of the city on either side. Every bench was occupied. They ended up sitting on the concrete embankment with their legs dangling high above the water.

Luna dug into their bags of goodies, uncovering the berries first. They looked perfectly juicy in their little paper baskets.

"If Simone were here, she'd be screaming at me for eating produce without washing it first," she said, popping one of the blackberries into her mouth. It burst on her tongue in a riot of tangy sweetness.

"A good thing she isn't here, then," Jean-Pierre said. He took his key ring from his pocket and opened—was that an actual fucking corkscrew?

Luna stared, impressed. "You really are always ready to picnic like a Frenchman, huh?"

"One must be prepared." He grinned as he worked the corkscrew into their bottle of wine, then pulled the cork free with a pop. He poured a generous glass and handed it to Luna before pouring for himself.

Luna took a sip. The white wine was smooth and crisp and light, playing with the lingering taste of the berry in a delicious duet.

They dug in, ripping off hunks of the crusty bread and piling on buttery prosciutto. Jean-Pierre produced a small folding knife with a wooden handle—when had he had time to even get that thing after the flight?—and began slicing the cheeses. One was creamy and tasted faintly of honey; another was sharp and had grainy crystals that popped like candy between Luna's teeth. Her favorite was the funky bleu with dark seawater veins running through it. She smeared it on a piece of bread and popped a fat red raspberry on top, shoving the whole thing into her mouth in one huge bite.

"Fuck, that's good," she said. It came out more like *ffphk, ffs goo* since her mouth was full, but JP seemed to understand nonetheless.

He broke off another piece of bread and began preparing it with soft cheese and berries.

"You know this is my favorite kind of meal?" Luna said, popping a cornichon into her mouth between chews. "Just, like, nibbling on a lot of different things? It's right up there with mac and cheese."

"I do know," Jean-Pierre said. He handed over the perfect bite of bread, cheese, prosciutto, and fruit he'd constructed. "I actually know it very well."

Luna took the piece of piled-high bread, her cheeks warm.

Between the two of them, they polished off nearly everything JP had bought. By the time the sun dipped below the spiky rooftops of Paris, they had only a few odds and ends and half a container of pickles left.

"We'll save this; it was really good," Luna said, carefully rewrapping the leftover cheeses and neatly separating everything into a take-home bag and a trash bag. "Want to head back now?"

"In a little while," Jean-Pierre said. "Look. She is just starting to wake."

Luna lifted her head to ask what the hell that meant, but then she saw what JP was talking about. Her mouth fell wide open.

As it got dark, the glowing streetlamps and yellow globes that lined the bridges of Paris came on all around them. The buildings lit up like they were a stage. Even the boats that were tooling along the river blazed to life, lined with strings of light. It was like a postcard, but better, full of the sounds of people and the smell of the river, the taste of wine still on Luna's tongue.

"Oh, *wow.*"

"I don't know how anyone could not fall in love with her," Jean-Pierre said softly.

"Yeah, no, I get it. Your city is really something." Luna turned to smile at him, but the smile melted away when she realized JP wasn't looking out at the view. He was looking only at her.

Chapter 20

Luna woke up in a strange bed in an unfamiliar country, but instead of panicking, she lay against the ridiculously soft Egyptian cotton sheets and stared up at the ceiling. Facts came to her slowly. Right, Paris. Jean-Pierre. Jean-Pierre's guest bedroom —which was inspiring no small amount of jealousy; what millennial could afford a place with a guest bedroom?

Let's not start the day with bad vibes, she told herself. She closed her eyes and put a hand on the fluffy comforter right over her stomach. Five deep Vedic breaths. Get centered, get in touch with all that nervous energy.

She could hear JP moving around in the kitchen in that quiet, careful way a host did when they didn't want to wake their houseguest. The barely audible clink of a coffee cup in a saucer, the sink running. When a dish clattered, JP muttered a quiet *merde*, which made Luna grin.

Then the grin slipped away. Memories of their late picnic dinner flooded back. It had been a perfect evening, the kind you want to capture in your mind in minute detail because you know, even as it's happening, that there won't be many evenings like it in your lifetime. When they had finally left the little island in the river and walked home under all the blazing lights, fingertips brushing, Luna had thought that maybe—

But no. They'd come back to JP's place, where he'd given her a plush towel from the linen cupboard before they said good night and went to bed. In very separate beds. Even though Jean-Pierre had had a look in his eyes, some dark sheen that Luna thought might have meant he was considering other plans.

The image was burned into her mind: JP half-turned in the hallway that connected their rooms, looking at her over his shoulder, clearly wanting something but saying nothing.

Luna groaned and rolled over to stick her face in the nicest, most supportive pillows she'd ever met. This was getting out of hand. She was falling prey to the charms of Paris, that was all. The whole damn city was built to make people think they were in love. And because she came from New York, a city designed to make people turn into the Joker, Luna was not immune.

She needed to get her head on straight; she was there to do a job, to fulfill a role. Nothing more.

There was a soft knock at her door. "Luna?" JP whispered through the wood. "Coffee?"

The smell of it had already reached Luna's nose, and she couldn't resist. Which was fine, it was just coffee. But she'd have to figure out a way to resist other things. Dark eyes and floppy hair and the worst manners except when he was being nice and—

Dear god, she needed coffee.

Luna dragged herself out of bed and into some semblance of decency. "Coming," she called in a sleep-rough voice.

Once she was dressed and had a cup of JP's delicious pour-over, Luna asked about the plan for the day.

"We have errands," Jean-Pierre said cryptically. "Get your shoes."

Luna let herself be whisked away once again.

Their first stop was a bank—an incredibly beautiful bank with statues of Greek goddesses displayed in alcoves all along the facade. Jean-Pierre was greeted by name by a man in a slick suit, and within the span of fifteen minutes, all the paperwork was signed to transfer the remaining balance of $550,000 (about €512,000, but who was counting?) into Luna's checking account.

She gaped at the tiny font on the receipt JP handed her. "I thought maybe I'd get paid when we were done with the test."

"I trust you not to run off before tomorrow," JP said simply. "After all, you spent all that time making the little cards and le tableur. I would rather we get this out of the way now."

Luna's head spun with the thought of having that much money all in one chunk. That daydream of retiring to the Catskills suddenly morphed into a real possibility.

He took her by the hand to lead her outside. "Breakfast?"

Jean-Pierre's neighborhood bakery was like something out of a travel influencer's Instagram. It was a picturesque shop flanked by an equally picturesque antique bookstore and florist. An awning with green-and-white stripes shaded the front. Hand-painted letters on the glass door spelled out *Patisserie Marie* in gold cursive. Two large windows displayed their glistening offerings: trays of perfectly shaped croissants, rows of tiny tarts brimming with colorful fillings, soldierly rectangles of mille-feuille with feathered icing, and about ten different types of eclairs, not to mention all the little confections sporting wisps of cream and lacy hats of spun sugar that Luna couldn't identify. She resisted the urge to press her nose against the window and let her breath fog up the glass. Truly, this was heaven.

JP whispered in her ear as they stood side by side, surveying the spread. "And they have the best madeleines in the whole city."

Back home, Luna would have had to travel below 14th Street to get baked goods on par with this level of perfection. "You're so lucky to have this right here on your block."

"Lucky?" Jean-Pierre tossed his head back and laughed. "Why do you think I bought this apartment? It was no accident. Come." He placed his palm on the small of her back and guided her to the door, opening it for her as the bell attached to the ceiling gave a cheery ting.

There was no line, just a handful of people milling at the counter. The front of the shop was a small, narrow space, so even those five or six bodies made it difficult to navigate. To further complicate the experience, some people seemed to be actual customers waiting for their chance to order from the aproned staff while others—two older gentlemen in particular—appeared to be there only to shout their opinions regarding last night's football match. Luna was happy to find she could follow the conversation. Apparently, England was terrible and god would strike them all down if there was any justice in the world; that was the only point everyone seemed to agree on. Luna, who didn't know the first thing about soccer, found herself siding with the Parisian grandpas.

Jean-Pierre directed Luna with a hand on her back, sidestepping through the confusion until they reached the counter. A woman with thick glasses and a huge pile of hair shot through with silver wiped her hands on her apron, shaking her head at the football argument. Her lined face lit up at the sight of JP.

"Jean-Pierre, mon garçon! Tu es de retour."

"Bonjour, Marie." He leaned over the counter (which, considering how short he was, was no mean feat) and planted kisses on both her cheeks. "Comment vas-tu?"

Luna smiled at the interaction. So JP did have people who loved him in this city. It was nice to hear the bakery owner so happy that he was back home. He must have been coming here for years and years, if she was referring to him as her boy—her son, really. With the French, it was all the same.

Marie turned her sparkling gaze onto Luna. "Et . . . qui est-elle?"

"Ah, pardon." He turned to Luna. "Marie does not speak much English; do you mind if we continue in French? She might struggle otherwise."

"Oh, I don't mind at all," Luna said. Maybe this was a good time to show off her newfound skills. "In fact, I can—"

But JP didn't let her finish. "Brilliant, thank you," he said, before turning back to Marie. "Elle s'appelle Luna. C'est la femme que je veux épouser."

Luna froze. She could feel JP's hand still resting comfortably at the small of her back, where she was certain he could feel her heart pounding.

This is the woman I want to marry.

What? *What?*

She blinked. If this was all part of their cover, JP was really laying it on thick. Just how quickly was their fake relationship progressing? Luna had always thought if she ever got married, it would be to someone she had known for at least a decade. She and JP hadn't even been together for a year! A fake year, at that.

Marie gasped. "Vraiment? Ah, Jean-Pierre!" She struggled to untie her apron strings in her excitement and hustled around the counter to clap hands on Luna. She couldn't seem to decide whether to pull Luna into a hug or kiss her twice on both cheeks, so she tried to do everything at once. "So nice to meet you," she said in English, then, in French, launched into a thousand questions about when the wedding would be, and did Madame D'Amboise plan on making the cake, and if she wasn't, could Marie please make it? What flavors did Luna like? She guessed berries, playfully running her fingers through Luna's purple-tinged hair.

Luna laughed along with her, but glanced over to JP for assistance. It didn't take much acting to pretend not to understand what was going on, since that was exactly the case.

Jean-Pierre caught Luna's wide stare and swooped in to pry Marie away. "Non, non, non. Un jour, un jour. Pas tout de suite." *Someday. Not now.*

Luna kept her confused smile plastered on her face. She tried for a light, devil-may-care tone. "What's going on?"

"Ah, nothing." Jean-Pierre shrugged. "Marie is just happy to see I've brought a friend is all."

Friend. Hm. Luna's taste for the dramatic urged her to give her fledgling French a try right then and there. Maybe she should ask Jean-Pierre what sort of friend he wanted to marry someday, s'il tu plaît? But that would embarrass him in front of a very sweet lady who was currently emptying out the bakery cases and shoving all kinds of delectable treats into white paper bags. If Luna was to be the recipient of those treats, she didn't want to ruin the moment.

"Here, please," Marie said in French, bustling back around the counter. "Jean-Pierre is like family. We love anyone who loves him."

Luna juggled the bags of pastries. "Merci?"

"We have a busy day today, Marie," JP told her, still in French. "I am sorry we cannot stay long."

"Ah, yes! I heard a rumor—you and your grandfather are having some sort of competition, is that right?"

Luna peeked into one of the paper bags and selected a fat eclair, taking a huge bite as she eavesdropped. It was a classic combination of vanilla crème pâtissière with a dark chocolate ganache on top—simple, yet it tasted better than flour, sugar, and eggs had a right to. Luna stifled a scream as she chewed.

Marie beamed at her. "Good, yes?" she said in English.

"Very, very good," Luna said as soon as she swallowed.

Jean-Pierre, meanwhile, was not to be distracted by baked goods. He said to Marie in French, "I am not sure if we are ready for the test, to be honest. We still have some time to practice but . . ."

Marie leaned in close to whisper, "I am cheering for you. It's past time Henri learned you're the only Aubert-Treffle worth a damn."

Luna would normally have let loose a heartfelt whimper at hearing that—she was a sucker for sentimental pep talks—but she wasn't supposed to know what Marie was saying, so she shoved a madeleine into her mouth instead and let the rich, buttery flavor shut her up.

"Okay, I don't think we can practice any more than we already have," Luna said. She stood in JP's kitchen and watched as he scratched out something in his Moleskine notebook. His apron was covered with streaks of chocolate and red wine, and there was a smear of cream on his cheek. "We've been at this for hours."

"But the test is tomorrow." Jean-Pierre looked up from his scribbling. "The tartare is still not quite right, and the timing on the salad course is—"

Luna held up both hands, and miraculously, he stopped talking. "It is what it is," she said. "That's what my mom always says."

He took a deep breath, glancing back down at his notes before tossing his pen onto the counter. "And here I thought you Americans were supposed to be endlessly optimistic."

"I am! I only mean—some things can't be improved, right?" She sighed. "We need to accept that."

Jean-Pierre's eyes shone with an emotion Luna couldn't name. Whatever it was, it seemed like a lot for some under-seasoned tartare. "When something's important," he said, "you want to get it right."

She rounded the kitchen counter and rubbed his arm in what she hoped was a soothing manner. "Tomorrow will be fine. Fifteen rounds. We just need to hang in there."

"Yes." He rubbed his fingertips over his eyes. There were dark shadows beneath them. Had he even been sleeping since they'd come to Paris? "Like Rocky."

Luna frowned. "Let's get you out of the kitchen, champ." She steered him forcefully toward the plush sofa. "Sit. Did we eat lunch?" She checked the clock on the wall. It was well past afternoon and into the evening. "Jesus, Mary, and Joseph, no wonder you look like death warmed over. All this cooking and you haven't had anything to eat since this morning." Marie's madeleines, while exquisite, couldn't be considered an entire meal.

Jean-Pierre went down on the couch with a thump and a groan. "Please, not my grandfather's food. I am sick of eating that."

"I'll handle dinner," Luna said.

Jean-Pierre eyed her. "You will?"

"Yeah. I'm now a semi-gourmet cook, too, you know. Chill here, okay?" She gave his knee a pat and then disappeared back into the kitchen.

For all her devil-may-care attitude, Luna was not a fool. She knew an opportunity when she saw one. There was no way to outright ask JP what he'd meant about wanting to marry her without revealing that her French was more polished than he realized, and Luna wasn't quite ready to relinquish that ace up her sleeve just yet. It was very useful, she found, to let people underestimate you. Given the circumstances, her best option was obvious: do something wifelike and bait Jean-Pierre into spilling the beans all on his own.

And Luna knew exactly what kind of mushy, wifey behavior she could perform.

Thankfully the fridge was well stocked. Luna retrieved the leftovers from their picnic dinner: a packet of prosciutto wrapped in butcher paper, a jagged hunk of Gruyère, a half-demolished wedge of Parmesan, the remaining pickles. Butter, too, and lots of it—French style in blocks with a fleur-de-lis stamped into them. A tiny jar of mustard from Dijon itself. Couldn't get more French than that. There were a ton of fresh herbs: some sprigs of thyme, a bundle of chives, and a wealth of parsley. She closed the fridge door with her hip, her arms now loaded down.

She arranged her haul on the counter and considered it. She wished she knew how to make Thai food, but in the absence of fish sauce, chilis, and fresh lemongrass, this would have to do.

First, the white sauce. Easy. Béchamel was the basis for the sauce that accompanied the poached scallop on The Menu, and Luna now knew how to do it with her eyes closed. Flour, butter, milk, salt, pepper: the gang was all there.

Luna dumped half a brick of butter into a heavy Dutch oven and clicked on the burner. As that melted, she chopped the herbs and cut four thick slices from a sturdy loaf of peasant bread. Then she eyeballed a scant half cup of flour and chucked it into the pot. If it was too dry, she could always add more butter.

Cooking was actually kind of fun once you realized it wasn't the end of the world if you got something wrong. With Simone's lessons under her belt, Luna now understood that most mistakes in the kitchen could be corrected with a little creative thinking, and creative thinking was her thing.

The pile of herbs on the counter grabbed her eye. Hm, at what point should they go in the pot? Thyme was pretty robust and could take some heat; chives were kind of oniony in flavor, so maybe they should be cooked a little as well? Except she always saw them sprinkled raw on top of things, so maybe not. Parsley was a fucking diva and would wilt into gray mush if cooked even a little bit, so—okay, she had her game plan. Luna scooped up the thyme, losing only a couple of green bits to the floor as she dumped it into the pot to cook with the roux. The other herbs would be mixed in after.

She clicked on the oven's broiler and started assembling the food. Once everything was ready to get browned and bubbly, she realized something was missing. With a smile on her lips, she retrieved a single egg and a frying pan.

A few minutes and only one singed knuckle later, Luna emerged from the kitchen with two plates in hand. Jean-Pierre was still on the couch exactly where she'd left him.

She cleared her throat. Time to wife it up and gauge his reaction. "Dinner's ready," she said, placing one of the plates on the coffee table in front of Jean-Pierre.

He stared at it like it had come from outer space. "You made . . . croque monsieur?"

Luna flopped onto the other end of the couch. "I made *you* a croque monsieur. With an herbed béchamel and artisan pickles." She held up her own plate. Her sandwich was topped with a lacy fried egg. "And a croque madame for me."

If her goal was to completely mess with Jean-Pierre's head, she was on the right track. The man was speechless, eyes fixed on the cheesy, greasy, decadent meal Luna had made for him.

"Maybe it's not as good as your grandma used to make but, you know." She shrugged and picked up her knife and fork, eating a bite of her own sandwich. Oh, damn, it was good. The prosciutto was maybe a tad too fatty for an already rich combination, but screw it, she was in Paris. Plus the tang of the herbs mixed in with the charred sauce provided a refreshing lightness. She broke the yolk of her egg and let it soak into the golden bread, sneaking a glance at JP's profile as she chewed. He still hadn't budged.

She swallowed. "I hope I didn't overstep or something. I know this is Lisette's specialty."

"No!" Jean-Pierre's gaze whipped up to her. His eyes were as big as the sandwich. "No, it's perfect. Thank you." He picked up the fork and knife that Luna had thoughtfully included and got to work sawing off a corner.

"Good." Luna ate another bite. "Now you can tell people your girlfriend makes your favorite foods to cheer you up, and it won't even be a lie." She cocked her head. "Are you having a hard time with that? Lying to people about us, I mean."

JP chewed and swallowed before answering. "No, not really. It's quite—quite easy." He spoke that last part at his plate. "I suppose I am an excellent liar."

"Oh." She directed her attention back to her sandwich, stabbing at it like it was the reason for her disappointment. "So you're just saying stuff? Straight off the top of your head? That's— Wow, that takes a lot of skill. You should be proud."

Something in her tone must have made her displeasure obvious, because Jean-Pierre let his knife and fork fall to his plate with a clatter. He looked at her like she was the only person in the whole world worth seeing. "I have *never* been proud."

That sounded like it had more than one meaning. Luna's heart gave a confused twinge in her chest. How could Jean-Pierre inspire both fury and heartache in her within the same five-minute span? He was good at that, at making her feel like the ground beneath her feet wasn't real.

While she was contemplating how to respond, a harsh buzz vibrated twice through the sofa cushions. JP lifted his hips to get his phone out of his back pocket, then checked it with a sigh.

"What is it?" Luna asked.

"My grandfather again." Jean-Pierre held up the phone to show her. Henri had texted him a photo of a line of gleaming metal trash cans arranged against a brick wall. Beneath that, Henri had written in English: All is ready for your first dinner service.

Luna hadn't been aware of having hackles until precisely that moment when she felt them rise. "What the fuck? Is he saying our food is going to be garbage?"

"That is the joke, I suppose." JP placed his phone facedown on the table. He picked at the remains of his sandwich with his fork, but didn't take another bite. "He is only trying to irritate me. Typical psychological warfare."

Guilt crept in as Luna recalled that had been her own goal when she'd made JP dinner. She didn't like thinking that she and Henri had anything in common, but apparently they both liked making Jean-Pierre's life harder. She set her plate aside and scooted closer. "You're not going to let him get to you, right?" JP didn't answer, just kept staring at his sandwich, so she tried another tack. She put her hand on his arm, rubbing in what she hoped were soothing circles through his shirtsleeve. "You know, it's not too late to back out of this whole weird test."

Jean-Pierre put his half-eaten dinner on the coffee table

as well. "I cannot do that. I have worked too hard—*we* have worked too hard to give up now." He scrubbed a hand over his face. "I've flown you across an ocean for this. Do you really want to go back home without at least trying to win?"

"Don't worry about what I want." She touched her fingertips to his stubbled jaw. His skin felt hot. She had never been so attuned to someone else's breathing in her life, following the cadence of his inhale with her own. "What about you? What do *you* want?"

"Ah, Clair." He turned his head to look at her, his eyes dark and damp. He moved close, letting their foreheads press together, letting out a shaky breath. "I want to kiss you."

By the time he said it, they were already halfway to each other. Luna let her lips graze his, a bare brush. It was meant to be a comfort, something grounding, but apparently it wasn't enough. Jean-Pierre lifted a hand to the back of Luna's head and pulled her deeper.

Finally, finally, finally.

Luna couldn't get as close as she wanted, not when they were sitting side by side and twisted toward each other, so she climbed into his lap and settled herself on his thighs. That was a pleasant surprise for JP, judging by the gasp he made. She cradled his face in her hands and kissed him while his fingers dug into her hips.

They parted for air, but didn't go far, breathing hot against each other's cheeks.

She leaned in again, helping herself to a nip of his bottom lip. "I'm glad we—"

He leaned back, putting a confusing amount of distance between them and closing his eyes.

"—aren't letting the tension between us get overwhelming, yes." Jean-Pierre nodded. "Good thinking."

Luna stared at him. She had been planning to finish her sentence with something like *glad we finally decided to stop pretending we're not actually into each other*, because that was how she felt. She could admit it to herself now. As weird as it was being with someone like JP—fussy, French, and full of shit, sometimes—she liked being with him. She wanted to be with him even after all this nonsense with the culinary test was over.

Apparently, she was the only one who felt that way.

"Tension," she said, unsure of what else to say.

"Oui, vrai, there is, of course, between us, naturally—" He opened his eyes, looking lost. "Some tension." He lifted one hand to run his fingers through Luna's hair, the purple a touch less vibrant than it had been a few weeks ago. "You are a beautiful woman, Luna. You cannot blame me for noticing."

Luna cleared her throat. She was still straddling him, so a graceful dismount was going to be tricky. "We said one time only, last time. Remember?"

Jean-Pierre stared up at her, his smile small. "But tomorrow we give our last performance as a couple, no? Perhaps we should"—he shifted his hips beneath her, not in a lewd way, but like he was trying to get more comfortable—"get it out of our system before then."

Luna's hands slipped down his neck to rest on his shoulders. "So . . . one more one-time thing?" Her stomach sank like it was weighed down with rocks.

"You can say no," he rushed to add. "It was merely a passing thought. A suggestion. Just for tonight."

Her hands came to rest on JP's chest, her fingers fisting the fabric of his impossibly soft shirt. She couldn't meet his eyes. The silence was stretching, but she didn't know what to say that didn't sound needy and terrible. *Hey, can I pitch something really quick? Have you thought about keeping me around more permanently?* That sort of thing had worked only with Delilah, and Luna wasn't sure she should push her luck.

"There would be no expectations," Jean-Pierre said, each word making Luna's heart sink further. "Nothing more than—this."

Luna thought about all the times she'd slept with someone knowing it was only a one-time thing, or nothing serious, or because she wanted to blow off steam. She rarely regretted any of those nights; some things were just simple. This could be simple, too. Who cared if it was just for tonight? She had her answer about his bakery comment, didn't she? Of course he didn't want to marry her; that would be off-the-wall wild. He'd never even dated her, not really. He never would.

"Fuck it," she said, and kissed him again.

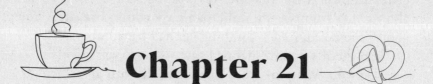

Chapter 21

Luna had never been a teenager. She had lived through the ages of thirteen to nineteen, sure, but that had been the only way in which she fulfilled the definition. All the fun things that teen girls were supposed to do—experimenting with makeup trends, shoplifting risqué panties, stealing the hottest boy in school's sweatshirt so your friends could take turns huffing it—had missed Luna by a mile. All part of growing up not knowing you were trans.

Which was why, for her, making out on a couch for an extended period of time was a thrilling new experience. Her past make-out sessions had all been as an adult, and they'd been hurried affairs, sometimes an afterthought, something to mark off the checklist before getting to the main event. Not so with Jean-Pierre. In fact, he seemed content to press Luna into the blue velvet sofa cushions and kiss her all night.

He really was a good kisser, so she was tempted to let him, but she was also overheating in her tight shirt.

"Here, let me—" She grabbed the hem of it and pulled it over her head. When she emerged, shaking out her long hair, JP was staring down at her with his mouth hanging open. Luna glanced down at the bra she was wearing, not her sexiest but also not her frumpiest, a utilitarian navy cotton bralette. "You good?" she asked, finger-combing her hair back into place.

Jean-Pierre's mouth snapped shut. "Good. Very good."

"Do you want to—too?" She fiddled with his shirttails, which had come loose from his waistband.

"Oh." He looked down at his own shirt-covered torso like he'd forgotten he possessed a corporeal form. He went to work on his buttons, fingers fumbling with each pearly stud. Once his shirt was stripped off, it joined hers on the floor.

Luna wasted no time in skating her hands over his bare chest. "Have I told you lately how hot you look?" She looked up at him through her eyelashes. It was important to keep things fun and flirty, she felt. Just like last time.

"You do not have to tell me this," he murmured.

Luna injected some teasing into her tone. "Oh, I see. You're well aware, huh? Don't need me telling you."

He stared up at her, his hands coming to rest on her hips again. There wasn't a trace of a smile on his face. It made Luna's own smile falter.

"I look—the way I look," he said. "I know on some level it is fine. But you—" He drew a hand up the side of her neck and cupped her cheek. "You were made to be worshipped."

Luna's breath caught. She tried to laugh because what else was she supposed to do? Who said stuff like that? Out loud, where it could actually be heard?

The laugh came out as more of an exhale. "Worshipped?" It didn't sound as teasing as she meant it to. It didn't sound teasing at all.

"Mm." He kissed the column of her throat, and she tipped her head back to let him. "Like a goddess."

She pasted on a watery smile, hoping to shake off the strange thrill those words sent through her. "Didn't peg you as a big talker," she said. "Last time you were pretty quiet."

"Last time my mouth was rather occupied," he said into the skin beneath her ear.

She dug her fingers into the thick hair at the back of his head. "Yeah. I remember." It was impossible to forget.

It was also impossible to herd them into safer territory. There was something heavy in the air, like the feeling right before a thunderstorm. Luna could sense that all her efforts to lighten the atmosphere would be met with more quiet declarations that would bring her right back here, underneath JP, with his careful hands and gentle mouth.

He kissed her while he unhooked her bra and drew the straps down her arms. Even that inconsequential scrap of fabric was set aside with a delicacy that felt ponderous. Any snarky remarks about it died on Luna's tongue the moment she looked down and saw JP's eyes staring back at her.

Like this mattered. Like she mattered.

She looked away, trying to find a minute to breathe. If she tipped her head back, she could see the night sky through the skylight. No stars in the center of the city, just the deep velvet of midnight blue, wisps of clouds like smoke passing over it.

Jean-Pierre kissed along her collarbone while she watched the sky. He whispered something in French, something Luna could barely catch through the haze of her pleasure. *You taste divine.*

It was impossible not to hear the intimacy of it in the closeness of the room. Especially in Jean-Pierre's stripped-raw voice. It was too much. Too—exposed.

"Hey." Luna tugged at Jean-Pierre's hair, forcing his head up so they could see each other. His eyes were nearly black, his pupils blown wide. She couldn't help petting his curls away from his brow. "Why don't we continue this somewhere with a door?"

"Yes, of course. Please, I— My bedroom." He nearly fell over in his haste to help her off his lap and the couch. Though Luna knew the way, he took her by the hand to lead her down the hall. She couldn't stop staring at their joined hands between them, connecting them like a garland.

"I like your room," she murmured when they crossed the threshold. Luna had seen only glimpses of it from the hallway, and now that she was inside it, she could tell it was his from smell alone. Coffee, lots of it, and that aftershave of his.

"Really?" He sounded incredulous. "Why?"

Luna could understand his disbelief. As a room, it wasn't much. There was a big bed, the bedclothes pulled up only on one side, like its owner had been in the process of making it and then given up. An armoire in a corner, a couple pieces of framed art prints on the wall, those blue Matisse cutouts. Very much a hotel room, a place someone passed through and did very little living.

"It smells good," she said honestly. She lay back on the bed, testing the bounce of it. Maybe that looked silly, her still topless and all, but JP was staring at her in a way that didn't make her feel silly.

Jean-Pierre moved to join her, shucking his jeans as he went. "Like my hair?" he murmured as he crawled onto the mattress on his hands and knees over her.

He kissed her like that, braced on his arms above her. Her hands were in his hair again. Whatever they'd done back in New York, it hadn't been like this, slow and strange and shivery.

JP kissed his way down her neck, between her breasts, low on her stomach. "Shall I . . . ?"

She made a noise of assent and lifted her hips so he could undo the buttons at her waistband and slip off her jeans. Then he disappeared over the edge of the bed.

She sat up, propped on her elbows. "Where are you going?"

His dark head lifted so he could look at her from his position kneeling on the floor between her legs. "Here." His hands slipped into the creases at the backs of her knees, his lips brushing along her thigh. "You seemed to enjoy yourself last time."

"Yeah, but—" He was too far away. He was practically on

another planet down there. Luna couldn't feel the whole press of his skin against hers. And if this was the last time she could have him, she wanted all of him.

Not that she could say any of that.

"Come on." She reached for him instead, waiting for him to put his hand in hers. "Come back up here. I want you to be more . . . involved this time."

He stayed on his knees for a long moment, looking at her hand like it was some kind of trick. "I don't mind," he said. "I like it. Pleasing you. I know I can please you like this."

Luna sat up fully so she could frame his stubborn, confused-looking face in her hands and kiss his frowning mouth. "You can do that lots of ways," she murmured. "I'm sure of it."

Jean-Pierre let out a ragged breath. For the first time the whole evening, a glimmer of a smile appeared on his mouth.

Her lips brushed over his upturned face. His eyes fell closed.

It occurred to Luna that maybe she was asking for more than a two-time thing allowed for. That this was too much, that she was too much.

She moved back onto her elbows again, shrugging. "If you'd rather stick with what you know, that's fine; I totally get it. Trust me, I won't complain either way."

JP got to his feet, standing over her now, head lowering so that their mouths almost met. His fists were planted on either side of Luna's hips, making the mattress dip. "I want to give you whatever you want," he said, the words falling against her lips. He had to be nervous; Luna could feel the tremor in his arms where she touched him, could hear it in his jagged breaths. "Only, I do not want to disappoint you."

Luna shut her eyes. Sex. They were just talking about sex. There was a limit to what Luna could ask of him, and she was taking them there. She picked up one of his hands and pressed a kiss to the palm. "You won't," she said. Faith enough for the both of them.

There were the usual practicalities to get through. Lubricant in the nightstand, pillows rearranged, sheets wadded out of the way at the foot of the bed. JP wriggled out of his purple briefs and got himself hard, and Luna wished he'd let her do that for him. But then again, he probably didn't want to drag this out any longer than they had to. The thought stabbed her in the gut.

But then he was back with her, and his skin was warm and soft where it pressed against hers, and his hand dug into the violet cascade of her hair. He kissed her while she opened around his slicked fingers.

"C'est bon?" he whispered against her cheek. "Tu aimes ça?"

"That's so unfair," she groaned. She buried her face in his shoulder as she clutched at his back. "You can't just say things like— Oh my *god*." How could he be this talented with his hands *and* mouth? It was really unfair.

A shadow of a smile pressed to the side of her neck. "You do not even know what I am saying." His fingers slipped free, leaving her feeling far too empty.

She considered telling him she knew exactly what he was saying, but it didn't seem like the right time to get into her self-taught French skills. Besides, if Jean-Pierre wanted to talk dirty in his native tongue, who was she to ruin his fun?

"It's not what you're saying, it's the way you're saying it," she huffed. Not a lie, not technically. His breathy murmurs were as intoxicating, if not more so, as the words themselves.

He seemed to take her consternation seriously because he became very quiet after that. Luna was about to tell him she hadn't actually minded—that she'd just been trying to lighten the mood again, obviously a losing proposition—but then he was inside her, and whatever they'd been talking about didn't seem important.

Luna had slept with plenty of people. Sometimes it was fun, sometimes it was very unfun, sometimes it was just whatever, and sometimes it was memorable for reasons completely separate from the sex itself. Very rarely was it like this.

She lay in Jean-Pierre's excellent bed, the softest pillows in the world under her hips, and she stared up into his dark eyes. Her mouth fell open as he moved in her. He mirrored her, his breath coming in sharp, staccato exhales. He looked as over-come as she felt.

Wordlessly, she slid her leg up around his waist. He was holding still above her, as deep as he dared go. She squeezed him with her leg and invited him deeper. His cock, that marvelous wonder, filled her up.

He did what she wanted. Like he always tried to do. He was more careful with her than anyone had ever been, and if she didn't love him before, she knew she did then.

"JP—"

He shushed her, kissing her before she could form any more words. They moved together, their bodies taking care of each other, slow and deliberate. When the kiss broke, Luna swore she could see the sheen of tears in JP's eyes.

It had never been like this. She wondered if it ever would be again. Where was she ever going to find this with someone else, this quiet devotion? She said his name again, not in a rush this time, just measured between her breaths. And he said hers, both of them. "Luna. Mon clair de lune."

It was the first time in her life she had two names and loved them both.

She fought against the impending wave of pleasure that shimmered in the distance. Once this was over, that was it. She didn't want it to end. Her fingers clawed into the muscles bunching in Jean-Pierre's shoulders, like she could hold on to this if she just tried hard enough. If she just pretended it was possible.

"Please," JP panted against her ear.

She had to let go.

"Please, darling—"

So she did. She let everything in her body go electric with the feel of him. She was lit up in every cell, every atom. It shouldn't have surprised her, but still she gasped. His arms held her so close, and his mouth was hot against her throat, and she could feel him shaking apart one step behind her.

And if she had to swipe some wetness from the corner of her eyes before untangling herself from him, well, hopefully he didn't notice.

"Come here, come." JP eased his cock out of her, curling a hand protectively over himself while he rearranged their positions. Luna found herself on her side with her cheek pillowed over his heart, his arm draped over her shoulders. His lungs were working hard still, her head rising and falling with his chest.

She wiped a hand surreptitiously at her eyes again. This was such a nice, peaceful moment, and instead of appreciating it for what it was, she was thinking about how much she was going to miss it when it was over. How much she was going to miss Jean-Pierre. It didn't seem possible that in a few days, she'd be back to her normal life in New York, and this would all be a distant memory. It all felt too real.

She should have never let it go this far.

"You are . . . all right?" he asked, lifting a strand of her hair and tucking it behind her ear.

"Mm," she said noncommittally. "I'm not too heavy on top of you like this?" She nuzzled under his chin, where the five o'clock shadow was becoming more like a ten o'clock one.

"Non." He kissed the top of her head. "You are as light as a feather."

Their height difference meant that his feet met Luna's shins, and their legs tangled together in a firm knot. Luna nestled closer to his still-heaving chest and sighed. *No regrets,* she told herself. One night like this was better than zero. Enjoy what you can while you can.

"Might just fall asleep right here," she whispered. "Do you mind?"

"Tu devrais." His tired fingers combed through her purple hair, trailing down her naked back. "Oui, reste avec moi." His lips touched her forehead. "Reste ici pour toujours," he murmured. *Stay here forever.*

Luna's eyes flew open. That was not something you said to a one-night stand. Or a two-night stand. That was not even something you said on a third date.

"Mon dieu," he said on a sigh, "je souhaite . . ."

What? Luna thought frantically. *What do you wish?*

She cleared her throat, trying for casual. "Did you say something?"

The gust of his breath went through her hair. "No," he said. "Nothing."

Right. Nothing. That was all it could be, if he couldn't even be bothered to say these things to her in English. They were probably just sweet nothings, vestiges of an orgasm that had reduced his brain to mush. Not everything had a deeper meaning. Some things just *were*; he'd been the one to teach her that.

They lay in the dark, skin-close but saying nothing, until eventually Luna fell into a troubled sleep.

Chapter 22

Luna stepped into the silence of Chef Henri Aubert-Treffle's flagship restaurant, Le Terrain, with her stomach somewhere around her ankles.

She'd never been in a restaurant outside of operating hours before, and it was really creepy. Only a few recessed lights were switched on, leaving almost everything in shadow. The dark dining room bristled with sleek padded chairs tipped upside down on the bare tables. Stacks of spotless white tablecloths were folded atop a banquet seating bench, waiting for someone to put them into service. Over by the hostess stand, plastic trays of fresh flowers sat on a sideboard, but whether they were decorative or edible, Luna couldn't say.

The kitchen was the centerpiece of the space. It loomed large on the far side of the cavernous room, its maw open for the world to see. A huge pass-through made it possible for chefs to hand off dishes to the waitstaff, all under the watchful eyes of the diners. Luna was starting to understand why people paid so much to eat here. She didn't *agree*, necessarily, but she understood.

It wasn't about food. It was about the performance.

Jean-Pierre stood at her side, his sigh loud in the quiet. "We can do this," he reminded her. His fingers brushed against hers like he planned to take her hand, but he must have thought better of it because the touch was gone as soon as Luna registered it.

She smiled stiffly at him. "Totally!" Rah-rah, cheerleader voice. Her smile faltered and she looked away, feigning interest in the pretentious art that hung on the walls between taupe satin drapes.

Their morning had been—not unpleasant, but awkward. Luna had awoken alone in Jean-Pierre's bed. He'd already gone for a run, had a shower, and made his coffee by the time she shuffled out of his room. There hadn't even been time to finish a single cup, let alone talk about what had happened the night before. Some agent of Henri's had arrived to escort them to the culinary test, informing Jean-Pierre in crisp, haughty French that he would be responsible for Luna's translations, as an interpreter would not be provided.

"Ah, look." JP walked ahead, pointing to another stack of white cloth on the gleaming pass-through rail. "Papi has left us some chef's whites."

"I love playing dress-up." Luna chose the smallest coat she could find, wishing that Henri had had the courtesy to find something cut for a lady. She shrugged into it, the boxy garment hanging awkwardly on her frame.

Oh, well. It wasn't like anyone but JP and Henri were going to see her wearing it.

The door opened just then, and a tiny blur of blonde hair rocketed straight for JP, calling, "Jean-Pierre, Jean-Pierre!"

"Chloé?" Jean-Pierre caught the bundle of energy in his arms and swung her around once before setting her on her feet. It was such a practiced maneuver that Luna was certain he'd done it a thousand times. "What are you doing here?" He spoke in French, naturally, and Luna was never so glad to have boned up on a language before.

"I didn't want to miss your big test," said the little girl. She peered up at Luna with all the undisguised curiosity of an eight-year-old.

Jean-Pierre switched to English. "Luna, this is my little sister, Chloé. Chloé, this is—"

"Miss Luna." Chloé stuck her hand out like an adult. "I am very pleased to meet you," she said in perfect English. Her big brown eyes and aquiline nose were the only features she seemed to share with Jean-Pierre, unless you counted her forthrightness. "Jean-Pierre has told me all about you. We text, of course."

Of course. "It's nice to meet you, too." Luna took her small hand and shook it. She didn't know much about kids, being an only child, but she figured just like grown-ups, it was best to meet them where they were. "I've heard a lot about you as well."

"Yes, I am a fantastic sister." She turned back to JP. "I am allowed to watch as long as I stay with Nanny and do not make any noise."

At that moment, a harried-looking young woman came through the door, looking around until her eyes landed on Chloé. "There you are! Your parents told you not to run ahead, did they not?" she said in French.

Chloé looked not the least bit guilty. "I barely jogged."

Parents? Luna opened her mouth to ask what that was about, but before she could, the door swung open and answered her.

In walked the most elegant older couple Luna had ever seen outside of a glossy advertisement for liver pills. The man was balding with his hair buzzed close to the scalp. He wore a lush plum turtleneck and eyeglasses in the same color, and his face was handsomely adorned with crow's feet. His hand was at the small of the woman's back, guiding her gently ahead of him.

She was small in stature but tall in heels that were as spiky as her gaze. Her silvery hair was coiled into a sleek seashell at the side of her head. She wore a black structured dress dotted with flashy buttons along one flank. It reminded Luna of a military dress uniform, if uniforms were featured in *Vogue*.

JP stared. "Maman?" he croaked. "Papa?"

Luna's hands instinctively rose to check her hair. It was still in its messy bun. She hoped it looked artful because it was the best she could do under the circumstances. She watched as Jean-Pierre wafted forward to speak to his parents. His incredibly stylish, fancy parents.

"You are also here?" he asked in French.

JP's mother kissed his cheeks without smiling. "Your grandfather has invited us to participate in the judging, of course. Did he not tell you?"

"No," Jean-Pierre said, cold. "He did not."

There was an awkward pause. The nanny took Chloé by the shoulders and led her toward a banquette seat at the back of the restaurant. "Come, we should stay out of everyone's way."

Chloé cast a forlorn look over her shoulder. "Good luck, Jean-Pierre. I will be cheering for you. Quietly."

He kissed his fingertips and puppeted them in her direction. "Be good."

Luna tried to shake off how cute JP was being and stepped forward to greet her fake boyfriend's parents properly. "Sir? Ma'am?" she said in English—she felt so nervous, she was afraid she'd mess up the French masculine and feminine identifiers. "I'm Luna. I've heard so much about you; thank you for coming." She stuck out her hand.

The married couple shared another meaningful look, and JP's dad accepted the handshake on his wife's behalf. His grip was a bit hesitant, not overly strong, but warm. "I must apologize," he said in heavily accented English. "My father, Jean-Pierre's grandfather, has a flair for the dramatic. I should have known he would not tell you of our coming." His voice was very similar to Jean-Pierre's, deep and smooth. He was giving Stanley Tucci. Luna had a passing thought that if this was what JP would look like in twenty or thirty years, it wasn't a bad deal.

Not that anyone was offering her said deal.

"And you are?" Mrs. Aubert-Treffle said, nudging her husband out of the way so she could stand directly in front of Luna.

"Uh, Luna. I said that, didn't I? My name is Luna O'Shea." She darted a look at JP. *Some backup, please?*

"She is my girlfriend," he said. "Surely Papi has mentioned her? He made such a fuss about including her in today's festivities." He placed his hand on Luna's back, mirroring the pose his parents had arrived in.

"She is transgender also?" Jean-Pierre's mom said in French. Disaffected, like these were just facts that weren't even that interesting. "She is very tall, and her voice . . ."

Luna supposed she should just keep smiling, since she wasn't supposed to understand what was being said. At least she was using the feminine pronoun.

Luna felt JP go rigid at her side, his fingertips digging slightly into her back. "Maman—"

"Ma cocotte," Mr. Aubert-Treffle said (Luna wasn't sure what the hell that word meant), "you cannot just ask that."

Her perfectly coiffed head swiveled toward him. "Why not? Is everything such a secret?"

"No one is keeping secrets from you," Jean-Pierre said. "Could you please stop being so paranoid?"

"Paranoid! If I am so paranoid, tell me, why do we not hear a word about this except through your grandfather?" she snapped. "He knows more of your life than us these days, I suppose. The tabloids, they know infinitely more! What do your mother and father know?" She made a violent gesture, exploding her hands apart in front of her. "Nothing."

Mr. Aubert-Treffle gave Luna a pained smile. "We are so pleased to meet you, of course," he said in English.

"Oh, likewise," Luna said between gritted teeth, forcing her lips into a tight grin.

The argument between mother and son continued without their input.

"When was I supposed to inform you, exactly? You were in Capri all last month, and before that, I only saw you for a moment at the reopening in Manila!"

"It does not take long to say, 'I am seeing a woman,' if that is indeed how you would describe this situation."

Luna's teeth ground together. Deep breaths. She had a lot of money in her bank account, so at least there was that.

"Is this your first time in Paris?" Mr. Aubert-Treffle asked, but Luna didn't feel like making any more small talk.

"I should familiarize myself with the kitchen. Excuse me," she said. She reminded herself to hold her head high as she retreated, but her progress was arrested by Jean-Pierre's hand on her arm.

"One moment, Clair," he said in English, and then, to his mother in French, "You will not talk about her that way. I will not allow it."

"Why are you so upset?" She laughed at the ceiling, like she was sharing a joke with the gods. "I only meant I do not know how you would characterize this—dalliance. That is all."

"That is not what you meant," Jean-Pierre growled. "If that is what you meant, that is what you would have said. You mean to be insulting."

His mother shook her head. "Now you are the one who is paranoid."

Luna glanced over to where Chloé and her nanny were sitting at the back of the dining room. The little kid seemed to be absorbed in some kind of school workbook and thankfully wasn't paying any attention to this awkward argument.

"Do you know why I tell you so little?" JP leaned closer to his mother, his hand hot on Luna's wrist. "Because of this. Because I know how you are. Why should I tell you anything if this is how you act? Make snide remarks about me all you like; I don't care anymore. But you will speak of Luna only with respect, or not at all. Do you understand?"

Could panties spontaneously combust through the sheer power of someone being a badass? Luna felt that if it were possible, she'd be experiencing the phenomenon at that very moment. She stared at JP's profile, his sharp chin and sharp eyes, that glare of his that wasn't backing down, and she was certain that, of all the people who had stuck up for her in her life, this one was the bravest.

Jean-Pierre's mother, for her part, shifted on her heeled feet and gave a click of her tongue. She looked to Mr. Aubert-Treffle, but he was not meeting her gaze. He only took her gently by the elbow with a murmured, "We should take our seats."

Mrs. Aubert-Treffle tightened her jaw the same way JP did when he was angry. She gave a curt nod and moved toward a banquet along the far wall. As Mr. Aubert-Treffle followed his wife, he stopped and looked over his shoulder at Jean-Pierre. His mouth opened, then closed like he didn't know what to say. He walked away, too, leaving them standing in front of the kitchen.

"Hey," Luna said to Jean-Pierre once they had the space, "this is all kinds of fucked up."

"Oui." He sighed. "Very much fucked." He glanced over at her, his hand still clutching her arm. "I would understand if you wished to leave."

The thought had never crossed Luna's mind. "It's your family; you make the call. If you say we stay, I'll stay. If you want to go, I'm right behind you, dousing this place in kerosene."

That made Jean-Pierre crack a smile. He ducked his head. "I would never ask you to commit arson for me."

"You don't have to ask," Luna said. "It would be my treat." She was smiling now, too, and for the first time since their night together, it felt like they were on the same page.

Then the cameras arrived.

Video cameras. And lighting. And boom mics. Lots and lots of them.

Luna's eyes widened at the sudden influx of Parisian videographers that flooded into the dining room. All the tables and chairs were rearranged to make space for the equipment. A woman with a high ponytail and aggressive eye makeup— a director?—was shouting orders to the crew.

"What the fuck?" Luna felt like a pebble in a chaotic stream. "What's going on?"

"I have no idea," said Jean-Pierre, who was also staring open-mouthed at this latest development.

"Did I forget to mention?" A booming francophone voice emanated from the depths of the kitchen. Luna turned to find Chef Henri himself striding toward her. Two incredibly similar young women—maybe twins; assistant twins—flanked him, one texting furiously on her phone and the other whispering into the headset she wore. "We are filming your little test. My producers, they suggested it." His English had a superior note to it. He stopped a few feet away from Luna and looked her up and down. His chef's whites, she noticed, were tailored perfectly to fit him.

"Chef Henri, I presume?" She gave a lazy raise of her eyebrows. "You look taller on TV."

The barb had the desired effect. While JP was busy covering his laugh with a cough, Henri turned a fun shade of brick. He faced his grandson, full of bluster. "I trust the cameras are no problem for you? I'm not certain what we will do with this footage; perhaps it will be packaged as a special. Christmastime, ideally, since it is a family affair."

"Papi, the agreement said nothing about filming," Jean-Pierre said.

"Well, we are in my restaurant, and I will do what I like," Henri snapped. "Unless you wish to concede?"

Luna rolled her eyes. "Film us, don't film us, we don't mind either way." She threaded her fingers through JP's. "Isn't that right, sweetie?"

Jean-Pierre didn't look away from his grandfather for a moment. If eyes could bore holes, Henri would be Swiss cheese. "That is right. It doesn't matter what you throw at us. We are going to win."

The front door opened again. Luna turned with a groan. Would the surprises ever end?

Then she caught sight of the figure sailing through the mess of the film crew setting up, and her mouth fell open.

"Is that?" She blinked hard. "Pim Gladly?"

It was. Delilah's ex-boss and Simone's nemesis, she of The Discerning Chef empire, celebrity guest judge on about half a dozen cooking shows, was here. She wore a giraffe-skin-print jumpsuit with bell sleeves and was inexplicably cradling a small dachshund in the crook of her arm in defiance of all food safety rules. Her sharp eyes landed on Luna, then JP, before finally settling on Henri.

"I need to be in Cannes by breakfast tomorrow," she said without preamble, "so this better not run long." The dog whined, and she shushed it.

Jean-Pierre squinted at her in confusion. "Madame Gladly?" Of course he would know her, or at least know of her. It was a small world, and the food world was even smaller. "What is this?"

Henri gestured expansively, almost striking one of his assistants in the side of the head. She ducked. "My dear friend Pim has agreed to be a special guest judge," he said. "It is only fair, no? Someone outside the family should taste your food as well."

Pim seemed to lose interest in the conversation and instead craned her neck to see who else might be in residence. She spotted JP's parents sitting at a carefully staged table on the other side of the dining room and gave a gasp. "Claude! Julia! Bonjour." She minced toward them in her heels, stepping delicately over the reams of cables that the film crew was in the process of snaking across the floor.

Jean-Pierre gave his grandfather a hard look. "You are making this far more complicated than it needs to be."

Henri looked strangely proud. "That is very funny," he returned in French, "especially coming from the likes of you."

Luna ground her teeth together. She wasn't just imagining the slimy judgment in those words. "Excuse me," she said with false innocence. "What does that mean?"

"Ah, yes, I forgot: your very serious girlfriend, she only speaks English," Henri said in that tongue. He finally addressed Luna directly—rude. "I was only saying if you do not like the terms of the arrangement, you are free to forfeit. I am happy to instead leave my fortune to some charity that"—he moved a hand vaguely through the air—"provides kittens with university degrees or some inane thing."

"We are so looking forward to the test, though," Jean-Pierre said with a smile that was all teeth. "The more, the merrier, I think."

"Très bien." Chef Henri clapped his hands. "We shall begin once the cameras are ready, oui? Bonne chance." He didn't even try to make that last bit sound sincere. He just oiled away toward the judging table, snapping his fingers to call his twin assistants to heel.

Luna watched him go with a wrinkled nose. "Hey, no offense—"

JP let go of her hand. "He is an ass. I know. Everyone knows." He took a deep breath and finished buttoning his coat into place. "Let's just get this over with."

They were a third of the way through the allotted time, and Luna was totally snowed. The Menu was coming together, but it certainly wasn't as polished as some of their practice rounds. It was an entirely different ball game in an unfamiliar kitchen under the watchful eyes of the cameras, not to mention all the interruptions from Henri and Pim for the sake of color commentary. The duck was greasy; the crème anglaise wasn't smooth; the salad dressing had split; and Luna couldn't find the kohlrabi no matter how many times she checked in the back.

"Did you look in the storeroom with the potatoes?" JP said

as he concentrated on slicing very thin medallions of something red with Pim Gladly hovering at his elbow, flanked by cameras.

"Of course I looked with the potatoes. The potatoes were the first place I looked!" She wiped her face with a kitchen towel. In the last three hours, she had sweated more than she ever had in her entire life. It was like trying to work in the bowels of hell with the ovens and cooktops going full blast.

"I'm curious." Pim poked her nose over his shoulder. "Do you think the rabbit will be cooked in time?"

"It only needs seven hours in the pressure cooker," Jean-Pierre said.

"But you only have six hours left." Her voice held a note of unholy glee.

"What will be, will be." Jean-Pierre dumped his red stuff in a pot and slapped the lid on. "Luna, did you check the walk-in?"

Before Luna could inform him—in a completely calm and collected tone, of course—that she had checked the walk-in *twice* already, Chef Henri materialized at her side. She barely managed to swallow her yelp of surprise. Cameras loomed over his shoulder as he gave Luna and her workstation an imperious once-over.

"Can you tell us what you are working on at the moment?" he said in his thick accent.

Luna gave the salad dressing another vigorous whisk along with another glug of oil, hoping it would come together. It didn't. "Uh, just getting the components for the salad course together."

"It does not look the way it does when *I* make it," Henri said in his trademark gruff tone.

She was approximately fifteen seconds away from setting his beard on fire with the broiler. "What a helpful piece of feed-back. Thank you, Chef." Luna looked directly into the camera and hoped that, whatever this footage ended up being used for, the viewers would catch her deadpan stare. "I need to find the kohlrabi; excuse me."

She ducked around Henri and the camera crew, hustling through the huge door of the walk-in fridge. Fully stocked shelves lined the frost-encrusted walls, and Luna tore through them trying to find the absent vegetable. The roar of the walk-in's motor was so loud, she could barely hear herself think. She turned around and leaned back against the freezing metal shelves with a groan, rubbing at her eyes and trying to get herself under control.

The door whooshed open and a nervous-looking crew member with a headset entered. "Ah, mademoiselle?"

"Quoi?" Luna snapped. She knew it wasn't the crew's fault that Henri was a kohlrabi-hiding dickhead, but she was on her last nerve. "Que voulez-vous?"

The PA stammered in French, "My name is Louis. If an ingredient is missing, I am supposed to fetch it for you. Is there something you need?"

"Yes, uh—" Luna racked her brain. Thankfully, she'd studied up on food vocabulary for just this kind of emergency. "Chourave. Deux kilos. Et les . . ." She turned around to point at the crate of fucking rhubarb that wasn't nearly ripe enough. "Ces rhubarbes, elles sont trop vertes."

"Les vertes sont mauvais?" Louis said. *Green is bad?*

Luna reminded herself that committing a murder in the middle of the cooking challenge was probably against the rules. She heard the click of the door behind her, but in her agitation, she didn't really register it. She was too focused on the rhubarb situation, a phrase that by rights should have had zero business being in her life. She held up two fingers in Louis's distressed face. "Deux kilos aussi. Très, très rouges. Comprenez?"

"Je comprends," said Louis at the same moment Jean-Pierre's voice echoed through the cold chamber.

"Since when do you speak French?"

Luna squeezed her eyes shut. Her hand fell back to her side. Wonderful. Now the situation was way bigger than rhubarb.

She spun on her heel to give JP a grimace of a smile. "Surprise?"

He was standing just inside the walk-in with the door sealed shut behind him. His mouth hung open, breath coming in huge clouds of steam in the chilled air. "Answer me. When did you learn French?"

"The core competency stuff?" Luna cringed. "About three weeks ago."

Louis began edging toward the door, but JP pointed a finger at him and barked, "Stay where you are." It sounded even angrier en français. He turned back to Luna, shaking his head in disbelief. "So last night, you understood everything I said to you?"

"I should probably go," said Louis.

"No!" they both shouted.

"Wait there just a second." Luna turned back to JP. "I'm sorry; I wanted to tell you but I didn't want to make things awkward."

Jean-Pierre gestured wildly between them. "And *this* isn't awkward?"

"Yeah, okay, you have a point." Luna sighed. She rubbed at her temples. Her headache was growing by the second.

Jean-Pierre exhaled sharply in disbelief. "I said things in front of you that— Putain de merde." He raked his hands through his sweat-damp curls, groaning loud enough to be heard over the walk-in's rumble. "Do you have any idea how foolish this makes me feel?"

Luna wrapped her arms around herself against the cold air. "Look, people say things in the heat of the moment. I get that. It's not the huge deal you're making it out to be."

"I am very uncomfortable right now," Louis told them.

But JP was giving only Luna his attention. He lifted his head, his eyes wide. "You think I didn't mean what I said?"

"Uh, obviously." Luna gave a laugh, as bitter as the radicchio she was fifteen minutes behind on washing and chopping. She kept her gaze on the floor. "You don't want me around forever. You definitely don't plan on marrying me. That's all part of—

you know—our whole thing." Her throat was tight, but she bit out the words like curses. "Temporary. A two-time thing. Nothing personal. Just business."

Jean-Pierre abandoned his post by the door to stand in front of Luna. He took her clammy hands in his, and she finally looked up. His eyes were as dark and deep as fond on the bottom of a good enameled pot.

"That is not true," he said. His voice was so quiet, she could barely hear him over the walk-in fans. "It is personal. Very personal. And I meant it. Every word."

Luna's lips parted. She wanted to say something sophisticated, charming. What she said was, "Wha . . . ?"

Somewhere over by the dairy shelf, Louis coughed meaningfully into his fist. They ignored him.

"I am sorry." Jean-Pierre looked at the tile floor beneath their clogs like it held all the answers. "I know this is just a job for you; I know none of it was real. I do not care. I want you. I want you forever." He picked his head up, a sheen of tears in his eyes. "Do you hate me very much?"

"I—" Luna clutched his hands tighter. "I don't understand. Why didn't you say anything before? Like, in English? I was so convinced that you couldn't— Because you never said anything."

He groaned and let his head fall again. "How could I? You were always reminding me this was just a ruse, a means to an end. The only reason you're even here is because of this ridiculous feud I have with my grandfather."

"I'm here because I chose to be," Luna said.

He looked stricken. "He can leave me out of his will entirely; it doesn't matter to me anymore. It hasn't mattered for weeks. But I did not want this to end." His fingers threaded more firmly with hers, holding tight.

Luna took a deep, shuddering breath. She thought about JP's terrible vaping habit and his inability to sleep like a normal person; his coffee snobbery and his colorful underwear; the way he loved his little sister and old women who could bake; how gentle he was with children. How well he kissed her.

She really, really liked pretending to date Jean-Pierre. He was the most real man she'd ever met. And she wanted to keep him—for real.

"I don't want it to end either," she said, "so let's just keep going."

JP lifted his head and stared at her. "Going?" He blinked. "Actually—not as an act?"

Luna smiled and shrugged one shoulder. "Yeah? If that sounds—"

He didn't let her finish. His hands came up to frame her face, and he kissed her as hard as he ever had. Right there between the crates of spinach and the shelves stuffed with cheeses, heedless of the cold air and the fact they were running out of time to cook this damn meal. Not that she was going to point that out when his tongue was dipping into her, inviting her to taste him, too. She smiled into it when she realized he was up on tiptoe to get to her. Her arms wound around his broad shoulders and stayed there.

"Excusez-moi." Louis was snapping his fingers to try and get their attention. "Am I going to the shop or no?"

JP pulled away from Luna's mouth just enough to murmur, "What do you think? Shall we just leave now? Spend the rest of the day in bed?"

"Tempting." She nipped his lower lip. "But on the other hand, we did work really hard learning how to cook."

"I do not want to cook this food. I hate this food, actually." His huff appeared like icy smoke in the frigid air.

"Well." Luna felt lit up from the inside, like the lights along the Rockaways, like the ones along the Seine. She was feeling downright petty, and if Jean-Pierre's answering smirk was any indication, he was right there with her. "We can cook something else. If you want."

"I do want." He kissed her again, lingering only for a moment. Then: "You," JP called to Louis over Luna's shoulder. "You are going to the shop. I will give you a list."

"And if you can't find pickled jalapeños," Luna said with a laugh, "fresh is fine."

Chapter 23

They cooked nine courses, in the end.

They just weren't the ones they were supposed to cook.

The chilled soup—which was an affront to god and all the saints, in Luna's opinion—was served hot. And instead of sunchokes, it was broccoli and cheese, a thick, hearty, incredibly American dish that was served in a hollowed-out round of peasant bread. The caviar course was done simply, on store-bought crackers with flecks of rosemary baked into them. Luna thought the two strong flavors might clash, but oh well. It wasn't like she was the one who'd spent upward of five hundred euros on a tin of fish eggs. The composed salad was now just a salad. Greens. Some chopped vegetables. A few sprouts and a hard-boiled egg and some bottled dressing. It was fine. It was a salad, and it didn't need to pretend to be anything else.

The beef tartare was nixed altogether, replaced by a single cocktail meatball sitting in a pool of soy sauce that had been reduced with apricot jam. Luna was very proud of JP for coming up with that one. He'd practically cackled as he formed the meatballs, taking care not to overwork the mixture: "Papi will have a heart attack when he realizes we have cooked this mince. He had to import it from Mongolia."

The scallop got wrapped in bacon, coated in bread crumbs, and deep-fried. It wasn't very successful but Luna felt it was important to take risks.

They had both agreed that the rabbit and duck could go fuck themselves. If they never saw another plate of Bugs Bunny and Daffy Duck in their lives, they would be content. Instead, Jean-Pierre made his semi-famous macaroni and cheese. Luna made a series of herby croque monsieurs with fried eggs on the side so that the individual diner could choose what gender their sandwich would be that day.

Luna regretted not being able to serve the floating islands, since she really did like the dish, but there was just no time to whip the meringue. Instead she used the crème anglaise in a simple parfait with caramelized pears and bleu cheese crumbles.

The gâteau was nowhere to be found once the countdown clock struck zero. In its place was the cheese plate to end all cheese plates: a bounty of French and English and even a few American-style cheeses, an overflow of fresh berries, dishes of pickles, spiced nuts, good, crusty bread that Louis had bought from the shop since they didn't have three days to make the perfect loaf themselves, and a dizzying assortment of jams, mustards, and chutneys straight from the jar.

Luna stood at JP's side, sweating from all the hard work and the damn lights. Her previously white chef's coat was smeared with butter and her hair was a mess, but she couldn't stop grinning at Jean-Pierre. A few scant hours ago, they were just business partners who'd fooled around a little. Now they were—well, they didn't have a label or anything, but they were something. Something good. He liked her. A lot. Luna had been liked (a lot) by plenty of people, but this one . . . this one made her feel giddy down to her toes.

She also couldn't stop smiling at the array of food they'd produced. It was the perfect meal, in her opinion. It sat before the judges on the huge table, ringed with cameras and all the sound equipment. Behind the crew, Luna could just make out little Chloé's ecstatic face, her mouth open in wonder.

Under the bright lights, Chef Henri looked like he was going to explode. His face was as red as the tomato medallions that had made it into the salad. JP's parents just looked confused. And Pim—she seemed to be taking it all in stride, actually. She leaned over the table to survey the offerings like a bird hunting for a worm in the tall grass.

"It's very . . ." Pim Gladly adjusted her designer eyeglasses. "Cheese-forward."

"I like cheese," Luna said.

"So do I," Jean-Pierre said. He reached out his hand, and Luna took it without even looking. It was sweaty, but she didn't mind. "I love it, in fact," he added.

Luna looked over at him then, her heart fit to burst. He met her gaze with a secret smile dancing around his lips.

"If you love it so much, why don't you marry it?" she said.

"Maybe I will." His smile grew. "Someday."

Luna bit down on the squeal she wanted to let loose.

A delicate cough from JP's father brought their attention back to the judging table. "I do not think," said Claude Aubert-Treffle, "that what you have presented to us fulfills the brief."

"This is not your grandfather's menu. It is not even a clever twist on the classic dishes," Madame Aubert-Treffle broke in. "It is just—a lot of cheese!"

"And a salad," Luna pointed out. "Something light, you know. A nice break between all that heavy stuff."

Jean-Pierre waggled his head. "Though there is some cheese in the salad."

"Feta is practically a vegetable," Luna told him.

"Ah, you are so right, mon Clair."

"I am not eating this," Henri said, pushing himself away from the table. His chair squealed as it was dragged along the floor. "It is a travesty, a joke."

"Ah-ah, Papi." JP held up a finger. "According to the rules, the food we present *must* be sampled and judged by the panel."

Luna gave him her widest grin. "So eat up, Henri. Quick, before the soup gets cold."

Henri glared at the woman with the clipboard on the camera crew. "Why aren't you putting a stop to this madness? None of this footage will be usable."

"Jean-Pierre is correct," the woman said in a tone that brooked no argument. "The rules are the rules. We keep shooting." She pointed with the tip of her pen at the soup course. "You start eating."

With an unintelligible grumble, Henri dipped his soup spoon into the cheesy broccoli bread bowl and took the tiniest sip. Claude and Julia exchanged looks before following suit, although Luna noticed JP's dad took a healthier spoonful and went back for more.

Pim Gladly seemed unfazed by Henri's brand of bombast, eating her soup with a steely expression. "Uninspired," she declared. "You could find this on the menu at any American chain restaurant, I imagine."

"Thanks." Luna smiled brightly. "That means a lot, coming from you."

Pim didn't even respond. She just tore a hunk off her bread bowl and fed it to the dachshund that sat in her lap. He gobbled it up without complaint.

Jean-Pierre's mother cleared her throat. "I find this soup quite heavy. It is better to start a nine-course meal with something light and silky, no?" She mimed rubbing fabric between her fingertips, looking to her husband for confirmation.

"I like it," Claude said. Luna beamed at him. "It would make a hearty lunch all on its own." He turned to his father. "What are your comments, Chef?"

Henri placed his soup spoon on the table with a thunk. "I have nothing to say."

What a big baby. Luna looked right into a camera, telegraphing all her thoughts before clearing away the first course and serving the second.

It continued in the same vein for several courses: Henri sat sullenly like an angry badger, Pim offered some snooty repartee, Julia largely agreed with her, and Claude, bless his heart, kept finding some bright spot in each ridiculous dish.

Then she and Jean-Pierre presented the entrée.

"This is a gratin de macaroni with Brie, grilled jalapeño"—since the local supermarket did not, in fact, carry cans of pickled ones—"and a pretzel crumb. Enjoy."

All the judges save Henri picked up their forks.

"I refuse to allow this to continue," Henri declared, and swept an arm over the table, knocking his TV-ready place setting onto the floor.

Luna and JP both hopped out of the way of flying cutlery. Forks and spoons clattered to the ground. A plate shattered into jagged pieces. The mac and cheese made a postmodern spray of white and yellow and green all along the tablecloth and on the floor. A boom mic operator cried out in pain; a steak knife had nicked her leg, and she was struggling to keep her boom lifted while simultaneously clapping a hand to her bleeding calf. Someone else on the crew screamed.

Jean-Pierre took Luna by the arm, sweeping his gaze over her. "Are you all right?"

"I'm fine but— Oh my god." Luna took a step toward the boom mic woman, wanting to help, but medics had already descended on her. Another crew member took the mic from her grip so she could be tended to. The director rolled her fingers through the air and stared pointedly at Luna. "Seriously? We're supposed to keep going? Someone is *hurt*."

One camera peeled off from the pack to follow the injured crew member as she was half-carried away by the medical team. Doubtless her teary commentary would make for good television.

Henri deigned a glance in the direction of the crew's panicked reshuffling. "Barely a scratch. The real hurt has been dealt to hundreds of years of French culinary tradition!" He puffed up at a camera lens. A perfect sound bite.

Luna turned to catch JP's eyes in all the chaos. His own gaze was locked on something in the distance, and Luna followed his line of sight to find Chloé huddled in the back of the dining room with both hands clapped over her mouth. She looked terrified, and JP looked furious.

"Get her out of here. She should not have to see this circus," he called to the nanny.

"But Jean-Pierre—" Chloé protested even as her nanny took her by the hand and dragged her toward the exit.

"It's all right. We will speak soon, Chloé." He kissed his fingertips again and sent them her way.

Chloé returned the gesture before disappearing out the door. Luna was sad to see her go, but she was pretty sure this was no place for a child.

Henri, for his part, just snorted. "She wasn't even that close."

"That was not the problem." Jean-Pierre turned back to Henri. "You don't like what I cooked? Fine. But you have a tantrum over it? You act that way in front of your granddaughter?" He scoffed, unbuttoning his chef's whites to hang open, exposing his simple black T-shirt. "And you think I am a spoiled child."

Pim Gladly chose that moment to take a bite of the mac and cheese that still sat undisturbed in front of her. "Too spicy for me," she said with a weak cough.

No one paid her any mind.

Henri stood, rising to his full height. He growled. Actually growled, like a bear. "You are worse than spoiled," he boomed at JP in French. "You have been, at every single turn, every step of the way, a disappointment." He gestured to Claude and Julia, who were cowering in his shadow. "This is a family of chefs and you, whatever you are, are not that." He angled his face so the camera could catch the arrogant jut of his bearded chin.

Jean-Pierre stalked to the very edge of the table, leaning over it to get right into his grandfather's face. "I decide what I am, not you. I cook for the people I care about. I say that makes me a chef—twice the chef you are."

Claude held up his palms. "Calm down, Jean-Pierre," he said, like JP was the one breaking dishes on the floor.

JP did not calm down. He swiveled his head, addressing his parents as well. "And if I say I am a man, then I am a man. That is what this is really about, yes? That I must prove myself in this ridiculous manner because you refuse to accept what is real—what I am."

Julia slammed her palms on the table and stood. Pim Gladly's little dog whimpered in the silence that followed.

When Jean-Pierre's mom finally spoke, her voice was as cold as that walk-in had been. "It took me years of hard work and determination to become the chef I am today. Now you come here with your childish food and your American—" Luna gave a start as she pointed at her.

Claude placed a hand over his wife's, lowering it back down. "My love, perhaps we should leave. This is getting a bit heated."

Julia ignored him. She huffed at JP. "You can say you are an elephant; that does not make it true. What you are doing here is mockery."

Pim Gladly, who didn't seem to be following the French conversation very well, hissed at one of the production assistants, "What are they saying? Is it juicy?"

Luna stepped forward so that Jean-Pierre wasn't standing alone at the judging table. She held his hand in hers and caught his grateful look.

He turned back to his mother. "Grand-mère can understand this simple thing; why can't you? She raised you better than this, surely."

That sent a ripple through the room. More than one sharp gasp could be heard, and Luna saw one of the camerapeople poke their head out from behind their equipment to gape at the scene. Julia went pale and her mouth tightened into a thin line, but she had no retort.

"Get out of my restaurant," Chef Henri said in dangerously quiet French. "Get out of my sight."

"Come on, Clair." Jean-Pierre squeezed Luna's hand. "I'm done here."

"I'm not." Luna stood her ground and said, in perfectly serviceable French: "I have a lot to say." She was really glad she'd boned up on podcasts with explicit language because she was not feeling PG-13 at the moment. She drew a little rectangle around the judging panel with her pointer fingers, making a picture of them. "You are all pieces of shit. And you can rot in hell for all I care." She singled out JP's wide-eyed dad with a nod. "And yes, Papa, that means you, too. Trying to play nice while you let your father and your wife tear your son apart? Shame on you."

The man ducked his head and removed his glasses, but the cameras were inescapable.

"Since when does she speak French?" Julia murmured to no one in particular.

Pim Gladly scratched her little dog behind its floppy ears. "I don't understand a word of this," she said in English. "Someone tell me when it's reached its natural conclusion."

"Get out, the both of you!" Henri stabbed a blunt finger at Luna and JP. "Out, out, out!"

Luna cupped a hand to her ear. "Sorry, can you repeat that one more time?"

"Leave!" he roared, his face turning a lovely shade of eggplant.

"My pleasure," Luna said, still in French. She squeezed Jean-Pierre's hand hard. "And since the rules of the culinary test state that if either party—that is, either Jean-Pierre *or you*—halts the proceedings for any reason, that party forfeits and the other automatically wins. And we haven't gotten to the dessert course yet. Which means that you, Chef Henri, have just made Jean-Pierre your sole heir."

JP looked at her askance. "Is that true? Really?"

"Really," Luna said. "I read the fine print. You know why?" She gave Henri the coldest look she'd ever given anyone. "I am an excellent fucking assistant."

"She is correct," the Frenchwoman with the clipboard piped up from behind the cameras. She unclipped some pages from the board and held them up in all their marked and highlighted glory. "It says so right here." She tapped her pen to the relevant paragraph.

"Isn't that interesting." JP released Luna's hand to shrug off his borrowed chef's whites, tossing them onto the judging table alongside the abandoned plates of food. "I suppose my lawyers will be in touch with your lawyers to draw up all the necessary paperwork, Papi. Maman, Papa, Madame Gladly." He nodded to them each in turn. "Bonsoir." He turned on his heel.

"By the way," Luna said, unable to resist a parting shot at Chef Henri, this time in English, "I'm trans, too. And yeah, I'm pretty, but not too pretty for Jean-Pierre. Exactly the right amount of pretty. Which is a lot. Also your food tastes like musty old ass. Go fuck ya'self." A middle finger for good measure, and then she was following JP outside, shedding her chef's coat as she went.

They both pushed through the restaurant door and stood on the narrow sidewalk outside, blinking in the harsh sunlight. Jean-Pierre turned to her, breathing hard. His face was flushed, his hair a wild tangle.

He spoke first. "You really—"

"Defended you amazingly? Yeah. I did." She tossed her hair out of her eyes.

"I was going to say you really should have stolen those cheese boards on the way out." His smile was small but growing. "I'm starving."

She made a face. "Damn, you're right. I hope the camera crew is allowed to eat all that food. It would be such a waste otherwise. How awkward do you think it would be if I popped back in and—?"

He leaned in and kissed her. Luna was only somewhat aware that they were blocking foot traffic in an extremely posh neighborhood, but she didn't care. She wrapped her arms around his shoulders and felt him take hold of her waist, and smiled against his mouth when he went up on tiptoe to kiss her deeper. It went on for long enough that Luna forgot what she was going to say, which was probably for the best. When it ended, Jean-Pierre stared at her lips.

"Thank you," he breathed. "I owe this all to you."

Luna shrugged. "Hey, one of those TV producers would have pointed out the rules anyway. Makes for a healthy dose of drama."

"No, not the inheritance. Although you do deserve credit for that. No, I mean—" He shook his head, then switched to French. "You let me be more myself than I have ever been in my life. Does that make sense?"

Luna smiled and placed a hand on the side of his face. "Tons." She gave him a peck on the cheek. "Want to take me back to your place, Chef?"

"Oui, Chef," he murmured, and kissed her through her giggles.

"Jean-Pierre!"

They turned as one to the doorway of the restaurant, where Claude Aubert-Treffle was stumbling out onto the street.

"Oh, thank Christ," he said in French. "I thought I would be too late."

"We were just leaving," Jean-Pierre said, sounding wary. He released Luna from his embrace but didn't go far, instead wrapping an arm over her shoulders. "What is it, Papa?"

Luna narrowed her eyes at Claude, wishing she had taken a cheese board if only so she could whack him over the head with it if he tried to mess with her—oh—her very real boyfriend.

Claude watched her carefully as if he could divine her intentions. His hands went up in a gesture of peace. "If you do not wish to speak with me—oh, my dear boy, I wouldn't blame you. I only wanted to let you know—" He glanced back over his shoulder like someone might be pursuing him, but they remained alone. Even the foot traffic had seen fit to leave them be. "I am sorry. I thought, with time, your mother and grandfather would come around. I even thought this silly test was a step in the right direction. An opportunity for you to prove yourself. That is the only reason I suggested it, I swear."

"Sorry?" JP blinked. "You—you were the one who came up with this whole elaborate scheme?"

Claude hung his head. "I did. I told your grand-père that if he did not go through with it, I would never speak to him again. That was enough, I suppose, to pressure him into this. I hoped that, even if you didn't succeed in passing his test, you could at least earn his respect—and you could have, Jean-Pierre. I saw you cooking his dishes earlier; you were brilliant. Especially for a novice."

JP stood there for a moment, looking into the middle distance, his lips mouthing like they were trying to find the correct words. At last he said, "You were trying to get me into a club I have no interest in entering."

"What?" Claude frowned. "What does that mean?"

Luna gave his waist a squeeze with her arm, telegraphing how proud she was of him in that moment. He turned and caught her eye. His smile said he got the message.

"I do not need the respect of Papi," he said to his father. "I have my own."

Claude had tears in his eyes. "Your mother, she loves you," he said. "I love you. We just don't know how to show it sometimes."

"You can start by not letting her talk to me the way she does."

Claude looked away. "I cannot make her listen to reason. You know how stubborn your mother can be."

"So can I," Jean-Pierre said. He sounded so determined. And so damn hot. "I don't need to listen to it, not anymore.

Not ever again. If that means not being around her, then that is what it means."

His father paled. "Do you want to leave your position? The family business?"

Jean-Pierre clicked his tongue. "I have not thought about it. This is all happening so quickly. And anyway—" He looked over at Luna. "Perhaps I will move to New York soon."

Luna's heart surged. "Wait, really?" She let herself picture it for a minute—Jean-Pierre's coffee every morning and his bad jokes every night—but then shook her head. "But you love Paris. You love traveling. You wouldn't be happy staying in the States, would you?" They had so much to talk over. It felt like a red carpet was being rolled out for the future, and the rest of her life would be spent walking it.

"I don't know," JP said thoughtfully. "We should sleep on it." He reeled her in closer to his side.

Luna tried not to laugh. She doubted there would be much sleep tonight, once they got their greasy clothes off and took about a half dozen showers.

Jean-Pierre turned back to his father, more sober now. "I need time, Papa."

Claude nodded, still teary, and looked like he was going to go in for a hug, but stopped at the last second. "Yes. Of course." He settled for a firm nod.

They parted ways, not awkwardly—Jean-Pierre was too self-confident for that—but bittersweet. Claude stood in front of the restaurant and waved goodbye as they walked in some random direction that Luna hoped would reveal a taxicab.

She looked at JP's profile, and for once, he looked relaxed, his lips even quirking at the corners. "You okay?"

"I feel like the longest shift of my life is over," he said. "And I can finally go home." His hand sought hers and squeezed. "With you."

"Avec moi," she said with a grin.

Epilogue

Luna stood at one of the baking stations on set at work, tapping away at her laptop. The nice thing about the set was that the counters where the contestants would soon be competing were the perfect height for her to use as a standing desk. Her day's task list was dwindling: Delilah's lunch had been delivered and eaten; the network meeting was scheduled; nothing else was really pressing. She glanced at her phone's lock screen, which now displayed the time in both New York and Paris. It was still the middle of the afternoon for her, but it was night for Jean-Pierre. She pictured him padding around his gorgeous apartment barefoot, probably drinking an ill-advised final cup of coffee for the day while checking every pocket for his vape pen.

Long-distance sucked. Like, really, really sucked, but they had agreed to give it a try. There weren't many other options, after all: Luna loved her job as Delilah's right hand, and the show was going to start shooting in just four days. Jean-Pierre was still busy with his own work, too, although he planned to take a leave of absence soon. He had told Luna during their video call the night before that he wanted to get all his affairs in order. Henri's lawyers were desperately trying to find some loophole in the agreement that they themselves had made iron-clad, and it looked like the legal squabbling might go on for quite some time.

"Still," he'd said, "it would be smart for me to start looking into ways my future inheritance can be put to good use. Perhaps there is a way I can fund more of these, for example." He'd made a brief gesture at the dash-like scars on his bare chest (it wasn't a sexy video call; those were reserved for the weekends; he'd just come in from a morning run).

Luna had laughed. "So the Aubert-Treffle fortune is going to bankroll transitions? Henri is going to love that."

There had been many interesting recent developments. In the weeks since Luna had come back from Paris, the gossip blogs that had been somewhat responsible for her new relationship were awash with tawdry tales of a new rumored *If You Can't Handle the Heat* special. Footage from their disastrous culinary test had been leaked online, including one memorable clip of Henri losing it and injuring a crew member. France was a country of strict labor laws, which meant Henri was embroiled in quite a few legal battles on that front as well. Not to mention his transphobic rant had also been caught on film. A huge PR disaster. Last Luna had heard, his network was planning to announce that another chef would replace Henri next season.

Jean-Pierre's smile had almost filled the whole screen. "He loves nothing but the sounds of his own voice. Why try to please him when I can please myself?"

"Just yourself?" Luna had teased. (*Not* a sexy call, honestly.)

That laugh of his still rang through her head. "And you of course, mon Clair. I will always try to please you."

"Luna?" Delilah came to a stop in Luna's field of vision and waved her hand back and forth to get her attention. "You in there?"

"Yeah. Sorry." She shook herself out of her JP-flavored day-dream and looked down at her laptop. It was open to her calendar with the start date for shooting highlighted in bright yellow. Four days until she was working on an actual television shoot—and yet her weird little French dude was taking up most of her brain space. "What did you need, boss?"

"Oh, I'm good." Delilah smiled knowingly. "But you have a visitor."

"A visitor?" Her mom wasn't due to come into town until next month; her friends were all at work at this hour. Who could possibly—?

"Bonjour," said a voice behind her.

Luna turned. There was Jean-Pierre, standing like a dream, like a vision, like an oasis if oases could dress all in black. And he was holding—

"Are those eclairs?" As shell-shocked as she was, Luna pushed away from the workstation and squinted at the paper bag. She recognized the stamp from Patisserie Marie.

"I am happy to see you, too," he said with a bitchy little raise of his brow.

"Oh my god, yes, of course. You're the greatest eclair of all." She put a hand in the thick black hair at the back of his head and drew him in for a kiss. "But what are you doing here?"

"I decided to take my leave early." His eyes softened. "I wanted to see you. Very badly. Is that all right?"

"Yeah, it's fucking fantastic. And you brought eclairs!" She took the bag from him and set it on a nearby countertop so she could root through it properly. There were about a dozen of the classic ones, her favorite.

"I'll leave you to it," Delilah said, slipping away from the edge of Luna's conscious attention. She only had eyes for her boyfriend and his baked goods right now.

"I brought you something else, too," JP said. "I know shooting begins soon and you will be very busy with that for several months, but I thought—" He stopped, chewing his lip. "Perhaps I should wait?"

Luna shoved half an eclair in her mouth. "No way," she said

with her mouth still full, but with a hand daintily placed in front of her lips. "Don't keep me in suspense; life is too short!"

"I agree." He took a slim, plain envelope from inside his leather jacket and held it out. "So here you are."

Luna licked some chocolate ganache from her fingers before taking the envelope. There was no writing on it and the flap was unsealed. She made her eyes huge with fake excitement. "Is it one of Henri's horses?" She gasped for good measure. "Can I call her Annabelle?"

JP laughed at her joke because he always laughed at her jokes, even the ones that didn't make much sense to him. "Would you please open it?"

"Fine. Rain on my parade." Luna opened the flap and took out the single piece of paper inside, unfolding it to read. It looked official with a business logo at the top, an abstract sun shining over a horizon. Luna scanned the words on the page. Then read them again, just to be sure. "Wait. What?"

The letter was short and to the point:

Dear Ms. O'Shea,

> *This letter is to inform you of your admission to the Sunspot Collective for Yoga Instruction and Radical Healing. The fees for your accredited yoga instructor certification course have been paid in full. We have several programs available throughout the year and invite you to visit our website to register for the timeframe that best fits your schedule. I will personally see that you are accommodated in whatever way is necessary to ensure a smooth, peaceful experience for you here at Sunspot.*

It was signed by the president of the school. Actually signed, not printed.

Jean-Pierre cleared his throat. "I thought maybe after season one is—how to say—wrapped, you could have time to do this. If you want." He paused. "Do you want this? Still?"

Luna shook her head, not in answer but in disbelief. "Of course I do. But you didn't have to do this for me."

"I wanted to," he said. "Your dreams are important to me, too."

Luna sucked in a breath. Getting her certification was just step one in a long, daydreamy plan that might not ever happen in the end.

But Jean-Pierre was still in her corner. And whatever else happened, that was what mattered.

She set the letter aside with great care next to the bag of eclairs and wrapped her arms around his neck. "You are—" She kissed him. "The best." Kiss. "Realest." Kiss. "Boyfriend a girl could ever ask for."

JP grinned between kisses. "You think so?"

"Yep. You know what else I think?"

He kissed her forehead. "What do you think?"

"I think," she said with a smile, "I'm going to go home early today."

Acknowledgments

I am bound by my promises to first say that my wife is the best and greatest wife in the universe, and if the good folks at Simon & Schuster could afford it, there would be another three hundred pages in these acknowledgments dedicated to the topic. Alas, paper is money, and money doesn't grow on trees—even though paper is made from trees. Anyway. Thank you, Kara, for making it possible for me to be more myself than I have ever been. Thank you for supporting my writing habit. Thank you for getting us a little treat every time you go to the store. I love you, I love you, I love you.

Also thank you for the joke about being a threat to women's sports; everyone should know that I did not write that joke. My wife is, annoyingly, funnier than I will ever be. There is no greater compliment I can give, so I'll leave it at that.

I owe so many people some thanks. Dana, for continuing to be the best first reader, cheerleader, and straight person I know. (Sorry, but all you other straight people have got to get on Dana's level.) Erin, for doing Luna's and JP's astrological charts and writing with me every weekday morning. P.M., for explaining Paris to me. Rachel, for explaining Parisian cocktails to me. (Sorry that plotline got dropped.) Darcy and Chloe, for coming up with The Rare Parrot. Memphis and the folks in the Q&T writing workshop—thank you for withstanding my corny, swagless nature. Del, who helped fix my awful French—I am so sorry about what I did to your language, and I cannot thank you enough. Everyone who said nice things about *Chef's Kiss* and listened to me rant about writing this book, you are all angels, especially Lauren, Shayne, Hadley, Alejandro, Megan, Kaila, Dani, Tony, the folks in the group chat, my mom, and Jesse.

To my therapist, thanks for helping me get to a place where I can write things like this book. I told you I was serious about the shoutout, Doc.

My wonderful agent, Larissa Melo Pienkowski, come get your flowers. Here's to the queer yoga retreat and pet rescue we will someday have in the Catskills, though it might be more metaphorical than actual. Thank you for believing in Luna and Jean-Pierre. You are, as always, the best champion I can ask for. And thank you for letting me double text you when I have Ideas.

To my editor, Lara Jones, what can I say that I haven't said with a million exclamation points already? You have supported my vision of Luna's story every step of the way, and just a few scant years ago I could have never in my wildest dreams thought that would happen. Your guidance has made me a better writer. Your enthusiasm has made it easier to believe in my stories. As any true Sagittarius would say: thanks for being rad.

To the team at Atria, there are so many people who touched this book and *Chef's Kiss* and I am overflowing with gratitude for all of you. Thank you to my fellow y'all'er Emily Bestler. Thanks to Libby McGuire, Dana Trocker, Paige Lytle, and Liz Byer. Thank you to Megan Rudloff and Karlyn Hixson for being my publicity and marketing powerhouses, respectively and re-spectfully. Thank you to Colleen Reinhart, James Iacobelli, and Min Choi for creating the beautiful cover. God bless the copy editors; I am in awe of your skills. And thank you to the literal miracle workers in the sales and library marketing teams! I don't know how you all do it, and I owe you a series of cupcakes baked to your individual tastes.

Thank you to every librarian and bookseller who hyped up *Chef's Kiss*. Your support is stunning. I could kiss you all on the mouth in the spiritual sense.

And since it wouldn't be a TJ Alexander book without something painfully earnest in the parting shot: Luna and Jean-Pierre's story is a celebration of the kind of love that exists between trans people. As I write this in 2022, there's a lot happening in the world designed to scare us, silence us, keep us closeted, deny us care, even kill us, but nothing can stop us from loving each other and ourselves. So if you're reading this, you beautiful, powerful, tired trans person, please know that this was my love letter to you. I hope it brought you a little joy; you deserve every bit you can get.

Turn the page for an exclusive look at
TJ Alexander's next rom-com,

Second Chances
in New Port Stephen

Chapter 1

December 15

Eli Ward counted four MAGA flags on his parents' street, and those were just the ones he could see in the dark.

They were mostly in tatters, having weathered years of Florida thunderstorms, some so raggedy as to be illegible. There were yard signs, too, one bent completely backward on its coat-hanger legs. Oh, and a couple matching bumper stickers slapped on the backs of SUVs.

In a perverse way, Eli was comforted by all this. At least those households were displaying their intentions; it was the homes with empty yards that made him wonder.

The truck trundled by a house that was positively festooned with star-spangled merchandise. Eli craned his neck to take in the scene on the driver's side. Jesus, they'd decorated the signage with red Christmas lights, giving everything a decidedly demonic cast. It wasn't the first time he'd seen a fervent display of right-wing sentiment—he'd been on the road during election season, when there were pockets of it everywhere: the Midwest, the South, Upstate New York—but it felt different here, where he'd grown up.

He glanced at his cousin in the driver's seat, but Max didn't seem to register the house, eyes firmly on the road. When had the kid gotten old enough to drive? he wondered. Eli's most enduring memories of Max were from Facebook photos of a toddler picking clover. It just didn't compute with the lanky beanpole in combat boots and a billion necklaces who'd picked him up from the airport. Bit of a queer vibe, but who knew what teens were like these days? He should probably make an effort to find out, at least when it came to his own flesh and blood.

Eli cleared his throat. "So, uh, how's school going?" Great opener. He only sounded about nine hundred years old.

Max gave an eye roll because that's what teens did; it wasn't because Eli was irredeemably uncool, surely. "It'll be better in a few months. When it's over."

That gave Eli pause. "Wait. You're graduating this year? Seriously?"

"I'm eighteen," Max drawled, guiding the truck along a snakelike bend. "I know the Florida public school system hasn't improved much since you were in it, but they did teach me simple addition."

Eli resisted the urge to fling himself from the slow-moving vehicle to hide in a ditch, where he could spend the rest of his twilight years without being sassed by young'uns. "And how is Port Stephen Prep these days?" Seemed polite to ask, like the school was some mutual acquaintance of theirs.

"Closed. Hurricane damage." Max shrugged. "No one's sure when Prep will reopen; some fight about who pays for the repairs. I might have to finish the year out at Southern."

"That sucks," Eli offered.

"Not really. It's all the same," Max said.

Couldn't really argue with that. Eli looked out the window, letting his breath make a circle of fog on the glass. The house he'd grown up in finally came into view. For the first time in almost twenty-five years, Eli was back.

The driveway was packed with cars, so Max parked on the street. Eli took his time unbuckling his seatbelt, staring at his parents' house through the passenger window. Of all the houses he'd seen so far, it was the most decorated for the holidays. Eli's dad had always gone a little overboard with the lights back in the day, but this was something else.

Eli got out of the truck to take in the full effect of the Christmas display. Strand after strand of multicolored lights flickered in a repeating pattern. The eaves were dripping in lights, as were the neatly trimmed azalea bushes out front. And the squat cabbage palm in the flower bed. And the mailbox. And the arch of the carport. And a million other things, probably, that Eli's overwhelmed eyes hadn't yet noticed. A half dozen holiday characters sat on the lawn, including a plastic Santa wearing a panama hat and an inflatable Rudolph with a glowing red nose. The rest of the reindeer were represented by pink flamingos with felt antlers glued to their heads.

"Dad really went all out, huh?" he said to Max, who was getting his suitcase from the bed of the truck.

"You should have seen it a couple years ago." Max slammed the tailgate shut. "It was like Disney World. Tons of people came to take photos." A shrug. "Uncle Wen said this year he wanted to scale it back. Tasteful or whatever."

Eli watched as a robotic deer outlined in bright white lights lifted its head from the front yard's grass, swiveled it around, and, apparently satisfied that no Christmas predators were close by, lowered back down to fake-eat.

"Huh," Eli said. "Tasteful." He took his suitcase from Max.

As they neared the wreath-bedecked front door, Eli could hear the clamor of overlapping voices and Christmas music. He took a deep breath and held his suitcase handle in a white-knuckled grip. Why had he flown in tonight of all nights? He should have waited one more day. He should have found another couch to crash on. He shouldn't even be here.

No. This was going to be fine. There were worse things than a family holiday party. A party was just a performance, and he was used to performing. Sure, he hadn't actually been onstage in over a year, but it was like riding a bike. Probably. He hadn't done that in decades, so he couldn't be sure.

The door was unlocked as usual, and Eli stepped inside. He had just enough time to get a vague impression of the house: covered in Christmas kitsch on every available surface and stuffed to the gills with people, most of whom he didn't recognize. Probably his parents' friends and coworkers. A few turned to give him polite nods, clutching their red Solo cups. Bluetooth speakers scattered around the room belted out that song that went, "So this is Christmas . . ." The John Lennon version, not Céline, because life wasn't fair.

"Eli's home!" A woman with gray-streaked hair swooped out of the throng of people, her caftan flapping. Her Bakelite bangles—red and green, naturally—clinked as she wrapped Eli in a fierce hug. She still wore plumeria perfume. "You made it," Cora Ward said right into his ear.

"I made it," Eli said, hugging back with one arm. She felt smaller than he remembered. Were his parents shrinking? He certainly wasn't getting any bigger. The T had done all it was going to do at this point. He closed his eyes and tried to enjoy a moment of floral-scented comfort.

"Hey, *son*." Giddy emphasis on the *son*. Eli opened his eyes to find his dad standing by with his arms held wide. What hair remained on his head was grayer than the last time Eli had seen him. He wore a navy sweater vest over his long-sleeved button-down, and his glasses were horn-rimmed. His mustache was neatly trimmed, but not too thin, because he felt that was the mark of a pervert, which Eli still thought about every time he trimmed his own Selleck-esque 'stache.

In short, Wendall Ward looked like a librarian, because he was one. Cora had been a librarian, too, until she'd retired the year prior.

"Hi, Dad." Eli released his mom to hug him.

A flurry of activity followed.

"Where's Max? Max, get in here!"

"Close the door; the cat's been trying to get out all night."

"How was the flight? Let me take that bag—no, no, I insist."

"Was traffic bad coming up from the airport? I swear, gets worse every year. Just last week—"

"My god, what did you pack? Bricks? Max, do me a favor, sweetie; put this in the back bedroom for your cousin."

"—it was shut down for four days, every single lane. That's why I always take the Turnpike."

"No, the *back* bedroom. That's the front. Wen, you can't take the Turnpike to the airport. It doesn't go to the airport."

"Yes, it does. You just have to exit before the dog track."

"Wow," Eli said in a desperate bid to interrupt their double act, "look at all these old photos, huh?" It was the first thing that caught his eye, the only thing he thought might derail another hour of patter about the Florida highway system. He slipped between his mom and dad to examine the framed photographs on the wall of the sitting room. A few partygoers obligingly stepped aside to give him a better view.

His mom took the bait. She cooed at the pictures of Eli in '80s and '90s film of varying quality. There was a second little kid in many of the photos: black hair, gangly legs, oversized T-shirt. "You two were the cutest," she said, tapping a fingernail against the glass that covered the other kid's tousled head. "Do you keep in touch at all? Facebook, that kind of thing?"

"No," Eli said, only half-conscious of the question. "No, I don't do social media anymore." He stared at the figure in the most central photograph. Aunt Honey and Uncle Hank's wedding. Must have been ten or eleven. Wearing a poofy purple dress. He didn't bother trying to discern a familiar nose or a tilt of the mouth. There was nothing about the kid in the picture that looked like him except maybe the haunted look in the eyes that seemed to scream *Get me out of here*.

That, Eli could sympathize with.

"His dad's here if you want to say hello." Wendall pointed over to the family room, where a dark-haired figure was standing next to a folding table covered in finger foods, chatting with Aunt Katie. "He still lives over on Papaya."

Eli could see only the back of Mr. Wu's head, and he had no plans to see much more than that. This day was stressful enough. "Yeah, maybe later," he said.

Wendall was called away to mediate a debate between his friends, but Cora stayed right where she was, like she couldn't bear to take her eyes off Eli. She was practically bubbling over with excitement. "So how is the new job going?" she asked.

Eli cracked his neck side to side. "Oh. You know . . ." There was only so much you could say when you didn't want to say anything.

Because the truth was, there was no job.

The truth was, after having a decent career in various writers' rooms for years, all that had evaporated like so much canned milk. The truth was Eli's plane ticket had been one-way because his apartment in Brooklyn was currently home to a subletter, and Eli had no idea how or when he'd be going back. The truth was Eli was possibly stuck in Florida for the foreseeable future while he got his shit together, but if he tried to explain this to his mom in the middle of her annual Christmas party, he was going to have to tell her how he was a huge disappointment, and then she would cry, which would make his dad cry, which would make Baby Jesus cry, and Eli was going to throw up just thinking about it.

"It's going," he finally choked out.

His mom beamed at him, oblivious to his internal whirlwind. "You'll have to tell me all about it later. I'm sorry I never caught that last show you worked on, but you know how your father and I don't care for raunchy humor."

"Yeah. I know." His parents subsisted on a media diet of public radio and the odd rerun of *Antiques Roadshow*, and he didn't expect them to start watching prestige streaming dramedies just because their only child was writing the material.

Or had been.

Cora sighed gustily. "Working in television must be so interesting. Much more interesting than our sleepy little town! I hope you don't get bored while you're here."

In the dining room, someone dropped a cup. His parents' cat—a hefty ginger named Sweet Potato (the third of his name)—tried his best to lick up the sticky concoction that had spattered onto the floor, despite being shooed away by the guests. Eli hoped that would require his mom's attention, but Wendall stepped in to clean it up instead.

"Hey-hey!" A meaty hand landed on Eli's shoulder, making him startle. "The prodigal . . . whatever returns."

"Son," Cora said in a singsong voice.

Eli turned to face his mother's younger brother. "Hi, Uncle Hank. How've you been?"

Hank's red face stretched into a grin. "Getting by, getting by. How's life in the big city? You doing all right in that crime-riddled hellhole?"

"Ridden," Eli's mom said. "It's crime-*ridden*. And Eli lives in a nice neighborhood, not one of the bad ones."

"Mom . . ." If he cringed any harder, Eli was going to implode.

Uncle Hank leaned in like he was imparting state secrets. "You heard about the new law they're trying to pass here?"

"Yeah, Uncle Hank. I heard," Eli said. "I don't live under a rock, so . . . yeah."

The proposed law was the subject of opening monologues on the late-night circuit, a topic of conversation for internet trolls, a headline for days when there was nothing else happening. It was the brainchild of the governor—a guy who looked like undercooked pizza dough and with a haircut to match. The poorly written law prohibited "cross-dressing" on the campuses of state-funded schools and universities, making it illegal for "biological" men to wear skirts or dresses and "biological" women to wear . . . pants. This last part, naturally, had caused so much confusion and uproar that the real issue—the fact that some douchebag in Tallahassee wanted to terrorize transgender people to the ends of the earth—was usurped by a bunch of round-table discussions about women's lib that had all the relevance of moldy cave cheese. It was so depressing and predictable, it made Eli want to crawl into said cave and sleep for a month.

"Ridiculous." Eli's mom clicked her tongue. "They wouldn't even be able to enforce that law."

Not its biggest flaw in Eli's opinion, but okay.

Hank pointed at her with the hand that was holding his plastic cup. "I told Honey, I said to her, I said, 'No way are they going to make my nephew wear a dress.' Not even if it's, like, a really nice one. I'll fight 'em. Sock 'em in the mouth if they try."

"That's some amazing allyship, Uncle Hank, thank you. I don't plan on visiting any school campuses while I'm here, though." Eli eyed the sloshing cup in Hank's hand. Smelled like rum. "How many of those have you had, by the way?"

"Why, do you want one? I can get you one."

Cora sighed. "You know Eli is sober."

"You can't even have *one*?" Hank's eyes went wide with disbelief.

"Oh, I can," Eli said. "I'll just have nine or ten more in quick succession and I'd rather not spend Christmas getting my stomach pumped."

It was an old punchline that Eli usually pulled out at parties. It was easier than explaining how bad his drinking had been when he first moved to New York, back in his early days on the stand-up circuit. How he'd woken up twice in an MRI after getting blackout drunk. How his closest friend, Margo, had not-so-gently pointed out that once might be classified as a funny story to tell in greenrooms, but twice was a pattern, and maybe he should talk to someone about it. How therapy had pulled off his alcoholism's Scooby-Doo mask to reveal—surprise!—repression! Gender stuff! All the things he'd been trying to avoid his entire life!

How he'd gotten sober and transitioned and pulled himself

together just so he could go on Christmas vacation in a state where the leading government body was actively trying to make his life a living hell.

Yeah. Much better to tell a joke.

Eli smiled tightly. "I'm going to get some water." He gave his uncle a manful pat on his arm. "*Incredible* seeing you again, Hank," he said, putting every sense of the definition into the word.

The kitchen was crowded, since that was where all the booze was. Eli squeezed between bodies and snagged a Zephyrhills bottled water from the fridge, then headed for the screened-in back patio for some fresh, albeit humid, air.

He closed the sliding glass door behind him. The sounds of the party were muffled instantly, and the noises of the night bugs took over. Eli listened to them trill and buzz while twisting the cap off his water bottle, then gulped it down in a long series of swallows. He just needed a second to regroup, then he could continue pretending to be fine and normal.

He could feel a headache coming on.

Is it possible your guilt is manifesting physically? said a voice inside Eli's head that sounded suspiciously like the therapist he had stopped seeing when he'd lost his health insurance. *Very helpful observation, doc. Thanks for that.* He paced around the porch, finishing off his water and leaving the bottle on the table.

The sliding glass door opened, and Aunt Honey stuck her head out. The sounds of various wails floated onto the porch. "Can I borrow you?" Her soft voice held a note of resignation. "Sweet Potato got outside. We're organizing a search party."

Eli felt deeply for the cat. He also wanted to escape this party even if it meant running into the scrub pine wilderness.

He left the porch via the screen door that led into the side yard, his aunt right behind him. Christmas lights and cell phone flashlights provided pools of illumination. Eli sensed movement on the edges of his parents' property, but he could make out only vague shapes while his eyes adjusted. The voices of the partygoers called out in all different directions: "Sweet Potato! Come here, boy. Come on, Tater!"

"He's a cat, not a dog," Aunt Honey informed the person closest to her in the back flower bed. "He won't come when you call." Her tone made it clear she found this a huge defect.

"I think I found him!" someone shouted. Then: "Nope, never mind, it's a plastic bag."

"Oh, dear god." Eli rubbed his forehead with the heel of his hand. Clearly he'd picked the wrong decade to stop drinking.

A figure appeared from behind the crepe myrtles and jogged up to him. It turned out to be Eli's dad, his glasses fogged from his exertion. "Can you give me a hand? Hank fell into the swale."

"What?" Eli couldn't hide his surprise. The swale, the gutter-like ditch that ran along the front of the properties all throughout the neighborhood to collect excess rainwater, could only be half a foot deep at the most. "Can't he just . . . stand back up?"

"Muddy patch. His foot's stuck." He grimaced. "I think he's had a few."

"You have *got* to be kidding me." Eli was tempted to suggest they leave him there for the rest of the evening, but he knew that would probably not go over well. The Ward family was famously polite in that buttoned-up, mainstream-liberal kind of way. Eli's parents had no doubt watched a PBS docuseries on the dangers of leaving uncles stuck in swales.

Several yards away, somewhere close to the street, Eli heard a collection of grunts followed by a wet pop. "Got 'im!" Max hollered into the shadows. Cries of relief came from all corners, so Max amended: "My dad, not the cat!" Huffs of disappointment from the Greek chorus. Eli's head throbbed.

Aunt Katie sauntered by with a margarita glass in hand. "It wouldn't be Christmas without Hank making an ass of himself," she muttered to no one in particular.

"Sis, can you please at least pretend to be looking for the cat?" Wendall called after her.

Eli was about to suggest opening a can of tuna, when a

Creamsicle burst of color rocketed out of the underbrush. Eli's dad yodeled in triumph. "There he is!" He took off running after Sweet Potato, with more verve than Eli would have given him credit for. He stood where he was and let everyone barrel past him as they pursued the escaped cat. Too many cooks, he decided.

Eli's mother trotted up then. "Oh, there you are, sweetie."

"Here I am," Eli said, like he couldn't believe it either.

His mom smiled at him, a hint of anxiety clouding her face. "You know what? Could you do me a favor and go to the store to get more drinks? We're running low somehow."

Eli looked over at the scene still unfolding by the swale, standing on tiptoe to see over some bushes. Aunt Honey was trying to swipe the mud off Uncle Hank's pant leg and was only succeeding in spreading it along the length of his khakis. "Yeah. Somehow."

Cora followed his gaze, shaking her head. "I'd ask someone else, but everyone's either had one too many or is underage. Please?" She held out her keys, a confused jangle of novelty book key rings and supermarket savings cards.

"No problem." Eli swiped the keys from her hand. Living in New York for so long meant his driving skills were likely rusty, but honestly? A fender bender sounded like heaven compared to staying at this party.

Cora bobbed her head in thanks. "There's a Wine Barn down on Route 1 where the Circuit City used to be. You know, the one they burned down for the insurance money?"

"That was never proven in court," Eli said automatically. Why was this town so goddamn weird?

His mom dug her Mastercard out of a pocket in her caftan. "Beer, wine, some of the hard stuff, mixers. Oh, and some more limes. They have everything there, so you won't need to make more than one stop. Drive safe, okay?"

"I'll be back as soon as I can." Lies. He was going to dawdle like he'd never dawdled before.

From deep in the woods out back, Eli heard the yowl of a cat who presumably had been captured by many sets of hands.